PENGUIN BOOKS
# THE WOMEN IN CAGES

Vilas Sarang was educated in Mumbai, and at Indiana University.
He has taught English Literature in Mumbai, Kuwait and Iraq.

Sarang's stories have appeared in India, UK, USA and Canada in
journals such as *Encounter*, *The London Magazine*, *Triquarterly*,
*The Malahat Review*, and in the anthologies *New Writing in India*
(Penguin), *The Penguin Book of Horror Stories* and *New Directions
No. 41*. His published books in English include a collection of stories,
*Fair Tree of the Void*, and two novels, *In the Land of Enki* and *The
Dinosaur Ship*.

# The Women in Cages

*Collected Stories*

### VILAS SARANG

**PENGUIN BOOKS**

An imprint of Penguin Random House

PENGUIN BOOKS

USA | Canada | UK | Ireland | Australia
New Zealand | India | South Africa | China | Singapore

Penguin Books is part of the Penguin Random House group of companies
whose addresses can be found at global.penguinrandomhouse.com

Published by Penguin Random House India Pvt. Ltd
4th Floor, Capital Tower 1, MG Road,
Gurugram 122 002, Haryana, India

Penguin
Random House
India

First published by Penguin Books India 2006

ISBN 9780143061847

Typeset in Sabon by Mantra Virtual Services, New Delhi

Printed at Manipal Technologies Limited, India

www.penguin.co.in

MIX
Paper | Supporting
responsible forestry
FSC® C043100

# CONTENTS

# acknowledgements

Many of the stories in this volume were initially translated from the Marathi by the author. Breon Mitchell also worked on the translations. (See 'The Making of the Text' on page 277.)

The stories in the present volume have appeared in the following journals and anthologies:

|  |  |  |
| ---: | :---: | :--- |
| *Encounter* | : | 'Musk Deer' |
|  |  | 'Return' |
|  |  | 'The Terrorist' |
| *London Magazine* | : | 'Flies' |
|  |  | 'An Interview with M. Chakko' |
| *The Malahat Review* | : | 'An Evening at the Beach' |
|  |  | 'On the Stone Steps' |
|  |  | 'Kalluri's Escapade' |
| *New Orleans Review* | : | 'A Revolt of the Gods' |
|  |  | 'Tree of Death' |
|  |  | 'The Departure' |
| *Tri-Quarterly* | : | 'Letter from Nikhil' |
| *Mundus Artium* | : | 'Spider in the Clock' |
| *Prism International* | : | 'An Excursion' |
| *The Red Rock Review* | : | 'An Afternoon Among the Rocks' |
| *Debonair* | : | 'Om Phallus' |
|  |  | 'The Phonemate' |
| *Indian Horizons* | : | 'Testimony of an Indian Vulture' |
| *New Quest* | : | 'The Life and Death of Manu' |

| *New Writing in India* | : | 'Rabbit' |
| *(Penguin, 1974)* | | |
| *New Directions; No. 41* | : | 'The End of History' |
| *(1990)* | | |
| *Man's World* | : | 'The Women in Cages' |
| *Post-Post Review* | : | 'A Tale of Two Generals' |

Some of the stories were reprinted in *The Penguin Book of Horror Stories* (UK, 1984), *Short Story International* (1983), *Keynote* and *Goa Today*.

A number of the stories have been translated in French, by Alain Nadaud, under the title *Le Terroriste el Autre Recits* (Denoel, 1989). Individual stories have appeared in *Le Monde, 40 Nouvelles du Monde* (1986), *L'Infini, Nouvelles Nouvelles, Quai Voltaire*, and in the German magazines *Der Monat* and *Meine Welt*. The translation of the Sanskrit verses in 'Tree of Death' is by Daniel Ingatts.

# preface

A collection of my stories under the title *Fair Tree of the Void* was published by Penguin Books India in 1990. It is now out of print. The present collection includes the substance of the earlier one; in addition, six of the stories in the present collection are previously uncollected. I have made some alterations in most of the stories included in *Fair Tree of the Void*. The stories have been regrouped, with a heading for each section, which, I hope will make the collection more reader-friendly. The section headings loosely point to the subject of the stories, and are not taken as 'defining' something. Needless to say, the stories—materializing several years apart in some cases—were not written to a plan. The grouping is only an afterthought.

Perhaps a brief explanatory note regarding Section IV (The Shadow of the Gulag) is in order. The three stories at the head of this section were written as the result (along with my novel, *In the Land of Enki*) of my five-year stay in Iraq. In none of the stories is Iraq mentioned, though 'The Terrorist' is vaguely set in Basra, without mentioning town or country. During the time I was in Iraq, the Emergency of 1975 ran its course in India. On my annual vacation to India, I took in the developments. All stories in this section refract my Iraqi experience as well as that of the Emergency, and also my growing awareness of the realities of what has been called the Third World.

As a practising writer of fiction for many years, I have tried to formulate my views on the state and status of the art of fiction.

Some notes pertaining to the issue are appended to the present volume, which may be of interest to those who are interested in literature per se.

February 2006                                        Vilas Sarang

. . . his power is the will to create and he is impelled by the powers of the things to be created.

—From the *Vishnu Purana*

# I

# The City by the Sea

# an evening at the beach

## 1

Bajrang arrived at the beach with Shalini. Winter in Bombay is seldom very severe, but it happend to be rather cold this year. A chill wind blew in from the Arabian Sea. Bajrang and Shalini walked along the beach, lifting heavy legs in the sand. Since it wasn't a Sunday the beach wasn't crowded. The sun had just set, and the sky was still bright.

They made a round of the small strip of beach. On this beach near Shivaji Park there is a huge gutter pipe which pours out the filth of Bombay into the sea. The gutter's giant mouth has a small dome-shaped structure of concrete to let out gases. Bajrang told Shalini how a man, obviously a visitor from some small town, had once approached him and asked solemnly: 'To which god was this temple built?' Shalini laughed, and Bajrang put his arm around her shoulder.

Bajrang started looking about for a place to sit near the walls by the beach. It wasn't dark yet, but later the walls would become crowded with couples and it would not be easy to find a secluded spot. Bajrang wanted to settle down in a good place while there was still time. Few people chose to sit beside the cemetery wall, so Bajrang selected a spot there. Bajrang liked to sit by this wall partly because it reminded him of a passage by Albert Camus, in which he spoke of Algerian boys and girls having assignations under the cemetery walls. It was thrilling to know that Bombay, together with a distant city like Algiers, contributed towards love's triumph over death. Bajrang saw a vision of cemeteries all over the world besieged by passionate youth.

Bajrang and Shalini sat against the wall. Bajrang had to listen to Shalini's chatter until it was quite dark. Playing with the fingers of her left hand, Bajrang gazed out at the horizon. The sea was darkening. The tide was low, and the water was far away from the wall. Near the water's edge, little waves rose and fell in tiresome sequence. Since it was turning dark, slum-dwellers were beginning to come onto the beach to defecate. They crouched at a modest distance from one another near the water, their silhouettes outlined clearly in the evening glow.

One man who looked rather old got up after his bowel movement, and went towards the water to wash himself off. Standing where the waves were breaking upon the shore, he lowered his buttocks. He didn't want to go into the water and wet himself any more than necessary. His idea was to clean himself against a wave just as it was about to break on the sands. He lowered his buttocks when he saw a wave coming in, but panicked thinking that the wave was high and would soak him to the waist. As he raised his body hastily, the wave passed beneath him without so much as touching his ass. He lowered his buttocks once more and waited for the next wave. Again he misjudged the height of the wave and it passed under him. This happened four of five times. It amused Bajrang to watch the old man alternately lowering and raising his buttocks as if he were engaged in a physical exercise, or practising the motions of a dance, or as though he were a puppet moved by invisible strings. Then the man seemed to have made up his mind, and remained still as the next wave came in. This time the wave was indeed a high one, and, breaking full against him, soaked him to his chest. It was dark now, and the man was far away, so Bajrang couldn't see the expression on his face, but he thought he could imagine it. Life's like that, Bajrang said to himself, and idly wondered if he should send this anecdote to *Readers' Digest*.

As darkness fell, the breeze turned colder. Shalini snuggled closer to Bajrang for warmth. Bajrang felt cramped after sitting for so long against the wall. He decided to get up and stretch before they began necking seriously. Gently pushing away from Shalini, he stood up and brushed off the sand. Stretching himself, he glanced around. Couples were sitting along the wall on both sides of him. Bajrang noticed that the distance between each pair was about the same as that between the slum-dwellers defecating on the beach. Turning around, Bajrang looked over the wall. A corpse appeared to have just been brought to the crematorium. As they waited for the crematorium attendants to build a pyre, men sat around the bier like ants around a dead beetle.

Bajrang was about to sit down again when someone stood up unexpectedly on the other side of the wall. Bajrang wouldn't have paid much attention, but something struck him. He looked across at the man. Good God, it was Kanchan Kothare, he thought. What the hell was he doing out here?

Kanchan had also recognized Bajrang. 'Hey, Bajrang,' he shouted. 'What brings you here?' Kanchan was one of Bajrang's close friends at college. He was somewhat hare-brained, and you could never be sure what he would say or do.

'I came to piss against the wall, and I hadn't the least idea you'd be on the other side, Bajrang,' Kanchan said.

'It`s a long time since I've seen you,' Bajrang said. 'But how come . . .'

'Oh Bajrang, my mother died, you know,' Kanchan's voice changed suddenly. Tears came into his eyes. 'I've come here for mother's cremation. Bajrang . . .' For a moment Kanchan seemed unable to speak further. Bajrang knew that Kanchan was extremely fond of his mother. 'Bajrang, you'll never know how wonderful my mother was.'

Bajrang didn't know what to say. Shalini, sitting beside him in the dark, looked at him with raised eyebrows. Kanchan was an old friend, but he had no business bothering Bajrang at this time, and in this place. Bajrang was about to say goodbye to Kanchan brusquely, when Kanchan cried, 'Bajrang . . .' Kanchan's body was shaking, and Bajrang thought he might collapse at any moment. Kanchan came forward a little and leaned against the wall. Bajrang felt Kanchan's breath upon his neck.

'Bajrang, how can I tell you my feelings,' Kanchan said. 'And I hate all these people.' He waved his arm towards the men in the distance. 'As for father, he sighed with relief when mother died. She was in bed for two years, you know. Then all these people who call themselves relatives came out of nowhere. Like vultures flapping down to the ground. I'd never seen any of them in my life. But you can count on relatives to turn up at funerals. And at weddings. They'll come from the most god-forsaken village in the country. Always willing to lend a hand. This one, he's an expert in tying the bier, he takes the lead. And so it went. They tied her up in no time. As tight as they could.'

Kanchan's cheeks were wet. 'Bajrang,' he said. 'Could you come over the wall for a while, just to keep me company. I'm frightened of these people, you know. You'll come, Bajrang, won't you?' Kanchan rested his hand upon Bajrang's shoulder. Bajrang looked into his eyes. Then he bent down and whispered into Shalini's ear. 'Shalini, darling, look. I'll be back in just a few minutes. Will you wait here . . . please? Please, darling.' Shalini shook her head. Bajrang wasn't sure if she meant yes or no, but without waiting to find out he jumped over the wall. He put an arm around Kanchan and walked with him towards the bier.

## 2

The pyre was built and Kanchan's mother was placed on it. Arms folded, Bajrang stood by the pyre as the last rites were performed. It was quite cold now.

Flames leapt up when the pyre was lit. The faces of the men standing round the pyre looked red, like painted masks. The warmth of the fire made Bajrang feel better. He watched the varying shades of red on the faces of the motionless men.

Kanchan dragged me away from the warmth of Shalini's body, but his mother's body is warming me anyway, Bajrang thought. And what about Shalini? She's beyond the wall, alone in the cold. Bajrang's heart was suddenly filled with tenderness for her.

The warmth of the fire had taken the edge off the cold. Bajrang felt invigorated. Then, looking at the silent men ringed round the pyre, it occurred to him that they might have killed this woman so that they could warm themselves on a cold day. He could see their faces gratified by the warmth of the fire.

Where would a person find this much warmth during a cold

winter in Bombay? They had certainly made a first-class bonfire.

Kanchan's the only one here who isn't in on the secret, Bajrang thought. He looked at Kanchan, who was staring vacantly into the distance. He seemed to have completely forgotten that he had specially asked Bajrang to come.

As the flames leapt higher, the heat became intense. Yet, Bajrang's hands and back hadn't received their share of the warmth. Stretching out both hands, Bajrang spread his fingers in front of the fire. He turned them around a few times, until both sides were properly warmed. Then he turned his back to the fire.

When his back had absorbed enough warmth and his front was beginning to cool off, Bajrang turned his face again towards the pyre. Then he noticed that the people around him were whispering among themselves, casting frequent glances towards him. Perhaps it's because they don't know who I am, Bajrang thought. He decided that this wasn't an appropriate time to introduce himself. He spread out his fingers again before the fire.

Soon he saw two men advancing in his direction. He thought one of them was Kanchan's father. 'This monster, has he come to attend a funeral, or to enjoy himself beside a bonfire?' Bajrang recognized the voice of Kanchan's father. Before he knew what was happening, the men fell upon him.

Bajrang extricated himself from the grappling arms, and dashed to the other side of the pyre. He crouched there for a few seconds planning his next move. Kanchan seemed to have caught on to the situation by now. 'Bajrang, Bajrang . . .' he cried out, and, pushing people out of his way, ran to Bajrang's rescue.

Bajrang made up his mind quickly. He couldn't escape towards the wall by the sea, where Shalini was sitting. He would have to run for the wall in the other direction. Once more, he made a quick dash around the pyre.

Looking back he saw that he had hit the pyre as he was running around it, and that the logs on one side were tumbling down. A glance over his shoulder revealed that Kanchan, who had started to move towards him, had tripped over the logs he had dislodged. Sprawled on the ground, Kanchan thrust his arms and legs into the air as charred pieces of wood fell upon him.

Bajrang reached the wall, climbed up and, before jumping down on the other side, had a last look behind him. Kanchan had disappeared under a pile of wood, and his mother's half-burnt body had slid down towards him. Kanchan, who had been shouting Bajrang's name, now started crying out, 'Mother, mother . . .' and violently hugged her body. Some of the men had seemed bent on following Bajrang, but when they saw what had happened to Kanchan, they faltered. Most of them abandoned the pursuit to pull Kanchan out of the mess. One or two men continued half-heartedly after Bajrang. Bajrang looked upon this scene for a few moments, and then leaped down from the wall. He kept on running.

### 3

One of Bajrang's beliefs was that he was a Great Indian Bustard, a species of birds now on its way to extinction. Bajrang alone knew the secret of the apparent contradiction in the name bustard: the bustard is a large swift-moving bird, but its name 'bustard' derives from the Latin *avis tarda*, 'slow bird'. You think you can catch me easily, Bajrang said to himself as he ran, but I'm a Great Indian Bustard. 'He's a slow bird,' you say to yourselves. 'We'll have him in no time.' But I'm gone before you've uttered those words. Try as you might, you can't lay hands on me. If you got me, though, it would be a sad day. The Great Indian Bustard is on the verge of extinction, and you might really wipe us out. As one of the few survivors of a vanishing species, Bajrang knew that it was his duty to protect his own life. Pride welled up in his heart, and a kind of wistful love.

Bajrang reached a street that looked deserted, and stopped for breath. He glanced in the direction of the cemetery, but didn't see anyone coming after him. He relaxed.

The area was in darkness, but there were a few lights here and there, as there always seem to be, wherever you go. Bajrang stood in the street undecidedly. Words floated upon his consciousness, taking advantage of the emptiness of his mind: *No one should be allowed into the royal household without proper scrutiny. Fires burn themselves up; stubs litter the roadside.*

*Stop and proceed*

*The state of my shoe-laces is not a subject openly to be discussed. Nor do I claim*
*Night-blind towers paralytic.*

Then Bajrang started walking, perhaps in the direction of home. He suddenly remembered the time he had been to the beach at midday. Everyone goes to the beach in the evening, so Bajrang once went at midday, just to see what it was like there then. There was no one on the beach except for a few dhobis, who had brought large bundles of freshly dyed saris, and were spreading them out. Under the blazing sun, Bajrang had stood that day watching long stretches of colourful saris drying on the sand.

# an afternoon among the rocks

It was two o'clock when Bajrang finished the rounds of the buildings in King's Circle. Then he locked the case in which he carried his samples and, taking a bus to Dadar, left it there with Ranjit, who ran a newspaper stall.

'Looks like you've finished your rounds early today,' Ranjit said. 'Yes, I have some of my own work this afternoon,' Bajrang said. 'And how's business?' Ranjit asked. 'Not too good,' Bajrang said. 'Too many people have got into this door-to-door salesman's business now. It's hurt my sales.'

Telling Ranjit that he would come and pick up the case in the evening, Bajrang took a bus again. He was supposed to meet Shalini at 2.30 near New Talkies in Bandra, but it was 2.35 when he got off the bus. As he started walking towards New Talkies, it occurred to him that he ought to have taken a pee while he was at Dadar. He was going to be among the rocks with Shalini the whole afternoon, and it would have been prudent to take care of that in advance. Where could he do it now? He would have to go down to the railway station, but that would take a few more minutes, and he was already late. Still, he went down to the station, then turned and went to New Talkies. Shalini was waiting for him.

'You're late!' Shalini said, frowning. 'It's miserable standing here. People keep staring.'

'I'm sorry, I had to wait a long time for a bus,' Bajrang said. They took a taxi to Band Stand, and went into the only restaurant there. The restaurant was deserted, except for a waiter idly gossiping with the man behind the counter.

'I hope it's not the same thing as last week,' Shalini said.

'Oh, no, people don't go and drown themselves every day,' Bajrang said.

They had come here the week before, only to find a small crowd gathered among the rocks beyond the restaurant. The waiter had told them that the body of a woman who had drowned herself had been washed ashore. How could they go and sit among the rocks with that in mind? They went back the way they had come.

'And you can't take time off more than once a week . . .' Bajrang said.

'No way. It's difficult enough making it once a week. To come over here, I have to take half a day off at the factory. I lose half a day's pay, and of course on pay day Father finds out. Then he grumbles about my taking too much time off.'

'I guess he's only interested in the amount of money you bring home.'

'But Bajrang, how can *you* afford to come here any oftener? Won't you lose business?'

'That's all right with me. I'm ready to come here every day. I don't care about losing business.'

'Oh, don't say that, Bajrang. You want to save money, don't you? Both of us have to save enough to marry as soon as we can. Otherwise, we have to go on putting it off. How long do we want to keep putting it off?'

'Do you need some sauce?' Bajrang asked, holding the sauce bottle over Shalini's sandwiches. Shalini nodded, and he tilted the bottle.

'Is business good?' Shalini asked.

'Fairly good.'

'And how long do you want to keep at this door-to-door job?'

'I don't know. I could go on for another year or so. Sooner or later I'll get a sales officer's job with some company.'

Slurping his tea, Bajrang noted that Shalini had eaten the meaty portion of the sandwiches, and left the crusts on her plate. Bajrang found it shocking and unforgivable to leave anything on the plate. He didn't like Shalini's doing so, as if she were rich. Was that the way she would keep house when they were married?

Paying the bill with a ten-rupee note, Bajrang made some calculations as he put the change in his pocket and figured that he had enough money left for the return taxi and bus. More than once in recent weeks he had had just enough money on him for the date. He hoped he wouldn't be reduced to cutting his dates with Shalini just because he didn't have the money. Still, going to Bandra with Shalini once a week did cost him quite a bit, what with the round-trip taxi and the restaurant. It couldn't be helped, though.

They came out of the restaurant, and walked towards the rocks. The sun was blazing, yet the heat wasn't oppressive because of the fresh sea breeze. Below the wall to the right there was the half-finished foundation for a building. 'They're going to build a huge five-star hotel here, aren't they?' Shalini asked.

'Yeah.'

'Once there's a big hotel here, we won't be able to come here in the afternoon any more.'

'Why worry about that? The hotel won't be up for another two or three years.'

'Yeah, and by then we'll be married. We may even have a child by then, don't you think? A son—or a daughter—'

'Hm . . .'

'But where will couples like us go three or four years from now?'

'Why do *you* have to worry about it?'

'You know, one day we'll bring our son here, and show him this place, and we'll say, "Darling, we used to come here before we were married." And he'll smile a big smile, even though he will not understand a word. Don't you think?'

There was a low, sloping hill on the left, overgrown with grass. The pathway went along the hill, at the end of which stood the fortress-like Byramji Point, overlooking the sea. On the right, there were rocks all around. As they descended to the rocks after leaving the pathway, Bajrang held Shalini's hand, and they picked their way carefully, watching their step. From time to time,

Bajrang looked round for a comfortable place to sit. There were no other couples among the rocks at this time of the day.

After looking around a bit, Bajrang found a suitable spot. A long, flat rock, with an even, perpendicular rock behind it: it was like a spacious sofa facing the sea, with its back to the pathway. Dusting off the sand with his handkerchief, Bajrang sat down. Shalini too cleared a place for herself, dusting daintily with her tiny handkerchief. She kept her handbag by her side, and Bajrang put an arm around her. A few feet away on the other side of him a few used condoms lay scattered about.

'These rocks are hot, aren't they?' Shalini said, as she leaned forward to cover her back with the end of her sari. 'Still, we're lucky the rock's not too rough. You know, when we were here two weeks ago—the rock we sat against was so jagged! It left deep impressions on my back, marks that hadn't gone away even by the time I reached home. I didn't realize it. Mother asked, "Where did you get those marks on your back?"'

'What did you say then?'

'What could I say? I got around the question somehow.'

'I wonder where exactly the woman's body was washed ashore last week,' Bajrang said. 'I hope it wasn't where we're sitting now.'

'Ough! Why do you have to bring that up?'

'Anyway, the waves would have washed the place clean in the meantime.'

'Please, let's not talk about it.'

They were silent for a while. Since they were sitting practically at sea level, they could see very little of the water. Between the rocks before them and the sky above, the sun glittered on a small strip of sea. Waves beat on the shore some distance away, and the sound of clothes being beaten by the dhobis on the rocks came from far away on the right. Bajrang's hair flew in the breeze.

Bajrang took off his wristwatch and put it in Shalini's handbag. He didn't want it to get scratched as they moved around on the rocks. Then he put his arm around Shalini again, and pulled her closer. They kissed silently. Even though his eyes were closed, the light glowed through his eyelids. The glow through his shut eyes, the sun warm upon his body, and the occasional cool breeze caressing his skin, all made Bajrang feel light in the head. With his eyes still closed, he started unfastening the hooks at the back of Shalini's bodice. Then he drew back and said, 'Why don't you come without a bra some day?'

Shalini merely smiled, crossing her arms over her chest.

'Every time I tell you, you just smile.'

'I'll do it next time, okay?'

'That's what you always say.'

Shalini laughed and said, 'Dear, you know I have to go to work for half the day. And to go to work like that—I'd have to keep myself wrapped up in my sari all the time.'

Bajrang slid down on the rock, and pulled the sari away from Shalini's chest. As his forehead pressed against her breasts, Shalini raised her neck and looked away into the distance. She gazed at the horizon in silence, like a cow staring patiently ahead while suckling her calf. Then Shalini turned her head a little to the left, stared for a few seconds, and pushed Bajrang hastily away. Bajrang looked up at her.

'There's someone standing over there,' Shalini said.

Bajrang looked over Shalini's shoulder. Some distance behind them, where the rocks began at the foot of the hill, a man was standing in a blue shirt and dark glasses. He must have been around twenty-five. From the shade of the Byramji Point wall, he stood looking in their direction.

Muttering a curse, Bajrang turned his head. Then he slid up again, and sat up straight. 'What a nuisance,' he said, wiping the perspiration from the sides of his nose.

'Isn't it!' Shalini said, as she adjusted her clothes.

They sat still in silence. 'Don't look back at him,' Bajrang said to Shalini. They watched the man from the corners of their eyes. The blue shirt didn't move.

'We'll just sit here quietly,' Bajrang said, 'He'll get bored and go away.'

'He's still there,' Shalini said after a while.

'Men like that are stubborn,' Bajrang said.

They watched the sea glittering under the sun.

'That's the trouble with coming here in the afternoon,' Bajrang said. 'It's nice in the evening after dark. Lots of couples come here then.' When Shalini didn't say anything, he added, 'But you can't make it in the evening, right?'

'No, how can I? If I came, I'd be so late getting home. Father wouldn't put up with that.'

'It's too bad.'

Shalini didn't say anything. Then, feeling as though she were to blame, she changed the topic and said, 'What part of town did you cover today?'

'King's Circle.'

'That's South Indian territory.'

'Yeah.'

'One thing I don't understand—why is it called King's Circle? What king was that?'

'Must have been some British king.'

'But they've changed the British names of places and streets now, haven't they?'

'Maybe they forgot this one.'

'Hm, King's Circle ... Which British king do you think it was? There were so many ...'

'What does it matter? Who cares about things like that?'

'King's Circle—the circle of the king. Strange, isn't it—the king is gone, but the circle remains.'

Bajrang turned his head and looked at the blue shirt. He stared for a few seconds, then turned his head again and said, 'You know, I don't think he's watching us. He's looking out to sea.'

'Why would he be looking out to sea? What's out there?'

'Maybe he's waiting for a boat. You know, fishermen from Mahim Creek go out to the sea this way. Maybe he's waiting for friends to return.'

'I don't believe that. I tell you, he's looking at us. He may be pretending to look out to sea. People like that are very cunning.'

Saying nothing, Bajrang put his arm around Shalini's shoulder, and fondled her arm. Then Shalini said, 'Bajrang, you'd better get a job in a good company. Then we can think seriously about marriage.'

'Yeah. An opportunity has to come up, though.'

'How long are we going to keep coming to these rocks?—

under the afternoon sun? What a horrible situation!—leaving the whole of Bombay behind, coming to these wretched rocks.'

'What's so bad about it? I like it here among the rocks. You have the sea—a nice breeze—'

'I'm beginning to wonder if we're going to spend all our life here. We have our own lives elsewhere, but our life together belongs almost wholly to these rocks—our only memories will be of them.'

Bajrang looked ahead in silence. Some distance to the right, another couple had seated themselves. Their heads were just visible above the rocks.

Bajrang turned his head again and looked at the blue shirt, who was still standing in the same spot, although in a different posture. Bajrang watched for a few seconds. 'I tell you, he's looking out to sea. He's waiting for a boat,' Bajrang said.

'You're just trying to convince yourself, Bajrang.'

'But if he wanted to watch us, he wouldn't stand in the open like that. He'd be hiding, and sneaking around.'

'People like that are shameless.'

'I'll tell you what—he's probably waiting for smugglers. They say boats come this way carrying smuggled goods, and go up the creek.'

'You're becoming more imaginative, Baju.'

Watching the blue shirt for a few seconds, Bajrang said, 'It's hard to tell, though. One moment you feel he's looking at you, another moment you feel he's looking at the sea.'

'Didn't I tell you he's looking at us? Suppose, as you say, he's waiting for a boat; even so, he must see us in between, right?'

'It's frustrating. If you know someone's looking at you, you can adapt yourself to the situation. But it's maddening when you're not sure if you're being watched or not. I mean, you begin to wonder if you exist.'

'What do you mean? We exist even if no one's watching us, don't we?'

'Yeah, sort of . . .'

Suddenly Shalini said, 'Baju, I—I need to pee.'

'Damn! Where can you go out here in the open? The restaurant doesn't have a toilet either.'

Shalini didn't say anything. Then Bajrang said, 'Why didn't you go when you quit work?'

'I left in such a hurry, dear. I'd been thinking about our meeting since morning. I was so impatient to see you, I didn't think of anything else. I started off in a hurry thinking I might be late.'

'Now there's no place to go. Maybe we'll have to leave early today.'

Shalini sat in silence feeling guilty. Bajrang turned his head, and looked at the blue shirt again. Then Shalini said, 'Why do you keep looking at him?'

'You know what, now I'm beginning to feel that he isn't someone else—'

'What do you mean?'

'I haven't told you about it before—sometimes when I'm here with you, when I'm holding you, I begin to feel I'm silently watching myself sitting on the rock. Do you see? I'm another person, but I'm myself watching me sitting with you among the rocks.'

'So?'

'So now I'm starting to feel that the person standing over there is that other me.'

'Oh, come on! It's obvious that he's someone else, a stranger.'

Without saying anything, Bajrang turned his head and looked at the blue shirt.

'But Baju, what's this strange feeling? There's another "I" hovering around you? Do you get that feeling often?'

'Not always. Only when I'm with you. Especially when I'm kissing you, and the rest.'

'And you never get the feeling at any other time?'

'No, I don't. I used to get it when I was a child, though. Father didn't care much for me, but my mother loved me very much. Even when I was nine or ten years old, she used to hug me and kiss me. When she hugged me like that, I used to get that feeling—that I was standing at the side, looking at myself.'

'That's weird.'

When Bajrang's hand began to wander, Shalini held it and said, 'Don't. He's looking.'

'It's all right,' Bajrang said, freeing his hand. 'He can't see on this side.' After a minute or two, he said, 'Why don't you slide down a little bit? He won't be able to see then.'

After a while, Bajrang's movements became insistent. Seeing what he wanted, Shalini said, 'No, Baju—not that—'

'Oh, come on—'

'No, dear—not that—'

'I can't hold myself back now—'

'Please—he's watching—'

'We'll finish quickly—'

'Baju—'

'Turn this way—'

'Ough!—what are you doing—right in front of his eyes—'

Yanking her by the shoulder, Bajrang said, 'That's just me over there—didn't I tell you it's just me—' Realizing that he had jerked her rather brutally, Bajrang released her arm and sat still. For a few moments, Shalini lay quietly, half-reclining. Then she looked into Bajrang's eyes and said, 'You frighten me sometimes, Baju.'

'You're making such a fuss—' Bajrang said, leaning forward again. 'Come on, turn this way—' he said, as he pulled a condom from his trouser pocket.

Shalini lay quietly, without moving. Bajrang didn't look at her face. Then suddenly Shalini said, 'Ough!—to do it here like this—under the sun among the rocks—right in front of someone—' She started crying.

Bajrang sat up again. Without saying anything, he folded his arms over his drawn-up knees, and leaned back against the rock. Shalini wiped her eyes. Then she stretched out her hand and said, 'Are you angry, dear?' Bajrang didn't move. 'Come on, dear—' Shalini said. Rising partially, she pulled Bajrang towards her.

Shalini lay down with her eyes shut, head turned to one side, as Bajrang heaved above her. With his neck extended, Bajrang could see the blue shirt in the distance. Because of the up and down movement of his body, and the heat and the perspiration that clouded his eyes, Bajrang saw the man's face as a hazy mirage. The 'I' that he often felt hovering near him while he was with Shalini now stood directly before him. It made him happy, this manifestation of the other 'I' in concrete form. The two had finally met, like the Atman meeting with the Brahman. A wave of joy surged up in Bajrang's heart, and a smile appeared on his face. He continued to move up and down as though riding on waves of joy.

Sensing a movement to his left, Bajrang looked in that direction. In the distance, where the road ended and the pathway began, a police van had appeared. The van was turning around to park. Bajrang watched it.

Then, feeling there was a movement in front of him, he turned his head again. The blue shirt, too, had seen the police van, and had quickly lowered himself to the ground. Crouching, he watched the van in the distance. Then he turned his head, and looked towards Bajrang. He looked at the van again, then rose and started running in Bajrang's direction. He ran doubled over. Seeing him coming in his direction, Bajrang stopped moving up and down. Shalini opened her eyes, and turning her head, looked up at Bajrang questioningly.

With the blue shirt so near, Bajrang moved off Shalini hastily. While he was buttoning his fly, Shalini too began rising, sensing that something was wrong. When she turned her head and looked behind them, the blue shirt was just a few strides away.

'Oh mother—' Shalini cried.

'Shut up! Don't shout—' the blue shirt said, as he came up and crouched in front of them. He brought out a knife with a long blade from his trouser pocket, and opened it with a flick.

Adjusting her clothes hurriedly, Shalini was trying to say something, but couldn't speak. Two streams of perspiration were coursing down Bajrang's already perspiring face.

'Don't make a fuss,' the blue shirt said. 'And don't be frightened. I'm not going to hurt you.' Turning to Bajrang he said, 'There's only one thing you need to do. The girl has got to come with me. Get it?—she'll come with me up to the road, and then I'll leave her at the restaurant. Okay?' He paused for a second, then turned to Shalini. 'Come with me quietly. When we pass the police, don't make a sound, or you'll get this in the stomach.' He held the knife up before Shalini's eyes. He turned to Bajrang again. 'And you—you sit right here. If you start anything while we're walking, I'll knife this bitch and run for it.'

Reaching out, he caught Shalini by the arm and said, 'Come on—'

'Oh mother—' Shalini cried, freeing her arm and moving closer to Bajrang.

'Quick,' the blue shirt said. 'There's no time to lose. I've got to get away.'

Shalini looked at Bajrang, who remained silent.

'Look, I've told you—I won't hurt you. I've had plenty of broads. All I want is to get away from here.'

Reaching out again, the blue shirt caught Shalini's arm once more. She didn't resist this time. He raised her up, and she stood whimpering. Shutting his knife, he put it away in his pocket, and kept his hand in the pocket. Then, putting his left arm around Shalini's shoulder, he started walking. Shalini walked with faltering steps. After a few feet, she halted uncertainly, and looked back at Bajrang. When the blue shirt tugged at her, she started walking again. They came out of the rocks, and climbed up to the pathway.

The dark blue police van was parked in the distance, a little way off the road. Two policemen got out, and were walking in the direction of the rocks, glancing sideways towards the sea now and then.

Shalini walked meekly next to the blue shirt, who had pulled her close, so that they looked a pair of lovers lost in their own world. Getting up, Bajrang sat down upon the high rock, and watched the two walking away.

'So he was a smuggler after all,' Bajrang said to himself. Watching the two moving away from him, he thought: all this while, he's been watching us, now he's taking her away, and I'm sitting here watching them. But after all, he's me.

The two policemen were coming down the pathway. When the couple came near them, Bajrang saw the blue shirt turn his face to Shalini, as though talking intimately with her. His right hand was still in his pocket, and his face was turned away from the policemen. The two walked like lovers cooing.

The policemen looked at the couple walking by, and came on down the pathway. There were two more couples among the rocks to their right. After a glance at them, the policemen continued walking down the pathway, looking up at Bajrang sitting by himself towards the far end of the rocks.

The blue shirt and Shalini were past the van now, and were walking down the road towards the restaurant. Bajrang's mouth was dry, but sticky mucus had accumulated in his throat. Hawking vigorously, he spat on a nearby rock, and, with his elbows upon his knees, awaited the policemen.

# musk deer

## 1

Waking up one morning he felt a kind of wetness in his
navel. He lifted the tail of his night-shirt and peered down.
His navel was indeed filled with a liquid, topped by a thin film.
He dipped a finger in the liquid and held it close to his eyes.
Then he sniffed at it. It had that odour peculiar to lint from the
navel. Disgusting, if you like, but also exhilarating in a way. He
sniffed again.

Of course he didn't know what had happened. But he was
amused rather than intrigued. 'Good God, am I turning into a
musk deer or something?' he asked himself. He had a vision of
himself as a puny deer roaming distractedly high in the thin air
of the Himalayas, searching everywhere, amid the rocks and the
bushes and the pure streams, for the source of the maddening
scent, not knowing that the scent originated in its own aching
navel.

He wiped off the liquid with the tail of his shirt. Later, he
forgot about the whole matter. He had to finish a book review by
that evening, and that kept him totally occupied.

Getting into bed that night, he had another look at his navel:
liquid had welled up again. Now he felt annoyed. 'Musk deer,
musk deer,' he muttered as he wiped away the liquid.

The next morning the level of liquid in the navel had risen.
There was a crust around the edges. The liquid was yellower
than the day before. He also noted that his navel hurt slightly.
'This is too much. I'd better go see a doctor,' he decided.

The doctor took one look at his navel and announced, 'Well, you've got an umbilical abscess.'

'Umbilical abscess?' Musk Deer said to himself. 'What's that?' he asked the doctor.

'It's like this,' the doctor said. 'When you are born, they cut the umbilical cord. The wound heals after a while. But in rare cases the wound does not quite heal. Later on it may become infected. Pus begins to seep out.'

'But doctor, I'm twenty-six years old.' Musk Deer said incredulously. 'How could the wound stay unhealed for such a long time? That's hard to believe.'

'Yes, it's hard to believe,' the doctor said. 'But such things do happen.'

It seemed to Musk Deer as if he were seeing the entire course of his twenty-six years in a wholly new light. Hell, he thought, I finished school, graduated from college, went to work for a living, and all these years my umbilical cord has never been properly severed!

He thought of Karwar, the place where he was born. His father had left Karwar soon after his birth and he had never gone back there himself. So he carried no memory of his birthplace. Not even a blurred picture of a house, or a street, a scene with trees or water. Nothing. His birthplace was just a name.

'So what do we do now?' he asked the doctor.

'I'll give you antibiotics,' the doctor said. 'Then we'll see. Perhaps the abscess will dry up. But if it grows and threatens to burst, it's better to get into a hospital.'

'How many days will this take?'

'Can't say. Maybe two or three weeks. Maybe more. But get as much rest as you can. Don't move around much.'

He left the doctor's room with a packet of sulphonamides.

## 2

After lunch that day he went to see Waghmare. Waghmare lived on the top floor of a building he owned. He had kept the entire floor for his own use. He had given Musk Deer a small room on the ground floor. In lieu of rent, Musk Deer went around collecting Waghmare's share of the money earned by his beggars. Waghmare had twenty-seven beggars.

Not many of Bombay's citizens know that the countless beggars in that city are under the thumb of a few bosses. The bosses keep beggars in their power by threat and force, and by protecting them from the police. In return each beggar gives a cut of his earnings to the boss. With two or three dozen beggars under his wing, a boss can make a good living.

Waghmare's servant opened the door and Musk Deer went in. Waghmare's face was hidden behind a newspaper, but, sensing the arrival of a visitor, he folded the newspaper and threw it on the table. He took off his spectacles and placed them on top of the newspaper. He looked up. 'Ah, so it's you,' he said.

Musk Deer noted that Waghmare had set his spectacles down right side up. One shouldn't leave spectacles that way if they're open, because it causes the frames to loosen. It's always a good idea to place spectacles upside down. It bothered Musk Deer every time he saw Waghmare put them down the wrong way. But he could never get up enough courage to teach the correct way to do it. That would not be politically correct.

Musk Deer told Waghmare about the umbilical abscess. 'Well,' he said, trying to sound jovial, 'I've become a kind of musk deer.' Waghmare showed a good deal of interest in Musk Deer's malady. 'The kind of illnesses a man may have!' he marvelled. 'So you are a musk deer now, eh? That's a delightful idea. You read a lot of books, I know. That's where you get such fanciful notions.'

As he talked, Waghmare kept pushing a finger up one of his nostrils. There didn't seem to be anything there. It was simply a habit. Over the years this habit had made Waghmare's large nostrils even wider.

Waghmare was now scraping hard at the inside of his nostrils, which were beginning to look red. Then Waghmare wiped his finger on his loincloth and, with the same finger, began to feel the hair inside the nose. Finding a somewhat longer hair, he pinched it between two fingers, shut his eyes, and gave it a tug. Opening his eyes, he was observing the hair when he was seized by a sudden fit of sneezing. The hair slipped from his fingers. Wiping his nose he bent down and began to look for the hair on the carpet. He couldn't see it. So he got out of the chair and, kneeling down on the carpet, searched for the hair. Musk Deer stared at the soles of his feet pressing against his buttocks. The soles of Waghmare's feet were pink and delicate.

At last Waghmare found the hair. He dropped it carefully into the wastepaper basket.

'What else, then, Musk Deer?' Waghmare asked.

'Well, here's how it is,' Musk Deer said. 'If this abscess gets worse, I won't be able to move around much. The doctor has told me not to anyway. So I doubt if I can make my rounds to the beggars for a while.'

Waghmare stroked his thigh thoughtfully for a minute or two. Then he said, 'All right, I'll send someone else on your rounds till you get well. But if we aren't able to locate a shirker, you'll have to go and find him, okay?'

3

Returning to his room, Musk Deer thought things over. Since he wouldn't be able to do his work for Waghmare, he decided to devote more time to his other job. The work for Waghmare had solved the problem of accommodation, but he still needed other work in order to make a living. Fortunately, this other job happened to be sedentary. The Literary and Cultural Academy had launched the gigantic project of compiling an Encyclopaedia of Indian Literature, and Musk Deer was helping out on it. He had gained a certain reputation for his knowledge of Sanskrit literature, and he was writing articles in this field for the Encyclopaedia. Besides this, he wrote book reviews for the Sunday edition of *People's Power*. On the whole, he was doing pretty well.

Musk Deer began to work on an article on Kalidasa's *The Cloud Messenger* for the Encyclopaedia. He swallowed sulphonamides at prescribed intervals. The abscess remained a mild irritation; some pus seeped out.

Three days later there was a message from Waghmare: the cripple at Bombay Central Station had vanished; also, Bansi Lal of Breach Candy was missing. Could Musk Deer go and look for them?

It was not yet particularly painful to walk, so Musk Deer said yes.

The next morning he headed towards Bombay Central. The cripple—who was known simply as the cripple—normally slept in a shelter beside the State Transport bus-station. He would beg in the lanes around the bus-station.

First, Musk Deer checked the cripple's shelter. Then he began to cover the streets around the shelter one by one. Here and there he asked petty shopkeepers if they had seen the cripple lately.

When a beggar is missing, three possibilities arise: he may be working for another boss, or he may be begging on his own, or he may have left Bombay. Hardly anything could be done in the third case, but it seldom occurred. People come to beg in Bombay from all over India, from obscure villages in distant regions. Why would they leave of their own accord? In the other two cases, one could usually trace a beggar by getting in touch with the men of the other beggar bosses.

Besides, this was the case of a cripple. How far could a cripple go on his own? A beggar woman called Bhagi lived in a shelter near a street-corner. The cripple sometimes visited her late at night. Musk Deer questioned her, and learned that she hadn't seen the cripple for four or five days.

Extending his search wider and wider, Musk Deer found himself near the Mahalaxmi area. It was past three in the afternoon. Musk Deer was tired. Earlier that day he had spent half an hour in an Irani restaurant over a cup of tea. That was all the rest he had had. But now a paanwalla told him that he had seen a cripple, who crawled on his back, go past his shop a few hours ago. Musk Deer's face brightened. And indeed, turning a corner, he saw in the distance a figure stretched out on the sidewalk. The figure appeared to be moving in Musk Deer's direction.

Musk Deer walked on a little further and waited near a shop. On the opposite side of the street, the cripple moved forward.

The cripple had lost both his legs up to the buttocks. He moved on his back. His method was to first pull his head and shoulders in the desired direction, and then drag his backside. He placed his small aluminium begging-bowl on the side towards which he was progressing. Before moving his head and shoulders, he pushed the bowl ahead. Then he dragged himself up to the bowl. Then he pushed the bowl further. The aluminium bowl rattled on the pavement. Passers-by dropped in coins. The cripple was also mute, but he made a kind of nasal sound. Making what noise he could, he stretched his arms towards people passing in the street. When someone walked behind his head, his eyes rolled upward. When someone passed below his body, his eyes rolled downward. His stretched-out figure took up most of the sidewalk, and people had to find their way past on one side or the other.

In a short while the cripple had moved to the point where Musk Deer was standing. He was, of course, on the opposite pavement, and therefore did not see Musk Deer. Being close to the ground, his field of vision was naturally limited. He kept on moving.

Musk Deer decided not to go to the cripple, but instead to keep a watch on him from a distance. He wanted to see where he went in the evening. Then he would know if the cripple had joined up with someone else.

Musk Deer shadowed the cripple. The cripple's pace was slow, and Musk Deer had to pause frequently. When the cripple started out down a street, Musk Deer walked to the end of the street and waited for him to catch up. The cripple crawled to the end of the street on the opposite side, then turned right or left, or continued straight ahead. Musk Deer would walk up that street and wait again for the cripple. Musk Deer noted that the cripple raised his neck at every corner to look about at the shops and buildings.

At sunset the cripple paused in front of a shop that sold roasted peanuts. He picked up two or three coins from his bowl, held them up to the shopkeeper, and made a noise. The man bent down to take the money, then handed the cripple a packet of peanuts. The cripple moved on and, lying beside a wall, ate the nuts. Then he moved on again, found an unoccupied space in a lane, and settled down.

By now Musk Deer was convinced that the cripple had not absconded deliberately. He had merely strayed beyond his familiar streets and lanes, and was unable to find his way back. Musk Deer crossed the street and went up to the cripple. The cripple saw him, raised his arms, and began to make urgent noises, like a child seeing its father.

'Hey cripple, you got lost, did you?' Musk Deer said.

The cripple made a louder noise.

'Okay, okay. We'll carry you back tomorrow morning. Do you want a little tea or something?'

The cripple nodded, and made more noise.

Musk Deer went to the nearest restaurant and brought back some tea in a tall glass. The cripple drank, and Musk Deer turned towards home. He had accomplished one of his two tasks.

Musk Deer was dog-tired when he got home. He ate, and stretched out on his bed. Because of the irritation in his navel, he couldn't sleep. He lay in bed with his eyes shut. During the day he had watched the cripple for so many hours that an after-image remained before his eyes: head and shoulders jerking, then the backside, head and shoulders jerking again, moving endlessly. The cripple's eyes are always turned upward, Musk Deer thought, so he must know a lot about God in Heaven. But then, the creature happens to be dumb. So what use is there in asking him about God? Maybe it was the perpetual sight of God that had struck him speechless.

Late in the night Musk Deer fell asleep. But he kept having unpleasant dreams. Once he saw the cripple at the end of a street. Suddenly the street tilted up like a see-saw board, and the cripple rolled to the other end. Then the other side went up, and the cripple rolled back again. The street's behaviour gave Musk Deer a terrible fright and he woke up in a sweat. He wiped his half-naked body, and then, after a while, went back to sleep again. The cripple reappeared. This time, as the cripple moved up the street, the other end of the street rose slowly. The cripple progressed forward, but found it more and more difficult to hold on. He was frantic. By the time he was nearing the other end of the street, it had risen so high that he rolled down again. His aluminium bowl came clattering down after him, and the coins scattered about. The cripple lay motionless at the lower end for some time. Slowly the street righted itself. Seeing this, the cripple collected his bowl and what coins he could gather, and started moving again. Once more the street rose slowly, and the cripple slid down. Musk Deer woke in the midst of his sliding. Giving up hope of getting any sleep, Musk Deer switched on the light and began to read a book on Kalidasa.

## 4

The next day Musk Deer informed Waghmare's men of the whereabouts of the cripple. Then he went in search of Bansi Lal. Bansi Lal, a leper, lived in a shack near Breach Candy. Usually he begged at a corner of the Bhulabhai Desai Road. Musk Deer checked there first. Bansi Lal was not at the corner. Then Musk Deer went to his shack. He peered in, and saw Bansi Lal lying on a tattered mat.

'Well, Bansi Lal, you're right here!' Musk Deer said. 'And they told me you had vanished.'

'Yes, sahib, I'm here. Why should I run away?' Bansi Lal lifted his head. A fly sitting on his atrophied nose rose into the air. Leprosy has made his nose insensitive, so he doesn't feel the fly's presence, Musk Deer thought. But, he wondered, when most of the nose has disappeared, doesn't the remaining part have any sensitivity?

'Then where were you,' Musk Deer asked, 'when our men came to see you four days ago?'

'The story is this, sahib. The other day my crow brought me a piece of meat and I ate it. Then in the evening I had a great pain in my stomach. At that time I was at Haji Ali. I began to vomit, and became quite ill. So I slept there in a friend's shack. I couldn't get up for two or three days. Only yesterday did I get back. I'm still not well, though, I'm too weak to go out.'

Musk Deer knew about Bansi Lal's crow. Instead of cremating or burying their dead, the Parsis throw them to the birds. The Towers of Silence—the wells into which they place their dead— were on the hill above Bansi Lal's shack. So there were always multitudes of kites, vultures, and crows hovering in the area. Once, a crow had flown down and perched on a tree near Bansi Lal's shack. He carried a large piece of flesh in his beak. The crow tried to tear at the piece with its claws, and the piece fell to the ground. Before the crow could descend, Bansi Lal pounced on the meat and, holding it between his atrophied fingers, went inside. It was nice, red meat. Outside, the crow raised a din. Bansi Lal cut up the meat and put it on the stove. Annoyed at the crow's squawking, he went outside and threw a few stones. The crow dodged the stones, and continued to hover around. The meat was cooked. Bansi Lal thought for a moment, then threw a piece of meat outside. The crow swooped down, grabbed the piece in his claws, and flew off.

The next morning Bansi Lal heard cawing outside his door. He ignored it. The cawing continued. Bansi Lal peered outside and saw a crow perched on a tree. The crow held a chunk of meat in its claws. Seeing Bansi Lal the crow dropped the meat to the ground. Bansi Lal was amazed. For a minute, he just stared at the piece of meat. The crow looked at him and kept cawing. Then Bansi Lal walked out and picked up the meat. After cooking it, he threw a piece to the crow.

This began to happen every day. The crow had developed a taste for cooked meat. Later the crow became half tame. It used to come to the door of the shack, and hop about and make friendly noises, though it never let itself be touched. Bansi Lal was happy. He was getting a good meal every day without much effort. Things were fine as long as Parsis were dying.

But this time something had gone wrong. 'Must've been some rotting bastard,' Bansi Lal said. 'Messed up my stomach.'

'Well, are you okay now?' Musk Deer asked.

'I'm getting better, sahib,' Bansi Lal said, 'I'm weak, as I said. But I'll be able to go out in two or three days.'

Musk Deer asked if he needed anything.

'It would be nice if you could fetch me some bread,' Bansi Lal said.

Returning with a loaf of bread, Musk Deer saw a crow on the tree in front of the shack. It was cawing.

'It came yesterday too,' Bansi Lal said. 'It had brought meat. Went on cawing for a long time. It must have wondered why I didn't come out. But I could hardly rise. Finally it went away.'

Musk Deer looked at the crow on the tree. There wasn't any meat in its claws.

'Throw a few pieces of bread to it, sahib,' Bansi Lal said.

The crow swooped upon the bread. 'Eat, my dear, eat,' Bansi Lal said, raising his head to look at the crow.

When it had finished the bread, the crow flew up to the tree. It kept cawing for some time. Then it went away.

It was noon when Musk Deer left Bansi Lal's shack and went to the bus-stand. He was hungry, and hoped to get home soon for lunch. But no bus turned up for a long time. In the distance, above the Towers of Silence on Malabar Hill, birds circled. Beside Musk Deer, two women and a man waited for the bus. None of them looked like a Parsi.

## 5

Musk Deer had carried out both the tasks assigned to him. For a whole week there was no further request from Waghmare. Musk Deer managed to do a good deal of reading and writing. The irritation in his navel did not diminish. The sulphonamides did not seem to have much effect. Now he was not able to walk erect. He had to stoop a little, and walk gingerly.

After completing the article on *The Cloud Messenger*, Musk Deer began working on a book review for *People's Power*. Then a message came from Waghmare saying that Narayan of the Mahalaxmi racecourse was missing.

Musk Deer's first thought was to refuse the task. He couldn't do much walking now. But then he thought of Narayan. Narayan was a newcomer. Musk Deer had visited him only two or three times for collection. Narayan had begged since he was a small child. Then, when he was seventeen or eighteen, a holy man called Jayaram Baba had taken him under his wing. In Jayaram Baba's company Narayan had travelled widely in North India. They had visited many holy places. At night Jayaram Baba would make love to him. After a few years Narayan was tired of slaving for Jayaram Baba. One day he ran away, and came to Bombay.

Narayan's only capital as a beggar was that his right arm was amputated. But he had a flair for begging, and earned good money. There were two or three bus-stops at which he usually begged.

The first time he saw Narayan, Musk Deer was struck by his own resemblance to him. Even their physical build, he thought, was alike. That first time, he gazed at Narayan as if he wanted to pierce his soul. An idea was taking shape in his mind. Many years ago, when his parents lived in Karwar, and some time before his own birth, his elder brother had vanished. Musk Deer had learned about this from his parents. His elder brother was five years old when this happened. One day his mother had taken him to a temple, and he got lost in the crowd. He was never found again. His parents thought that he was carried off by some band of dacoits or beggars. When Musk Deer was a child, his mother used to hug him and talk to him of his missing brother. 'He looked so much like you,' she used to say, and wipe her eyes.

The idea that was now forming in Musk Deer's mind was this: could Narayan be his missing brother? It was an electrifying idea. It made Musk Deer look at Narayan with quite different eyes. He observed Narayan's every movement closely, as if he expected to find some clue to his identity.

Although Musk Deer had obtained some information about Narayan's earlier years, he had never asked Narayan about his childhood. Nor had he spoken to Narayan about the hunch he had. He thought he would raise the subject when he had come to know Narayan better. And now Narayan had vanished.

Musk Deer thought it over. If it were only a question of obliging Waghmare he would have said no. But here his own feelings were involved. After much deliberation, Musk Deer decided to go in search of Narayan. The abscess would make it painful, but it was something he had to do, out of some obscure compulsion.

Musk Deer checked the places where Narayan usually begged, and where he slept. There was no trace of him. Musk Deer didn't know where else to look for him. Since Narayan was a newcomer, Musk Deer knew next to nothing about his friends, or about the places he frequented. All he could do was wander around Bombay. He recalled that Narayan had once mentioned to him that he liked to sit in a park in the evening. So Musk Deer decided to look for him every evening in the public gardens in Bombay.

He wandered for hours each day. Because of the abscess he had to walk with a stoop, like an old man. People in the street were often intrigued at the sight of a young man walking in this manner. Boys teased him. To prevent the pus from running down, Musk Deer taped some cotton wool over his navel. it was summer. The pad of cotton wool got soaked with pus from the inside, and with sweat from the outside.

For three days Musk Deer walked countless Bombay streets. He searched in all kinds of places. He did not see Narayan.

At a railway station Musk Deer saw a man in a dark suit, wearing dark glasses. On Bose Road he saw a taxi-cab with its hood opened like a jaw, and the cabman peering into it. He saw an old man at a crossing waiting for the lights to turn green. He looked as if he had been waiting forever. He saw a man sitting on top of an empty handcart. He saw a man leaning against a lamp-post, reading a newspaper. He saw a small boy pressing his nose against the glass of a shop-window. He saw a man trying to light a cigarette, his back to the wind. He saw the film actor Dilip Kumar pass by in his Cadillac. He saw a woman on the second floor of a building shut the window. He saw a man on a ladder painting a huge film poster, and the man's raised arm holding a brush. He saw on the poster the head of a woman with only one eye painted. He saw a dog sniffing the dirt on a garbage heap, and another dog sniffing the first dog's behind. He saw a man in a red shirt come out of a restaurant. He saw three men sitting upon a parapet by the sea, looking out at the lifeless water. Downtown at dawn, passing by the rows of beggars and vagrants sleeping in front of office buildings, he saw a boy masturbating. He saw the wrapper of a loaf of Britannia bread on the sidewalk. He saw the unhooked strap of a woman's bra inside her bodice. He saw a postman enter a building on Lady Jamshedji Road. He saw men hanging in the doorways of a suburban train. But he did not see Narayan.

Three days of wandering left Musk Deer in a state of exhaustion. The pain became worse. On the fourth day he stayed in bed. He realized that he had little chance of finding Narayan. How could you track down a man in a vast city like Bombay? But then, what else could he do except wander in whatever direction his feet took him?

The next day Musk Deer went out again. Two days later he had a stroke of luck. Wandering at evening in the Five Gardens at Matunga, Musk Deer saw a man on a bench with his back towards him. The figure looked just like Narayan. Back bent, Musk Deer ran towards him, breathing hard.

'Narayan, Narayan,' he panted.

Narayan sat on the bench, legs stretched out and eyes shut. He opened his eyes. 'Oh, sahib, how did you get here?' he said.

'But why did you run away, Narayan?'

Narayan smiled. 'I got bored with begging at the same bus-stands everyday. It was nicer in a way when I was with Jayaram Baba. As holy men we begged with honour. People gave freely, and with respect. We went from town to town. We could travel everywhere free on the train.' He scratched the stump of his amputated arm. 'I thought I'd leave Bombay, grow a beard, and become a holy man. Having been around with Jayaram Baba, I know the ropes; I know where to go, and when. Then I thought I'd move around a bit and see Bombay before I left. But sahib, it's incredible that you hunted me down!'

'Look here, Narayan. Don't leave Bombay, at least for a few days,' Musk Deer said. Suddenly he realized that he was very tired, and that the abscess hurt more than ever. He sat beside Narayan. 'I'm not asking this for Waghmare's sake, Narayan. It's for my own sake.'

Then he told Narayan about his missing brother. He spoke about the idea he had. Narayan listened, a smile on his face. When he wasn't begging, Narayan always wore this faint smile on his face. It was as if he were amused at everything.

Musk Deer finished talking. Then Narayan said, 'What's all this you've got on your mind, sahib? It doesn't make sense. There are so many people who look alike in some way or the other. Why take it so seriously? It would be unbelievable if I turned out to be your brother among all the thousands of beggars in this country. I think you had better forget the idea.'

With one hand over his abdomen, Musk Deer looked at Narayan. He didn't speak. It was Narayan who spoke again. 'And look at it this way, sahib. Suppose I turn out to be your missing brother. What good is that? Your life has been so different from mine. You're educated. I've begged all my life. In Jayaram Baba's company I've had all kinds of experiences. So what's there to bring us together now? Why do you take all this trouble?' Stroking the stubble on his chin, Narayan looked towards the top of the tamarind tree standing before them. 'Nowadays, sahib, even brothers who have grown up under one roof don't care for one another. And you're getting all worked up about a brother you've never seen! These days one doesn't worry much over others. All one can do is live off someone. I live off the people, Waghmare lives off us, you live off him. Why bother about anything else?'

'Narayan, we'll talk about that later,' Musk Deer said. He lifted his hand from his navel and placed it on Narayan's shoulder. 'Tell me, when did you lose your arm? And how?'

'I don't know,' Narayan said. 'My arm has been like this as long as I can remember.'

'It's curious you should lose your arm at such an early age. Probably the beggars who kidnapped you cut your arm off to make you fit for begging. Now, tell me where you lived as a child?'

'As far back as I can remember, I begged at Nasik under the shelter of my uncle. Uncle used to say that my parents died soon after I was born. Then one day Uncle vanished, and later Jayaram Baba picked me up.'

'Hm . . .' Musk Deer said thoughtfully. 'What's your earliest memory? Describe it as well as you can.'

'My earliest memory?' Narayan pondered. 'Yes, I see a dim scene. There is a sea at one end, then palm trees, further on a house with a tin roof, a narrow lane . . . it meets a paved street near a fig tree . . . chickens feeding in the courtyard of the house.'

Eyes shut, he rested his head on the bench. 'There's another blurred picture. A room. Not well lit. A bed on the right hand. A mat spread near the bed. Two trunks in a corner, one above the other. Near them, a toy horse.' Narayan fell silent. He didn't open his eyes, or raise his head.

Musk Deer's eyes shone. 'Look, Narayan,' he said. 'There's no sea at Nasik. But Karwar's on the sea, right?'

Narayan didn't speak. Musk Deer thought things over. It occurred to him that if he himself had some memory of Karwar, he might have been able to say if the house Narayan remembered was their own. 'But damn it, I don't remember a thing,' he said to himself.

Then he said, 'I've got an idea, Narayan. See, the two of us will go to Karwar. We'll look around. We could find out if a house like the one you remember is still there. Or the lane, or the fig tree. Maybe you'll recognize something else. Then we'll know. Yes, we can find out.'

Narayan opened his eyes. He looked at Musk Deer and smiled.

Musk Deer persuaded Narayan to go with him. 'We'll take a bus tomorrow, or the day after tomorrow,' he declared.

The two got up. As he rose, Musk Deer felt a sharp pain in his abdomen. His face twisted. When the pain subsided he began to walk, his hand on Narayan's shoulder. Yet with every step he had the sensation of a nail being driven into his navel. But they had only to walk as far as the Dadar Tram Terminus. There they could get a bus. The abscess was causing more pain, and yet Musk Deer felt so light, so free. He had found Narayan.

Now it was dark. The two reached the main road. In the distance they could see the glitter of the shops of Dadar T.T.

Musk Deer wondered if he could make it to Karwar in his present condition. He knew he would suffer. But there won't be much walking to do, he thought. What was the point in waiting till his illness was over? He couldn't tell when it would be over, anyway.

He mustn't speak to Waghmare about the planned journey with Narayan, he thought. And what happens after the trip? Musk Deer was convinced that Narayan was his missing brother. Would he let Narayan beg in the streets after their return? Oh no, he thought, I'll look after him, help him make it in life. No doubt Waghmare would be angry. He wouldn't like it at all. In matters of business Waghmare was ruthless. Perhaps he'll fire me, Musk Deer thought. I'll have to give up my room.

His train of thought was broken by a fresh bout of pain. He crouched clutching at his abdomen. 'Sahib, sahib . . .' Narayan called, bending towards him.

There was another stab of pain. Vaguely, Musk Deer realized that this was due to all his wanderings over the past week. He waited for the pain to subside. But it didn't.

He couldn't bear it any more. 'A cab . . . stop a cab,' he said to Narayan.

Narayan tried to hail a cab. When they got a good look at him, cabmen sped away. They didn't want beggars or bootleggers in their cabs. Finally, a cab did stop. Musk Deer crawled towards it. Narayan opened the door, and Musk Deer got in.

'Don't you come in,' the cabman said to Narayan.

Musk Deer looked at Narayan. Silently Narayan shut the door. 'I'll visit you tomorrow, Narayan . . .' The taxi sped away before Musk Deer could say anything more.

'To J.J. Hospital,' Musk Deer told the cabman.

Musk Deer groaned in the back seat. The cabman drove rapidly, without once looking back at him. Large and small lights flashed by on both sides of the street. A breeze blew in. Then suddenly Musk Deer shut his eyes tight. At that moment the abscess burst. He felt as if a thousand lotuses were blossoming at once within his navel.

For an instant a picture flashed before his eyes: the sea at one end, then palm trees, a house, chickens clucking in the courtyard, a lane.

He opened his eyes, and looked at his abdomen. His shirt was soaked in blood. He passed out. For a moment before he lost consciousness, a strange, incense-like scent overpowered his senses; then, in bright morning sunlight, he saw a small temple high on a hill, and heard the tolling of a bell.

The taxi was entering the hospital gate when Musk Deer came

to. I won't be able to go to Karwar soon, he thought. But I'll go, he thought. I'll go as soon as I get well. Narayan will wait for me. He won't run away. I'll go to Karwar with Narayan, he thought. It's just a question of a few days. The taxi stopped.

*The Women in Cages*

# an excursion

## 1

Since daybreak I'd been hearing the roar of airplanes in the sky. Were air force exercises under way, or had war broken out overnight? I thought I should go up on the terrace, and check to see if there were actually airplanes zooming above. Perhaps the roaring sound was originating in my mind. That kind of thing had happened before. Once I lay in bed all day listening to the patter of falling rain. Towards evening I rose, went to the balcony, and looked around. The sun was shining brilliantly, and the road and buildings before me were dry, without a trace of rain.

Whenever I hear a voice, I look around me. If I observe a person nearby, and see his or her lips moving, I conclude that that person is speaking, perhaps to me.

Before I had time to climb up to the terrace, the sound of airplanes ceased abruptly. Perhaps peace had been made. Anyway, I was preoccupied more with a toothache than with the chances of war or peace. I'd been to a dentist the day before, and he'd told me that he would have to pull out the tooth that was hurting. I was horrified. For some reason I had always thought that teeth were a part of the skull, and thus solidly connected to the entire skeleton. When I mentioned this to the dentist, he laughed and said that wasn't true. This fact shocked me even further. To realize that teeth, which looked so firmly embedded in the body, were just clinging precariously to our flesh was distressing. That day I lost faith in teeth.

This was my wash-day. I spent an extra hour or so in bed, put off by the thought of having to struggle with lumps of soggy clothes. Then I bounced out of bed, went to the bathroom, and got through the chore with great speed and verve. In fact I think I expended more energy than the job required, strictly speaking. With a sense of exhaustion and relief I went to the balcony. Leaning upon the parapet, I watched the traffic flowing below. Numerous little pieces of paper floated down from above, danced around lazily, and landed upon the ground. I fancied that it was God in Heaven, writing a poem, or drawing up a legal document, and, not happy with the drafts he was making, tearing them up. Leaning out, I looked up and saw a small boy two floors above tossing pieces of paper into the air. I watched the pieces floating down. One landed on my balcony. I picked it up and drew a picture of the Sun-God on it, complete with mouth, nose, large eyes, and a Stalin-type moustache.

In the afternoon I went out for a walk. I have a habit of walking straight down a street as far as I want to go and then returning the same way. Not for me the adventure of right or left turns, of weaving through alleys, or of wandering in a bazaar. The only thing is, when I want to go back home, I cross the street, and walk back on the other side. I don't have the heart to simply turn around and start walking straight back, as if it were an innocent and inconsequential act.

This afternoon I walked farther than usual. The sun was hot, and I felt enervated. I didn't see a restuarant anywhere nearby. Then I saw a bus-stop, which was really just an iron pole painted red and capped with a sign. There was no one at the stop. I walked up to it and leaned on the pole. It was not the most restful of positions, but it was better than nothing. Then a bus rumbled by and stopped in front of me. A couple got off. The bus-conductor, with the bell-string between his fingers, looked at me impatiently and shouted, 'Come on, hop in quick.'

I was confused. I was vaguely aware that I wasn't standing at the bus-stop to catch a bus, but I didn't know how to explain this to the bus-conductor. For one thing, he obviously had no time to listen to explanations of this sort, and, moreover, I thought that he would start laughing at my words. To make matters worse, I didn't seem to have much time to think. The conductor stood at the door of the bus, ready to pull the bell-string the moment I got in. Like a somnambulist, I stepped into the bus, the conductor rang the bell, and the bus hurtled on.

The conductor came up to my seat. I took out some change. 'Where do you want to go?' the conductor asked. 'Oh give me a ticket anywhere,' I said. 'Don't get on my nerves, man,' the conductor rasped. 'Tell me where you're going. I'm not a tour guide.' What a nuisance, I thought. I wanted to tell him that I hadn't wanted to get onto his bus in the first place, that I had got in only at his insistence, and that he had no right to ask me now where I wanted to go. But I saw that this might sound silly, and therefore kept my mouth shut. The conductor stood before me; his punching machine held out like a knife.

'Okay, give me a ticket for Parel,' I said. 'Sorry, this bus doesn't go to Parel,' the conductor said. I got more annoyed. 'Where does it go then?' I asked. 'Wadala, Sion, Kurla . . .' The conductor click-clicked his punching machine. 'I'll have one to Sion,' I said. Stuffing the ticket into my pocket, I looked out of the window with relief.

The bus passed Wadala, and headed towards Sion. When it was nearing a stop, an old woman sitting in front of me got up excitedly.

'Have we gone by Wadala?' she asked loudly, as if she were putting the question to everyone on the bus. 'Why didn't you call out the stop?' she asked the conductor. 'I did; maybe you didn't hear me,' the conductor said. They went on bickering for a while. Finally the old woman got off at the next stop. Although I had bought a ticket to Sion, I didn't care if I went there, so I hopped off too.

The old woman walked back towards Wadala. I walked behind her, without meaning to follow her. The woman was carrying a large bundle, and walked with difficulty under its weight. Her legs were bent with age. Though I walked in a leisurely fashion, I soon caught up with her. I was about to pass her when I turned round and said, 'Give me the bundle. I'll carry it for you.'

The old woman looked at me with a frown, thinking that I was a coolie looking for work. Then she seemed to wonder if I was a conman. When she had made up her mind that I was neither, she smiled and said, 'All right, young man. Not that I can't carry this; I'm strong enough, God be praised. But today the bus kept me waiting a long while, and I'm a bit tired. I'm glad to see that there still are nice young men like you in this world. Here, take it.'

While I walked alongside the old woman carrying her bundle, she told me about herself. The bundle contained a huge doll and a few other things. The woman lived in Wadala with her granddaughter. The child's mother was dead, and the father had married again. The child didn't want to live with the stepmother, so she lived with her grandmother instead. The old woman had a brother living elsewhere who helped her out. Once she took her granddaughter to his place, where the child saw a huge doll and wanted it very much. At home, she kept asking for the doll all the time. The old woman finally went to her brother's place and was now bringing the doll home.

We reached the building where the old woman lived. On the second floor, as she informed me. 'I'll come upstairs and leave the bundle,' I said. We climbed the stairs. 'Open the door, Chima,' the old woman shouted. 'It's me.'

There was no response. The old woman knocked loudly upon the door. 'Such a wicked, wicked girl,' she said, 'I wonder what she's doing inside. I wouldn't normally leave her alone at home. But today I wanted to go and get back quickly, so I didn't take her along. I told her to sit quietly and not open the door unless she heard my voice. I didn't want her messing around in the kitchen, so I locked it up. Still, I can never trust that kid.'

The old woman called again. I put the bundle down and knocked hard upon the door. Still no response. Now the old woman got panicky. A few neighbours gathered and deliberated, wondering what was the best thing to do. Someone suggested calling the fire department. The old woman became more and more agitated. I leaned over the parapet along the passageway and looked along the left side of the apartment. The living room had a large window with bars, but one of the bars was missing, leaving a fairly wide gap. I thought for a minute, then jumped over the parapet, and gingerly made my way towards the window. I got to it and wriggled through the bars.

Taking a deep breath, I looked around. Chima was right there, lying in bed. I didn't go up to her, though. I went straight to the door and opened it. The old woman rushed towards Chima. I had thought that she was just sound asleep, but she didn't wake even when the old woman shook her. Then I checked if she was breathing. She was. Perhaps she had fainted. Someone went and got a slice of onion, and held it before Chima's nose. At that, she began to cry, 'I'm dead, I'm dead. Why did you do that? I'm supposed to be dead, don't you understand?'

It took us a little while to figure out that Chima had taken it into her head to die, and had simply done so. She expected her decision to be respected, and was annoyed by our meddling.

'What devilish games you play, Chima,' the old woman said. 'I almost died myself a few minutes ago.' But Chima was in no mood to pay attention to her granny. Fixing her large eyes upon the ceiling, she was lost in thought. She seemed to be puzzling over her existential status: *I was dead, these people woke me from death; now what am I?* Then she seemed to have found an answer. She clapped her hands loudly, and declared that she was a ghost. Spreading her arms out and making weird noises, she walked about the room. She seemed to like that particular category of being. She didn't want to be her old self again. Her granny opened the bundle and placed the doll before her. 'Look, Chima,' she said. 'I've got the doll that you wanted so much. Aren't you happy now? Come on, give up all those silly notions.'

The old woman had thought that Chima would forget about being a ghost as soon as she saw the doll. But Chima obviously had a one-track mind. She stared at the doll for a minute or two, and then announced: 'There, *that* is Chima. The dead Chima. And *I* am her ghost. Do you see?' And she made another round of the room making noises and flapping her arms about. When her granny talked to me, Chima said, 'Quiet, Granny. You mustn't speak when there's a dead person in the house. Didn't you tell me to be quiet when Mama died?'

So far Chima hadn't paid any particular attention to my presence. But then I became aware of her eyes fixed intently upon me, as though she were determined to discover my role in the scheme of things. I became uncomfortable.

'Oh yes,' Chima screeched. 'I know who you are. You even look like the man who came to take Mama away when she died. Now you've come to take away Chima, right? What do they call a man like that, Granny? I *know* the word. But . . .' she looked at Granny. 'Yes, undertaker. That's it—you're the undertaker.'

I shuddered, as if I had suddenly been blinded by a searchlight. An undertaker! Numbly, I looked at Chima.

Then Chima insisted that I should take away the dead Chima, that is, the doll. I gave a start. Carry away a doll! And what would I do with it?

Her granny was about to lose her temper. 'What's all this silliness, Chima? I went all the way to Bhai's place to get the doll, and now you want it taken away? You're driving me crazy. The next thing you'll be wanting us to sit in front of the doll weeping and moaning!'

'But we mustn't keep a dead body in the house, Granny,' Chima said, following up the inexorable logic of the situation. 'When Mama died, didn't you tell me that we couldn't keep her body any longer?'

The old woman made tea for me. After tea, I rose to leave. Chima went into a terrific tantrum. 'Take her away! Take her away!' she screamed, pointing her finger alternately at the doll and at me. Finally, in exasperation her granny picked up the doll. Holding it towards me, she said, 'Take it away then. I can't stand this anymore. You've been so nice, though. Come to think of it, I didn't even know you a few hours ago, and you've done so much for me. I wonder how many boys as decent as you there are today. You know, I had so many hopes for Chima. I've done so much for her, but I can see what it's all going to come to.' For a moment she stared past me into emptiness, then looked at me. 'Here,' she said.

Gingerly I stretched out my arms. With sad eyes that lingered over me, the old woman placed the doll across my arms. It was quite a large doll, and heavy too. It was almost like holding a child in my arms.

I turned and walked towards the door. I didn't even remember to say goodbye to the old woman. The doll lay across my forearms. I didn't hold it with my hands. With slow, careful steps

I climbed down the stairs. I got to the bottom and stood on the sidewalk, holding the doll in front of me.

## 2

Now I faced the task of getting home. On my countless little forays into the world, how my heart used to leap up at the thought of turning homeward! But today was not the same.

I decided that the wisest thing would be to take the same bus that I had caught earlier. Like a fool, I hadn't even noticed the number of the bus I had taken. I went to the stop at which I had alighted and read the sign. It carried only one number: 315. So I crossed the street intending to catch a 315 going the other way. I went to the bus-stop on the other side of the road, but couldn't find 315 on the sign. It showed number 314 instead. I was puzzled. Then I asked someone and learned that number 314 did go to Mahim, where I wanted to go. Number 315 and 314 were circular routes, which meant that I could not only go home by taking a 314, but also, if I wished, by getting onto a 315 and continuing along the same way that I had come. I found the idea of returning home without retracing one's steps, as it were, fascinating. Crossing the street again, I went back to the stop for 315.

I got home, placed the doll upon the table and stretched out in bed. After some time I began to feel that something was wrong. I felt as if I had gone out, and never returned! I tried to persuade myself that I had in fact returned home, that I was now lying cosily in my bed, and that nothing was amiss. But it was no use. Then I got out of bed and switched on the light. Like a magnet, the doll upon the table attracted my eye. Propped against the wall, it looked so large in my room! It occurred to me that I hadn't as yet had a good look at it. I sat on the edge of the bed and looked at the doll. It was a woman in a Rajasthani dress. She wore a long red skirt with a bright green bodice. She held her arms in such a way that you felt she was about to clap her hands, or begin to dance. Her eyes were large and shining, like the eyes of goddesses in pictures. On her feet she wore silver anklets.

I rose and went towards the table, and stood in front of the doll for a few moments. Then I gently lifted her skirt and peered underneath. She wore yellow panties, bordered with white lace. I returned to my bed.

Later I warmed some food, and ate. While washing the dishes, I realized that I was thinking again about my excursion during the day. I was still puzzling over the experience. There was this nagging feeling, for instance, that I hadn't returned home, and I didn't know what to do about it. Then I noticed how the doll on the table appeared to have arranged everything in the room around itself. With a quiet self-assurance the doll had made itself the centre of my room. And it's only the dead body of Chima, I said to myself. It's strange how something dead becomes a kind of centre, whereas the living never keep still, and therefore can hardly be the centre of anything.

I wondered what I would do with the doll. Maybe, I thought, I should give it away to some child living in the building. Or maybe I should go to the beach and bury it in the sand. Or I might visit the old woman's house again and return the doll. Perhaps Chima would forget the idea of the doll being a corpse, and might welcome the doll's return. Then my tooth started hurting again. In the excitement of the day I had forgotten to take the pain-killers the doctor had given me. I took the tablets now, and switched off the light. Lying in bed, I pondered over the difference between natural and artificial light. You switch off an electric light, and instantly plunge into total darkness. On the other hand, sunlight graduates gently into darkness, almost imperceptibly. I remembered the evenings when I used to sit among the rocks by the sea and watch darkness growing, enthralled by the metamorphosis of day into night. Yet darkness increases only to a certain point, beyond which it cannot grow at all.

# on the stone steps

## 1

The monsoon had usually set in by the time school began each year in early June. It was the first week of July now, and there was still no trace of rain. The days were hot and dry. Clouds gathered one evening and the air became sultry, but it didn't rain. The next morning I rose early. My third form composition exercises had to be graded. I corrected a few, and then felt so enervated that, leaving my pencil inside an exercise book, I simply sat listlessly in my chair.

The fan churned the humid air above my head, and the pages of the calendar on the wall fluttered in the breeze. One or two leaves flew up, came down, and flew up again, while one end of the towel thrown over the back of the armchair flapped back and forth ceaselessly. Flapping back and forth, back and forth, for hours on end! Heavy things are better off. The chair I sat on, the bed upon which I stretched out my legs, the small table beside me, the exercise books with their thick covers—things like that stay put. But it's different with a calendar or a towel. Let the fan begin to whirl, and they know no peace. How can they stand it? If the calendar were human, it would keep its pages in place by sheer will power, or, if that proved impossible, it would get up and leave. A man will at least protest somehow if life becomes unbearable. Even if he is helpless, his mind can still rage within him. He doesn't simply sway with the breeze. Suddenly the mindless fluttering of the calendar filled me with loathing. I thought of finding a nail and pounding it through the bottom of the calendar. But I didn't have the energy to do it at the moment.

After a while I got up, went to the sink, and splashed water in my face. Wiping myself off, I looked into the mirror above the sink. My hair was thinning faster of late. Like a hidden truth, the oily skin of the scalp was showing through. I had tried all sorts of shampoos, and many different kinds of hair oils. Nothing had worked. It's not pleasant to go bald at twenty-eight.

Hair transplants have become quite common in England and America nowadays, I thought. If only I could go to England, I could get a hair transplant. But how could I, a mere school-teacher, hope to make such a journey?

Shashank left for America last week. I went to see him off at the airport. He said he didn't ever want to return to this wretched country. Before entering the embarkation area, he made a point of visiting the men's room. 'Let me piss on this country before I leave,' he said.

He was able to get a green card because he's an architect. As a schoolteacher with a BA (Third Class), I could never hope to get a visa to go to America. Then I thought, what's so wonderful about America? One would only end up in a different sort of mess.

It was time to leave for school, and I went and knocked on Gunjikar's door. Gunjikar was my neighbour, and we taught in the same school, so we usually left for work together. Gunjikar was twenty years older than me, and had, in fact, been my own teacher at the school in which I now taught.

As a schoolboy I had never dreamed that I would one day become a teacher in my own school. I would have been angry if someone had made such a prediction. Whenever I was asked as a child, 'What do you want to be when you grow up,' I invariably answered, 'A pilot.' That remained just a flight of fancy, however. School is something one leaves behind in order to join the rough and exciting world outside, but I never got beyond the schoolyard, so to speak. Four or five years for the BA and a teacher's diploma, and I was back in school. What's more, there wasn't even the sense of making another start in a new environment. The school happened to be in a crowded part of Bombay, but it had a good reputation, and, more important, it was close to home. There

*The Women in Cages*

seemed no point in looking for a job elsewhere.

Even in the sort of weather we were having, Gunjikar came out in his usual brown jacket. I had seldom seen him without a jacket. As a matter of fact, I used to see him in this same brown jacket when I was his student, except that by now it looked quite faded.

Gunjikar was shutting the door behind him when his wife shouted from within, 'Didn't you say you'd bring vegetables from the market in the evening? You forgot to take a bag.' Gunjikar went in again and came out folding a cloth bag.

On the way to school we had to cross one end of Tilak Bridge. There are steps up to the bridge which are made of dark, smooth slabs of stone. The bridge was built many years ago, which probably accounts for its stone steps. A more modern bridge would have used cement, for who carves stone steps these days? The stairs make a turn halfway up, and one invariably sees a beggar sitting in the corner. Beggars are smart. They find the perfect place to sit, not quite in the way of passers-by but not quite out of the way either. Anyone climbing the steps couldn't help noticing the figure at the edge of his field of vision.

Gunjikar dropped a five paise coin in the beggar's bowl. He often does this, and I never do. Gunjikar once said to me, 'Don't you ever feel pity for these creatures? Remember that the Lord Buddha saw only one old man, one sick man, and one corpse and his heart overflowed with compassion. It changed his life.'

'Now listen, Gunjikar,' I said. 'For one thing, the Buddha only saw *one* old man, and one of all the rest. But when you look at the hordes of beggars, lepers, and cripples infesting Bombay, how can compassion continue to well up in your heart?' After a pause for effect I continued, 'Secondly, the Buddha's life until that moment had been spent in pure happiness and pleasure. Not only had he not had any unpleasant, ugly experiences, but he hadn't even heard of such things. Naturally, a person like that is bound to be deeply affected when he sees things of that sort. But that's not the story of my life.'

'Still, what does that have to do with the suffering of any particular beggar?' Gunjikar asked me. Then we ran into someone we knew and the topic was dropped.

That evening Gunjikar went to the market, so I walked back home alone. I crossed the bridge and was going down the steps when I suddenly halted. The beggar at the corner was gone, and a twenty-paise coin shone at the place where he had been sitting. Without thinking I bent down, picked up the coin, and put it in my pocket. I went on down the steps. A moment later an incident from my childhood flashed before my eyes.

From my earliest schooldays, there had always been a beggar at the turn of those steps. Of course, the beggar sometimes changed. One day the regular occupant would vanish, the place would remain vacant for a few days, and then a new beggar would appear on the scene. A strategic location like that didn't remain unoccupied for long.

Sometimes the beggar was gone before I descended the steps in the evening on my way home from school. On one occasion, as I skipped down the steps, I saw a four-anna coin in the corner (we had annas in those days). I stopped, bent over and picked up the coin hastily, and hurried on down the steps. No one had seen me.

The blood raced in my veins. In those days four annas was quite a bit of money. It would've bought plenty to eat during the afternoon break, and I didn't get much pocket money at home.

Then it struck me that the four annas must have belonged to the beggar who sat there. He had overlooked the coin when he left. Suddenly I felt unclean. It was one thing to pick up a coin someone had dropped in the street, and another to pocket a beggar's money. My mind was in turmoil. I was beset by feelings I couldn't quite understand, feelings of having been somehow polluted, of having done something common and mean. For a while I thought I ought to throw the coin away, but I couldn't bring myself to do it.

The next morning, on my way to school, I saw the beggar in his corner. My heart fluttered, as though I were afraid he was going to demand his money back. Perhaps if he had done so, I might actually have felt happier, but he scarcely noticed me. He had a businessman's eye: schoolboys didn't give money, and he had no interest in them.

For three days the coin remained unspent in my pocket. Each

*The Women in Cages*

day I passed the beggar. Then on the fourth day, as I was going past him, I took out the coin and dropped it into his bowl. I hadn't actually planned on doing anything of the kind, and was surprised myself that I had. I had dropped the coin in the same impulsive manner in which I had picked it up. The beggar appeared surprised that a schoolboy had given him a coin, and a four-anna one at that. He stared at me. I walked away briskly.

## 2

And now something similar was taking place. As I went down the steps my heart was beating rapidly. I was fascinated by the repetition of this incident after so many years. But then I realized that it wasn't really so unusual. I had gone up and down those steps countless times over the years; it wasn't odd that the same thing had happened again one day.

I came home and hung my shirt on a peg, with the coin in its pocket. Stretched out in my armchair, I contemplated the shirt pocket. Then I was seized by a kind of rage at being caught again in this childish situation. And why had I picked up the coin? I couldn't buy anything but a couple of cigarettes with it. Although the circumstances were almost the same as when I was a boy, there was one difference: twenty paise were worth less today than four annas had been fourteen years ago. Also, I was a schoolboy at the time, and wasn't earning anything. Today I had a job. Still the fact was that I had picked up the coin. Nothing else made any real difference.

Then I thought, I'll go and return the money tomorrow, and get myself out of this situation. But my mind inexplicably rebelled at this thought. If I gave the coin back, then everything would have happened exactly as it had fourteen years ago. I didn't like that. No, I said to myself, I won't give it back. I was surprised at my own decisiveness. Why was I being so stubborn? It was as though something that had been bothering me for a long time was coming to a head.

I had made my decision, but my mind didn't seem to be at rest. After supper I sat down with the unfinished composition exercises from the morning, but wasn't able to concentrate. Then I suddenly banged my fist upon the table and said to myself, What's all this nonsense? Why am I getting worked up over nothing? I have lots of other things to do and to worry about.

It's amusing how one's mood can change. Instantly I felt carefree. I attacked the composition books with great energy, and finished them well before bedtime. I was pleased.

The next day, getting ready for school, I put on my shirt. I put my hand casually inside the pocket and felt the cold touch of the coin. I gave a start, as though I had touched the forehead of a corpse. I never keep money in my shirt pocket. I realized that my mind was not really at peace. I went out. The clouds that had gathered the day before had vanished and the sky was as dry as hot sheet-metal. I became tense as I walked past the beggar on the steps. Seeing that I was uncommunicative, Gunjikar kept silent most of the way.

In the evening clouds reappeared in the sky, and the weather became sultry again. Eating a light supper, I sat under the fan. As I watched the calendar fluttering upon the wall, I remembered that I had intended to pound a nail through its lower end. Then I heard children clamouring outside. I rose and looked out. Large drops of rain had begun to fall, and children had gathered in the courtyard below, dancing and shouting in the rain. The heat will let up now, I thought, the night should be pleasanter.

It rained all night, and in the morning there were puddles in the streets. School finished early, since it was a Saturday. I had to bring some records up to date, so I stayed late. Gunjikar too remained to teach a small group of students who were going to be taking a scholarship exam. I didn't think he would be free soon, and left when my work was finished.

The school was practically deserted, but there were a few boys in the courtyard at the back. Being in a crowded part of the city, our school lacked a proper playground; all we had was a vacant lot behind the school building. Rain had turned the ground into mud, and the boys were playing tag on the slippery surface.

I remembered when I was in the fourth grade at school. In the middle of the monsoon season we decided to play tag in the courtyard. Running about on the muddy ground demanded skill;

every so often someone would slip and fall, covering himself in mud. The constant danger of falling made the game exciting. Rows of boys standing in the school corridors watched the game, and laughed and shouted when one of the players slipped and fell. The presence of spectators added to the thrill. Soon the game became popular, and the number of spectators grew. Then the school principal got wind of this new form of entertainment and quickly put an end to what he termed our devilry.

## 3

The boys before me now had discovered the same kind of fun, although there were no spectators. I watched as they ran about trying to keep their balance on the muddy ground, and occasionally slipping. I became absorbed in the game, and the thrill of running over the slippery ground seized me. It was as though I were a boy again, running with the others. What if I joined them? It was an outlandish idea. A teacher wasn't supposed to get involved in such tomfoolery. If the principal happened to pass by, it would be embarrassing. He didn't think very highly of me as it was.

Without noticing it I had drifted towards the courtyard. At first the boys didn't know why I was approaching. When I said I wanted to join in, they were excited and welcomed me with shouts. I heard one of the boys refer to me as 'tubelight', and saw him stop short when he realized that I was within earshot. Lately I had noticed that the boys had taken to calling me 'tubelight', which is schoolboy lingo for 'baldy'.

I was soon engrossed in the game. Then it was my turn to chase the others. Those little boys were nimble-footed, balancing themselves effortlessly, and scrambling to their feet quickly when they slipped. I was no match for them on the slippery ground. I was becoming tired, but felt I had to prove myself and ran about madly. Then, before I knew what had happened, I tumbled face down in the mud. Pain shot through my right arm. As I raised myself up, I saw the twenty-paise coin from my shirt pocket sinking into the mud before me. I tried to reach out and pick it up, but my arm seemed paralyzed. I was confused. I lifted my right arm with my left, and then realized that it was broken.

The boys gathered around me and helped me up. 'Teacher has broken his arm, teacher has broken his arm,' they shrieked. For a while I stood there trying to catch my breath. Then Gunjikar, who had finished teaching at last and was passing by, saw me amidst the boys and walked up. 'What have you done to yourself?' he said, pushing the boys away. 'Why did you get mixed up with these kids? You know your bones or mine aren't as supple as theirs.'

My clothes and hands and face were smeared with mud. Mud was caked in my eyelashes, blurring my vision. The raw, pungent smell of clay tingled in my nose. But the pain in my arm made me oblivious to these things. 'Let's go,' Gunjikar said, supporting me with both hands. I started to take a step, then halted and said, 'I dropped twenty paise somewhere around here. Could someone have a look?'

The coin had disappeared into the mire, and I didn't know exactly where I had dropped it. One or two boys groped about in the mud for it. Then Gunjikar said, 'Oh, forget it. What's twenty paise? We've got to get you to the doctor as quick as possible.'

'Let's leave the coin in the mud,' One of the boys said. 'Then it will sprout, and become a tree. Then money will grow on the tree, lots and lots of money.' Some of them laughed. Boys will be boys.

We moved out, with Gunjikar supporting me, and the boys crowding around. In the midst of my agony the lost coin still nagged at my mind. But, I thought, even if I had returned the money to the beggar it wouldn't have been a real repetition of the incident from my childhood, for all things change. On the other hand, if I had stubbornly refused to return the coin, that wouldn't have made any difference either, for nothing ever really changes. You walk up the steps, or down the steps, you finish school and become a schoolteacher, or an architect, an engineer, or a pilot, and there is always a beggar at the turn of the stone steps, a shadow that is little more than a coarse voice that you can't help hearing, or a gesture of the arms that is deliberately ignored, or eyes that turn away as you turn at the corner.

Now I would have to take a few days' leave. What would the principal say, I wondered. Then I realized that I couldn't pound a nail through the bottom of the calendar after all, now that my arm was broken.

# a revolt of the gods

## 1

It was the time of the Ganesh festival. In the evening I had to go out to photograph one of the numerous festival shows that were being staged all over Bombay. It took me longer than I expected, and the next morning I rose late. Dalvi was already at the studio when I arrived and was busy developing negatives in the darkroom. We had been getting a lot of extra business during the festival, having been called in to photograph several shows. Amateur singers and actors were particularly eager to be photographed on stage. While Dalvi handled such jobs expertly, I was much happier doing portraits in the studio. During the festival, however, there were often two assignments on the same evening, and then I had to go out too. Dalvi enjoyed these stints; I hated making my way among the noisy crowds, toting a camera and other paraphernalia, and moving from one end of the stage to the other in search of a better angle, often crouching awkwardly in order to catch someone in a good pose. It's different in the studio: an elegant curtain in the background, lights placed at strategic points, and in their midst the customer seated silently and meekly, if somewhat uncomfortably. This was the last day of the Ganesh festival, and I was relieved that there would be no more spells of working late. There was still a lot to do in the studio of course—making prints, enlargements, and so on.

I set about touching up some passport photos. Touching up—that's my forte. It's mostly Dalvi who looks after developing and printing; he's better at it than I am. We've set up our studio in partnership, relying largely upon Dalvi's technical skill; I take care of things like touching up, cutting prints, and keeping the accounts.

A young man who looked like someone in search of a job came in to have some passport photos taken. I asked him if he wanted to wear a tie, and he said yes. Inspecting the tie I handed him, he remarked that it seemed old-fashioned and asked if we had another one he could use. We only had one tie, I said curtly. I was annoyed. If he was so particular, he should've come with his own tie, I thought. He couldn't even manage a decent knot, and had probably seldom worn a tie before. I had to tie it for him.

I found it difficult to keep working until one o'clock, and my eyes were heavy from lack of sleep. Just as we were about to close down, a blind man walked up tap-tapping his cane and asked if his pictures were ready. Four days ago he had come in, feeling each step with his cane before climbing it, had stood at the counter for a few moments taking in my presence, and then asked, 'Is this the Gajanan Photo Studio?' Apparently some institution was sending him to the US to study music, and he needed pictures for a passport. He was talkative, as all blind persons seem to be, and was excited about his prospective journey. He told me that the blind had a difficult time in India, and how a blind person could hope to develop his abilities in Western countries. I listened absent-mindedly as I led him to the seat. It occurred to me that I was taking a blind man's picture for the first time. I switched on the lights; he stared with eyes wide open. Usually, people blink in the glare, or turn their heads away. The blind man sat motionless, with his sightless eyes shining defiantly under the violent lights.

I had told him that he could pick up the pictures today; I searched about but couldn't find them. They must be lying somewhere amidst the heaps of festival pictures, I thought. 'I'm sorry, could you come back in two days?' I said. He went away, tap-tapping his stick. I locked the studio and went home. I was glad that the studio was closed for the day. That evening Dalvi had to go to witness the immersion of his household Ganesh.

I slept for an hour after lunch before being awakened by the noise of kids in the courtyard below. The members of the festival commitee for our building were getting things ready for the Ganesh immersion. Like countless other buildings in Bombay, ours too had its Ganesh, with shows every evening for eleven days, the whole affair financed by donations from each tenant. I got out of bed and made myself a cup of tea. Refreshed, I went out for a stroll. I thought I'd catch up with the procession bearing our building's Ganesh somewhere along the way.

The evening shadows were lengthening. I walked, looking at the shadows of buildings, of electric poles, and of men and women. I like observing shadows more than watching things and human beings. Buildings and poles and men remain the same for years, or change very little, very slowly. On the other hand, the shapes and angles of shadows change minute by minute. They are sometimes clearly etched, and at other times like badly focused photographs. Men, stolid and heavy, merely dream of transfigurations, while shadows change endlessly. A man is nothing compared to his shadow. Without shadows, life would have been far duller.

The main street was crowded. Small groups of people went by with their household clay figures of Ganesh. One man carried upon his head a small figure on a wooden platform, and the rest walked behind him singing hymns. The large civic figures were brought down later in the evening. I sat in an Irani restaurant on the way to the sea-shore. After some time I observed people from our building approaching with the clay image. I got up and merged into the tail-end of the procession.

As always at the yearly immersion, the beach was swarming with people. Amid the sea of human beings milling about one could spot here and there the colourful figure of the elephant-headed god. The civic images, perched comfortably upon handcarts and trucks, were in greater evidence. The figure from our building was medium-sized. Members of the festival committee had complained that the collection was unusually small this year. I was sure, though, that they had managed to pocket their usual share of the money. Anyway, I didn't take much interest in their dealings.

The roads had become so congested that all the processions

*The Women in Cages*

had more or less ground to a halt. The sea was only a short distance away, but it would take a long while to reach the water's edge.

Then I noticed a disturbance at the head of our procession. Being at the tail-end, I didn't know what was wrong at first. I craned my neck, but couldn't see our Ganesh figure and wondered if it had fallen off the handcart. Then someone said that the Ganesh had jumped off. Naturally, I thought he was joking. But the commotion seemed to be spreading. Indeed the figures in the different processions had begun to disappear, apparently deserting their seats on the wooden platforms and handcarts and trucks. In the melee I couldn't quite see what was happening, but I did observe a huge civic figure jumping down from a truck. I saw a man fall to the ground at a blow from its trunk.

Here and there one glimpsed clay images that had come to life, as it were, and were sprinting away. But scarcely anyone possessed the composure to watch this miraculous spectacle. Confused and terrified, everyone ran back towards the city. Even the traffic cops had abandoned their positions and were running with the rest. Knocked about in that disorderly retreat, I lost one of my slippers. For a while I ran with one slipper, but then realized that there was no point in returning that way. I cast it off too and ran barefoot.

When I reached the building, I noticed that almost everyone else was already there. People gathered in the courtyard and discussed the event in excited tones. Since everyone was talking at the same time it was hard to understand what was being said. The women, many of whom chanted prayers breathlessly, looked particularly frightened. Children cried.

After some time the clamour became more intelligible. An attempt was made to discover the significance of the supernatural event. At first everyone seemed to be convinced that it was a manifestation of divine wrath.

Mr Kini—who was an accountant in a government office, and was commonly known as Accountant Kini—appeared even more excited than the rest. 'Look,' he said in a cracked voice. 'For a long time I've had the feeling that sooner or later something of this sort was going to happen. True, Lord Ganesh is called *lambodara*—pot-bellied—but how many sins can you expect him to swallow? I bet now he won't return to heaven without giving a good lesson to all the black marketeers, smugglers, food adulterators, and politicians. They're the ones who've brought this on.'

'But all these images that have come to life—just what are they going to do now?' Akshikar, who lived on the third floor, asked. 'How will they punish the guilty?'

It was something to think about.

'Well, who can tell what the gods will do?' someone said. 'We just have to face up to whatever happens next without complaining.'

Professor Matkari had a different view. He said, 'I see no reason for being so frightened. You must have seen that the gods just jumped off their seats and went away. It didn't seem as if they were lashing about at people, or wanted to hurt anyone.'

'That's right,' Subodh, who was studying physics in college, said. He was on the festival committee in our building. 'I see no point in talking about sin, and the like. The gods have not arisen to dispense punishment. They could've done that without resorting to miracles. They're gods, after all. I think they were simply outraged by the whole spectacle—the sweaty crowds, the hurly-burly, and the disorder. Why should the gods put up with it? When they couldn't stand it any longer they just got up and walked away.'

The discussion continued. I slipped away and went upstairs to my apartment. I stretched out in bed. The excitement and the exertion had tired me.

## 2

The next day there was a great stir in the city. People wondered if the absconding gods had vanished completely, or were still prowling about. At first it seemed that they had disappeared, but then fleeting glimpses of them were caught here and there. The elephant-headed god's trunk would appear around a corner, or, climbing a flight of stairs, one would suddenly become aware of a shadowy figure disappearing ahead. A lonely passer-by might receive a blow on the head from a god's trunk. No one was hurt seriously, but some people were sent into a state of shock for a few hours. They would behave strangely for a while, say unintelligible things, and then gradually return to normal life. That was all the gods did. They didn't unleash any terrifying forces, or throw the daily life of the city out of gear. In a few days people calmed down and went about their business. And of course the people of Bombay have a reputation for not being thrown off balance or surprised by anything. Still, people tended to return home earlier in the evening, and avoided walking through isolated areas. There was no telling when one might receive a blow on the head.

The day after the revolt of the gods I didn't go to the studio. Like everyone else, I thought I'd see how things turned out first. Then we went back to business as usual. For a week or so, there were very few customers. But we had plenty of work at the studio. Dalvi spent most of his time in the darkroom. I had taken pictures at the show in the Makarand Housing Society, and they had all come out poorly. The entire roll of film had been exposed at the wrong speed. Dalvi wasn't happy about it. I told him not to worry; I'd touch up all the pictures and set them straight.

One day the blind man returned. I had forgotten about his pictures in the meantime. I searched for them again without success. I didn't know what to do. I didn't feel I should make a blind man come back time and again. For a moment I thought of handing him someone else'e pictures: after all, he couldn't see them. I said, 'Please come back in four days; I'll definitely have them ready.' He seemed upset and went away tap-tapping his cane noisily.

Another day Accountant Kini came to my room with a roll of film. Photography is his hobby and that has made us friends. He comes in often to talk over technical matters. Some of his pictures of flowers and the like have appeared in the Sunday newspapers, so he feels he is an artist.

While leaving Kini said, 'For the last two or three days we've been bothered by mice. We've never had them in our apartment before. These must have come in recently. Last night I set a trap;

in the morning I found two. Then it suddenly occurred to me—when the Ganeshas arose and left, the mice that had invaded my house were the same ones on whose back the gods are supposed to ride.'

'What did you do then?' I asked.

'Well, I didn't know what to do,' Kini said. 'I was appalled at the idea that the mice I was going to kill might belong to the gods.'

'You could've taken the cage with the trapped mice to the sea and drowned them,' I said. 'As it is, don't we immerse the mice along with the Ganeshas anyway?'

'Oh, no,' Kini said. 'It's one thing to carry Lord Ganesh and his mouse reverently to the sea for immersion, and quite another to drown mice.'

I saw no difference, but didn't have enought interest in the matter to argue about it.

Touching up the pictures I had taken at the Makarand Housing Society show turned out to be an exhausting job. It wasn't the same as touching up a studio portrait. There were often a number of persons in a single picture, with faces much smaller than in a portrait. Touching up each little face was tedious. Then one day their man came and picked up the pictures. The next morning he was back at the studio. 'Are these our pictures, or someone else's?' he asked. 'We can hardly recognize a single face.' I shrugged. 'What's so special about a face?' I said. 'We won't come back next year,' he said.

Then I spent an entire morning looking for the blind man's pictures, again without success. I was exasperated. I decided that I'd take his picture again, free of charge of course. He was supposed to come in the next day. The next morning I waited for the sound of his cane, but he didn't turn up.

As I was getting ready to go to bed that evening there was a knock at the door. My first thought was of the blind man. Then I laughed, realizing how absurd the idea was. He didn't know where I lived; besides, photographers aren't called at night like doctors. I wondered who it could be. Opening the door, I saw Accountant Kini. I thought he had come to ask about the roll of film he had given me the other day. I said I hadn't been able to develop it, what with all the work on the festival pictures. But he stayed on, making small talk. I saw that his mind wasn't in the conversation, but on something else he wasn't mentioning. He kept fidgeting.

Then the conversation faltered; I deliberately remained silent. Kini looked around aimlessly at the calendar on the wall, at my books, at the curtains. Then he looked at me and said, 'There's something I wanted to talk to you about.'

'Go ahead,' I said.

'I've never mentioned this to anyone until now. My wife is the only person who knows about it,' Kini said. 'In the last few years I've developed a strange habit—that of cursing the gods.'

Kini paused and stared at the foot of my bed. I remained silent.

'In our family we worship Lord Ganesh,' Kini continued without raising his head. 'I've known the hymn to Ganesh by heart since childhood. Yet, instead of hymns and prayers, what comes into my mind are curses. Unspeakable, abominable curses. I was brought up well as a matter of fact. Never learned bad words as a child. Even today I wouldn't say something like "damn". And yet when I think of God my mind literally spews out curses. At first I was shocked to discover that I knew so many.'

There was a knock at the door. 'Papa, papa,' little Sushma shouted. 'What a nuisance,' Kini said, and rose to open the door. 'What do you want?' he asked his daughter.

'Mummy's calling you,' Sushma said. Then she seemed to want to get in. But Kini pushed her away. 'I'll be back in a few minutes,' he told her.

'And don't you come knocking again.'

He bolted the door and returned to his seat.

'So that's my story. Usually, the cursing goes on silently in my mind. Often, when I'm at home, I mutter to myself. On a few occasions, when my wife and Sushma have gone out, I've shut the doors and windows and, standing in front of the images of the gods, shouted curses until I was hoarse, I found it nauseating to my own ears, but my mouth wouldn't stop.'

Kini paused. He suddenly looked tired.

'At first I tried to control my mind, but without success. Then

I tried different kinds of charms and amulets. I made offerings to many deities. Nothing worked.'

'Perhaps it's due to something nagging at your mind,' I said. 'Deep in your mind there may be resentment at some injustice, or some disappointment. Perhaps it comes to the surface in this way.'

'Oh, no,' Kini said. 'I'm as happy in life as anyone could be. My only son—a bright boy, and well-behaved—is studying to be an engineer. We're all in good health and there's no great worry on my mind. Oh yes, I've been happy. And yet, there's this horrible thing that won't go away.'

'Have you been to a psychaitrist, then?' I asked.

'I don't believe in that sort of thing. This isn't a matter of mere chemicals, or of nerves. Scientific mumbo-jumbo would be of no use. It's only God who can save me.'

From Kini's apartment came the sound of his wife shouting, and then of Sushma crying. Kini listened for a moment and then ignored it.

'Then this thing happened the other day,' he said. 'The gods became angry. Since that day, I've been thinking—did that happen because of my dreadful habit? I had a feeling that something of this sort would happen one day. Sins must bear fruit, sooner or later.'

For a few minutes I didn't speak. Then I said, 'Look, Mr Kini, what you've said doesn't make much sense. Think about it— hundreds of Ganesh images in Bombay got up and went away. That couldn't be the fruit of one person's sins. I mean, there'd be too large a gap between cause and effect. God doesn't watch you alone. His eye is on everyone, you know.'

I lit a cigarette and continued, 'But I don't find it strange that such an idea came into your head. When a shattering public event like this occurs, everyone begins to see his own life in its light. I'm sure thousands of persons in Bombay at this moment have similar ideas. On the other hand, your petty sins may not count for much in God's account books.'

Kini remained silent. My words seemed to have made some sense to him, but I doubted that he would change his mind.

Lying in bed, I thought for a long while about what Kini had told me. It was past midnight when I fell asleep, but I woke up almost immediately. I was wondering what had awakened me, when I heard small noises coming from the kitchen. I listened. Mice, I thought. I hadn't had mice in my apartment before. Then I remembered that Kini, too, had spoken about mice the other day. Mice must be invading the whole building, probably because of the squalor in the new shanty town growing up behind it.

The noise of the mice made it hard to get back to sleep. Sounds in the dark are particularly irritating. As long as things are visible, noise recedes into the background. But once things have become invisible, noises—be they loud or small—begin to rule. I got out of bed, went into the kitchen and knocked a knife-handle upon the kitchen table. I went back to bed. Things were quiet for a few minutes. Then the noises began again. Suddenly I remembered Kini's notion: these were Lord Ganesha's mice. Sacred mice. I smiled.

Listening to the sound of mice in the dark, it seemed to me as though someone were scratching words that I couldn't decipher upon a black slate with a rough slate-pencil. It occurred to me that I had some rat poison in the house, and I thought of scattering some on the kitchen floor. But instead of getting out of bed I lay in the dark with my eyes wide open. Perhaps someone was photographing me under powerful lights, although I was unable to see them. Then the photographer, with a black cloth still over his head, began to help me knot a tie around my neck. I pulled away the tie with both hands and jumped out of bed. I switched on the light and splashed cold water on my face. Then I dressed and went out.

### 3

The streets were deserted. I felt like roaming about, and thought of going to the beach. I often went to the beach at night. In the evenings the beach is crowded. It's nice at night, with few people around and the sea babbling in sleep. Once in a while a plane passes overhead, blinking red and green lights.

It was different now, though. It wasn't safe to wander around alone at night any more. You didn't know when you might be struck by an elephant's trunk. I thought it over for a minute or two and decided to go to the beach all the same. I didn't care. Perhaps somewhere inside I wanted that blow on the head.

I arrived at the beach and sat on the huge pipe that pours sewage water into the sea. I could see a few forms wrapped in blankets sleeping by the beach wall. The sea shimmered under the moonlight. It was midway between high and low tide, and a cool breeze was blowing in over the calm water towards the beach.

After an hour or so I saw two or three figures walking towards the beach. Some sleepless wanderers like me, I thought. The figures were short, and I wondered if they were children. What were children doing out by themselves at this hour? Then I saw something waving like a tail, and thought they were dogs. The figures came forward, and walked out onto the sand. Then I realized in amazement that they were Ganesh images.

More figures began to arrive. The ones that had come first reached the water and went straight in. I watched them disappear under the surface, legs first, then belly and shoulders, and then the elephant head. One after the other the images came down to the beach and entered the sea. Their sleek bodies shone in the moonlight. They walked with such an air of freedom, with such grace! As each entered the sea, the water seemed to make way for the god, compliantly breaking into ripples. Some of the gods, as they entered the water, playfully waved their trunks in the air. All was quiet, and the gods were disappearing noiselessly one by one into the sea.

Spellbound, I watched the unearthly sight. The gods were quietly going home, spurning all rituals. They had come down the beach in a wave of pure joy; their clay figures melted into the sea like lumps of sugar. I thought their melting figures would make the salt sea sweet.

Somewhere in my mind questions were fluttering. Why were the gods leaving so suddenly? Had they accomplished their mission? Why had they risen up? Were they returning because they had failed to achieve some objective? Perhaps they had decided to leave the affairs of men to men themselves. Perhaps they had undertaken this experiment to undo some divine entanglement of their own which had nothing to do with the world of men. Or they had staged the uprising for fun, and now, having tired of the game, they were departing. I remembered the tale of the Pied Piper and the rats. I thought that a Pied Piper who can lure away the gods must be very powerful indeed.

But such questions and ideas didn't linger long in my mind. They appeared pointless, entranced as I was by the sight before me. I watched for a long time. Then the number of figures coming down to the sea grew smaller. In the end a very small god came skipping down and threw himself into the water with abandon. Then the beach was deserted; the water shimmered quiescently. I fell asleep without realizing it.

The sun was up when I awoke. Slum-dwellers were coming down to the edge of the sea to defecate. The sea was low. I felt stiff. I stretched myself and started for home.

I pondered over the previous night's spectacle as I walked. I wondered if it had really happened, or whether it was just a dream. Who was I to be blessed among all men with the sight of such a vision? I thought I could find out the truth when I got back to the city. If the gods had truly left, people couldn't fail to have noticed it. Also, on other beaches of the city a few people must have seen the gods leaving. But then I didn't really care if what I had seen was real or the play of my imagination. To have seen it was enough.

I recalled an incident from my childhood. In the village where I grew up there lived an old astrologer who was something of a crank. One day he made some calculations and declared that on a certain day there would be great floods and storms and everything would be washed away. He began to warn the villagers, telling them to leave their huts and go to the top of a mountain on the appointed day. Everyone laughed at him.

The astrologer became increasingly frantic, running about to save the villagers from what he believed was their folly. On the day before the world was to end, he packed a few of his belongings and, warning the people for one last time, climbed up to the top of the mountain behind out village. It was a hard climb, and the old man must have been half dead with exhaustion when he reached the summit. That night there arose by chance a great storm; sheets of rain poured down for hours, and trees fell. In the morning, when the sky had cleared, a small band of villagers climbed the mountain. The found the astrologer's stiffened body.

When I was small I hadn't realized it, but many years later it struck me: braving the violent winds and the rain, the old man must have died in the conviction that he was indeed witnessing the end of the world. That was the truth as he saw it; and, in the final analysis, what other truth is there?

I reached the building where I lived. Climbing up to my room, I stopped and knocked on Accountant Kini's door. Kini opened the door, and looked at me with sleepy eyes.

'Mr Kini,' I shouted. 'They've gone. The gods have left.'

'What, the gods have left?' Kini muttered, rubbing his eyes. 'How? And when? Why did they leave?' And, with half-shut eyes, he began to mumble curses as though he were reciting prayers.

*The Women in Cages*

# II

# Libido Zones

# the missing link

It was after Ratna went away that Rumi made the discovery. Rumi was about thirteen at the time, and Ratna was two years older. Rumi at first thought that her elder sister had gone away, in the way that people in the village go away for a few days and then return. But weeks passed, and Ratna didn't return. It was then that Rumi knew that her sister had gone away in a special sense.

Rumi asked her mother. 'Mother, what about Ratna? Where has she gone?'

Her mother was tossing the grain in a wicker basket to separate the stones and the chaff from the grain. She stopped for a moment, but did not speak. Then she continued her chore.

'Where has Ratna gone, Mother?' Rumi persisted.

'Ratna has gone to Swarg,' Mother said, in a flat, unemotional tone.

'That means she's dead?'

'No, she's living in paradise. She's living in great luxury and happiness. Such luxury that you cannot even imagine.'

'Oh, how exciting! I know about the luxuries in Swarg, because Manik's Granny has told me a story about it.'

For a moment, Rumi was lost in thoughts of Paradise.

Then she asked, 'So Ratna will not return?'

'No, she will return. She will return home.'

'When will she return?'

'In a few years. About the time that she is thirty years old. Then she will return.'

Rumi mulled over the information. It had to be assimilated to her little store-house of knowledge.

Then she said, 'Ratna's friend, Manik, has also gone away. She too went to Swarg?'

'Yes. She too.'

'And she too will return?'

'Yes, yes.'

'At the age of thirty?'

'That's right.'

This was additional information. Rumi took time to digest it. Then, as if in a flash, it dawned upon her; in the village, there were girls of her age; and there were middle-aged women, and old women. But there were no young women, women in the prime of youth. Where had all the young women gone?

'Mother, do all the girls go to Swarg at fifteen?' Rumi asked.

Rumi's mother tossed the grain in the air and halted. She looked at her daughter.

'Yes, they do,' she said.

'And they all return after they have enjoyed the luxuries of Swarg to the full?'

'Yes. They go at fifteen and, God willing, they return at about thirty-five.'

'But why at fifteen? And why return at thirty-five? Why don't they live in Swarg for ever?'

'God ordained it so. You mustn't question God's will.'

'But mother, some women don't return. Kaveri's sister never returned.'

'Yes, some women don't return. They live in Swarg for ever.'

So much new knowledge. Rumi had to strain her tiny brain to the utmost.

After some time, she had another question.

'And Mother, what about the boys? They don't go to Swarg? Why not?'

'No, they don't.'

'But why not Mother?'

'Boys must do the work at home, must go to the fields. Mustn't men work when the women go away?'

'Yes, Mother,' Rumi said. Then she asked, 'So Purna won't go to Swarg?'

'No, he will stay with us.'

Purna was Rumi's brother. He was ten years old.

From that day on, the seed of the image of Swarg was deeply embedded in Rumi's mind. The seed rapidly grew into a whole cluster of images, of scenes of unearthly beauty and joy, of divine foods and nectar, of beds which made you swoon with pleasure instantly, and of a thousand other luxuries and comforts which she could hardly imagine with certainty.

Rumi kept this knowledge to herself, she didn't talk about it to her friends. She instinctively seemed to understand that it was far too precious. And fragile. To disclose it to others was to risk seeing it shattered.

For the same reason, Rumi did not want to ask mother a further question: would she go to Swarg, very soon? There were some puzzling strands in the narrative. Rumi knew a woman in a neighbouring hut who had returned. The woman looked gaunt and prematurely old; she seemed to be always ill, with some disease that nobody would describe clearly. The village women said she was going to die soon.

The thought of that woman, and other perplexing thoughts, evaporated when Rumi was with her doll. Her imagination soared when she was in the company of her doll. She thought of the doll as an apsara, a celestial beauty, who had condescended to come down to earth. Rumi was lost in images of the paradisal happiness that her doll symbolized.

She was careful to keep her doll out of sight at other times, hidden in some corner. If Purna came across it, he might vandalize it. He relished taking things apart, or dismembering them. The doll was beautiful once, but now much shopworn and faded. One of its eyes, made of beads, was missing. Its long red skirt was now an apology for red. One of Rumi's maternal uncles had brought it from Mumbai years ago. He had struck it rich in Mumbai, selling brown sugar. Whenever she remembered her only brother, Rumi's mother shed a few tears. This uncle of Rumi's was stabbed fatally in a brawl in Mumbai three years ago.

The day of reckoning soon came. That evening, Rumi's father came home as usual. All day since early morning till sunset, he worked as a farm labourer. He was one of the few men in the village who didn't come home drunk. Rumi's mother always thanked the deities for giving her such a husband.

After eating his rotis and dal in the light of the kerosene lamp, Rumi's father called his wife.

'Tomorrow morning Patel is coming to our house.'

'What for?' Rumi's mother asked, a bit alarmed.

'He wants to see Rumi.'

'What do you mean?' Mother's voice sank.

'We will send Rumi away. Patel wants to see her before he decides on the deal.'

'O God! You want to send her away so soon?'

'Oh, she is already running fourteen. And it's never too soon.'

'But you could have waited! At least till she has completed fifteen.'

'Maybe. But things are getting more and more difficult. The burden of the loan is getting larger and larger. The bania came to the fields today and warned that I pay up or else.'

Rumi's mother was silent. Then she said, 'How much will Patel pay?'

'That is to be decided. He will quote a figure when he's seen her.'

Rumi's mother was silent for some time.

Then Father said, 'Tell Rumi that Patel is coming tomorrow. She must behave herself in his presence.'

Mother called Rumi, who was herding the chickens in the coop.

'Rumi, Patel Uncle is coming to visit tomorrow morning.'

'What for?'

'To see you. If you are nice, he will agree to take you.'

'Take me where?'

'Don't you know? Where all the village girls go.'

'You mean to paradise?'

'Yes, here's your opportunity. If you are selected, you will be rolling in luxury forever.'

'But—'

'But what?'

'I didn't know I will have to go so soon. I wanted to—.'

'What?'

'I wanted to live with you a little longer, mother, really I wanted to very much.'

Mother swallowed her saliva with difficulty. Then she said, trying hard not to show the choking of her voice: 'But you are going away to live in great luxury and happiness.'

'I know. But . . . all the same, I wanted to be with you both . . . and with Purna . . . a little longer . . .'

'It's not in our hands. Patel Uncle may never come again.'

That night Rumi didn't fall asleep immediately. Her mind was torn between contrary emotions. In a way, she was excited at going away, with a whole new world opening up to her, a world of undreamt of luxuries and enjoyments. But the thought of saying farewell to her parents and to her younger brother created an unbearable ache in her heart. Her mind swayed this way and that, leaving her in a state of confusion and perplexity. Buffeted by contrary winds, her mind went numb.

The next morning Father did not go to work early; he would go a little late. Mother asked Rumi to bathe, then to put on her best clothes which were ragged anyway. They all awaited the arrival of Patel.

Patel came after an hour or two. He sat on the cloth that Rumi's mother had spread on the ground.

Patel and Rumi's father chit-chatted. Tea was given to the guest in the only cup in the house, with a broken handle.

Rumi had been ordered to sit in the inner part of the hut separated by a sari hanging on a line. Then she was called out by her father.

Putting the tea-cup down, Patel looked at Rumi. Patel had a large moustache, its points turned upwards. His lips were red with betel-leaf juice; now he inserted a fresh betel-leaf roll inside his cheek.

'You have a beautiful daughter. In a couple of years she will be stunning,' Patel said.

'It is God's grace,' Rumi's father said.

'Do you cough a lot?' Patel asked.

Rumi shook her head to convey a negative reply.

'There has been no sign of TB?' Patel asked.

'None at all, by God's grace,' Rumi's father replied.

Patel aimed a gob of red spittle at a corner of the hut.

'Let us talk about the deal, then,' he said.

'Yes, Rumi dear child, go out and play for a while.'

Rumi went out. Mother called her only when Patel had gone away. Rumi's father had already left for work in a hurry.

'What did Patel Uncle say?' Rumi asked. 'Am I going away?'

'Yes. Tomorrow,' Mother said.

'Tomorrow?'

'Yes,' Mother said, without looking at Rumi.

Rumi stared at Mother. Tears streamed down her face. She tried to rein in a sob.

Mother looked at her. She hugged Rumi. 'Don't cry,' she said, with her own voice choking.

Rumi held mother tightly in her embrace.

'I told you, you are going to paradise,' Mother said. 'Or a place like paradise. There will be much luxury in that place.'

'But I want to stay with you.'

'Don't worry. After some years you'll come back with much money. Then we'll all live happily. Now have food and then go out to play. No work for you today. The whole day you enjoy. Play with your friends. But listen, don't tell anyone that you are going away with Patel Uncle.'

Rumi went out. But she had no desire to play. She just stood outside the hut, or aimlessly strolled about. It occurred to her that she may be seeing the village for the last time, or will not set eyes upon it for a long, long time. Yes, the village where she was born and where she had spent all her life; it had been her whole world. A thousand memories of her life in the village crowded her mind; hundred trivial memories, but all suddenly invested with new meaning. For the first time, she realized that she loved her little village—a collection of a few huts high in the hills at the foot of still higher mountains in the northern part of the subcontinent. She looked at the cluster of huts, the small patches of cultivation on the slopes of the hills, the valley and the far mountains. It was a windy day, and the wind, blowing every which way, tossed Rumi's hair about. She took deep breaths in the clean mountain air as if she instinctively knew she may not breathe this air again.

Most of the day Rumi spent wandering about the village, staring at things, or at nothing. In the late afternoon, she returned and lay on her bedcloth in the hut with eyes open. She lay rigidly for a long while. Mother was preparing some sweet, the smell of which filled the tiny hut. Then Mother called her to eat some pieces of the sweet. Mother filled a small rusty tin with pieces of the sweet. 'This is for you to take along tomorrow,' she said smiling.

After the family had eaten their evening rotis by the light of the kerosene lamp, mother quickly extinguished the lamp. Kerosene was costly, and not to be burned without good reason.

Rumi returned to her bedcloth behind the sari spread over the clothesline. Purna also slept beside Rumi. The flimsy sari-cloth dividing a part of the hut was all the privacy that the hut afforded.

Purna was soon fast asleep. Rumi lay in bed, eyes closed. Her doll was in her arms, as was her wont. But there was no sleep for her. She lay in bed, still as a corpse, for what seemed like hours.

Late into the night, Rumi heard a soft sound on Mother's side of the sari-cloth. It was a muffled sound, but unmistakably the sound of sobbing. Mother was sobbing.

Rumi's father called after his woman in a hoarse, sleepy voice. Then he called again, slightly louder, slightly more awake.

Rumi's mother said, 'I can't sleep. Rumi is going away tomorrow'.

'Oh, girls go away anyway. And we have Purna . . .'

'I know, but . . .'

Father didn't say anything. It was Mother who spoke again, between sobs:

'I can't bear the thought of Rumi in that city . . .'

'Oh, she will be all right.'

'There will be rape, beatings . . .'

'That's not true. She'll make money. She'll be comfortable. She'll be happy'.

Mother knew that Rumi's father knew that that was not true.

'What is the use of money?' Mother said. 'To spend her life like that . . . in a cage . . .'

'Look what can anyone do? All the girls of the village go the same way. If I refuse to send Rumi, Patel's men will kill me, and take away Rumi.'

'I know. I am not blaming you. But . . .'

There was silence for a few moments. Then Mother said, 'Horrible . . . it's horrible . . .'

'It's better not to think of it. What's written on your forehead, will come about. Now, go to sleep.'

Husband and wife had been talking, under the impression that both children were safely asleep. Wide awake, Rumi had heard every word of it. She did not quite understand what was said, and she strained her understanding to grasp the meaning. When it was clear that the talk between her parents was over, Rumi, on the other side of the sari-cloth, turned her face away from her parents, and lay, still clutching the doll to her breast. Every night, the village dogs created a ruckus late into the night, by which time Rumi was usually asleep. But tonight she listened to the dogs fighting and howling in the silence of the night. The dogs fell silent after a while, but a solitary animal wailed periodically long into the night.

# the women in cages

## 1

Gulshanbai's *kothi,* or bordello, had two cages, in two adjacent rooms. The cages were, in reality, shop-windows of a sort, for customers to survey the goods on display as they strolled down Foras Road—the name being a metamorphosis of the British era Foreshore Road. Foras Road is not far away from the now internationally known Falkland Road.

The women stand at the bars of the cages, and try to attract the attention of potential customers. Gulshanbai's kothi had eight women, four in each cage. The cages were rooms with an adjoining door, but the four on one side of the dividing wall always stood on that side, and the other four on the other side. The women could move freely on both sides of the bars, and in the passage and the cubicles adjoining them. The women generally ordered tea and food from the boy employed by Gulshanbai, so there was little reason to step out. If needed, a woman could go out for a brief chore. But, as a courtesy, she told Gulshanbai where she was going, and Gulshanbai, effortlessly but sharply, kept an eye on her women all the time. No woman would dream of an escape, anyway. In that sense, the women could be said to be caged. But then, a housewife looking out of the bars of the window of her tiny flat, and obediently providing sex to her husband whenever desired, could also be said to be in a cage.

Sarsa—the name was an abbreviation of Saraswati—was the senior-most employee in the establishment. She had been under Gulshanbai's care for over fifteen years. In her profession, being a senior member was in no way an asset. Quite the contrary. Sarsa was getting old, too old, to continue in her profession much longer. She didn't know her precise age. It was on the wrong side of thirty, to be sure. When asked, Sarsa said she was twenty-five years old. But nobody believed her.

It was becoming increasingly difficult for Sarsa to find customers. Her old customers, who had faithfully given her patronage for years, had deserted her. One or two still came to her, but they were occasional visitors, not regular customers. Then there was the odd novice who plumped for her as a less challenging, and less threatening, choice. A sort of a motherly figure, they unconsciously thought of Sarsa.

Getting ready by eleven o'clock that morning—it happened to be Mahatma Gandhi's birthday—Sarsa stood in front of the cage bars. There weren't many people in the street at that hour, and there were even less today on account of Gandhi Jayanti, which was an official holiday. There was, of course, no holiday for the women in the cages, whether it was Gandhi Jayanti or Gandhi Punyatithi, the day the Mahatma ascended to Heaven. As a matter of fact, a holiday meant there would be a greater turnover of customers that day.

At that hour of the morning, only rarely would a customer walk in. But Sarsa stood at the cage on the off chance that some passer-by might be stirred to pay a visit. The other women of Gulshanbai's kothi were fast asleep, and would not appear in front of the cage bars till late in the day. The day began late on Foras Road. The women went to bed early in the morning, and woke up late in the afternoon. At that hour, when the competition was asleep, and snoring in attitudes of despair, Sarsa hoped to hook a customer.

Her anxiety had taken on a deepened sense of urgency since the day before. Gulshanbai had summoned her, and given her notice that she would have to leave exactly in a month's time. The spectre of unemployment, and of being without a shelter, grew threateningly large, and much more real, before Sarsa's eyes. What would she do? She had no relatives worth speaking of, and no place to go. She would be out in the streets. No doubt she had collected some money, which was deposited with

Gulshanbai; additionally, Gulshanbai would give her some money, a gratuity of sorts. But Sarsa knew that the money, though it seemed like a goodly sum, would evaporate in no time. Nobody would give her any job. At best, she could become a street hawker, selling flowers or something. In the end, it will be begging in the streets. And a death as a homeless person, a numbered cadaver in the Government hospital waiting for the edification of medical students.

The chain of thoughts was broken, as Sarsa spotted Padhye ambling along the street in the direction of the kothi. Padhye was one of the few customers of the old times who had remained loyal all along. He visited about once in fifteen days, more to keep in touch than for sex. He had turned fifty, and sex didn't matter much to him. He was one of the few intellectual customers that Sarsa had had: he was a journalist in a Marathi paper. Padhye supplied Sarsa with interesting tidbits about the goings on in the world, the kind of information that Sarsa, who was practically illiterate, could seldom hope to get. Sarsa valued Padhye's patronage for that reason; added to that was a sort of friendship that, over the years, had developed between the two. Padhye disappeared from view as he entered the building, and Sarsa turned away from the bars of the cage to await Padhye's entry.

2

In their cubicle, Padhye sprawled on the bed, and Sarsa sat on the edge. Padhye was never in a hurry for the physical part. They talked, joked, smiled. Uppermost in Sarsa's mind was Gulshanbai's ultimatum, and the question of her own future. She wanted to ask for Padhye's advice on the matter. But, in this country, it was impolite to raise the matter on one's mind the first thing on encounter; it was usually kept to the last. What's more, Padhye was, after all, a customer; it was one's duty to attend to the customer first, and not to annoy him with questions of day-to-day life.

'What's happening in the world?' Sarsa asked, as she usually did.

'Oh, nothing unusual. The same old thing. Terrorist attack; election in Uttar Pradesh; the row over the Ayodhya temple is getting worse.'

Padhye paused. 'I am sick of all the politics. So I write about the politics-free topics, whenever they allow me.'

'Like what?'

'Oh, cultural happenings. You know "culture"? Things that don't really matter.'

'I know, I know.'

'Like I wrote a story about the latest Nobel Prize winner.'

'What is the Nobel Prize?'

'It's the topmost prize in the world. Indians seldom get it, naturally.'

'Of course.'

'You know, Sarsa, this guy I wrote about, and who is a writer, publicly thanked the prostitutes in Europe for giving him comfort in the years he was engaged in his creative labours.'

'Really? How nice! It was very thoughtful of him to think of the women who gave him enjoyment. Otherwise, who thinks of us prostitutes?'

'I guess you have a point there.'

'If he had come to me, I would have given him company free of charge.'

'Oh. A world-famous writer coming to you—here in Foras Road! Are you dreaming?'

'All the same, I would have given him pleasure free of charge, if he had appeared.'

'Come to think of it, Sarsa, the writer's ancestors belonged to India. They were poor peasants in Uttar Pradesh.'

'Really?'

'Yeah. So if they had stayed in Uttar Pradesh, maybe one of the descendants might have come to you!'

'There, you see!'

'But wait a minute. If he had stayed in India, he couldn't have become a world-famous writer. How about that?'

They tired of the subject, and got down to the business of sex. It was sweaty, as it is almost invariably in Mumbai. It was a relief to get it over with, Padhye thought. A repeat erection would take half an hour, Padhye knew from experience. It was best to lie down patiently. They were both silent.

Just when Sarsa was about to broach the subject of her retirement, Padhye spoke suddenly, 'You know, Sarsa, I came to you today because I was very, very upset yesterday. I thought your company might clear away the blues.'

'What made you so upset?'

'Yesterday, the paper I work for had sent me to the K.E.M. hospital for an interview with a chemistry researcher. He is doing some research on mosquitoes, malaria and that kind of thing. He had a room full of mosquitoes. And how were the mosquitoes fed? They slid a rabbit into the mosquito room, and shut the door. The hungry mosquitoes jumped on the rabbit. Thousands of mosquitoes competed to suck its blood. The rabbit was white, but for a minute, it looked absolutely black, covered with mosquitoes. A mosquito rabbit! We watched it from a glass window. Within a minute, the mosquitoes had sucked the rabbit dry. It lay down in the cage like a bloodless creature. I was so shaken by the whole spectacle. I couldn't sleep last night. I kept seeing that white cadaverous rabbit.'

Sarsa said something she considered appropriate, but, all the time, she was thinking of the terrors of her future. Padhye was ready with a second erection; the sweaty business, again. It was over and Sarsa knew that Padhye would now prepare to leave, his customary quota of sex fulfilled. She broached the subject that was on her mind all the time.

'Ah yes, it's a big problem—a real problem—.' Padhye said thoughtfully. 'But, Sarsa, we all face this problem sooner or later. Look at me—I am a journalist. I have changed papers several times. When I retire, I won't get much pension or gratuity, or whatever.'

'But Bhai, you will work till sixty or even later. In our profession we have to retire at thirty-five or so. How to get on with life when one has to retire so early in life?'

'Yes, I see your point. It is indeed a great problem.'

Padhye pondered over the problem. Then he said, 'You know, Sarsa, in the army they retire from active service at thirty-five or so. You women of pleasure are in the same situation. In the Army, of course, they get a handsome pension at that age.' Padhye paused. 'I will tell you what,' he exclaimed. 'The government should give you women a pension on the same lines. The women should get the same deal as the men from the army. We should have an army of comfort women!'

Padhye laughed at his own witty remark. He rose from the bed. With the rabbit story narrated to Sarsa, and sexual juices emptied at her feet, his own catharsis was complete. Sarsa had served her purpose.

'Well, I ought to be going,' Padhye said. 'I have to report on some Gandhi Jayanti programme in the evening.' Standing by the bed, he put on his trousers. He took out his wallet from his pant pocket, and rolled two one hundred rupee notes into a roll narrowing at one end. He stuck the roll between Sarsa's legs, who still lay naked in bed. Padhye smiled. That was his customary way of bidding goodbye to Sarsa in an affectionate and whimsical manner.

'I am giving you one hundred extra today—towards your retirement fund!' Padhye smiled again.

At the door, Padhye turned and said, 'I will remember about your problem, Sarsa. I will see what I can do.'

Padhye left, and Sarsa deposited the earnings with Gulshanbai. Sullen and disappointed, she did not think Padhye would be of much help, beyond a small gesture of personal charity.

## 3

The women woke up in the late afternoon. They ate, made up their faces, and stood in front of the cage bars. The eight of them, all in a row. They smiled and waved to the passers-by; they smiled and laughed among themselves. As the evening progressed, they were picked up one by one by customers. As often, Sarsa was the only one left standing. Her inability to attract customers was underlined by her aloneness, and made her more miserable.

All the other women of the house carried on merrily; they were young and carefree, at least on the surface. Against their youth, Sarsa could not compete. Four of the eight women were

Nepali; all of them sixteen to twenty years old. In the old days, it was not so. In recent years, there had started a steady supply of teenage girls from Nepal. They were catapulted from the clean air of the northern mountains to the stifling slums of Mumbai by agents who had set up a regular chain. Apart from being young and sturdy, the Nepali girls were usually fairer than average Indian women, and thus in greater demand. In a brief period, they were soon out of business on account of TB, which they almost invariably contracted owing to the drastic change in climate they underwent. If it wasn't TB, they soon ended up with AIDS. Sarsa felt that, because of the easy availability of the Nepali girls, her own chances in business had become more difficult. Sarsa regarded the Nepali girls with venomous spite.

There was a young Nepali girl that had joined Gulshanbai's brood only a few months ago. Barely thirteen or fourteen, she had fought viciously when she first came. Gulshanbai's protectors raped her and beat her repeatedly, but this girl, who was called Rumi, would not give in. For some days, she even had to be chained to a bed. But after a month or two, she gave in. Now, she smiled at customers, and was jovial with them. Once or twice, Sarsa asked her about her past life, about her parents, and so on. Rumi replied curtly—her Hindi was poor—that she had no past life; there was nothing, nothing she could remember or tell.

As the evening progressed, Sarsa became more desperate. This happened every evening now. As the other women served their customers briskly, and Sarsa watched helplessly, her desperation increased. Oftentimes nowadays, she resorted to a glass of country liquor. The women had to keep company with drinks if the customers so desired, and Sarsa had done so for years. But she had never liked liquor, and she had a drink or two out of a sense of duty. Even now, she detested liquor, especially country liquor, but now she forced herself to gulp two or three drinks rapidly, which considerably alleviated her desperation. At such moments, she usually re-lived her past, when customers used to queue for her services, or used to book her in advance; that was the time when she used to imperiously refuse a drink, and tell her customers, 'Drink the urine of a donkey yourself!' She then had youth; she saw a lot of money passing through her hands. Now it was all gone.

Many women died by the time they were of Sarsa's age: TB, venereal disease, and now AIDS. AIDS had come as a godsend to the women. It spared them the misery of a long-drawn-out end. At moments of extreme despair, Sarsa wished she had contracted AIDS. But, by some stroke of luck, she had not been visited by any devastating disease.

## 4

That evening, Sarsa gulped a couple of drinks quickly and stood at the bars of the cage for what seemed like hours. And it *was* hours. Her legs ached. Then she heard a familiar voice call from behind, 'Sarsa—'

Yes, it was Babloo. Babloo worked in the area as a male prostitute. He was a jovial and carefree fellow. He regularly dropped in for a chat, and Sarsa liked his company.

'How are things, Babloo?' Sarsa asked.

'Oh, good.'

Sarsa thought there was a change in Babloo's tone. He looked ill and gaunt.

After a while, Sarsa asked: 'Tell me, Babloo. What's the matter?'

The smile was wiped from Babloo's face.

'Sarsa, I have AIDS. I got to know yesterday.'

'Oh God,' Sarsa said.

'It goes with the job. It isn't something unexpected, really.'

'But still—'

Both were silent for a while. Both gulped their drinks.

'How's business, Sarsa?' Babloo asked.

'Bad, very bad.'

'I have told you so many times, Sarsa, you should have offered anal intercourse to your customers long ago.'

'I can't do it. Babloo. It hurts. Hurts very badly.'

'It's nothing difficult. You have to follow the proper technique. When the guy rams it in your ass, you have to respond as if you're about to shit. Your sphincter muscles open up automatically, and the thing slides in smoothly.

'Yes, that's what you said a month ago. I tried it.'

'Then?'

'I opened up my ass, as you said, as though I were about to shit—and actually shit came out of my ass. The guy was wild, furious. He slapped me and went away, shouting. Gulshanbai scolded me.'

Babloo used to boast that a passive homosexual like him had no reason to worry about finding customers. A woman of the cages had a working life till about the age of thirty-five. But a passive male prostitute could go on working into old age. Passive males were always in great demand. Their looks, their age did not matter; only the hole mattered. It was as if the hole were a disembodied, abstract entity.

On this occasion, Babloo did not repeat his boast. AIDS had changed everything.

'Is it bad?' Sarsa asked.

'The doctor said it's not so bad. But I don't trust him.'

'Oh, Babloo—'

They were silent for a while.

'That's why I came to see you today, Sarsa. Who knows. I may not see you again.'

'Oh Babloo, don't say such things.'

When Babloo was gone, Sarsa resumed her vigil at the cage-bars. She had had more than her usual quota of alcohol, and her head was spinning. She wasn't much aware of her surroundings, but she clung on to the bars of the cage in desperation. The reels of images from the past rolled before her eyes automatically. Tonight, the archives of memory went back further. Sarsa saw herself as a small girl. She was dressed in a beautiful dress, a 'frock' they called it. She was in a strange, flowery land. The scene was actually from a story which a neighbouring woman, who was a school teacher, had told Sarsa in her childhood. The little Sarsa in that scene saw a rabbit, who was busily going somewhere. The rabbit hurriedly consulted a watch in his pocket. Sarsa accosted him, and was asking him directions politely, when, all of a sudden, thousands of mosquitoes descended upon the rabbit.

They covered his entire body, so that it looked black with mosquitoes. When the mosquitoes sucked the blood in the rabbit's body, little Sarsa felt the pain of the bite of mosquitoes. Very soon, the rabbit was only a skeleton, with all his blood drained. Little Sarsa wept inconsolably. But then, miraculously, the dead rabbit was metamorphosed into a young Babloo. He told little Sarsa that he was a prince who had been cursed by a rishi with AIDS. When Babloo pleaded for relief from the curse, the rishi turned him into a rabbit.

The ordeal of the mosquitoes had purified Babloo's body and soul, and he was restored to his former state. The handsome prince bowed before Sarsa, and kissed her hand like in the movies. Prince Babloo danced with little Sarsa as they do in Hindi films, and all the women in the cages, like 'extras' in the films, danced around the pair joyfully and festively.

# the odour of immortality

## 1

Champa was one of those girls who had come to Kamathipura from Nepal. After the initial shock of finding herself transported from the free air of her valley in Nepal to the claustrophobic atmosphere of Kamathipura in Mumbai, and the brief rebellion she indulged in, Champa, tamed soon, settled down to life in Kamathipura. She was fair like most Nepali women, she was pretty, and she was young. She had no dearth of customers. The madam of her house promised that if Champa earned fifty thousand rupees for the house, she would be free from her bondage, and would be allowed to go home to Nepal. The thought of going back to her valley in Nepal was electrifying. Champa worked towards the goal of making enough money to win her freedom. She took in ten or twelve customers every evening.

With that kind of regimen, Champa used to be dog-tired at the end of the day. She lay in a stupor late into the next morning, with a wooden body. With overuse of the muscles of that part of the body, her vagina became tender and painful.

'God! I wish I had ten vaginas all over my body,' Champa said, 'Then I'd be able to take on ten customers at a time and make money much faster!'

The idea stuck in her mind. Back in Nepal, Champa had known many tantriks, for her father had been very much into tantra and mantra. Champa herself had seen strange manifestations of the human form: a child with two pairs of eyes, one in the front and another at the back of its head; a child with two penises; a woman with several tongues lolling out of her vagina; a woman with two pairs of breasts; one above the other. Some of these phenomena might have been God's quirks; but Champa knew for sure that powerful tantriks could shape the human body like clay. Magic and supernatural powers could work wonders. Champa thought of Satyendra Mahant, a tantrik well known in the villages of eastern Nepal. Champa's father knew Mahantji very well. (Her father had died a year ago. It was after that that she was sold to an agent from Mumbai.) Now that she had put by some money, Champa decided to invite Mahantji to Mumbai all the way from Nepal. She sent him a letter, urging him to come, and promising that she would pay for all his expenses on travel and stay in Mumbai. She received a reply from Mahantji, saying that he did not, as a rule, travel outside of Nepal, and certainly not as far as Mumbai; but that he would make an exception in this case, seeing that it was the daughter of his bosom friend that needed him, a girl whom he remembered affectionately as a sweet child. Champa was overjoyed; she shed a tear in gratitude for Mahantji, and in memory of her late father.

It was a tough task, Mahantji said when he arrived in Kamathipura. But, God willing, he would succeed. After all, the god Indra was blessed with eyes all over his body. (Mahantji preferred to use the euphemism 'eyes' to refer to Indra's transformation.)

'Yes, Mahantji, I've heard the story of Indra. But I wonder why Lord Indra was blessed with vaginas—I mean "eyes"—all over his body. What's the use of it to a man? If a woman was gifted with many organs, it would have been a boon to her.'

Mahantji merely smiled, beneath his Chinese moustache, and small glittering eyes. He began his arcane supplications and obscure ministrations. Champa co-operated devoutly.

After two weeks, Champa complained of itching all over her body, with a burning sensation arising fitfully in various parts. Then she thought an ulcer was blossoming on the left side of her body, along the latitude of her belly. She lifted her left breast like a bag that was in the way, and peered at the left side of her trunk.

There was indeed an ulcerous growth on her body, the nature of which could not as yet be ascertained; it was like a volcanic island that had newly erupted in the geography of her body, or like some obscure pattern detected on the Martian surface.

A day or two later, it became apparent that a vagina had formed itself on the left side of Champa's body. Soon she could boast of several. Like small-pox, the organs covered her body. The few days it took for this transformation to materialize, Champa was in a strange state of delirium. She felt as if her body was opening up to the world, like a tender, exotic red flower, with innumerable petals.

Mahantji announced that his mission was accomplished, and prepared for the long journey to the north. Before departing, he told Champa: 'Remember that all this has been possible on account of what Lord Indra had suffered on mortal soil long ago. Always worship Lord Indra along with the other gods in your daily puja.'

## 2

It took time for people to get used to Champa's new look. The initial reaction was close to horror, as it might be to someone transformed into a giant insect. And, indeed, Champa had the appearance of a giant beetle, with a head like a turtle's head protruding out of the shell of a body thick with a surfeit of vaginas. Champa had not only grown vaginas, but also thick, bushy hair around each growth. The sprinkling of bushes of hair on her body gave her the appearance of a patch of land covered by cracks and desultory growth of stunted grass. All the organs were vertically placed on the erect body, which gave Champa's figure a striking degree of verticality. When she reclined, she had the appearance of a hill dotted with caves, like the Buddhist caves not far from the city.

Adventurous customers soon tried the pleasures of Champa's new body. To their delight, it was astonishingly pleasurable. The organs she had grown seemed to be more adept in yielding sexual pleasure. Anyone who tasted it once, was bound to come back for more. Ancient texts have compared sexual pleasure to the bliss of the taste of Brahman. The pleasure offered by Champa's divinely doctored body seemed to be far greater.

Word spread round that Champa's kothi had strange, exciting phenomena on display. Customers crowded her establishment. They were not disappointed, neither in satisfaction derived, nor in readiness of service. Instead of the traditional practice of one customer at a time, Champa was able to service ten customers at a time or more.

Her business acumen was sharper than that of a modern hamburger joint. It was an open house, sort of; customers were welcome to join in, to find a chink in the crowd already surrounding her body. For more efficient utilization of her assets, Champa abandoned the traditional bed to service her customers. She adopted a standing position in the middle of the room, with both arms raised, hands tied securely above her head (there were vaginas under the arm-pits). Since most of the additional organs were above the level of the natural organ, customers had to cope with the new obstacle of achieving access to the organs with the male organic counterpart. To this end, chairs and stools were provided to the customers so that they could penetrate the vaginas above waist level. During rush hours, Champa looked like a woman with so many leeches clinging to her body. Her body was a hunk of flesh on a kebab spit, where you could slice off meat anywhere round the spit, allowing the meat to cook slowly all round.

The vaginas engaged in intercourse were, naturally, noisy. With so many female organs busily emitting sounds of pleasure, Champa was like an organist expertly producing a variety of notes on the instrument. But there was harmony in all this variety. The orchestration in Champa's organ-fest gave the male accompanists the experience of heavenly harmony.

However, once a month, the army of men round Champa's body fled with their noses held in cloth. The menstrual period was a period of test, and of great stress, for Champa. A normal human female goes through much stress during menstruation; imagine then the stress borne by someone in Champa's condition. Keeping the innumerable orifices staunched with pieces of an old sari was a Herculean task.

The prosperity that Champa enjoyed did not last for long. True, she made a lot of money in a few weeks. She had enough stashed away for her to buy her freedom from her madam. But, as usually happens, she was by now so inured to life in the metropolis that she didn't care about going back to her birthplace; she didn't want to admit it to herself, either, so she kept putting off the idea of bidding farewell to life in Kamathipura.

The sudden intrusion of the new marketing conditions introduced by Champa had an unsettling impact upon her competitors. Champa effortlessly captured a large share of the market, drastically reducing the share of others in the trade. The marketing departments of other establishments in Kamathipura— or pimps, in short—raised a hue and cry.

The underworld of magic and black magic got busy. The madams of the other houses in Kamathipura hired powerful tantriks to counter what they perceived as an assault on their freedom to earn their bread and butter in an honest manner.

Black magic bore black fruits, before long. It became apparent that anyone who visited Champa became, as a consequence, impotent. Her organs were affected by a virus that left the male organs that came into contact with them permanently crippled. Lord Indra had also been afflicted with a similar curse in ancient times. A displaced imitation of that Puranic precedent had enabled the evil-doers to deflate what they perceived as a challenge.

3

As soon as the news of this affliction spread around Kamathipura—and news of this kind spreads amazingly fast— the large clientele that Champa had commanded instantly vanished. Nobody came near her.

Suddenly Champa found her situation reversed: from a woman busy as a bee to a woman who had nothing to do. The great transformation in her body that she had brought about with such resourcefulness was now utterly useless.

So far, the cage-bars were for others. Champa, since her transformation, never had to stand at the cage-bars putting herself on display. She had customers licking her fingers without her going to the cage-bars. But now she sat near the cage-bars for hours on end. Not for the purpose of attracting customers. No customer came anywhere near her. She sat at the cage-bars only to while away the time, looking at the people going about in the street. She didn't have to worry about money; she had enough put away. She paid her dues to the madam for room and board.

Champa usually sat a little away from the cage-bars, so that she was not readily seen from the street below. If she allowed herself to be seen, passers-by might revile her and curse her. So she preferred to keep herself out of sight. Sitting at the cage-bars, with her head held just high enough for her to get a view of the street, Champa thought of her future. What was she going to do? It seemed unlikely that her situation might change. She had to more or less think of retiring. This was by no means an exceptional situation. Premature retirement was usually one's fate in the world's oldest profession.

One afternoon Champa was looking down the cage-bars on the street scene, when a ragged creature who looked like a beggar caught her eye. Beggars were a common sight in the street, for the women in that profession gave money generously to supplicants and mendicants.

Champa sent a couple of rupees to the beggar through the house tea-boy. But the beggar was still there on the sidewalk after a while, looking up at the upper-story cage-front like a dog looking up expectantly for a bone from his master.

Champa sent the tea-boy again to inquire why the beggar was still waiting at the door. The tea-boy came up smiling.

'Champaji, this beggar wants something more!'

'Like what?'

'He wants a sexual favour!'

'Wants what?'

Aslam the tea-boy, who often doubled as a pimp, explained the beggar's wish in coarser terms.

'Good God! Even beggars have started visiting us demanding sexual favours!'

'Tell him to get lost,' Aslam suggested.

But Champa told Aslam to send the beggar up.

'Champaji, if you encourage beggars to have a free fuck, we'll all be out in the streets pretty soon.'

'Send him anyway, Aslam.'

Aslam hailed the beggar. The beggar climbed the rickety wooden steps slowly. Aslam disappeared in the inner chambers, as he did not want to be seen in such company.

'You have made such an odd request, strange man,' Champa said.

'What's so strange about it? True, normally we beggar-men handle such things among ourselves. Beggar-women dispense sexual favours, for a consideration, of course. But I wanted a real professional woman, for a change. I went down the entire Foras Road, asking for a favour. When they heard my request, the women laughed; they ridiculed me, humiliated me. The pimps drove me away, manhandled me.'

The beggar spoke with a strange dignity. Beneath his beggarly accoutrements and exterior, the unkempt beard and all, he was a handsome man in a way.

Champa's heart stirred.

'Come with me, stranger,' she said.

Champa took the beggar-man from the cage-room to her cubicle. Her cubicle was in an uncared for state. The bed-sheet, the clothes were all in disarray.

Champa undid what buttons there were on the beggar's shirt. As she was engaged with the buttons on his trousers, from the man's hairy, stained chest, she could make out a peculiar scent, the unmistakable odour of immortality. A mixture of sandalwood paste and rare Himalayan heavenly plants from the scent of the stranger's naked body captivated Champa. She immediately knew the stranger's identity.

'Lord Indra! You have, in your mercy, blessed my poor home!'

Bending down reverently, Champa touched Lord Indra's feet. Indra smiled wanly.

'O God! I do not know, Lord, if I can satisfy your desire, even if you blessed me with a thousand vaginas!'

'Don't worry. A beggar-man respects all the victuals he has been offered.'

While the god was taking his pleasure from Champa's body,

Champa had a look of anxiety and dread. When Lord Indra was satiated, and resting after his exertions, Champa said with fear in her heart: 'Lord, I have wronged you grievously. I would not blame my fate if you turned me into a stone like Ahalya.'

'What grievous wrong have you done me, earthly woman?'

For a moment, Champa did not speak. Then she said: 'Lord, anyone who has a sexual union with me is cursed with impotence. I acquiesced in your desire knowing that this may be the consequence.'

Lord Indra laughed a bitter laugh. 'Foolish woman,' he said. 'Do you think that I dallied with you without knowing what may happen?'

Perplexed, Champa stared at the god's face, forgetting that one should not stare at a god.

'Do you mean you knew, O Lord?'

'Yes, I did.'

'Then why did you do it, my Lord? You could have had your pleasure with any woman on earth, or in paradise.'

Indra did not answer.

'Why did you imperil your manhood by embracing me, my Lord?' Champa repeated her query.

'I don't care,' Indra said.

'Don't care? What do you mean, my Lord? I just don't understand.'

'I am sick of desire,' Indra said.

'Sick of desire, my Lord?'

'Yes, I am sick of it all. People think of me as a lecherous, fornicating god, a mirror of their own lusts. Anyway, that was in the past. I am sick now of lust, greed, all desire.'

'But impotence, my Lord?'

'Yes, why not?' Indra looked at Champa, perhaps for the first time as a human being may look at another.

'Impotence is wonderful! A blessing! For the first time, I feel free, light, free from anxiety. I shall go lightly into the mortal world, free of the baggage of my masculinity, blessed woman. I can now see you as a human being, not as a creature with so many holes. As if you were a golf course!'

Indra laughed at his own joke.

'Yes, you know, woman, I met a man in this city. For years, he had been a compulsive fornicator. Then, in the middle of his life, he was rendered impotent. I asked him how he had taken it. He said, "I enjoy this state of being. No more the anxiety of having to seduce a woman, or of not being able to; no more the burden of seeing a man as a threat, a rival. My wife can no more complain that I regard her only as a sexual object. Isn't that wonderful?" I can see his point now.'

Champa took some time to digest what Indra had said. Then she said: 'My Lord, I am beginning to see what you mean. And am I different? With all these useless holes spread over my body, like the moon with her craters, I am forgetting that I am a woman.'

'I am, after all, immortal,' Indra said. 'But I am thinking of the world of men. Death was ordained for mortal beings by Brahma as a counterpoint to sex. Maybe if sex is overcome, you will be nearer to the goal of immortality?'

'Perhaps, my Lord,' Champa said tremulously. 'But I feel fear, I feel strange and bereft.'

Indra laughed and said: 'You are, after all, a woman, and a mortal being.'

'Yes, my Lord.'

'In your new life, you will have new eyes,' Indra said. 'All these sexual organs—they aren't of any use to you any longer, right?'

'That's right, my Lord.'

'So I'll change them into eyes—an organ much more useful! I hope you will see things much better!' And Indra turned to go. On the landing, Indra turned and said to Champa: 'Walk with me down the stairs, blessed woman. My eyes are already growing dim, in my present condition.'

4

Men—and women—found Champa's new appearance quite startling and unsettling. Before, Champa used go about with a thick robe that covered all her body, except the head. Now she felt no need to do that, to cover her body as if it were a shameful secret. With a light sari thrown about her, she confronted the world with equanimity. Men and women found the gaze of her thousands eyes unbearable; to look at her was like looking at the Sun-God. People averted that gaze; but they went about reverently in her presence.

As time passed, the fierceness of Champa's gaze mellowed. With what money she had, she gave herself to the service of the women of the cages, and of the beggars in the locality. Like premature retirement, premature death is often the fate of those in the world's oldest profession, more so in the age of AIDS. In her heyday, with numerous sexual vehicles vulnerably open on her body, the worm had already gotten into her. She survived for some months even after she had got AIDS, then finally succumbed to it. All the innumerable eyes on her person changed into lotuses, and all the lotuses closed petal by petal. A black bee remained hidden in one of the enfolded lotuses, to wake when the lotuses bloom again.

Champa was remembered for a long time in Kamathipura, and even today, an image, bearing little or no resemblance to her actual looks, is displayed during the nine nights of the Navaratri festival; along with numerous images of gods painted on canvas and propped up on wooden cut-outs, the image of Champadevi, with numerous gaudy eyes illuminated by tiny colourful bulbs, stares garishly at the milling crowds.

# om phallus

## 1

I awoke one morning from strange freakish dreams and found myself transformed in my bed into an erect phallus. My head was round and smooth, with a small slit at the top. Completely hairless, it rested upon the pillow, while the rest of my straight, round body stretched out on the bed beneath the covers. When I moved my head this way and that, the rest of my body turned with it. I realized that, lacking a neck, I wouldn't be able to turn my head any more. I lacked ears and eyes and a nose, and yet, I don't know how, I was able to see. True, my vision was blurred, like a picture out of focus and under-exposed, but I could see. Could I hear? I listened for sounds. Yes, I could hear my neighbour Rambhau gargling noisily in his apartment, and also a radio blaring in the apartment further down. How about smells? The borders of my pillows smell of the blood of bugs I've killed. I turned my head—and, of couse, the rest of my body—and tried to see if I could smell the bugs' remains. I couldn't, which probably indicated that I had lost that faculty. I didn't regret that in particular. I'd never cared much for smell, pleasant or unpleasant. Smells are so useless. Then I wondered if I could still speak. This was an important matter. To hell with smells; speech was essential. I tried to speak, but immediately realized my efforts weren't properly directed. My lips weren't where they used to be. They were now located on the top of my head, and it was through that opening that I must now attempt to utter words. With much difficulty I move these lips, attempting to say 'Hare

Rama Hare Krishna'. But the sounds that actually came out were quite inadequate, something like 'Harr ... harrr ... kerrr ...' These new lips of mine needed practice enunciating words. This wasn't surprising, since their sole job up to then was excreting fluids. Yet, it was encouraging that they could emit sounds at all, and I felt confident that, in the course of time, I'd be able to train them to speak.

But what about my straight, round body that now had neither arms nor legs? Could I get up and move around, or would I be confined to bed forever? Alarmed at the latter possibility, I gathered all my strength and flung myself out of bed. The covers flew off, and my bottom hit the floor. I swayed unsteadily for a few moments, then remained upright on the floor. I stood there for a while, observing my room. I was pleased and relieved to see that even though I had undergone a radical transformation, the things in my room were exactly as they were before. Then, gathering my strength again, I jumped. In two hops I reached the door of my apartment. I stood there for a few seconds; then, jumping again, returned to the side of my bed. So I *could* move about. I was so happy about this that I bounced around my room in joy like a rubber ball in a Walt Disney cartoon.

I hopped over to the window and looked outside. The morning bustle had begun in the street. I watched, even though I couldn't see very well. Then it occurred to me that, from now on, seeing the world from my window would probably be all the contact I would have with it. For, in my new incarnation, how could I dare to venture out? People would laugh at me, boys would pursue and ridicule me, dogs would bark at me. Henceforth, I would have to spend my life behind closed doors. And why should I find it necessary to go out anyway? I no longer needed to eat and drink and excrete, and had no need to earn a living. Free from these worldly encumbrances, I could live happily in the solitude of my apartment. As for my job, I didn't need it either. I was fed up with it anyway. I no longer had to get up early, take my bath, breakfast hurriedly, and catch the suburban train to reach my office in time. I could now live a leisurely life free from all the demands of the outside world. The idea pleased me. While I entertained such thoughts standing at the window, I became aware that a few people had gathered in the street and were looking at me with curiosity. I jumped back quickly from the window.

I spent that day sitting around in the house: 'sitting around' is not really the right expression, since I could only stand up or lie down. Although I was not cut off from the outside world, I decided that I must learn to speak properly. It was a practical necessity, for even if I didn't open the door of my apartment, in all probability I would have to answer anyone who came to my door. The neighbours were bound to knock sooner or later when they saw that my door was always closed. I would have to answer without opening the door and try to get rid of them. Otherwise they might get suspicious and call the police or the fire department. Moreover, I regarded speech itself as inherently valuable, an important attribute of human existence. I must be able to speak, to utter words, if I was to be fully human. So that night I stood in the middle of the room and, concentrating hard, began to recite verses from the *Bhagvad Gita*. At first I was unable to form individual words, and only emitted vague, harsh sounds. But after an hour's determined effort, I found that I was making some progress, and that the words were beginning to emerge, even if only indistinctly. Then I grew tired and called it a day. I felt confident that after a few day's practice, I'd be able to articulate sufficiently well. I hopped into bed, wriggled under the covers, and, saying my prayers, went to sleep.

I spent much of the next day practicing talking, and made substantial progress in pronunciation. In between, whenever I was tired, I went to the window and gazed out. I had drawn the thin curtain across the window, so that I remained invisible from the street. Once in a while, I hopped around my apartment aimlessly.

One morning three or four days later was a knock upon the door.

'Mr Rao, Mr Rao,' Rambhau Purohit, my neighbour, called out. I went towards the front door and stood before it in silence. Then I spoke trying to articulate as clearly as possible, 'Who is it?' 'It's me—Rambhau. I haven't seen you around for four or five days. Your door was shut all the time too. And you hadn't mentioned going on a trip. So I thought I might have a look.'

'Well, I've been down with a cold the last few days.' 'Are you all right now?' Rambhau asked. 'Oh yes, I'm quite all right now.' 'Why does your voice sound so strange?' Rambhau asked. 'I've got a bad cough,' I said. Then I quickly added, 'Look, Rambhau, I'm going away tomorrow on company business. I'll be gone for over a month. Please keep an eye on my apartment.' 'Okay,' Rambhau said, and went away.

The day after this exchange with Rambhau, the mailman dropped a postcard through the slot in the door. It was from the company I worked for. Though I couldn't read very clearly, I went over it slowly word by word. The company wanted to know why I hadn't turned up for work for the last three days, and demanded that I return immediately.

I didn't care about the job any more, but another thought kept bothering me—that of seeing my girlfriend Latika. I wanted to see her badly. Even prior to my metamorphosis, I hadn't seen her for a fortnight. We had had a minor quarrel. Latika was haughty by nature, and I knew she wouldn't come to me first to make up. On the other hand, if I didn't go and see her soon she might feel that I had been seriously offended, and this would further sour our relationship. To be sure, there was scarcely any possibility that our relationship could survive my metamorphosis. Would she accept me in my new avatar? They say that true love conquers all, and I knew that Latika loved me truly, and yet it was difficult to believe that one might conquer the ultimate illusion behind all. Filled with sorrow, I was prepared to say goodbye to Latika, to bury our love forever in the depths of my heart. Still, I yearned to see her once, just once, for the last time. But how might that happen? Latika, who was studying for a degree in commerce, lived in a girl's dormitory. The dormitory wasn't far from my place but how could I cover that distance without being seen? And even if I managed to reach the dormitory, would the watchman let me in? Seeing Latika seemed an impossibility.

I mulled over the problem for three or four more days, then suddenly made up my mind—I'd go and see Latika. I stayed up late that night, and when I felt certain that the street was quiet and empty, I went to the door of my apartment, leaned on the latch and pushed it open, and took a hop into the hall. The building was silent, and all the doors were closed. I bounced down the staircase and reached the gate. I stood there for a few moments, looking right and left. Then I stepped out onto the street, and, with quick hops, headed towards Latika's dormitory. The night air was cold.

I had covered some distance when I saw two men coming in my direction, gossiping as they strolled along. I quickly turned aside into an alley and stood in the darkness against a wall. When the men had passed on down the road, I resumed my journey. A few minutes later, a man suddenly emerged onto the street from a side alley, almost directly in front of me. I didn't panic, but just kept going along briskly. I saw that the man was weaving about, and appeared to be quite drunk. He stared at me unsteadily, rubbing his eyes, as I passed him. I have no doubt he kept gazing at me wide-eyed even after I had left him far behind. It occurred to me that he could tell his friends about a fantastic sight—but no one would believe him.

My excitement and anxiety increased as Latika's dormitory came into my view. I slowed down and came to a halt in front of the iron grilled gate, which was closed. I looked through the grill, and saw a watchman sleeping upon a cot at the door of the narrow hallway. I retreated a few steps, got a good strong start, and leaped high over the gate. Landing inside, I cautiously passed by the watchman. The doors of the rooms on both sides of the hallway were closed. Latika's room, Number 37, was on the first floor. I went up the staircase, and first stood silently in front of the door, then knocked upon it gently with my head. I waited for a few moments, then banged again at the door a little more loudly. There was a noise inside, and then the light was switched on. 'Who is it?' I heard Latika's sleepy voice say. And again a little louder, 'Who is it?' 'It's me,' I said, 'Open the door.'

The door opened partially, and Latika looked at me with sleepy eyes. Realizing that she was about to let out a scream, I said hastily, 'Don't shout, Latika. It's me—Anil! Let me in first. Then I'll explain everything.' With the back of her hand before her open mouth, Latika stepped slowly backwards. I got inside the room, and pressed the door shut behind me. 'Latika, Latika!' I said pleadingly, with all my heart. Stepping backwards, Latika had stumbled against her bed, and was now sitting on its edge. Tears had welled up in her eyes, and the hands she had held over her mouth trembled. I stood in front of her. 'Listen, Latika,' I said. I narrated my tale to her. She listened with tears streaming down her face. I finished. She only managed to mumble, 'Anil, Anil!'

Then I said, 'Latika, I know very well that I must say goodbye to you forever now. There's no alternative. And I'll go; I'll never in my life bother you again. I just want you to marry some nice boy and be happy.' I paused, then said, 'Before going away, Latika, I just have one small favour to ask. Will you give me one last kiss—please?' I took a small hop forward. 'Anil!' Latika choked out in a smothered voice, and stood up from the bed. Kissing her was going to present a bit of a problem. I didn't have arms to embrace her. Besides, since my lips were at the top of my head, I'd fall to the ground. 'Please, Latika,' I said again and leaned forward a little. 'Anil!' Latika said again in a suppressed voice and stepped back quickly. Latika had run to the other end of the room and was standing against the wall, her whole body shaking. Without trying to rise, I rolled across the floor in her direction, but got caught between the bed and the writing table. Stuck in that cramped space, I couldn't even get up. 'Latika, Latika!' I pleaded in a smothered voice. 'Help me up. Latika, Please!' Looking down at me with an uncertain expression, Latika remained motionless. Then she slowly stepped forward, bent down and raised me up. How pleasurable was the touch of her soft hands! The sensation assuaged my desire, even when I noticed that she quickly withdrew her hands and held them behind her. Yet, a small gesture may restore our faith in illusions. 'All right, Latika,' I said, 'I'll go now. Goodbye for ever, my love.' For a few moments, I stood there and watched her face; if I had had arms, I would have wiped those tears gently away. Latika opened the door with a trembling hand, and in two jumps I was out of the room.

'O my God!' a number of female voice cried out in unison, and I looked around in surprise and alarm. I was surrounded by a bevy of girls. I figured out quickly that, hearing voices in Latika's room, they had surmised that there was something going on in her room, and had gathered at the door to try and listen.

'O my God, what a prick!' 'Man, so big!' 'Latika, where did you find such a big one?' Amid such reactions, one or two girls touched me with their hands. Deciding that I must break this siege quickly, I jumped forward vigorously. The girls in my way backed up. With a giant leap, I broke out of the circle, and headed for the staircase. 'Hey, wait, wait!' some of the girls shouted and started in pursuit. I went down the stairs quickly, and continued down the hallway. The noise had awakened the dormitory matron, who was coming down the hall now in my direction. She took one look at me as I came leaping along, then screamed, fainted, and fell to the ground. That woke up the watchman sleeping at the end of the hallway. I was by him before he was up, reaching the gate and leaping over into the street. I proceeded speedily down the street in the direction of home. I reached my building without further incident, went up the stairs and through the door, which was still open as I had left it, shutting it behind me.

After this encounter with Latika, I spent the next four or five days in bed in a despondent mood. There were one or two more cards from the office that I didn't even bother to read. After a few days I began to move around the apartment, but spent most of my time standing for hours at the window, looking out absent-mindedly. A great deal was passing through my mind. I pondered over my life, and my future. I had undergone a transformation; wouldn't my future, my destiny also change? I felt convinced that there was something different written in my fate. It was my duty to fulfil my destiny. I was no longer an ordinary human being called Anil Rao. Shedding the skin of that existence, I had now gained a clear, purer state of being. To live as an imitation of Anil Rao, to live the life of a timid creature afraid of the daylight, that was surely not my destiny. I must step outside my closed rooms, I must leave Anil Rao behind me.

It was with this conviction that, late one night, I left my apartment again, never to return. Hopping quickly along, I followed a road that led out of town. I had no idea where I was going. I felt certain that if I didn't find my destiny, it would find me.

I arrived at the outskirts of a town. There were no street lights there and it was still dark. I found the cold night air exhilarating. On both sides of the road there were fields and stretches of vacant land. From time to time, a truck or a car went by, and I hid by the roadside until the vehicle passed. After a while I left the road and followed a path meandering through the countryside. I had gone quite a way when I saw the outline of huts ahead in the distance. It was clear that the path led towards a village, and I had no intention of ending up in one of those. Leaving the path, I took off across the open fields, away from the village. To my right I could make out the shape of a small hill, and I continued in that direction. In a few minutes I arrived at the foot of the hill. It was a lonely, barren place. I was tired. Dawn was at hand. The sky had acquired a faint red tint behind the hill.

The sun came up. I surveyed the hill with its dry, yellowed grass, a few dwarf shrubs and a large number of boulders. Around me stretched a plain covered with the same dry grass, with scattered shrubs and stones, and a few tall trees. I was standing under one of those trees. I liked the place. It had an ancient, primordial air about it that I felt was closer to my new avatar. A cement structure no longer suited me. If there was to be any kind of construction around and above me now, I preferred it to be of stone, done in some ancient style.

While I entertained such thoughts, I observed a villager in the distance walking in my direction. He came nearer, I didn't move. He was almost upon me when he looked up and noticed me. He froze. Wide-eyed, he watched me. All of a sudden, he turned and started running in the direction of the village. After some time I saw a small crowd of villagers coming towards me hurriedly. Almost running, they came and stood around me. Uttering words of surprise they looked at one another. I caught the words 'The lingam of Shiva, the lingam of Shiva.' I gathered from their talk that they believed they had found a self-created lingam, and that they planned to carry me and set me down in an appropriate place in the village. Some of the villagers left and went back to the village, and returned bearing various items. Then they all sat around and worshipped me with flowers and other offerings. Some of them had brought along musical instruments. Then two of them raised me up in the air, and with cries of 'Long live Lord Shiva,' they all started walking back to the village, to the tune of drums and pipes.

They brought me to a large stone platform on the outskirts of the village, which seemed like the remnant of a temple that had crumbled or been destroyed. A huge crowd collected round the stone platform, and the whole village came to see me. Women and children were shouting with excitement, and were making gestures of worship from time to time. The two men who had borne me—one of them appeared to be the headman of the village—were discussing something with other leading villagers. Some of them touched me, as though to see what I was made of. I gathered from their talk that they were puzzled by the fact that I didn't seem to be made of stone, but felt warm to the touch like living skin. I listened to their talk for a while, then, in a loud voice, I said: 'Listen, O people!'

The crowd was struck dumb to see me speak like a human. 'Listen, O people!' I said again. 'Many years ago, the three highest gods, Brahma, Vishnu and Shiva, emerged from the waters that enveloped the earth. Brahma and Vishnu bowed before Lord Shiva and said, "Lord, you are all powerful, the greatest among us. We beg you to create the world, according to your wishes." "I shall," said Lord Shiva, and submerged himself again in the waters to meditate upon the matter. He remained submerged for thousands of years. In the meantime, Lord Brahma and Lord Vishnu debated what they should do. Then Vishnu said to Brahma, "Lord sir, why don't you create the world yourself? You have that power." So Lord Brahma created the world, moving and still. Then Lord Shiva emerged from the waters, all set to create the world. But he found that the world had already been created by Brahma. He didn't like Brahma's creation at all. He was disgusted to see all those animals and birds with their poor mental powers. Even more deplorable was the creature that Brahma had created as the crown of creation: Man, plagued by anxiety, fear, and confusion, and living a pitiful life owing to his thousand weaknesses. Flaring up with anger, Lord Shiva said, "What kind of a world has this

Brahma created! I would have created Man a thousand times better, a perfect Man, free from anxiety, fear and confusion, and from all weaknesses. What I was going to carry out slowly, giving everything full thought, has been done by this Brahma in too much haste, and quite inefficiently. Now I have no interest in creating the world all over again. On the contrary, I shall burn and destroy this poor, second-rate creation." With these words, Lord Shiva expelled a huge flame from his mouth. Then Lord Brahma pleaded with him not to destroy the world, moving and still. "We shall worship your sacred image—the lingam—perpetually," Lord Brahma said. With a bitter laugh, Lord Shiva said, "All right, I won't destroy your creation. But as for my lingam, it was going to be used to create a perfect human race on this earth. Now it's of no use any more." With these words Lord Shiva broke off his lingam and threw it upon the surface of the earth. O people, it is the sacred lingam of Lord Shiva himself that you now see before you.'

When I finished, there was not the slightest sound or movement around me for several moments. Then a cry emerged from all the mouths: 'Glory be to Lord Shiva! Glory be to Lord Shiva!' Many of the people came forward and prostrated themselves before me. Throughout the day men and women, young and old, came to worship me. This became a routine from that day onward. As the news spread, people from far off villages also began to arrive. Then the headman of the village decided to build a temple around me. Labourers came and began to chisel stones. Within a few days a domed, stone temple arose around me.

A village woman called Rakhmabai took to my worship with whole-hearted zeal. Her husband had died prematurely and they had no issue. Now practically abandoning her house, Rakhmabai spent most of her waking hours in my service, going home only at night. She supervised the devotees. Many of the devotees asked me questions regarding their life, their future, their problems. I answered them if I felt like it. Those who received answers went away happily. The fact that I answered such questions increased my fame. The whole day I stood upon a pedestal in the domed temple for the benefit of visitors. Sometimes late at night, when Rakhmabai had gone home, I hopped out of the temple and wandered about the countryside strewn with stones. At that quiet hour of the night, under the gentle light of the moon and the stars, I felt very happy, and a deep, deep peace enveloped my mind. After I had wandered to my heart's content, I returned to the temple. Sometimes at night I saw how I appeared upon the earth. I saw Lord Shiva breaking me off from his body and throwing me down upon the earth. I—Shiva's lingam—pierced the entire globe and stretched far into space. Brahma assumed the form of a goose and began searching for one end of me in space, while Vishnu assumed the form of a boar and searched for the other end in the belly of the earth. But they could find neither end of me, so vast had I become. Then the two gods heard a voice from the sky: 'If the lingam of the god with braided hair is worshipped, it will grant all desires that arise in the heart.' When they heard that, Brahma, Vishnu and everyone else began to worship me.

I had found my destiny. I now knew my extraordinary place in the system of the universe. I, the lingam of Shiva, was the image of the three times; past, present, and future. I was the axle of the wheel of time. Yet I felt a certain sadness. It was not a good thing that Lord Shiva broke off his lingam and threw it away. Without doubt, the chaos that was now the hallmark of life on earth was the result of Lord Shiva's wrathful act. If I could be reunited with the Lord, peace and love would prevail upon the earth. When would that be? When would I rejoin my lord?

3

Rakhmabai continued to serve me faithfully. Now she didn't go home even at night, but slept inside the temple. She was wholly devoted to me, and I had a deep affection for her. Late one night, when everyone else had gone away, I asked her to massage me. Pouring coconut oil over me, she rubbed me with both hands. From top to bottom, her hands moved over me faster and faster, and with increasing passion. She became so absorbed in the act that she didn't even notice her sari becoming wet between her thighs. I too became more and more excited, so that in the end I was possessed with a wild desire to send a burning jet of semen leaping from my mouth. But I knew that couldn't be. All that would emerge from my mouth would be words, words, words. Then I was filled with despair and sorrow. Enough of this vain, barren exercise, I said to myself. Rakhmabai too became tired, and lay on the stone floor with both her arms around me.

Sometimes she used to beg of me, 'My lord, will you bless me with just one drop of your seed? I shall have a son who will be covered in glory, and who shall rule the world. He shall establish the kingdom of peace and love upon the earth.' Then I told her, 'Rakhmabai, you know that is not possible at the present time. It will be possible only when I am reunited with Lord Shiva.' 'But won't you forget me when you rejoin him?' Rakhmabai asked with anxiety. 'No, Rakhmabai, I shall never forget you.' Then she hugged me with even greater fervour. Such are the experiences of despair and regret, and of luminous glory, that constitute life on earth, and which I have undergone like everyone else, witnessed by stones and stars.

The regret in my mind increased as time passed. I no longer cared for fame among men; it didn't give me the inner peace I longed for. Now I rarely answered the questions put to me by devotees. My mind was possessed by only one question: when would I rejoin my lord? I was upon the earth, but not of the earth; I was the image of divine power, and yet powerless. These underlying contradictions in my being became more and more vexing. And then, one night, I suddenly underwent another transformation; I lost my state of erection, and collapsed limply to the floor. I, who was over five feet tall, was now reduced to two feet. Rakhmabai, who was sleeping in one corner of the temple, woke up and came running to me, 'My lord, my lord, what's this?' she cried out. Getting no reply, she squatted by my side, and caressed me gently, wiping her eyes with the end of her sari from time to time. After a while, I began to speak. As my voice had now become extremely feeble, Rakhmabai had to bend her head down so that she could hear me. I said to her, 'Rakhmabai, I don't want to remain here in this state. Lift me up, and carry me to some deserted place before daylight. Tell the people tomorrow morning that I went back to the heavens during the night.' At first, Rakhmabai was unwilling to do this, but in the end she agreed. She held me in her arms like a child, and stepped out of the temple. After walking a long way in the dark, she placed me upon a large rock in a deserted spot. She tore off a large stretch of cloth from the end of her sari and wrapped me in it; thus she protected me from ants and crows and other creatures of the wild.

Here I am now on this plain, far away from village and city, from all human habitation. But what oppresses me is not my personal fall; it is the larger significance of the sign. Lord Shiva first broke off his lingam and threw it away; now he has also deprived it of power. Does this mean that my lord has lost all hope for the world? What will now become of the earth, of the world of men? Is this world, already ravaged by chaos and confusion, to sink further into that wretched condition? It is this that worries me. Stretched out upon a rock in my helpless, abandoned state on this barren plain, I continually pray to Lord Shiva that he may have mercy upon the world of men and bless it with his regenerating power.

# an interview with
# m.chakko

INTERVIEWER: Mr Chakko, you say that the island on which you spent so many years was named Lorzan, is that right?

CHAKKO: That's right.

INTERVIEWER: Where exactly is it located?

CHAKKO: I never learned that. When our ship went down, four of us drifted for several days in a lifeboat. Our food had all but run out and we were nearly at death's door when we came upon Lorzan. All I can say is that the island lies somewhere to the far south in the Indian Ocean.

INTERVIEWER: So four of you landed on Lorzan?

CHAKKO: No, two men died at sea. Vaiko was the only one who made it to Lorzan with me.

INTERVIEWER: And, as you testified in court, all the women on this island had only half bodies. Not a single woman possessed a whole, normal human body?

CHAKKO: No, they all came in halves. The upper half, or the lower half.

INTERVIEWER: But the men were normal?

CHAKKO: Yes, that's right.

INTERVIEWER: How did that happen?

CHAKKO: Apparently their genes had undergone some strange mutation.

INTERVIEWER: And what about reproduction?

CHAKKO: They had test-tube babies.

INTERVIEWER: Which suggests a fairly advanced civilization.

CHAKKO: Yes, indeed it does. In some respects they were far in advance of us.

INTERVIEWER: What race were they?

CHAKKO: I was told their ancestors had migrated centuries ago from somewhere in East Asia. Since that time they had avoided all contact with the outside world and developed their own civilization.

INTERVIEWER: And they accepted you among them?

CHAKKO: Well, yes, I can't say I had any problems fitting in. In fact, they wouldn't let me leave the island. They were afraid I'd tell the outside world about them if I left. After a while, I simply settled down there.

INTERVIEWER: In spite of the peculiarity of the island women?

CHAKKO: It didn't bother me all that much. One can get used to almost anything, you know. I got a job in an engineering firm. Once I had established myself, I applied for a wife at the government marriage bureau. Since the female population of the island was smaller than the male, there was a waiting list. Then one day I was allotted a wife. Her name was Ka Sirinom.

INTERVIEWER: But tell me, was living with half a woman really satisfying?

CHAKKO: Well, why not? Children in Lorzan were raised in government nurseries, and the family as an institution didn't exist in any real sense. What it came down to was men living by themselves in apartments, and they simply enjoyed having another person about the house, that's all. It didn't matter much if the woman had a whole body or only half of one. You must keep in mind that what one needs is simply someone else around. It doesn't matter who. I'm sure you know the difference it makes, if you're living by yourself, just to discover a spider or a mouse in the room, or even to have a fly buzzing about you! Let alone sharing the house with a cat or a dog. The point is, half a woman can fill the need quite well.

INTEVIEWER: You lived happily with your wife, then?

CHAKKO: Ka Sirinom became a part of my life in the course of time. At first, living with a half-woman was a strange experience. I often had the feeling that there was an invisible upper body floating above her waist like a ghost. Wandering about on heavy feet, she sometimes came and stood before me, and I felt that she was staring at me with invisible eyes. Once, when I was copulating with her in a standing position, I suddenly had the sensation of unseen arms embracing me, and I jumped back in fright.

INTERVIEWER: Didn't experiences like that make you miserable?

CHAKKO: I was involved in a research project in engineering at the time which kept me occupied. I had little time for Ka Sirinom. She wandered about the house, or rested in bed. Whenever I felt the need, I went to her and tapped her on the legs—like tapping at a door, you might say. She had nice, large hips, and nice, soft legs.

INTERVIEWER: Did you remain with Ka Sirinom for all your stay in Lorzan?

CHAKKO: (not having heard the question) No, she lived at my house for about five years. Then things went wrong for me at work. I made a series of terrible blunders on the project. I used to come home very depressed in those days. Then I would fall wildly on Ka Sirinom. I sucked her toes so hard that the skin was raw. She put up with everything.

INTERVIEWER: (seeing Chakko lost in thought) And then?

CHAKKO: I soon realized that it was no use. My frustration only became worse. If Ka Sirinom could have listened and talked, I would have spoken with her, would have told her about many things and unburdened myself to her. But she could neither listen nor speak. All she knew was how to open her legs. So one day I returned her to the bureau, and got myself another woman—this time of the Lin class. Her name was Lin Rabaya.

INTERVIEWER: But couldn't you get another wife without giving up Ka Sirinom?

CHAKKO: No, I couldn't. Since there were fewer women than men, one was allowed to keep—to marry, that is—only one at a time. There was, however, a method which people sometimes resorted to. A man with a Ka wife would team up with one with a Lin wife. They'd tie their wives together with a rope, thus making 'one' woman out of them, and then take turns sleeping with 'her'. I tried this with Ka Sirinom a few times, but it really wasn't very satisfactory. In a way you could make one woman from the halves, but in your heart you knew it wasn't real, you were merely fooling yourself. Besides, the two half-women were never smooth and flat at the waist and therefore never joined perfectly, which was annoying. On one occasion I was heaving up and down on top of the bound bodies, when the rope suddenly slipped and the two halves began to slip apart. The Lin woman was embracing and kissing me passionately, while down below Ka Sirinom had clasped her legs tightly around me. They were sliding in opposite directions, pulling me apart. It was like the earth splitting beneath my feet.

INTERVIEWER: Well, then, did you get what you wanted from your second wife?

CHAKKO: After I brought Lin Rabaya home, I used to talk to her a lot. There were times when we talked through the night. Lin Rabaya was an intelligent woman. She had read a great deal. You might even call her an intellectual. In the course of time, I think I genuinely came to love her.

INTERVIEWER: What about physical satisfaction, though?

CHAKKO: Oh, there were her hands, her lips . . . you understand.

INTERVIEWER: Yes, I do.

CHAKKO: She had nice, full lips—and she knew how to use them. But in winter they were chapped, and that was unpleasant. Then I gave her a salve for her lips. We got along fine, on the whole. Once during the holidays we went to a beach resort. I took her to the sea-shore on long excursions, although it was tiring pushing her wheelchair in the sand. We used to sit on the beach and watch the sunset. I told her about the country I came from. When I said that the women there had whole bodies just like men, she laughed and gave me a pat on the cheek. 'That's some fantasy of yours—something you dreamed about,' she said.

INTERVIEWER: If the Lorzanians were as advanced as you say, they must have known about the outside world?

CHAKKO: The government did. The common people were generally kept in the dark. The government took pains to see that the people looked down on the outside world.

INTERVIEWER: I see. Please go on with Lin Rabaya's story.

CHAKKO: After a while, I became disaffected with Lin Rabaya. I would whisper to her, 'I love you, I love you,' and she'd say, 'I love you too.' But she didn't really mean it. She showed little interest in any emotional involvement. She was a sensualist, a pleasure-seeker. She fondled and stroked me endlessly. Then I used to hold her hands and say, 'I love you, Lin Rabaya,' and she'd smile and say, 'I love you too, Chakko.' But as soon as I released her hands, they began moving all over my body again. You'd think she was groping in darkness for something she had lost. Her fingers became so avid that at times they seemed to be trying to penetrate beneath my skin. Gradually we spoke less and less. I lay still as her lips and fingers explored my whole body. It was like soft hail falling upon me, burying me slowly. Then I started spending most of my time away from home.

INTERVIEWER: So you abandoned Lin Rabaya too?

CHAKKO: Not right away. I lived for a year without anyone. Then I brought home a Ka woman. Not Ka Sirinom, who had gone to someone else. This one was called Ka Punnasarto.

INTERVIEWER: Tell me about her.

CHAKKO: Ka Punnasarto was different from Ka Sirinom. She wasn't as plump and fleshy. She had long, tapering legs. You might call her thin. But she had an attractive, delicate walk. I didn't pay much attention to her, at first. I had taken her only because I thought I ought to have someone about the house. Ka Punnasarto always got beaten in the women's games, and that put me off even more.

INTERVIEWER: Women's games? What were they like?

CHAKKO: We use to have these games in each residential block once in a while. Everybody brought his wife to the Community Centre hall. A few Ka women, along with an equal number of Lin women, were put inside a circular area. The Ka women, who couldn't see of course, groped about with their legs, and kicked when they came across a Lin woman. The Lin women tried to grab their legs and pull the Ka women to the ground. That was the nature of the game. Ka Punnasarto wasn't able to kick very powerfully; on the other hand, she was usually pulled to the ground fairly easily because of her long legs. That embarrassed me.

INTERVIEWER: So you sent her back like the others?

CHAKKO: No, I didn't. As time passed, I came to know her better. Whenever I drew her near, she clung to me and brushed herself against me affectionately. There was an intelligence, and a certain understanding, in everything she did. She didn't open her legs abruptly as Ka Sirinom did. She deliberately pressed her thighs together, and then parted them gradually and coyly. Sometimes she used to dance by herself. It was marvelous to watch that dance of half a body! The intricate movement of her legs, so swift and yet so graceful, entranced me. Usually, when she had stopped dancing, I would lift her gently and place her on the bed. I massaged her legs. She used to like that. She would hold my hand between her calves, and rub herself against it. She had a peculiar habit. She would press one of her toes on my body, lift the toe, then press again, then lift and press elsewhere, as you might test the softness of the ground. She once pressed the toe of her left foot at the very base of my spine, and instantly a strange sensation spread throughout my body. Eyes shut, I lay still for I don't know how long. I didn't stir even when she lifted her toe. At other times Ka Punnasarto placed her toes over mine, and pressed them alternately, as though she were sending a telegram. She pressed her toes passionately, as if she were desperately trying to tell me something. I too pressed my toes upon hers. This went on with increasing fervour. But it was never clear what she wanted to say. Then in despair she would open her legs and pull me closer with her feet. But I would gently extricate myself and lie quiet beside her. Wearied, we would lie still, clinging to each other. In this way I lived with Ka Punnasarto for several years. Then I noticed that she was becoming thinner. Her legs first became like dry sticks, and then they began to swell. I called in a doctor. He gave her a series of injections, but told me that her disease was incurable, and that she wouldn't live long. Ka Punnasarto's legs continued to swell. Her feet cracked and began to ooze a watery fluid. To me it seemed as though they were literally weeping—shedding tears. I caressed her cracked feet, and brushed my face against them. My tears mixed with the water oozing from her feet. She tried to move her feet, but they had become too heavy. In a few days she was dead.

INTERVIEWER: (after a pause) But tell me, Mr Chakko, how did the Lorzanian women manage to live?

CHAKKO: They were given injections of life-sustaining fluids at regular intervals. A medical van visited each house for this purpose.

INTERVIEWER: You must have been very unhappy at the death of Ka Punnasarto?

CHAKKO: For a few years after her death I lived alone. Then one day I took in Lin Maulafa. Lin Maulafa was a quiet, loving wife. But my relationship with her remained a superficial one. She stayed with me until I left Lorzan.

INTERVIEWER: Tell me, Mr Chakko, in a country like Lorzan wasn't homosexuality widespread?

CHAKKO: Not in the least. Homesexuality was commonly regarded as a great sin. Anyone indulging in it was sentenced to life imprisonment.

INTERVIEWER: What happened to the other man you mentioned—the one who reached Lorzan with you.

CHAKKO: Vaiko met with a strange end. That wasn't in Lorzan but in Amuraha. Did I tell you about Amuraha?

INTERVIEWER: No, you didn't.

CHAKKO: Some distance from Lorzan was the island of Amuraha. The situation on this island was exactly the opposite of that on Lorzan. Which is to say, the men there had half bodies, whereas the women were normal. The legend was that centuries ago Zem, a prince, and his sister Zemna, a princess, came there from the eastern regions of Asia. They had been driven out by their uncle, cast away on the ocean on a ship with a supply of food and water. Zemna, along with her seven husbands, landed at Lorzan, while Zem, along with his seven wives, reached Amuraha. What you find on the two islands is their respective progeny. The Amuraha women had normal bodies—you'll naturally wonder why Lorzanian men didn't marry Amurahan women. The answer is that since time immemorial, relations between Lorzanians and Amurahans were taboo. They believed that if a Lorzanian man so much as touched an Amurahan women the two would perish instantly. Any relations between them were, therefore, out of the question.

INTERVIEWER: What became of Vaiko?

CHAKKO: Oh yes, I was telling you about Vaiko. Vaiko too married a Lorzanian woman. But he wasn't happy. When he learned about Amuraha, he came to me and said, 'Look, Chakko, let's both go to Amuraha. Who wants to spend his life in a country of half women? There's no harm in our going to Amuraha. The taboos of these people don't apply to us, since we don't belong to their race. Think of the great time we'll have in a country where the women have never seen a man with a normal body! A complete male body in all its splendour! I tell you, they'll literally grovel before us. We'll live like kings over there!' The idea didn't appeal to me, in spite of Vaiko's great enthusiasm. I didn't want to risk my life on the sea again. Things weren't so bad in Lorzan, after all. I said no to Vaiko. He said he'd go alone. We were both under surveillance, but one night Vaiko stole a small boat and headed for Amuraha. For about a year after that, I had no news of him. Then one day I found out what had happened. Apparently, he reached the Amuraha shore, and the women in a coastal settlement there gathered about him. Seizing Vaiko's arms and legs and head, they started pulling him in every direction. They tugged at him so ferociously that his limbs were almost torn off.

He was screaming in the midst of rapacious women snarling at one another like a horde of hyenas. Vaiko was dead before the Amurahan policewomen arrived on the scene.

INTERVIEWER: It was a good thing you didn't go with him, wasn't it?

CHAKKO: Perhaps.

INTERVIEWER: Were the conditions for Amurahan men the same as that of Lorzanian women?

CHAKKO: They may have been. I don't know much about Amuraha.

INTERVIEWER: So by and large you were about happy in Lorzan? You didn't feel like returning to the world where you see normal women?

CHAKKO: Not particularly. Risking my life at sea solely on that account didn't seem worthwhile. How would I know in which direction to sail? To set out to the sea simply trusting to luck seemed suicidal.

INTERVIEWER: And yet, in the end, you returned. How did that happen?

CHAKKO: Towards the end a change came over me. For one

thing, I was getting on in years. I thought, am I going to die without ever holding a whole woman in my arms? But that wasn't the only thing. I was becoming homesick, too. I had spent the prime of my life in Lorzan. Now with the prospect of old age before me, the desire to return to my homeland took hold of me. This sentimental yearning to return 'home' became stronger and stronger. One night I lay alone on the terrace of my house. The stars shone in the clear sky. A cool breeze blew in from the sea. Suddenly I said to myself, 'I've got to go back!' The government didn't keep a strict watch on me any longer. They didn't think I'd make an attempt to escape after all these years. Taking advantage of this, I piled as much food and water as I could in a motorboat, and said goodbye to Lorzan. I drifted at sea for several days, until at last a tanker picked me up. I was back.

INTERVIEWER: Didn't you find it exciting to return after all those years?

CHAKKO: Of course. I visited places I knew, saw some people. Things had changed a great deal.

INTERVIEWER: And how did you react to seeing women with normal bodies?

CHAKKO: For the first few days, I simply stared at every woman I saw, whether she was beautiful or not. Then I went to a whore. I told her to undress, sat down and stared at her. Then I went nearer and stroked her all over gently. She looked at me strangely. She must have thought it odd, a man of my age behaving like a kid! Well, I was a kid in a way. When I landed in Lorzan I was not yet twenty, and had never had a woman. The rest of my years had passed in Lorzan, It was only now, in late middle age, that I was touching a normal woman.

Some time after my arrival, I married Lakshmi. Lakshmi was an independent widow. She wanted company in her declining years. Even in middle age, she had preserved her figure and remained attractive. Her late husband had left her a sizeable estate, so neither of us had to work. We stayed at home all day, spending hours in bed petting or teasing one another. We went out whenever the mood came over us. In spite of our age we lived like newly-weds. Lakshmi's late husband had been a withdrawn person with little appetite for sensual pleasures. Now, in my company, Lakshmi blossomed. She even said that for the first time she felt she was married in the true sense. But then little by little, I grew dissatisfied. Not that I had anything against Lakshmi. It was just that I didn't like the idea of women with whole bodies. When I returned from Lorzan, I was fascinated by the sight of normal women, but now in a few months I had lost interest in them. Perhaps this wasn't so very unusual. We sometimes desperately want to get somewhere, and when we arrive we wonder why we're there. That kind of experience isn't unusual, is it?

INTERVIEWER: I must say it isn't.

CHAKKO: So my attitude towards Lakshmi changed. I detested the sight of all women. Lakshmi was greatly disturbed at this change in my behaviour. 'Are you bored with me? Are you in love with someone else?' she kept asking me. I said no.

INTERVIEWER: May we talk about this in some detail, Mr Chakko? I'm interested in finding out why this change came over you. I wonder if, after all those years in the land of half-women, you had got used to it, and couldn't accept women with whole bodies?

CHAKKO: (after some thought) No, I don't think it was merely a question of habit, or getting used to something. There was more to it than that.

INTERVIEWER: Perhaps you believed that women should always be imperfect and inferior. You didn't like the idea of women being physically the same as men.

CHAKKO: (after some thought) No, I don't think it was that either.

INTERVIEWER: What was the reason for the change, then?

CHAKKO: First I should admit that I've never given it much thought. But it seems to me that the half, the partial, gives something that the whole, or what appears whole, doesn't.

INTERVIEWER: Could you expand upon that a bit?

CHAKKO: (throws up his hands.)

INTERVIEWER: Never mind. Please go on with your story.

CHAKKO: All I know is that day by day I grew more unhappy. I spent my time sulking, curled up in an armchair. Then one day I got up and went out. I went down to the blacksmith's lane and bought myself an axe. I hid it under my bed. That night after

Lakshmi had fallen asleep I brought the axe out, and, in the pale glow of the night-lamp, I aimed at her navel. In four or five blows I cut her exactly in two.

INTERVIEWER: (Opens his mouth, but does not speak; Chakko remains silent.) And then?

CHAKKO: Then? Then there were the usual things. The police and everything.

INTERVIEWER: You confessed to the crime, didn't you?

CHAKKO: What else could I do? I assumed that I was going to hang. But the other day my lawyer came to see me and said that the psychiatrist had certified that I was mentally incompetent, and that the death sentence had been suspended. I'll remain here as long as the psychiatrist says I'm insane. I thought, fine, good for me. If that idiot think I'm nuts, and if it saves me from the hangman's noose, why should I complain?

INTERVIEWER: (Looking at his watch) Mr Chakko, there were many more things I wanted to ask you, but there's not much time left now. Let me ask you a final question: do you have anything to say to our readers—I mean in general?

CHAKKO: (Lost in thought.)

INTERVIEWER: (Sees the Superintendent standing in the doorway.) Sorry, Mr Chakko, I've got to go now. I wish you luck. Goodbye, Mr Chakko.

CHAKKO: (Remains silent.)

(Interviewer's Note: *After the interview, I hastily leafed through a book of Freud's. I chanced upon this sentence, which I offer the readers to ponder over, if they care to: 'It is my belief that, however strange it may sound, we must reckon with the possibility that something in the nature of the sexual instinct itself is unfavourable to the realization of complete satisfaction.'*)

# barrel and bombil: a love story

'Call me Ali, or Ibrahim, or Ismail,' the man said, with a faint smile on his salt-dried lips. 'I've had various names. Each time I go on a voyage to the Arabian Gulf, I take on a new name. I tell them, on a whim, "I'm Ismail," and then, for the rest of the voyage, I'm Ismail. Nobody ever bothers to find out if it's my real name.'

'Don't they check your papers?' I asked.

'Papers!' The cracks in his peeling lips distended. 'Nobody has ever dreamed of papers! Our dhows have been going to the Arabian Gulf for centuries. Before anything like official papers was invented. We're all illiterate, anyway. The *darya sarang*—the captain—included. Nobody has any use for papers.'

'I myself was in Basra many years ago working for a construction company,' I said. 'I used to see dhows from India anchored in the Shatt-al-Arab.'

'Yes, Basra was a favourite port. It was on a trip to Basra that Bombil came with me.'

'And then you came across Barrel?'

'Precisely. It was an unforgettable voyage. I still remember it with a strange flutter in my heart.'

I sensed the promise of a salt-dried yarn from the old sailor's mouth. 'Tell me about Bombil and Barrel, dear Ali, or Ibrahim, or Ismail.'

The old sailor's face acquired a faraway look, as if he was throwing a fish-hook into the depths of the distant past.

'Bombil had joined our crew at the last minute. He begged the sarang to take him on, said he was starving. Indeed, he was thin as a bombil.'

'What's a bombil?' I asked.

'You don't know what's a bombil? I thought you were from the Konkan, a native of the coast.'

'Well, I spent most of my life in the up-country town of Kolhapur. And I'm Brahmin. I don't eat meat or fish.'

'Ah! A pure vegetarian, as they say. By the way, I've never been able to figure out why they say "pure" vegetarian? Are there "impure" vegetarians?' The old sailor's beard was laced with a sardonic smile. I didn't think he expected a reply. 'Oh well, bombil is the thin, long fish that seems to have no backbone. We usually eat it dry, stock it for long voyages. You see rows of bombil hanging to dry on the beaches, in season.'

'Yes, I've seen long rows of the fish drying in the sun near fishermen's huts here.'

'Our man Bombil got his name because he was thin as a bombil. Somebody called him Bombil, and the name stuck.'

'And what about Barrel?'

'That's a whale-shark. Off the coast of Gujarat, one sometimes encounters the whale-shark. There are fishermen who specifically hunt the fish. It gives a lot of meat. And a lot of oil. It's lucrative to hunt for whale-sharks.'

'You encountered a whale-shark?'

'Yes.'

'And why did you call it Barrel?'

'Barrel is not a proper name. It's a common name. These whale-sharks are commonly called barrel by the local fishermen, because the whale-shark is caught by harpooning. The fish is harpooned and empty barrels are tied to the harpoon. The huge fish dives into the depths, and the fishermen track it down by looking for the barrels that float upon the water.'

'I've seen it in American movies.'

'You don't need American movies to see it. Anyway, the barrel Bombil fell in love with was just one of the species.'

I kept quiet, not wanting to interrupt the flow of the sailor's yarn.

'I was on a dhow which, as usual, was loaded with various spices meant for the Gulf ports. We were going to unload the cargo, take on a fresh cargo of dates from Basra and other nearby ports, and sail back to India. Three days into the voyage, we sighted Barrel. Barrels, as I said, were not uncommon in these waters.

'Some of the sailors had done barrel-hunting earlier, and they watched Barrel with greedy eyes. "It's a huge barrel," one of them said. "We rarely see such a giant barrel. I wish we could harpoon it, and kill it. It'll give loads of meat, and fill buckets of oil." But we were on a dhow headed for the Gulf ports, and barrel-hunting was not on our agenda. So we had to let this specimen be.

'We thought Barrel would disappear after some time. But, strangely, Barrel kept on following our vessel. Even when half submerged, it towered above our eyes, and it swam steadily, at a measured pace, right after the dhow, its huge, bulbous eyes following us.

'Whale-sharks are not dangerous or fierce. It is we humans who turn them into maddened prey, with our harpoons and our axes.

'We were not going to harpoon this barrel, so it was not in danger, and it posed no danger to us. It just kept company with the dhow. It followed us, temporarily submerging completely, and again surfacing triumphantly. And its huge eyes followed us.'

'May be it felt lonely in the vastness of the sea?' I suggested.

'I don't know. Such ideas come into our human heads. I doubt that they'll make sense to whale-sharks, or to any other fish, for that matter.'

I kept quiet.

'Barrel kept us company. We kind of got used to its presence. A presence strangely comforting, I must say.

'Bombil was most fascinated by Barrel. He watched Barrel for hours. Bombil was the deck boy. He had work to do on the deck. But, every so often, he would go to the aft-end of the vessel, and watch Barrel. They communed with their eyes.

'After a couple of days of this, Bombil announced he was going to have a swim in the company of Barrel. The sarang allowed it, seeing that the boy was so eager, and so innocently boyish. He told him to be careful, and to get back soon to the vessel.

'Bombil dived into the ocean. He submerged for unbelievably long periods, but surfaced again. He played around with Barrel in this fashion. He seemed be to enjoying it. Barrel swam calmly, eyeing the boy with what seemed like kindliness. Almost love, one fancied.

'The dhow was making slow progress over the ocean. We didn't have mechanical engines in those days. We managed with sails. The wind was not favourable. As a matter of fact, there was no wind. The sea was like glass. I guess this suited Bombil and his lover.

'Yes, by now the two were head over heels in love. Bombil submerged in the water for long periods. And so did Barrel. The two spent as much time as possible under the vast sheet of water.

'Since the day he joined the crew, Bombil was a shy, withdrawing kind of person. He spent most of his time by himself. I was the only one who somehow struck a chord of fellowship with him. He used to come to me sometimes, and chat. Of course only if no one else was with me. Perhaps he came to me because I, too, spent most of my free time alone on the deck.

'Bombil told me he had the strange power of communing with whale-sharks through low-frequency sound waves. When they were under water, Bombil and Barrel communed by sonar signals. It was a strange kind of conversation, perhaps not much of a conversation by our standards. But they were happy in their own world, communing soul to soul, it seemed to me. Perhaps the two sang songs to each other, perhaps a duet, a passionate declaration of love. When Bombil zoomed up from the depths of the sea after one of his sorties, one of his trysts under water, he shot out of the water like a rocket, the upper half of his body standing above the surface almost vertically for a moment, and there was such a smile on his face, the face with water dripping from his hair and skin and his incipient beard and moustache, such a smile, innocent and joyful, oh, it was such a smile, out of this world, the smile of a puny, minor god, it seemed to me. I'll never forget that smile.'

The sailor was momentarily lost in his memories, and silent.

'Bhai,' I said. 'This Barrel, this whale-shark, was it female, or a male?'

Woken out of his memory-world, the old sailor smiled broadly, and said: 'Oh, sir! I never bothered to find out. And I'm sure it made no difference to Bombil. The love between Barrel and Bombil superseded sex, it seemed to me. Well, there may have been some kind of sex to it. Sometimes, as Bombil surfaced above the water, I could see that his penis was erect under his short pants. I don't know. Whatever sex was there, it transcended all ideas such as male and female, fish and man. The bond between them was unworldly, in a way.

'Our dhow made slow progress. But, eventually, it reached a point beyond which Barrel could not travel. Apparently, there was an invisible line beyond which whale-sharks did not travel in the Indian Ocean.

'Bombil had to bid farewell to Barrel. The massive presence of the whale-shark was blotted out. We all missed the comforting presence of Barrel behind our vessel. Bombil was inconsolable. That night, I slept; but my sleep was haunted by weird, disturbing dreams. I awoke early. Beside my bed, I found a crumpled piece of paper with a note scribbled upon it: "Friend Ali, I am going to join Barrel. See you all on the return trip. Bombil." We searched on the ocean. We even retraced part of our way upto that point. Bombil was not to be found. I was the most distressed. Others soon forgot about the reticent lad that had been on board.

'We offloaded our cargo of spices at Basra. We spent a few days at Basra Port. Then we loaded a cargo of the year's fresh dates, and sailed back.

'We reached a point at which Bombil had disappeared. I had a fond hope that we would encounter both Bombil and Barrel in the waters that we had gone over. I kept a watch around our vessel. It was fruitless. Neither Bombil nor Barrel was to be seen. I desperately hoped that at least the massive presence of Barrel might be visible on the horizon. If we did, I would wildly hope that, like a dolphin carrying a boy, Barrel might have carried our lad to the safety of some beach. But nothing of the kind became a reality.

'We reached Verawal port on the Gujarat coast, the port from which we had started. The sailors were joyous at the prospect of meeting their near and dear ones, and at being paid for the trip. The voyage was successful, and without a mishap. We docked. Some of the sailors were busy offloading the cargo of dates. Others were busy gathering their belongings together. I was the only one without a family. I carried no souvenir, nor gift, for anyone. I still carried the hope in my heart that I would see Bombil on the beach. I half expected to find Bombil's slim body emerging from the crowd at the port, greeting me with the innocent, broad smile, a smile that concealed the depths of passion that sustained it.

'Instead of this, what I saw was quite a different scene. I saw a large crowd gathered upon the beach. Above the heads of people towered the huge body of a sea creature. That of a whale-shark, I could make out. I approached the scene. I made my way through the excited, noisy crowd. I stood before the gigantic beast, myself a puny presence, among so many puny presences, in front of that almost other-worldly being.

'I gathered from the people around that the whale-shark had not been hunted and caught; it had itself beached, for a reason that was not clear. Looking up at the gigantic creature in front of me, it struck me that it was none other that our Barrel, Bombil's lover. Now, one whale-shark is like another, you might say. But several days' familiarity gave me the confidence to know the creature as an individual.

'The whale-shark had beached for unknown reasons; perhaps it was sick, or in pain. The fishermen at the head of the crowd began tackling what they saw as a godsend. Axes and machetes were produced and the men began hacking at the mountain in front of them. Dismembering the giant fish was an arduous task, requiring much patience and perseverance. They hacked on.

'The fish, by the way, was still very much alive. The men were hacking at it, trying to dismember it, while the creature stared into the distant space with wide open eyes. Watching him die in that excruciatingly slow manner, I thought of the prophet Yeshu who died on the cross in a like manner. It was horrible, horrible. It was unbearable, that slow enactment of live death. But I did not turn my face away.

'And, looking up at that giant of the sea, with his huge, wide open eyes, I saw, or fancied I saw, a look of kindliness in those eyes, the kindliness that I had glimpsed in the creature's eyes as he watched Bombil cavorting in the waters around him. It was as if the creature had, in his tiny brain, still preserved the image of that frail, wispy human figure. Slowly, the fishermen made headway with the creature's corporeal substance. At some point, I suppose, the creature died as Yeshu must have died at some point of time during his long agony on the cross.

'The fishermen were cutting up the huge carcass. Huge chunks of meat were being distributed among relatives and friends amidst cries of joy and gratification. It was mostly offal; the choice pieces were collected in sacks for the market. Such a hullabaloo; excited cries of women and children were carried away by the sea breeze. I watched the proceedings with a heavy heart. Such was the end of Barrel, a sad end.

'Already somebody had started a fire for the purpose of melting the blubber. A large drum was kept on the fire; pieces of blubber were thrown into the drum. The fish-oil had started gathering at the bottom of the drum. It was bubbling. A cloud of acrid smoke rose from the spot, a thick, black cloud. The smell would have made you throw up, city-bred people like you. I was used to the sights and smells.

'The operation was only beginning. The butchers attacked the offal, the stomach parts. The body was still to be dealt with.

'One of the butchers raised an excited shout. He bent down, and picked up something from the innards of the huge beast. He held it up for all to see. It was a copper bracelet such as men wear. I recognized it as the bracelet of Bombil. Bombil used to wear a copper bracelet on his left arm.

'There were no other remains of Bombil inside the whale-shark's stomach. No pieces of clothing, or physical remains. I beseeched the butcher to let me examine the bracelet. I held the copper ornament in my hand. On one side of the bracelet, there were the peculiar markings that convinced me. Yes, it was Bombil's bracelet all right.

'As I held the bracelet in my hand, I fainted. People thought it was because of the gory sight, and the acrid smell and smoke. They carried me away, and laid me in the sand at some distance.

'After a while, I came to. I got up and left the scene, without once looking back. That was the end of Barrel and Bombil.

'Brother, I have told you the story. Let me go now. We shall meet again some time. Inshallah!' Ali, or Ibrahim, or Ismail, placed his skinny hand upon my shoulder; his hennaed red beard, sans moustache, shook in the breeze; he transfixed me momentarily with his pale eyes; then he turned and walked away, leaving his bare footprints in the wet sand of the low tide.

I went home, and, searching in my library, leafed through some books. I gathered some interesting facts about sharks. Sharks can detect sound waves. They can also sense electric and magnetic fields. As for whales as a species, they emit low-frequency sounds that can travel hundreds of kilometers. The whales sing long songs. I couldn't find much information about whale-sharks; it was unclear to me if whale-sharks also sing songs. The whale-shark is the largest of the sharks. The sharks generally are not blood-thirsty. The whale-shark, especially, is not dangerous to humans, as it is a harmless plankton eater.

The most interesting fact that I noted was that sharks are solitary animals. It is the solitaries—animal or human—that interest me, like the tiger in the forest, which, after the brief mating season, continues with his unattached, contemplative existence.

When the boy Bombil abandoned the dhow for the sake of Barrel—I speculated—he must have established communication with his ichthyian lover through low-frequency sounds, even though they may have been several kilometres apart. For all I know, they had a joyous and passionate reunion, a lover's reunion. What happened after that, I don't know. Nor I suppose, does anyone else.

I gathered some information about Bombil, too. I mean, about the name Bombil. This fish, known as Bombay Duck in what is now Mumbai, is apparently found only in the sea around Mumbai, and nowhere else. A six- to ten-inch slim, slippery fish with extremely soft flesh, it is considered a delicacy by some, and eaten fried or curried fresh. For others, in upcountry towns and villages, it is stocked in dried form; for upcountry people, it is a cheap and savoury source of protein.

I also came across an interesting folk-tale about the fish. The

Bombil was one of the adversaries of Lord Parashurama in ancient times. Lord Parshurama or Rama with a *parashu*—an axe—is supposed to have conquered Deccan India, including the coastal region of Konkan. Bombil was such a stubborn adversary of Parashurama that the Lord, in anger, hurtled Bombil into the sea. Bombil landed in the sea with all his bones broken. But still he survived, and became a fish in the local sea. Bombil is now a kind of symbol of triumphant survival.

As for Barrel, I learned that the Indian Government has now banned the killing of whale-sharks. If the ban had been in effect earlier, the barrel that Bombil was in love with might have escaped a gruesome fate.

Whatever barrels are there in the sea off the western coast of India now move freely and safely, I like to imagine, sending their songs far over the ocean. Their solitary meditations in the depths of the ocean, like those of the sages of ancient India in the depths of the forest, are undisturbed and exempt from the greed of men. As for the boy Bombil, tragically dead at a young age, I take comfort in the thought that his species represents the archetypal survivor. And I like to believe that the spirit of Bombil endures, and answers the call of love from some ichthyian lover, note for note.

# III

# Small Creatures

# flies

## 1

I read all day. I drag an armchair near my bed, rest my legs on the bed and go on reading, a book on my lap. But there are too many flies in my room. They keep buzzing over my head, land on my head, or my cheeks, nose, arms, legs, or on the bed. I hate the touch of a fly on my body. I boil with rage whenever a fly carelessly descends upon my limbs. I wriggle my arms furiously.

## 2

So now I keep a folded newspaper by my side. As a fly alights on my body, or on the bed, I raise the folded newspaper gently in the air and bring it down squarely upon the insect. The fly rarely escapes; on the other hand, it seldom dies. How can you swat and kill a fly on a floppy bedsheet with a limp newspaper? Yet the fly is dazed for a few moments and, with these precious moments in hand, I am usually able to deliver a few more blows to the reeling creature.

## 3

Sometimes an unlucky fly gets its wings—or one of its wings—badly damaged with the very first blow. Then I don't have to hurry to hit it again. It tries to get up, to fly away, uselessly. It crawls across the whole, white bedsheet.

4

I still remember one obstinate fly. When I struck, it lay there for a few seconds, almost in the middle of the bed, with a crumpled wing. Then it seemed to regain its senses. Under my intent gaze, it started to crawl slowly. To my amazement, I noticed that it was dragging itself to the other side of the bed, that is, away from me. I was surprised at the insect's awareness that its huge enemy lay on this side, and that it was I, crouched in an armchair with a newspaper clutched between moist fingers. With fascinated eyes, I watched the fly trotting painfully, hobbling, limping, through the desert whiteness of the bedsheet. When it had crept a good distance, I realized that I was letting it go too far. It wanted to get across the bleached desert, away from my sphinx-like face on this side of the bed. If it continued to crawl onward, it would soon be on the edge of the sheet, there to huddle in a crease, or topple onto the floor, a prey to ants. I didn't want that to happen. So I dragged it gently with the folded newspaper to the middle of the bed again. There it lay for a few seconds. Then it started to crawl almost in the same direction, as a blind man would. I was bored by now. So I whacked it with the folded newspaper, just once.

## 5

There is another fly that I remember. I had spotted it far down the bedstead and, leaning forward cautiously, was slowly raising the folded paper in the air, when I saw a spider drop onto the sheet from the bedstead and advance in the direction of the fly, step by step, with great patience. Instead of bringing my scimitar down upon the fly, I stayed still, looking at the two dark spots on the sheet, one winged, one many-legged. The fly didn't move as the spider advanced with immense steadiness and I watched with astonishment. When the spider was just a short distance from the fly, it stopped. I held my breath. But, for a long time, nothing happened. Under my gaze, below the upraised newspaper, the spider and the fly were utterly motionless.

The spider was now so close to the fly that I wondered whether the fly had seen it. It must have. But then, why didn't it fly away? In a moment it could be in the air, buzzing happily, with the powerless spider squatting below on all its ridiculous legs, watching in dismay. And yet the foolish creature remained there. Had the spider hypnotized it? That sounded fantastic. Then what was it doing there? Apparently nothing, nothing whatsoever. I felt helpless not knowing how the creature's mind worked.

Suddenly, before I knew what was happening, the spider was upon the fly, all its legs firmly encircled around the fly's body.

## 6

While I was applauding its skill, the spider started limping back towards the bedstead, somewhat awkwardly because of the prey under it, which was almost of equal size. So I quickly hauled it back with the newspaper. It was helpless. It wouldn't let go of the fly. When it started moving again, I manoeuvred it to my side of the bed. Then I pushed it over. It fell onto the floor, still with the fly clutched between its numerous legs. 'A creature with a will to live!' I muttered scornfully, and put my slippered foot upon the twosome. Only two sticky balls remained on the floor, one slightly darker than the other, almost mingled with each other like a copulating couple.

## 7

There was another fly that I had badly maimed. It lay unconscious upon my pillow. My pillow itself, as we Indians say. It may have been dead, but, with my long experience of flies, I knew it wasn't. Flies are tenacious, obdurate creatures. Some flies that I had taken to be dead and left to themselves after the first blow, suddenly came to life and got away before my eyes. So I should have given this fly one more blow right then, the way some cautious hunters do with tigers or leopards they have shot. But I didn't. Somehow I didn't feel like rapping the newspaper again on that battered body. So I continued to read (I was reading Spinoza at the time, I remember distinctly), and when I looked up again to see whether it was trying to get away, I found that another fly had alighted just next to it.

## 8

Here was an interesting situation. I'd be able to observe what a fly does when it finds a member of its own species in distress. I watched without the least movement so as not to scare away the newcomer. Soon enough, the second fly came upon the battered one. It stood before the first fly, face to face, for a few seconds. Then it went around it, as if inspecting its body. Then it climbed upon the dented fly, who reeled under its weight. All this time I had been watching intently. But, with all my attention, I couldn't make out a thing. What had the two flies done, face to face? Was the battered one conscious at all, in the first place? Had they just looked into each other's eyes, or had they communicated? 'He . . . him . . . that monster . . . he's going to kill me . . . oh, do something, whatever-your-name-is, please, quick,' and 'Don't worry, my dear, I'll set you right in a minute,' and so forth. But this sounded funny. Then what had happened? Again I was helpless before these tiny brains whose emotions and intentions I could barely know. I felt humiliated. And, watching the second fly on top of the battered one, I wondered if it was not copulating, or trying to copulate, with the other. What a thought! But wasn't it possible? What did these creatures know of virtue and wickedness? It was quite possible, it was quite possible. I could only see them lying there, one on top of the other, and guess, and know nothing for certain. So what my bizarre creatures had conjectured might very well have been true. Yet, it might have been that the other fly was merely inspecting the crumpled wings of its friend and trying to set them right, if it could.

## 9

Then the fly got down from its friend's body, circled it and stopped on the other side. Then it put its mouth close to the other's body and stayed there for a while. Then it circled again, got to the other side, and put its mouth to the body there. Here was another problem. What mysterious treatment was it rendering to its wounded companion? I couldn't even guess.

## 10

Having performed its strange rites, the fly seemed to have done with its companion. It jogged on a bit and stayed at some distance, perhaps watching the other to see if it was recovering. But the dented fly was still unable to stir. I must have wounded it badly.

## 11

At this point it occurred to me that the other fly might fly away now, content with having done its duty, or in despair at having been unsuccessful, or with a pleasant after-copulatory drowsiness. It also occurred to me that I could kill this fly now, and that I could have killed it long ago, and very easily. No one, no one on earth could doubt that. And in fact, I should have killed this fly, I thought, there was no point in letting it go. I had watched what I had wanted to watch; and had only got enmeshed in a mystery. So why should I let this one go, who had appeared before me so readily?

## 12

And yet I didn't strike. I merely looked at the two insects, one alive, the other near-dead.

Then the live one suddenly shot up into the air and was away.

# 13

In this way, I let the fly get away. I don't know why.

# 14

Yet, in my time, I have killed many flies and I don't regret that I let this one get away. Besides, killing flies has never been my principal ambition. It was only to facilitate my reading that I took to killing flies. And although it is true that killing flies did in itself hamper my reading to some extent, it was a lot better than trying to read with flies buzzing around you.

# 15

Having read my books all day, and having killed a fly or two from time to time, I get out of my armchair in the evening and collect all the flies on the bed and floor, and throw them out of the window. Then I go for a brief walk along the sea-shore. After supper, I go to bed directly for a sound sleep. I don't masturbate much nowadays.

# spider in the clock

I awoke and opened my eyes in darkness. How does the darkness of closed eyes differ from the darkness of open eyes?

But I didn't have time to ponder the question. I had to write down my dream, as quickly as possible.

I sat up in bed. I reached for the light switch. I sat in bed until my eyes were used to the light. I looked at the slippers near my feet and noticed that one of them pointed towards me and the other away from me. I was puzzled. Before lying down in bed, I always leave my slippers pointing away from the bed. Then why did one of them point towards me now? I wasn't so very sleepy before going to bed that I would have done something like that. But I had no time to puzzle this out either. I rose and went to the desk. I opened my book of dreams. It was a two-hundred page notebook, two-thirds full already. In a few days I shall have to ask for another notebook.

As I took the cap off the pen, I remembered that I had to wind the clock. I put the cap on the back of the pen and placed it in the open notebook. I rose and went towards the clock upon the shelf. I have made a strict rule: wind the clock whenever you get up. It would take just a few seconds. I couldn't forget the dream so quickly.

Holding the clock in my left hand, I was about to start winding it, when I saw an unusual black dot on the face of the clock. I held the clock close to my eyes.

A spider. It was a tiny spider. He was under the crystal, inside the clock.

A spider in the clock! Does he want to weave a web in there?

Idiot. If the clock stopped, he might have a chance.

With my right hand I tapped twice on the glass where the spider stood. He scurried away. I tapped again at the spot where he stopped. He ran again. I tapped on the glass again.

Then I realized he had gotten in somehow and now he didn't know how to get out.

I smiled. I shook the clock in my hand. Then I tapped on the glass again where the spider was. He ran. The moment he stopped, I tapped over the spot. Then again. Then again.

The spider kept running from place to place. Then I stopped tapping for a few seconds. I watched the spider.

Then I shook the clock violently with both hands.

When I had stopped shaking the clock, the spider crouched at a spot near the rim of the face. He started crawling slowly towards the minute hand.

I watched him.

Then I gripped the knob that turns the hands and turned them as fast as I could. The unsuspecting spider was knocked aside by the blow. I turned the hands again.

This happened three or four times and then I realized that the spider was trying to keep away from the rim of the face, that is, to stay near the centre of the clock. I soon saw why. The minute hand was not entirely straight from end to end. It turned inward near the rim. Near the centre that hand was at a greater elevation from the surface of the face. So when the spider was near centre he was more or less safe in the space between the hand and the white surface.

Smart little bastard, I said to myself.

For a few seconds I watched the spider and the hands of the clock. Then I turned the knob again. This time I concentrated my attention on the hour hand. The hour hand moved more slowly, of course, but it was below the minute hand, and thus close to the surface of the clock. The spider couldn't escape a blow by the hour hand. I went on turning the hands quickly and kept the spider moving. When he got out of the reach of the hour hand, I would hit him with the minute hand. When he ran toward the centre, I was after him again with the hour hand.

This went on for a while. Then I found the spider at the very rim of the face, in the narrow strip between the numbers and the rim. Actually he was quite safe here, for the minute hand does not reach beyond the numbers. If he stayed in this no man's land, the spider had nothing to fear from me.

But I was smarter. I spun the minute hand as quickly as possible, close past the spider. Although the hand did not touch him, its pointed end, like a sword, swept so near him that he panicked and foolishly ran towards the centre. Then I hit him again with the hour hand. This happened two or three times.

By now, the spider had taken quite a beating. He wasn't able to move quickly any more. He was dazed, staggering like a bull in the ring. Later, he could only crawl about with difficulty.

My clock's alarm hand is in a small circle just above the centre of the clock. This hand practically grazes the surface of the clock. When the hour hand sweeps over the upper part of the clock, it intersects the circle of the alarm hand.

Hitting him with the hour hand, I forced the spider to move to the upper half of the clock. Then, skilfully, I turned the alarm hand and passed it under the hour hand. The space between the hour hand and the alarm hand was extremely narrow. The spider's body was crushed between the two.

For a few seconds I kept standing with the clock in my palm. Then I put the clock on the desk. I watched the spider hung on the cross formed by the hour hand and the alarm hand.

Then I was hit by a sudden shock.

I had forgotten to wind the clock.

Not only that, I had turned the hands!

I had turned the hands, round and round, without a moment's thought. And, before doing such a thing, I hadn't even noted what time it was!

I had gone to bed at about three-thirty. But who knew what time it was now? I might have slept any number of hours. Two hours. Three hours. Six hours. Eight hours. Or perhaps just half an hour.

The hour hand now stood between twelve and one, and the minute hand near six. So it was twelve-thirty. But did that mean anything? That wasn't necessarily the correct time. The correct time, at this moment, was probably very different from what the clock showed. A clock will tell the time you want it to. That doesn't mean it's telling the correct time.

It wasn't twelve-thirty. And I didn't know what time it was. For I had turned the hands of the clock, as though I were out of my mind.

I could never again anwer the question, 'What time is it?' For so many years I had taken care of my clock. I had made a habit of winding it whenever I got out of bed, so that it would not stop. It was a good clock, very accurate, something you could rely on. And now that was all over.

I sat in the chair with my chin upon my arms, my arms crossed upon the desk.

Suddenly I lifted my head and looked at the clock. I had a great idea.

Why not believe it was twelve-thirty? Actually twelve-thirty?

All it needed was a moment's decision. It's twelve-thirty, I would say to myself. In two hours it would be two-thirty. Three-thirty after three hours. Five o'clock after four-and-a-half hours. No argument, no misgivings. An act of faith.

The idea gave me life.

But only for a short time. In my heart I knew it wouldn't do, that I could never really swallow it. I might say, 'Well, it's a quarter-to-four,' but deep down inside I would know it was a damned lie, that it was NOT a quarter to four.

I had to admit that henceforth I couldn't truthfully answer the question, 'What time is it?' Thus it is that a man, one day, finds himself unable to answer simple questions.

I rose from the desk.

I ran my fingers through my hair and went to a corner of the room near the bed. I looked at the clock. Then I walked to another corner, where I keep my book racks. I stood there, looking at the clock as if it were a time bomb that might go off at any moment.

Then I went towards the light switch. I put my finger on the switch, turned and looked at the clock. I pressed the switch and the room was in darkness. In the darkness, in the spot I was still staring at, was the clock.

Slowly, step by step, I started moving in the direction of the clock. When I was about four paces from the desk, I could hear

*The Women in Cages*

the faint ticking. I took another step. The ticking grew louder. Another step. Then another. I bent down. I placed my ear close to the clock. I listened to its ticking.

Who could have realized that this careful counting was a hoax? The damned clock was ticking away as if it told you nothing but the correct time.

I quickly rose and went and switched the light on. I looked at the clock. As if I expected it to give a start!

It ticked away, mindlessly.

It was at this point that I noticed my dream-book lying open upon the desk, and realized that I had forgotten the dream.

But I merely took note of the fact; I didn't particularly feel anything. I quietly went to the desk, closed the notebook and put it away in a desk drawer.

Then I threw myself on the bed and lay there for some time.

I got out of bed and stretched myself. I must think of other things too, I told myself. I decided to get some exercise. First, I did some yoga. Then I opened the door of my room and stood in the doorway.

I was standing where the light from the passage in front of my room intersects with the light in my room. The lights in the passage give out a bluish light, whereas the light in my room is very white.

Outside my room the passage extends left and right. At regular intervals in both directions it curves slightly. So you cannot see very far in either direction. There are lights in the passage too, but on the right there are no lights beyond the third bend. I don't know why. On the left, as far as I know, the lights never end. I go jogging frequently, to the left of course.

Today I turned back at the fifth bend in the passage. By the time I got to my room I was breathing hard. I wiped the sweat from my face. I wondered if they had cut down on the oxygen recently.

I relaxed in my armchair for a few minutes. Then I was hungry. I got out of the chair and went to the food room on the left. A fresh supply of cans had arrived a few days ago. I selected two or three.

As I ate I noticed a picture on one of the cans. It showed a sunrise. Or perhaps a sunset. For a while I thought about the life of the people on earth's surface. I thought of the day and the night, the sunshine, the rain.

I finished eating and returned to my room.

I picked up the clock on the desk and put it back on the shelf. After a moment's thought, I turned the clock around. No use looking at the clock any more, I said to myself.

I sat again in the armchair with a book. But the sight of the clock with its back to me almost made me cry, so I got up and turned it around again.

I found it hard to concentrate on reading, so I got up again and put the book back in the rack. I didn't know what to do next.

I don't know why, but I felt like going for a walk in the passage to the right, where there are no lights beyond the third bend.

I walked up to the third bend. The last light is just before the bend. I walked past the bend and stood in the dim light, looking into the dark tunnel ahead. I had never walked beyond this point in the passage. This time I walked on. I couldn't even see a dim glow at my back. It was as if the passage were made of cement darkness.

Then I stopped. I waved my arms in the dark, for no reason. I didn't even see them. I knew only because they were my arms.

I kept standing for a few minutes. Then something unexpected happened. I remembered the dream. I remembered it very clearly, as if I were actually seeing it.

It was like this: I was jogging down the passage to the left of my room. Suddenly the lights in the passage went out and it was pitch dark. I stopped dead in my tracks. I was so terrified that I forgot whether I was running away from my room or towards it. So I didn't know whether to go on running in the same direction or turn around.

Here I had awakened.

I turned back. In a few minutes I could see the glow of the light around the third bend. I came into the light again. I walked briskly to my room. I opened the desk drawer, pulled out the notebook and wrote out the dream.

I was tired. I switched the light off and went to sleep.

When I woke up my head was lightly heavy. I don't think I slept long.

Out of habit I reached for the clock. My hand froze in mid-air.

The clock wasn't ticking.

It had stopped.

In all the excitement I had forgotten to wind the clock.

I picked up the clock. I held it close to my ear. Then I held it before me.

It had stopped at a quarter of seven.

I thought, if a man dies you can't tell what time he died by looking at him, but if a clock stops you can tell what time it stopped by looking at it.

I put the clock on the desk and sat on the edge of my bed.

I didn't have any feelings now about having let the clock stop. Not even about having turned its hands.

I got up, went to the desk and picked up the clock. The alarm was set for four. I began turning the minute and hour hands. It was like dragging a dead man's body.

The hour hand came to four. Instantly the alarm began ringing. Like the frantic tolling of a death-knell.

Or an incessant clamouring: *Arise, arise.*

# r a b b i t

To the Editor, the *Times of India*

Sir,
Are the zoo authorities aware of the manner in which their
animals are often harassed by visitors—children and
adults? I have seen the same attitude in zoos all over the
country so it must be a peculiar Indian characteristic.
Unfortunately, we cannot change it overnight. Parents and
schools will have to teach children to show genuine interest
in and kindness to animals. But in the meantime, zoo
authorities must be keenly vigilant.

Bombay, September 23            (Miss) Sushna Kumar

1

**M**y father disliked the rabbit. When it came hopping
near his reclining chair, he'd scare it away by tapping his
palm-leaf fan against the floor; then, as the rabbit scuttled away,
he would lean back in his chair and continue to fan himself
languidly. (In summer, beset by prickly heat, he used to scratch
his back with the handle of the fan.) The chair's canvas had blue
and green stripes, and when he reclined back into it, it curved so
deep that he looked like a ship at rest on the floor of the sea.
   Everyone fussed over the rabbit when I first brought it home.
It was white as snow, and had red glass-bead eyes, and the insides

of its ears were pink. It was so very white that it looked out of place in our house. Sometimes, as it sat serenely upon the floor, the evening sun coming in through the window illuminated its entire body, and caused it to glow softly.

We had to keep the rabbit indoors all the time and make sure that the front door was always closed. At night I shut the windows too, to keep out alley cats. The rabbit would wander around the house all day, from room to room, nibble at the cauliflower leaves I gave it, and sometimes become lost for hours in some kind of samadhi in the corner of a room. It always went to a particular corner of my bedroom to pee, and slept under my bed at night. It never uttered a sound. As it hopped from room to room, its paws were equally soundless. It had a strange habit though. If you happened to be standing in a room (perhaps because you didn't see any point in going out, and yet were tired of just sitting around), the rabbit would come hopping in and start going around you in circles. At first you'd be amused, and you'd wonder why it did that, but after a while, after it had gone round and round noiselessly several times, you'd begin to feel a little uneasy; for it whirled around you like a feather in a whirlwind, and you were the desolate eye of the storm, you'd get annoyed at its mindless behaviour, you'd begin to lose your temper, not knowing what was happening. And if you kicked it gently on its ear, it would freeze in its tracks for a few seconds, as though it were surprised and puzzled, and then begin to circle you again, and you wouldn't know whether to laugh or to cry. You'd have to break the circle being spun about you by jumping outside of it, and then the rabbit would be taken aback, seeing that it had lost you, and would hop away noiselessly, perhaps a little disenchanted.

There were times when the rabbit would sit absolutely still, with its eyes sometimes open, sometimes shut. At the slightest sound, one of its long ears would dip, then straighten, and while it continued to sit quietly, the ears would keep moving in this mechanical manner. If a sound were suspicious, it would be immediately on the alert. Oddly enough, loud noise like that of a car wouldn't bother it at all. But once I picked up the little bell that my father used in his morning worship and tinkled it close to the rabbit's ears. This almost frightened it to death. It tried to scurry away, but its nails kept slipping on the smooth tiles of the floor, and it remained in one spot, its legs moving frantically. I laughed aloud. And why, of all sounds, the tinkling of a bell frightened it so, was something that I never came to understand.

Later, the rabbit developed unhealthy habits. It started eating all kinds of things. Sometimes it would chew at a sandal, sometimes a newspaper. My father began keeping his sandals on the top rack of the shoe-stand and putting the *Times of India* in a safe place. Then the rabbit began to lose its fur. If you pulled at its coat, clumps of fur would come out between your fingers. It began to look like a mangy ghost. By then, nobody in the house cared for it. One day I took it out and gave it to Victoria Gardens, Bombay's zoo.

## 2

Flinging the newspaper away, I got up from the chair, looked out of the window, and yawned. I stared at the dust-covered trees brightened by the evening sun.

I'd been reading newspapers all day; my eyes were tired and my body ached. I don't really like reading newspapers, but then I suppose we all need to read them from time to time. It's more than I can do to read each day's newspapers daily, so once in a while I sit with a month's worth of newspapers piled in front of me, and go through them meticulously, reading the news, the ads, everything. I feel better doing this. Where would we be without newspapers? But human beings are clever. They publish newspapers, produce films, make speeches, listen to them, stage cultural events, or overthrow governments. That's why very few persons in this world go mad. As a child, I used to be terrified at the though that I might turn out to be mad. (My other childhood fear was that I was congenitally impotent, but that's another story.) Now, the idea of going mad seems itself a bit mad to me.

I've got into the habit of cutting out from the newspaper anything that catches my fancy. I have large piles of these clippings. My mother is annoyed at my habit, for the man who buys old newspapers from us pays less for the ones with bits cut out.

I stood leaning my elbows against the bars of the window. There was a soft breeze. It was towards the end of November, and I thought we wouldn't have to wait for long for the cooler days of winter, the most pleasant days in Bombay. The sky would become bright blue, and out of it, like unfamiliar thoughts, migratory birds from distant lands would descend upon the sea which, for the rest of the year, looked grey and brown, but in this season became green and blue. My elbows against the bars, I watched the palms outside swaying lazily in the breeze.

I heard a sound behind me but didn't want to turn around. My father coughed, as though in complaint, and I heard him pick up the newspapers I had scattered about the room. He arranged their pages carefully, tapped them lightly against the table to even out their edges, and, folding them double, placed them neatly on a shelf under the table. There was something about the hollow tapping of the newspapers on the table that terrified me. I gripped the bars of the window. My father coughed again and went slowly into an inner room. After a while my fingers loosened, but I felt the day's reading had been wasted.

## 3

NEW YORK, October 15: The Foreign Ministers of Israel and the UAR were among a big crowd of diplomats who attended a gala reception for the Indian Prime Minister, Mrs Indira Gandhi, here last night.

Observers noted that Mrs Gandhi had accomplished a rare diplomatic social feat by securing the attendance at the same function of the Arab and Israeli representatives. Arab diplomats usually refuse invitations here to parties to which Israelis have also been invited.

SYDNEY, November 4: Everything from chickens to doormats and soap are being consumed by armies of Australia's native bush rats as they march across the country, heading south in search of more edible fare.

BOMBAY, October 3: Most people in Bombay had to make do with the old national integration and national solidarity pledge at various 'unity' meetings in the city on Wednesday—Mahatma Gandhi's birth anniversary.

Excepting at one or two gatherings, the revised pledge could not be taken at unity meetings because the text of the pledge was received from New Delhi too late to be circulated. The integration and solidarity pledge can, however, be taken on any day till October 9.

*The rats, which are a foot long and covered with long hair, have gnawed their way through doors and tins to get to food. The only thing that seems to deter them is concrete.*

LONDON, October 13: Gold prices see-sawed in world bullion markets yesterday as anxious dealers awaited the outcome of gold sales policy talks at the International Monetary Fund meeting in Washington.

In London, where some dealers were convinced that a multi-nation sales agreement is imminent, the morning price was fixed at 39.00 dollars an ounce and the afternoon at 39.17 dollars.

—AFP

*Millions of rats have been described as covering the Barkly Tableland near the northern territory's Queensland border 'like a huge grey blanket'.*

SAIGON, September 24: The Beatles were 'just not ready' for yoga, according to Maharishi Mahesh Yogi. He arrived here from New York last night.

Although he did not explain why the musical group was not ready for the benefits of transcendental meditation, he said: 'I always work on hope. If they should come back to me tomorrow, I would gladly take them in again.'

—AP.

*'Cats are no match for them and even the dogs sh— off,'*

*said a worker at Avon Downs station. 'They are going for the cattle now—eating through their hooves and laming them.'*

MOSCOW, October 1: The Soviet Government sent a congratulatory message to the Chinese Government on the nineteenth anniversary of the foundation of the Chinese Peoples' Republic, which broke all traditions by omitting a reference to the Party. The message, sent yesterday, mentioned only the Chinese people and the Soviet people.

*The rats have ruined homestead gardens, ring-barked trees and attacked drovers and stockmen in their swags at night.*

VATICAN CITY, October 28: The Vatican today called for a wide-ranging dialogue between Catholics and atheists, but said communists who try to manipulate such an exchange for political ends could not be included.

A 32-page document setting forth the Vatican's views on a dialogue was made public by the Secretariat for Non-believers, a body set up by Pope Paul VI three years ago.

It urged a dialogue on 'all subjects accessible to human reason', such as philosophy, religion, politics, ethics, sociology, economics, the arts and culture in general.

—Reuters

*An English schoolmistress at Avon Downs station, Miss Jay Inkster, said: 'It is hideous. I have never imagined anything like it. The rats are into everything. One night I scrubbed a pair of sandals, three pairs of shoes and a pair of thongs and put them out to dry. Next morning I had one sandal left.'*

COPENHAGEN, October 8: A Bill which will recognize polygamous marriages, marriages between brother and sister and homosexual marriages, is to be put before the Danish Parliament.

The Bill, which will abolish marriage in the normal

accepted sense, is being tabled by the extreme left-wing
Socialist People's Party.

Political experts said it had no chance of becoming law.

—UPI

*When there is nothing left to eat the rats eat one another.
This is already happening in some parts of the northern
territory.*

—A-ANS.

# the end of history

## 1

Study your palm when you wake up in the morning: that's a well-known Sanskrit saying. One has to admit that the young people of today may not be familiar with it. What do you read in your palm, they might ask. It is pointless to answer such questions. What can those who have no strength in their arms see in their palms?

As always, I woke at five. I inspected the palm of my right hand. The life line is very strong indeed, I said to myself. God be praised.

I rose from the bed and approached the calendar on the wall. The corner laundry gives away calendars to its customers each year before Christmas. As a matter of fact, I usually wash my clothes at home. But every year, a few days before Christmas, I take my two woollen jackets to the laundry, and make it a point to ask for a calendar when I collect them. I like to have this particular calendar, because it shows each date on a separate slip. Each day you tear off a date. Such calendars are not popular anymore, but I prefer this type to the calendars common now. Tearing off a date daily is an excellent way of reminding yourself of the passing of time. It is like handing Him a receipt for each day you've been blessed with. I prefer acknowledging receipt promptly in this way, instead of doing so at the end of a month, or even of two or three months. The large stock of slips that one sees in January diminishes gradually. The other day I thought: little by little one cuts away this cancerous knot, and yet it reappears obstinately each year! Such bizarre notions often come into my head nowadays.

I went to the calendar and tore off the date. With the torn slip wadded up in my fist, I stared at the new date.

June 11. Today I am seventy, I said to myself.

I went to the door to throw away the ball of paper, but, forgetting to do so, I stood in the doorway pursuing a train of thought. I remembered that in my childhood my birthday used to be a holiday, for it was also the birthday of King George V. He is no longer on the throne, his successors have left this country, and I cannot take childish delight in my holiday-birthday anymore. Another thought that occurred to me was that, according to the Bible, a man's life-span is seventy years, whereas our Hindu faith considers it to be a hundred years. I have reached seventy, God be praised. Now, if I am to live to be a hundred, how am I going to spend another thirty years?

At this point I realized I was crushing the wad of paper in my fist. I flung it outside, and gripped the door-frame with both hands. A number of incoherent questions crossed my mind. What has this door-frame got to do with my being seventy? What is my relationship to persons born seventy years ago and no longer living? What proof exists, except a few pieces of paper, that I have lived for seventy years? Should I buy a new pair of sandals for my birthday? Or would I prefer a pair of fancy cuff-links?

I decided that finding solutions to these questions would take a considerable amount of time, and therefore turned from the doorway and occupied myself with my daily chores. I had decided upon one thing: I wished to spend this day like any other day. Except in one respect—I intended to devote more time to contemplation than I usually did.

Squatting over the basin in the lavatory, I found myself still thinking over the questions that had assailed my mind. After relieving myself, it is my custom to study the stool, although it is admittedly somewhat difficult to do so in a squatting posture. Also, one might wonder what benefit accrues from the exercise. Does one expect to have disburdened oneself of rocks or stones, or to have been relieved of gold and diamonds? All that one ends up observing are slight changes in colour and firmness. Sometimes there are tiny worms, or, if a hemorrhoid has bled, bright little red banners. Profitless though it may be, my habit persists. On this occasion, however, my mind was so preoccupied with the questions besetting it that the faeces slid down the drain before I thought of peering down. Not that this mattered much. And yet I was somewhat upset.

Before setting out for a morning walk, I slipped a slice of guava into the parrot's cage. When he saw me leaving the house, he screamed as usual: *History is on our side.* This is the only sentence the parrrot can speak. Whenever I go out, or return, or when someone comes to visit, or leaves, he shouts this message. With these confident words ringing in my ears, I stepped out.

The morning breeze was exhilarating. The nights had been unduly warm. I noticed a few clouds in the sky. The monsoon was almost upon us. I'm going to see yet another season of rain, I said to myself. In recent years, I had watched monsoon showers mostly through the horizontal iron bars of my windows.

As usual I went to the Mahatma Gandhi Garden. I sat upon a bench.

The sun was rising. Small birds chattered.

I rose and turned for home.

Nearing my house, I found that the roadmen had arrived with barrels of asphalt, heaps of gravel, a steamroller, and other paraphernalia of their trade. They had put up a sign in the middle of the road: Road Closed, Under Construction.

It appeared that the municipality was intent upon repairing the roads before the onset of the monsoon. Then traffic would flow smoothly. Automobile drivers would not curse the municipality, pedestrians would not curse automobile drivers for spraying them with muddy water, and bier-carriers would not curse the dead. I went into my house.

2

At half-past nine I heard a knock upon the door. I was a little surprised, for I didn't expect anyone. (I seldom expected anyone, for that matter.) I opened the door. It was a man, about fifty, and his face seemed familiar. Then I remembered: it was Sadanand Karkare. It was quite a surprise. I hadn't seen Sadanand for twenty years or so. He used to be a thin young man, but now he looked plump.

I was nearing fifty back then. Sadanand was one of my rare history-major students. In the small-town college where I taught, few students got to the stage of specializing for the bachelor's degree, and fewer still majored in history. Sadanand turned out to be an intelligent man. We used to talk for hours, and he helped me with my research on several occasions. He often remarked that he wanted to remain single and devote himself to research, following my example. I warned him that it was an arduous, austere life. Then he graduated, and went to another town as a schoolteacher. Both of us were sorry to part. A few months later I received a wedding card from him, and then a letter; I didn't write back. Two or three years later someone informed me that Sadanand's wife had died during her first pregnancy. Then for years I had no news of him. And now he stood in front of me, holding his baggage.

Sadanand put his bags down, and wiped the sweat off his brow. He sat in the chair to which I pointed. *History is on our side*, the parrot screamed. Sadanand gave a start.

Sadanand stared at me. I observed him. Twenty years ago his face looked somewhat boyish and delicate. Now, at fifty, the face had withered, and yet it carried a suggestion of the dew of youth, or so I fancied. He said: 'I've been teaching school all these years. I'm not tied down, but I've never been able to do the research I wanted to. And I wanted to see you, or at least to write, but I didn't. I was eager to see your study on the battle of Kurukshetra. When it came out, I read it again and again. Now I too have started on a piece of research. I felt I needed your advice. Finally, I decided to come down. I knew today was your seventieth birthday, and I thought it offered a good occasion to see you after so many years. Congratulations!'

Sadanand opened a box of sweets, and held it out to me. As a rule I refrain from eating between meals. Also, I avoid sweets, and prefer foods that have a bitter or astringent taste, which help the system to avoid ills like biliousness. But on this occasion, I did not have the heart to refuse the gift that Sadanand, whom I was seeing after so many years, was offering with such affection. So as not to hurt him, I selected a small laddu from the box.

'I was captivated by your book on the battle of Kurukshetra,' Sadanand said. 'Approaches to the writing of history have become extremely hackneyed. I believe you have successfully broken new ground, and developed new techniques.'

The story of my book on the Kurukshetra battle is this: I set out to write an account of the battle, but the fact that the battle between the Moguls and the Peshwas was fought at the same site centuries later kept intruding into my thoughts. Things became more complicated when I found details of the Arab–Israeli wars, the India–Pakistan wars, and the Vietnam war getting mixed up in my mind with the Kurukshetra battle. My book finally took the shape of an unusual amalgam of these different wars. I had the book published in Poona by investing part of my savings. I knew that historians would fail to see the significance of my method. As I expected, there were few reviews, and those that appeared were virulently denunciatory.

'What fascinated me was your technique of telescoping different wars,' Sadanand said. 'It should open totally new vistas in the field of historical writing.'

'I didn't exactly invent what you have called the technique of telescoping.' I explained. 'It just happened that way. I cannot claim much credit for it.'

'You say that out of modesty, sir,' Sadanand maintained. 'But what distresses me is that so-called historians should so criminally ignore the breakthrough you have made.'

I didn't say anything.

Sadanand said, 'Now let me turn to my own ideas, however poor they might appear in comparison to your magnificent insights. I have come to believe that traditional methods of writing history, such as studying documents and ancient inscriptions, are in the final analysis inadequate. The question is, can we arrive at the true nature of historical personalities by such methods? Perhaps there are things in their life that never get into documents or inscriptions. It is my opinion that we must focus our attention upon these other things, hidden in the darkness of the unspoken.

Convinced of this, I have now embarked upon a biography of the emperor Chandragupta. I have completely ignored what are called, with charming naivete, primary sources. I sit down with nothing but blank paper before me, and write.'

I said, 'I sincerely wish you success in your experiment. If young men like you begin to display such an intrepid spirit, I am sure historiography will witness a renaissance. I only hope that I shall still be in this world to see your work on Chandragupta completed.'

'Please don't say things like that,' Sadanand said quickly. 'I'm sure you will live for many more years. With your blessings I hope to complete my project, and to dedicate the monograph to you.'

I have to admit that I was rather touched. It seemed to me that the seventy years of my life had not been altogether wasted.

Sadanand rose from his chair, and went towards the parrot's cage. The parrot leered at him with one eye, and screamed: *History is on our side*. Sadanand turned and walked to the window by the door. He gazed outside. One could hear the rumbling of the steamroller outside, and the voices of the labourers. I watched Sadanand.

Then Sadanand unpacked his bags. He lifted a large box and placed it on my desk. 'Look,' he said. 'A tape recorder.' I was somewhat surprised. How could a mere schoolteacher afford to buy a tape recorder? Sadanand seemed to discern my thoughts. 'I invested much of my savings in this,' he said. 'Another of my plans is now materializing. The idea is to record the silence of historical places. It occurred to me that people only take pictures of historical places. How much can we learn from pictures alone? Auditory reality is important too. So I decided to visit various historical sites and record the silence there. Naturally, the silences are perforated by background noises. For instance, my recording at the Red Fort in Delhi caught the tourist guide's commentary; luckily, one can't make out what he is saying. The recording in front of the Taj Mahal picked up the sound of a small stone a boy threw into the water. In the caves on Elephanta Island near Bombay there was the screeching of a solitary monkey. However much you try to keep out sounds, they intrude. But if you listen carefully, you will hear the silence behind the sounds. I haven't been able to travel about a great deal. How can one afford it on a schoolteacher's salary? Now that I'm here, I'd like to record the silence in the Mogul tomb outside town.'

Then Sadanand played his tapes for me, and the silence of ancient places held me in thrall.

At lunch Sadanand reminisced over our days together, but I noted that he avoided talking about his marriage. The laddu that I had eaten that morning had taken away my appetite. My stomach cannot digest sweets easily. I ate a little lunch merely to keep Sadanand company.

After lunch Sadanand went out with the tape recorder. I lay down for a siesta, but was unable to sleep. I listened to the steam-roller thundering outside in the afternoon silence.

After a while I felt the need to relieve myself. This was unusual, for I am extremely regular in my habits. I seldom have a bowel movement except early in the morning. I assumed that the laddu I ate in the morning was responsible for the present situation. My body was in a hurry to purge itself of a substance that was not agreeable to it. I felt it was a mistake to have eaten it. Yet, nothing was gravely amiss. All would be well after a satisfactory evacuation.

I went to the lavatory. I stepped in, and saw a lizard on the wall, close to the ceiling. I stood still.

This was not the first time that I had seen a lizard on the lavatory wall. There is a small attic above the lavatory, and the ventilator at the back extends to the attic. So the lizards in the attic often slip into the lavatory in search of insects, especially at night.

I have a horror of lizards, and killing them is not easy. A blow with the broom is not really effective. Usually only the lizard's tail remains in front of you, twitching in a maddening manner.

What offends me particularly, however, is the sight of a lizard in the lavatory. I have found a way of exterminating them. With a raised broom, I slowly get as close to the lizard as possible. The lizard regards me with beady eyes, ready to break away instantly. Deftly I give it a lightning blow. It usually falls to the floor, knocked out momentarily, but not yet dead. Quickly I shove it into the lavatory basin, and immediately pull the chain. Before it has had a chance to come to, the lizard vanishes down the drain. The strategy demands special dexterity at two points. First, when the lizard falls to the floor, you must toss it accurately into the basin. If you miss, it will regain its senses and get away before you have a second chance. Secondly, you have to pull the chain quickly, or the lizard may climb out before the water flushes it down. If all goes well, it is an extremely effective way of eliminating lizards.

Now, too, I advanced towards the lizard with a broom in my hand. I struck, the lizard fell, and I hastily tossed it towards the toilet basin. I missed, however, and the lizard landed on the other side of the basin. Before I could strike again, it had climbed up the wall, reached the ventilator, and disappeared into the attic.

I went and put away the broom. If I had killed the lizard, I would have sat down to relieve myself with a sense of satisfaction. Nevertheless, it was all right to sit down now, for there was little likelihood that the lizard would descend again soon. I squatted, but without success. I was annoyed, for this had seldom happened. Many years ago I suffered from hemorrhoids, but I have never had to submit to the miseries of constipation. I wondered if the laddu I had eaten was causing all this trouble, or if it was due to the disquiet generated by my failure to dispatch the lizard. I came out of the lavatory. I paced about.

There was a knock on the door. Sadanand came in, put his tape recorder down on the desk, and announced, 'For once I was able to record pure silence.' He played the tape. I could hear the faint but sharp sound of a nightbug, a cicada. 'Oh, I didn't even notice that there was a nightbug chirping,' Sadanand said. If it chirps at midday, why does one call it a nightbug, I wondered.

It occurred to me that Sadanand's return had made me feel better. I had lived alone for many years; I did not need anyone. I do not mean the kind of thing one refers to when one says, for instance, that one needs a servant. I mean a terrifying need from which a man must do his best to keep his distance. I have seen people possessed by this need, and have seen what they came to. I had never let myself be ensnared by such a desire. It would be ironic indeed, I thought, if at this late age I seemed to be ambushed by it. I comforted myself with the thought that the need was momentary. I was a man of seventy, and not likely to be carried away by fleeting desires. I also reflected that Sadanand would not stay for long anyway. Once he had left, I would resume my placid life. It is all right to feel a need, and then to try to satisfy it, but often you simply drift into somebody's company, and *then* the need arises. A man must be wary of such insidious perils. But there was little chance that this would happen to me now.

I could not, however, conceal the fact that at the moment Sadanand's presence gave me pleasure. Moreover, I was agitated by recollections of the past. I was not at ease in this state of mind, and therefore suggested to Sadanand that we play a game of *bhendi*. We used to particularly enjoy this game; we played it with place names, though it can be played with other kinds of names. If I said *Ahmedabad*, Sadanand had to pick the final consonant and say, for instance, *Daulatabad*. Then I would come up with something like *Dakar*, and Sadanand might surprise me with *Rio de Janeiro*, and so on. In this way scores of places are joined together, however distant from one another they might be. It is like weaving a net, based simply on the fact that the first consonant of a name is identical with the final consonant of another. What is more, the net is woven by an alliance of two minds. It is as if the two coalesce; they do not collide, as in chess.

Slowly we warmed to the game. At first I could not think quickly of appropriate place names, but then I began to toss them off rapidly. At one point Sadanand had to rack his brains for a long time.

While Sadanand was thinking, I realized that I had to make another trip to the lavatory. I told him to take his time, and went to the lavatory assuring myself that, this time, I would surely be successful. Self-confidence is of great importance in life.

The trick paid dividends. Not to repeat the negligence of the morning, I quickly peered down into the basin. The stool was not of normal consistency and colour. It looked soft, and pale yellow. But the feeling that my stomach had cleansed itself gave me a sense of relief. By the time I returned, Sadanand had found a place name, which he announced triumphantly.

Soon we tired of the game. As the net of names spreads wider, one begins to wonder if one will ever catch anything in it. Also, what difference does it make if I say *Ahmedabad* and the other person says *Daulatabad*, or the other way round?

Then my stomach started to rumble mildly, and we abandoned the game. For a few minutes the two of us watched the road repairers at work below. Gravel was being mixed with asphalt, labourers shouted, and the steamroller boomed like the beating of a demon's heart. It is in this manner that they make the roads we saunter over.

I was constrained to make yet another visit to the lavatory. This time I found that the lizard had reappeared on the wall. On this occasion I successfully tossed it into the toilet basin, and sent it down the drain. My performance elated me.

The stool resembled the earlier one.

Sadanand inquired if my stomach was disturbed. He said he had some pills with him, but I declined firmly. I avoid medicines, as far as possible. I affected an unperturbed expression to mask my discomfort, but Sadanand seemed aware of it. He thought up something to entertain me. He took down the parrot's cage, asked me to make the parrot talk, and switched on his recorder. *History is on our side*, the parrot shrieked. Then Sadanand kept the parrot's cage in front of the mirror and played the tape. *History is on our side*, the recorder announced. The parrot in the cage was tricked by the sight of his own reflection in the mirror, and sound from the recorder. He thought that there was another parrot in front of him. He shrieked, and beat his wings, and lunged against the bars frantically.

The parrot's exertions made Sadanand laugh. He played the tape again, and the parrot fought against the bars more desperately. Sadanand howled with laughter. I watched. Simply because of Sadanand's merriment, there may have been a smile on my face. But in reality I was apprehensive. For one thing, the growing pain in my belly was driving me to distraction. Secondly, I felt that there was something wrong with playing such a prank on the parrot. Whose side is history on, I asked myself, watching the parrot in the cage, and the mirrored parrot in the mirrored cage.

The parrot's struggle made me uneasy. Until now my parrot

had lived peacefully. Only once, when a flock of wild parrots passed above the house shrieking, had the parrot in the cage listened tensely, and sat motionless for a long while. Otherwise, he was a cheerful companion. And now, observing a parrot in the mirror, he was driven to desperation. With my face contorted by pain, I alternately looked at the parrot in the cage, his reflection in the mirror, and at Sadanand. Outside, the steamroller rumbled, crushing gravel to dust.

The parrot's struggle against the bars had rumpled his feathers, and his eyes were dilated. After some time he looked exhausted. His movements slowed, and his shrieking became shrill. But he continued to struggle fitfully, until he could hardly move. Then suddenly he screamed, *History is on our side*, and, with a convulsive movement of his legs, dropped to the floor of the cage. He made no further movement or sound. For a few moments, Sadanand did not realize what had happened. He wiped his eyes, which were watering with laughter, and continued to laugh. Then he noticed the parrot's condition. He froze, and stared at the cage. Then he stood up, and looked alternately at the cage and the mirror.

Sadanand walked towards the cage, and stood in front of it for a few seconds. He opened the door to the cage, and watched intently, as if he expected the parrot to fly out at any moment.

Gingerly Sadanand inserted his hand into the cage, and prodded the parrot with his forefinger. The parrot rolled over, legs in the air. Sadanand reached in further, and clutched the body. He took it out, opened his hand, and stared at the dead parrot. Then, as if something had stung him, he flung the parrot's body into the cage, and quickly shut the door. He turned and looked at me. In his eyes I could read fear and contrition.

I was shaking with each stab of pain in my belly. To make matters worse, my parrot was dead, thanks to the prank played by Sadanand. The parrot that had kept me company for many years was gone, and as for Sadanand he would leave in a day or two.

Was it so hard to do without my parrot?

Perhaps it would have been better if I had not kept a parrot. If I had not kept a parrot—if Sadanand had not visited me—

my mind whirled. Suddenly I was filled with rage against Sadanand. He had killed my parrot. He had made me eat some stale sweetmeat, and caused me misery. Perhaps he had put something in the laddu? Maybe some kind of poison? Did he come all the way merely to congratulate me on my birthday? No, he had planned to do away with me. He was envious of my book, of the scholarly and dedicated life I had led. He had deceived me by flattery.

My face, twisted with pain, became even more crooked. In a voice that surprised me by its hoarseness, I commanded Sadanand to sit in front of the mirror. Sadanand obeyed, and I switched on his recorder. 'Speak,' I said.

Sadanand spoke: *The solitary one wears his shoes out. The Other takes one by surprise at the end, one day or another, a gun in his hand. Whose steps are imprinted backwards?*

I rewound the tape. 'Look into the mirror,' I told Sadanand, and played the tape. Sadanand stared at his reflection, and listened to his own words. I rewound the tape, and played it again. Then yet again.

I watched Sadanand. He didn't struggle like the parrot. Motionless, he looked wide-eyed into the mirror, with beads of sweat forming on his forehead. After a few minutes, his whole body began to perspire. Then, very slowly, he rose and walked backwards with measured steps, like a somnambulist. I thought he was going to stumble against the wall behind him. But just as he reached the wall, his legs gave way, and he collapsed to the floor. For a few moments his fingers twitched, as if they were trying to catch hold of something. Then he lay still. I sat looking at Sadanand's body. Then I rose and rushed to the lavatory. When I returned, I felt very weak. My stomach continued to churn. My head swam.

I approached Sadanand's body and, bending down, touched his forehead. Cold as marble. I lifted his hand, and groped for the pulse. There was none. I let go of his hand, and it dropped to the floor. For a moment I stood beside his body, then I turned and went to the window. It was evening, and becoming dark. The workers had gone home. Like a slumbering demon, the steamroller lay by the roadside, a shadowy, elephant-gray presence.

Sunk in my reclining chair, I watched Sadanand's body. There
was no sign of the pain in my stomach decreasing. I got up, and
took from the cupboard the bottle filled with some powder
Jambhekar Shastri, an Ayurvedic savant, had given it to me many
years ago. I swallowed a spoonful of the powder in water, and
lay down on my bed. Then I had to visit the lavatory again;
stumbling out of the bed, I made it to the toilet basin just in time.
A few moments' delay, and my dhoti would have been soiled.
The stool was thin as water. I sat on, in case my bowels had
more to discharge. I wanted my stomach to be purged thoroughly
once and for all, and had no inclination to keep repeating my
visits to the lavatory.

Squatting over the toilet basin, I discovered that, for no
particular reason, I was thinking about the lizard I had disposed
of earlier. I was trying to imagine how a lizard died in the water
gushing into the basin. Does a lizard really die, I asked myself.
In the whirlpool of my mind, the question fluttered without answer.
Then I had a strange feeling. In the multitude of thoughts,
emotions, and sensations raging in my mind and body, I did not
at first clearly apprehend the nature of this feeling. But it grew,
and then I realized that it felt like a lizard, which had emerged
from the lavatory basin, was entering my rectum. I did my best
to suppress this feeling, and endeavoured to convince myself that
such a thing was inconceivable. My attempt was fruitless. More
and more powerfully I had the sensation of a lizard squirming its
way up my rectum.

Giddily I came out of the lavatory, and threw myself into
bed. I stared at the ceiling. Then I sat up and, moving with
difficulty, walked towards Sadanand's body. I stooped, and
attempted to lift it, but to no avail. Somehow I dragged him to
the bed, close to the wall. I puffed heavily. I had exerted myself
knowing full well that, in my condition, it was not wise to do so.
Probably owing to the strain of this activity, I had a fresh urge to
relieve myself. I scarcely had the strength to go and squat upon
the basin, but, telling myself that this would be the last time, I
made it to the lavatory.

Nothing came. I continued to sit uselessly. And then, as I had half expected, the sensation I had felt earlier rose again. I had killed countless lizards in this lavatory. You could say I had become addicted to these little occasions for excitement. And now all those lizards were clambering up the basin, and jostling to invade me. My whole body shook.

After a while it became impossible to remain squatting. It appeared equally difficult to stand up, but, supporting myself against the wall, I managed it. I staggered into the bedroom, and collapsed on the bed. The sensation of lizards slithering up my rectum one after the other became unbearably acute. The reptilian invasion was unstoppable. I thrashed my legs upon the bed.

I thought that I should not have done what I did to Sadanand. If he were alive now, he would have helped me. Sadanand was a nice man. He would have helped me, and taken care of me. And what terrible thoughts I had entertained in my mind regarding him! He played with the parrot only to amuse me. He had come from so far away to congratulate me, and I had suspected his intentions. Now all that remained of him was the cold body beside me. With my mind in tumult, I stretched out my arm, and touched Sadanand's face. Gently I moved my hand over his face, and over his chest. I let it rest on his chest. I could scarcely stand the feeling of creatures squeezing in between my legs, but I clamped my thighs together. In my mind, the reptiles took on weird, outsized saurian shapes, muscling their way into the exposed, exhausted passage with brute force.

Late in the night I thought I heard the sound of rain. Then there was the peculiar smell of the first monsoon rains falling upon the dusty ground. Things were already beginning to assume their daylight shapes when I fell asleep.

# testimony of an indian vulture

## 1

It's been four days now since one of my wings was disabled. The wing isn't completely broken, so it's not totally useless. I can move it, though with great difficulty. I can even fly a little, but it hurts, it hurts.

I've been put in this condition by nothing other than the irrational, unreasonable behaviour of human beings like you. Four days ago, along with a dozen other vultures, I was feeding on a dead cow in the barren plain on the outskirts of town. We were competing for the best morsels, grabbing whatever we could. Engrossed in the feast, we didn't even notice a youth passing by who picked up a stone from the path and hurled it in our direction. The stone hit me right on the joint of my left wing. The sudden, unbearable pain of that vicious blow caused me to drop the sizeable piece of intestine that I held in my beak and try to fly away. Trying to fly made the pain even worse, so I gave up the attempt and just started hopping along. Some of my fellow diners also rose up in the air in alarm. But when they saw that the youth who had hurled the missile was continuing nonchalantly on his way, they resumed their meal. I remained standing alone, gazing at the man walking away from the scene. What was it that drove him to pick up that stone and throw it? He obviously had no material interest in the dead cow. I know that some of you humans eat cows, even cows that have died of natural causes. But the carcass we were devouring had already begun to rot, and I'm sure no human, however famished, would have touched it. So what harm was there in a flock of hungry vultures who had decided to put the abandoned carcass to good use? The man had no good reason to throw the stone that rendered one of my wings practically useless. That's the sort of thing you humans do—and yet you complain about the irrationality of the universe.

Dragging my broken wing, I hopped towards a tree, a tall tree standing alone in the middle of the bare plain. I somehow managed to fly up and land on a branch. This is my favourite tree. I love to sit on its topmost branch, enjoying a bird's-eye view of the surrounding emptiness. Now, with one of my wings crippled, I had to be content with clinging to one of its lowest branches.

I sat on that branch all day. My companions, having finished their meal, had flown away. Who wants to stay around someone who has been disabled by misfortune? That's the way of the world, and inescapable solitude was now my lot. I accepted it, and waited patiently for my wing to heal. I spent two full days sitting in the same spot, but the wing showed no sign of improving. Once, when I was younger, it would have healed in no time. But I've grown old, and my bones and limbs have lost their former vigour. You may ask, why should an aged vulture stretch his wings? But I wasn't the sort of bird to croak 'Nevermore', I wanted to live, I wanted to live. Circling high in the sky, surveying the meaningless complexity of human life, I still wanted to seek my nourishment.

When it became clear that the wing wouldn't heal, I started to wonder what I should do next. Then I remembered the bird hospital in town. We vultures only knew of this hospital by hearsay. I had learned that it was run by a doctor who belonged to the Jain sect. I am, of course, aware that the majority of people in our country are Hindus, and that they set great store by humanitarianism; I also know that the Jains champion humanitarianism and non-violence even more fervently. It was undoubtedly on the basis of such noble ideals that the Jain doctor set up an exclusive hospital for birds. And a highly praiseworthy idea it was.

From our viewpoint as vultures, though, there was a grave lacuna in the idea behind the hospital: it was open only to

*The Women in Cages*

herbivorous birds. Carnivorous birds such as crows, kites and vultures were strictly excluded. Pretty little birds like pigeons and sparrows were looked after with great care at the hospital. Circling above the hospital out of curiosity, I had often observed what went on inside through the windows. Patients were housed in little pigeon-holes, some with broken wings, or injured legs, some with other maladies. They were given appropriate medical treatment, and food and water, then released from the hospital windows, or from its terrace, when they recovered. I had often watched pigeons and sparrows flying away happily from the hospital. Although I knew that this privilege was not available to vultures, I had never taken it much to heart; strong and healthy all my life, I never thought that I would ever need the services of the hospital.

Things were different now. I was disabled, and the thought of the Jain doctor's hospital kept coming back to me. Was there no chance for me to find admittance there? Wouldn't the good doctor's heart melt with pity when he saw my condition? As the hours passed, and the pain in my wing increased, I felt more and more confident that I would receive treatment at the hospital. The logic of social segregation is doubtless unshakable, but it cannot withstand a creature that wants to go on living.

The hospital was a long way from my tree. I would have to pass through streets flanked by many houses to get there. Since I couldn't fly that far, I decided to try it late at night. When I felt certain that the town had gone to sleep, I descended from my tree, and taking cover from time to time, hopping mostly, but also flying now and then, I reached the hospital. I flopped up and over the wall with some difficulty, landed inside the enclosure, and crouched under a shrub in the darkness.

## 2

The sun came up, and after a while the bird doctor arrived. I gave him time to go on his daily rounds. When I saw that he was almost finished, I gathered all my strength and flew up and perched at one of the windows. The windows had no bars, but I didn't have the courage to fly straight in. It wouldn't help me anyway, I thought. Checking the condition of his patients one by one, the doctor stopped right under the window where I sat. He didn't notice me, busy as he was with his work, leaning over his patients. So, with great care, I made as soft and friendly a sound as possible. The doctor gave a start, and looked up. I could read the anger, the astonishment and the revulsion written upon his face.

'Shoo—shoo,' the doctor shouted, gesticulating in my direction.

'Please listen, Doctor—' I said in a tone of supplication.

'Shoo—shoo—go away!' the doctor shouted again.

'Doctor—Doctor—please hear me out—'

'Hey, anyone over there? Will someone get me a stick, please?' the doctor said, turning to his right. But both his assistants seemed to be out of hearing.

Realizing that I'd better state my case quickly, I said in haste, 'Please listen to me, Doctor—I haven't come to your hospital looking for food. I'm not going to harm your pigeons and sparrows. I've come as a patient—as a patient!'

The doctor continued to glower at me.

'Look, Doctor—look at my wing!' I spread my injured wing, ignoring the stab of pain that shot through my body as I did so. 'Look! It's injured. I think a bone's broken.' I noted that, almost involuntarily, the doctor had looked towards my wing, and that the anger in his eyes seemed to have diminished slightly. Encouraged, I said in an optimistic voice, 'It hurts a lot, Doctor. And if my wing is permanently crippled, how can I stay alive? Will you treat me, Doctor—please?'

'No way!' the doctor shouted, throwing an arm into the air, 'We don't take in birds of your kind. Go away, go away!'

'Please don't say that, Doctor,' I pleaded again. 'You're so compassionate towards birds. You've been performing such an invaluable service for them. And am I not a bird too, Doctor? Then why treat me like a step-child?'

'You—you eat filth—meat—any kind of meat—rats, dogs, cattle, anything!—ugh!'

'Yes, Doctor, I do. I can't deny that. But you won't throw me out just because my food is different, will you? Such hard-hearted treatment just because of what I eat?'

'Go away! I don't want to hear any more! Keep your wisdom to yourself!' the doctor cried out, his anger rising even higher.

Without abandoning the cordiality in my voice, I continued arguing doggedly. 'Just think it over a bit, Doctor. When you get right down to it, it really doesn't matter who eats what, not at all. Pigeons and sparrows eat grain, while we eat flesh—it's all *maya*, all illusion. Everything is one at the bottom of this world of illusion.'

'Ah! So now you're teaching me philosophy, eh!' the doctor said with scornful irony. 'Very clever, eh? Well, I've had enough of it. Get out, I say, get out!'

Making a last effort I pleaded, 'All right, Doctor. Don't admit me as an in-patient if you don't want to. But won't you at least treat me as an out-patient? If you'll do that, Doctor, I'll never forget your kindness for the rest of my life.'

'Ugh—a filthy creature like you!' the doctor said, turning up his nose. 'I wouldn't touch you with a ten-foot pole. You are unclean, polluted; Even your shadow will pollute all of us: Go now, go. How stubborn can you be!'

Just then one of the doctor's assistants entered the hall. 'Go get me a stick!' the doctor ordered. I saw that, instead of receiving medical treatment, there was a possibility I'd end up with a few extra broken bones, and decided to beat a retreat. I flew down from the window, reached the hospital wall, flapped over it, and, dodging people, somehow got out of town.

3

Now I'm back at my perch on the tree. My mind is filled with sadness. But this sadness is not just for myself, it's for you humans too. I pity you now more than I ever did before. So many things have created dissension among you. But should a simple thing like food divide you too? I believe no other country in the world is like ours in this respect. In other countries almost everyone eats flesh; it's only our country that's divided into those who eat meat and those who don't. It's most unfortunate. Tell me, what hope can you have for a country where food divides people? Can such a society ever prosper?

Sitting on one of the lowest branches of my favourite tree, I contemplate such questions. My weariness increases hour by hour, and the pain in my wing seems to be spreading throughout my body. It seems I may not remain in this world much longer. I wonder what I'll be in my next life. All I ask of the Lord is that I'm not reborn in this same country as a man.

It's evening now, and the western horizon is radiant with orange and purple stripes. The sky is darkening rapidly. It's one of those immemorial Indian evenings. There's no sign of the moon anywhere. Perhaps she will rise late, or perhaps it is the night of the dark moon. Gazing upon the darkening emptiness of the plain at this sombre hour, an unaccustomed sense of peace steals over me. I have a feeling that it may be on this dark night that my soul will take wing, soaring high and free in the sky.

# IV

# The Shadow of the Gulag

# r e t u r n

## 1

Experimenting with different ways of relaxing his mind and limbs, he tossed about in bed. Thrusting the pillow aside, he tried sleeping with his head flat on the bed. When that didn't help, he pulled the blanket over his face, then pulled it down again when he began to suffocate. He stared at the rectangle of yellow light cast on the wall by the street lamp. Moths must have been hovering around the lamp, for vague shadows circled in the patch of light. Thinking that it was the light that kept him awake he drew the curtains, making the room even darker. After a long while he got out of bed and groped about for a glass on the shelf. He filled it with water from the sink in the room and drank. Sometime later he got up again and went to the bathroom. Getting up much later once more, he switched on the light and sat reading. After an hour or so he returned to bed hoping that he might be able to sleep at last. It went on like that until he awoke.

For a moment, Sudhir marvelled at how real it all had seemed. He really had felt as though he was suffering helplessly from insomnia. How long had the dream lasted? He felt he'd been dreaming all night, but then it occurred to him that, however long a dream might seem, it might actually have lasted only a few seconds. Perhaps he had the dream just before he woke up. Looking at the clock, he saw that it was almost eight. He had in fact slept longer than usual.

In the bathroom Sudhir noticed that his eyes burned slightly, and that he felt a bit washed out, exactly as if he had in fact spent a sleepless night. That insomnia experienced in a dream should have such palpable effects was fascinating. Then Sudhir realized that he ought to have suspected something immediately, for he never suffered from insomnia. Karen, who could seldom sleep without popping a pill, used to say to him, 'How come you never have trouble getting to sleep? I know you have things to worry about, but they don't ever seem to affect your night's rest.' Then Sudhir had laughed and said, 'It's my Oriental ability to live in peace with myself. What you Americans try to achieve through TM and Krishna Consciousness and that kind of thing comes to me naturally.' So he should have seen through the dream right away. But is it possible for the dreamer to question his dream while he is still asleep, Sudhir wondered.

The dream continued to linger in his mind even after he was finished in the bathroom. There was something unusual about it, but he couldn't put his finger on it. Then he knew: the dream had transported him back ten years in time to his life in Bombay. The room he had tossed about sleeplessly in was the one he had back then as a lodger, studying for the MA. That room, like the one in the dream, had a wash-basin in one corner, and, as in the dream, the street lamp used to throw a rectangular patch of light upon the wall. The room he had dreamed about was doubtless the same one, for where had he slept in a room with a wash-basin since he came to America? But it was remarkable that that shabby room in Bombay should reappear in his dreams after so many years. He would have thought that the room, like much of his life in those days, was lost in oblivion. And yet it had now surfaced from some neglected corner of his mind, coming to life in minute detail. Was it because he was finally returning to India after all these years? Perhaps his mind was struggling to restore its ties with the past.

Sudhir checked his suitcases once again, though he had packed things to his satisfaction the day before. He went over everything mentally again to see if there was still something to be taken care of. He didn't like rushing about at the last minute, or doing things sloppily. At half-past nine Sudhir called Karen long distance in Buffalo, and talked for over twenty minutes. 'Come back if you're bored with India,' Karen said. As he replaced the receiver it occurred to him that he had probably heard Karen's voice for the last time in his life.

He sat for an hour in his favourite chair, stretching his legs out before him. Then Abhijit called: 'We're leaving at eleven-thirty, right? It's two-and-a-half hours to New York. It's good to start a little early, though.'

'I'm all set. I'll be waiting for you,' Sudhir said.

Patricia came along with Abhijit to say goodbye. Sudhir blushed a little when she kissed him lightly on the cheek. Even after eight years in this country he hadn't quite got used to it: deep in his mind Hindu taboos were still alive.

Dropping Patricia off on the way, the two hit the road for New York. Sudhir reminded Abhijit about the apartment key, the telephone bill, and one or two other small things. 'Don't worry,' Abhijit said. 'I'll take care of everything.'

They stopped for hamburgers at a McDonald's. 'The Last Great American Meal,' Sudhir said with mock pomposity. Abhijit laughed. Sudhir gazed at the huge sign proclaiming SEVEN BILLION SOLD. I'll be back in India and they'll go right on selling their millions and billions, Sudhir thought.

Abhijit drove in silence. Sudhir didn't speak either. His eyelids were heavy with the feeling of not having slept well, and the car's motion made him even more drowsy. Then Abhijit said, 'Write when you get there. Just let me know you're okay. Don't say anything about how things are in the country; the letter might not make it.'

'Oh, you're too cynical,' Sudhir said. 'They're not that strict any more.'

Abhijit shrugged his shoulders.

'You wouldn't think of returning yourself, then,' Sudhir said.

'Oh no, certainly not. It's okay for you. But I happen to be working actively for "Free India". There's no way I can go back—not until the regime changes.'

As a matter of fact, they had talked along these lines a number of times before.

Sudhir's plane took off from Kennedy airport at half-past four. He was flying in a Boeing 747 for the first time. When he flew from Bombay to New York eight years ago the 747 was not yet widely used. Sudhir had a seat somewhere in the middle of a row. There were so many seats to each row that the windows on either side seemed a long way off. Sudhir didn't like the airplane at all; it seemed to have been made for the sole purpose of herding together as many people as possible. It didn't matter much, though, because all he wanted to do was sleep. Asking his nieghbour to tell the stewardess not to bother him, Sudhir shut his eyes, and only awoke when the plane was nearing London. Rubbing his eyes he got up and went to wash. As the plane banked in its descent, Sudhir had a wonderful view of the city of London brilliantly lit with thousands of lights. He was fortunate enough to have a good connecting flight, and didn't have long to wait at the airport. On the next flight he had a window seat. It was past four a.m. by London time, but since he had slept well on the earlier flight Sudhir stayed awake. It was still dark outside. He stared vacantly ahead, lost in thought.

## 2

Eight long years in the US, and at last Sudhir was returning home. When he went to the States, he didn't expect to live there for that long. But within a year of his arrival there'd been a military coup in India. Like many others he was shocked at the news. Sudhir asked Abhijit, who had just arrived, 'How did it happen? I never thought anything like that could happen in India. I used to think Indians would never put up with military rule.'

'Well,' Abhijit said, 'that's how one feels until it actually happens. Once the upheaval is a reality people who used to say they couldn't live under a dictatorship shut up and go about their business as if nothing unusual had happened. And what makes India so special anyway? Look at the foreign students here— Africans, Latin Americans, the ones from the Middle East, and from South-East Asia—in practically everyone's country there's a dictatorship of one kind or another. It was bound to happen to India some day.'

At first there had been no strong reaction to the military takeover from Indians in the US. But voices of protest emerged as news of repression at home began to arrive. The Indians who had jobs in the US, and who had acquired immigrant status, didn't show much concern, but the students adopted a militant posture. The Indian students' associations in many universities expressed indignation at the developments. Even some officers of the National Association of Indian Students in America were openly critical. Then the Indian Embassy pressured them out of office and made sure the organization remained harmless. The rebellious students formed a new organization called 'Free India'. They distributed leaflets and broadsides publicizing stories of repression at home. Sudhir, who had little interest in politics, joined the movement in a moment of fervour, but quit within a year.

Sooner or later every Indian student faced the prospect of returning home. In the first flush of outrage many had been vocal in their opposition to the new regime, confident that it would crumble within a year or so, and that they would then return home in triumph. Contrary to their expectations, the new government's grip on the country tightened. How could one go back now? Even those who hadn't voiced opposition were unwilling to return, knowing that life would be difficult in the changed circumstances, and that their careers might suffer. Worse prospects confronted those who had actively expressed opposition. A few such students had not been heard from after their return to India. There were rumours that they had been thrown into jail and tortured. Even students who had stayed away from politics were frightened by news of this kind. Since a majority of them had been hostile, the Indian government looked upon all returning students with mistrust. This made returning difficult for everyone.

But there was also the difficulty of remaining in the US. Those on student visas were naturally expected to leave once they had finished their studies. It was no easy thing to find a job, the employment situation in the US was getting worse, and the government had more or less stopped giving immigrant status to foreign students. Sudhir completed his work for the Ph.D in four and a half years, and started sending out dozens of job applications, to no avail. His field was mathematics, and it seemed flooded with Ph.Ds. Without submitting his dissertation Sudhir continued mailing out applications. He was staving off the day when he would have to leave the university.

With funds drying up, the university began to cut down on assistantships. Since Sudhir had had an assistantship for four years, his department told him they couldn't give him one any longer. He had to look for a part-time job. He worked in a cafeteria for a while, then found a job in the university library. The library was a giant matchbox: eleven immense floors crammed with books, and with no windows. Once you entered the building you had no idea if it was raining or snowing outside, or whether the external world had been annihilated. Sudhir's job was to collect books from the study desks, put them on carts, and shelve them. It was boring, of course, but there was plenty of opportunity for loafing. Hiding among the stacks one could browse, and pretend to be busy whenever a supervisor seemed to be approaching. Sudhir got to know a lot of books he had never come across before—books on history, geography, and so on. The large geography books filled with pictures were especially nice to leaf through. Sudhir thought of his job as a never-ending struggle with the forces of chaos. You were striving to bring about order in this closed universe by keeping everything where it belonged, and people came and took out books, creating disorder. And so the struggle continued. There were times when Sudhir dreamed of all books at rest, each in its place; with perfect order established in his universe, and with no one else in the entire building, Sudhir would glide contentedly about in the stacks, a Buddha-like smile glowing on his face. But, of course, that state of nirvana could never become a reality.

Months passed, and then years. Clinging to the university, Sudhir was just marking time. He was often filled with bitterness at wasting some of the best years of his life on a trivial job. If he returned to India, he could find a good teaching position. And how long could he keep on like this? One way of acquiring immigrant status, and of settling down, was to marry an American girl. Many Indians, including Abhijit, had done just that. Abhijit used to say to Sudhir, 'Why don't you marry Karen? How long are you going to keep living in uncertainty?'

Sudhir had been at the university for seven years, which was the maximum period for completing the Ph.D. He received an extension for one more year, but things couldn't continue that way much longer. He would soon have to take the degree and quit. Matters were coming to a head. Sudhir knew a Bangladesh student who had a Ph.D in physics, and was living illegally in the country driving a taxi. Would he too come down to that? But an illegal stay carried the risk of arrest, which Sudhir, with his middle-class Indian upbringing, could not face.

Then came news of a change of leadership at home. The new generals in power had announced a liberal policy. No one was to be put in jail without a trial. The President himself appealed to Indian students living abroad to return home without misgivings; the country needed their talents; their educational achievements would be rewarded; their political record would be overlooked. Those who gave an undertaking not to become involved in politics on their return would be granted clemency for their activities in the past.

People talked about the credibility of these declarations. Some believed in them, arguing that the military regime felt the necessity for a better image. Others like Abhijit said, 'It's all eyewash. Don't believe a word of it.'

Sudhir decided to bide his time and see what happened. He heard of a few people in other cities who went back. There were confusing reports as to whether or not they had faced trouble; some said there was no news at all from them. Sudhir wrote to a few friends at home, but their replies didn't shed much light on things. He had a talk with Abhijit, who had no intention of returning himself. Having been active in the 'Free India' movement, Abhijit was sure he would be persecuted if he returned. Sudhir's case was different. He had been a member of 'Free India' for only a short time, and had no connection with the movement since. To be sure, since Abhijit was a close friend, he had sometimes helped out with reproducing handouts and the like.

In his uncertain state of mind Sudhir had sent applications to some universities at home. Then an offer came from Bombay. The urge to return grew stronger. Sudhir persuaded himself that he had been needlessly suspicious, that if he didn't go now he'd have only himself to blame for missing a fine chance all because of a lack of courage. For a few days his mind was in turmoil; then he wrote to Bombay saying he would come. He started packing.

## 3

After a stopover in Rome, the plane took off for Bombay. Sudhir leafed through a few magazines, since there wasn't much to see outside. The plane was flying over a bank of white cumulus. But, passing over the Middle East, Sudhir saw burning gas flaming in the vast sands below. He had seen the flames one night eight years ago, travelling the other way. At the time he didn't know what the flames were, and had wondered if houses were on fire. He hadn't known that the flames had anything to do with oil, for in those days people had little awareness of the Middle East and its oil. In the intervening years these had become everyday conversation points. How times change, Sudhir thought.

It was the monsoon season in India, and the weather changed as the plane approached Bombay. The ride became bumpy as the plane entered rain clouds. Then the sea was behind them and, as the plane emerged from the clouds from time to time, one had glimpses of the land. The hills near Bombay looked emerald green, and the fields were flooded. It had obviously been raining for quite some time.

The plane was approaching the airport, and began its descent. Long rows of shanty huts near the airport were now visible. After eight years, Sudhir was seeing the slums again. They clearly hadn't been reduced under the new regime, but seemed in fact to have spread. Sudhir watched intently as the plane circled above the airport. Suddenly an odd craving came over him—a craving for Bombay Duck, a kind of fish seldom found except along the Bombay coast. Sudhir wondered if it was the season for Bombay Duck; after eight years he couldn't quite remember. Then there was a thud of wheels, and the plane had landed at Santa Cruz airport.

Sudhir's nose was suffused with damp, salty air as soon as he stepped out of the plane. He realized it would be some time before he got accustomed to the warm, humid climate of Bombay. The airport building had been enlarged, Sudhir noticed. At one end construction was still in progress. Inside the airport things seemed to be working better than in the old days. There was little to remind one of the confusion and disorder of the past. Since he was returning for good after a long residence abroad, Sudhir was sure he would get through customs without much difficulty. Then he saw that in front of the customs there was a barrier with the sign, 'Security Check'. The security inspector rummaged through Sudhir's bags. Picking up the magazines, he looked at the names: *Scientific American, Psychology Today*. He put them down. Then he took out the cassette tapes. 'What do you have here?' he asked.

'Music,' Sudhir said, 'Mostly rock. Bob Dylan and that kind of thing, you know.' The tapes weren't bought pre-recorded; Sudhir had recorded them himself.

'We'll check these,' the inspector said. 'Come back in three or four days. If you want them mailed, give us your address.' He immediately wrote a receipt for the tapes. Then he looked at Sudhir's passport more closely. Student in the US. For how long? Eight years. Eight years? Yes.

'Go over there and take a seat, please,' the inspector motioned him to a room on the left. 'I'll keep your passport for now.'

Sudhir picked up his bags, went into the room and sat on a long bench stretching from one end of the room to the other. On the opposite side there was an identical bench. A long, wide table was placed in the middle of the room. Alone in that large room, Sudhir gazed at the President's picture hanging on the opposite wall.

Half an hour passed, but no one came. Annoyed, Sudhir kept looking at his watch every few minutes. Another fifteen minutes went by. He wanted to get up and go outside to ask what was happening, but thought better of it. Wiping off the perspiration he leaned on the arm of the bench. In the sticky monsoon weather he perspired even while resting. After about an hour a policeman walked in. 'Let's go,' the policeman said.

Sudhir was ushered into an officer's room. His passport was on the desk, next to a thick register. Behind the officer's chair stood a long row of similar registers. There was one vacant space in the row. The officer asked more or less the same questions the inspector had earlier, but in greater detail. Then he became absorbed in the register before him. As he watched the officer's balding head, Sudhir suddenly said, 'I must join the university as early as possible; I'm already late. The term began over two weeks ago.' Then he immediately wondered if he had said the wrong thing. Why had he mentioned that? The officer hadn't said anything about detaining him.

Raising his eyes from the register, the officer laughed loudly. 'Don't worry about that,' he said. 'The university has been locked for the last two weeks. It's not likely to reopen soon.'

The officer turned the pages of the register for a while. Then he called someone. A policeman entered and saluted. 'Take this gentleman to the Inquiry Block,' the officer told the man as he handed Sudhir his passport.

The Inquiry Block wasn't far. Sudhir had heard about a new five-star hotel that had been built near the airport; the Inquiry Block was close by the hotel. From their van, Sudhir could see the large hotel's windows shining in the evening light.

The officer in the Inquiry Block took Sudhir's passport, summoned a policeman and told him something. Turning to Sudhir he said, 'This man will take you upstairs.' Sudhir hesitated for a moment, then asked, 'Can I take my bags with me?' 'Certainly,' the officer said. 'This isn't a prison. Think of it as a sort of hotel.'

The policeman opened a room on the first floor for Sudhir, then showed him where the bathroom was. When he was gone, Sudhir shut the door and sat on the edge of the bed. Then he removed his shoes and lay down. All the fatigue of travelling seemed suddenly to have overcome him. It grew dark in the room.

Sudhir got up from the bed and switched on the light. He went to the window and looked out through the large horizontal bars. Outside the compound there was an open sewer, and beyond it were the huts of the slum, where women were busy cooking evening meals. Small fires burned, and streams of smoke arose. Children shouted and ran in front of the huts. In the distance, lights had come on in the five-star hotel. The revolving restaurant on top of the hotel was apparently not yet open, for it was still dark.

Returning to bed Sudhir tried reading a magazine. He got up once and went to the bathroom at the end of the hall. Walking back he watched the policeman seated at the other end of the passage. A light burned just above the man's head, so that his face remained dark, but the smoke rising from his cigarette looked luminous.

Sudhir's watch was still set for London time, since he had forgotton to reset it at the airport. He calculated the difference now and turned the hands. At half-past eight there was a knock on the door. A man entered, set down a meal tray, and went out without saying a word. Sudhir looked at the tray: two chapatis, a helping of rice, a bowl of dal, and some sort of curried vegetable. His first Indian meal.

## 4

Around ten Sudhir changed for the night and switched off the light. It was good to go to bed early. The long trip had been quite tiring. It would help to be fresh the next morning. After an hour or so, Sudhir felt unusally thirsty: he went to the wash-basin and drank a glass of water. Then he stood before the window in the dark. It was silent in the slum huts, and the revolving restaurant above the hotel shone with light. One couldn't actually see it turning, but after a while Sudhir found that it had in fact moved slightly. A light in one of the hotel rooms went off and came back on the next moment, as though it had blinked. Sudhir remembered working on the late shift in the library. The library closed at midnight, and a few minutes before closing the lights were blinked on and off three times as a signal to everyone inside. Three times in quick succession, though only for a few seconds, everything was plunged into total darkness. Sudhir had never quite got used to it. Every time it happened it gave him a start.

Back in bed, Sudhir looked at the luminous dial of his watch: half-past twelve. It was hard for him to get to sleep because of the time change. His limbs craved rest, but it was as though his body had forgotten how to relax. Much later he rose again, and, switching on the light, went to the wash-basin. He splashed cold water on his face, then sat on the edge of the bed drying off. It was a quarter-past two by his watch. It was drizzling outside, and a child wailed in the slums.

Sitting on the edge of the bed, Sudhir sensed that there was something odd about his room, but he couldn't identify it. Then it struck him: a room with a wash-basin, just like in the dream. To be sure, the room he was in now wasn't exactly like the one in the dream, but now too he was restlessly trying to get to sleep. He wanted to laugh aloud. It was all clear now: he was dreaming the dream again. With a few changes, the narrative was being repeated. He knew dreams often repeated themselves in that way. For years his father had been haunted by a recurring dream in which he found himself perched on top of a temple, encircled by flood waters rising almost to his feet.

When did he last fall asleep? On the flight from New York to London. And he was still asleep. Everything that seemed to have happened after that was all part of the dream, an anxiety dream that was quite natural given his situation. Suddenly he experienced a tremendous sense of release. It all seemed fascinating now. And he had only to wait for the dream to end. It would end, and then he would get up, wash, and wait for the plane to land. Sudhir got out of bed, switched on the light and opened the door. A lean, middle-aged man wearing glasses looked up at him and smiled broadly. 'Oh, you're awake,' he said. 'I thought you'd be fast asleep. I brought along a master key, thinking I'd have to let myself in to wake you up.'

Sudhir glanced at his watch: it was five minutes to four. On such occasions, Sudhir thought, one usually expects two heavy-set men in uniforms, with steely faces. The man standing before him had the look of a petty office clerk, with a cheap, white shirt and well-worn trousers.

'Come on. We want to ask you a few questions,' the man said. 'You know, this sort of job is best done at this hour. It's quicker, for one thing. Get dressed; I'll wait for you.'

This dream is becoming too complicated, Sudhir thought with annoyance, as he walked down the hall behind the man with glasses. They walked mechanically in the silence of the night, as in a dream. From one of the rooms came a faint sound of moaning.

'Sounds like someone's ill, doesn't it?' Sudhir said casually. The man with glasses didn't seem to have heard.

Sudhir wondered if he should scream out loud so that he could wake up, and free himself from the clutches of the dream, then get up and see how close they were to London. Then thousands of lights would shimmer brilliantly ahead, and the plane would glide towards them as though into some strange galaxy in space.

# kalluri's escapade

## 1

Jattu had been miserable ever since Kalluri went away. Escaping from his mother's watchful eye he roamed about, throwing stones into trees, sometimes at fruit and sometimes at birds. Other boys of his age did chores for their parents. Jattu's mother Elha often scolded him and tried to put him to work, but Jattu couldn't be controlled. The villagers said he hadn't had a disciplined upbringing, his father having died four years earlier.

Jattu often went to the edge of the village and climbed on top of a boulder there; with his back towards the village, he looked into the distance. The ground sloped down before him, and further away there was a small hill covered with bushes. This was the way one would leave the village, although there was no beaten track. How could there be one? Paths are made when people go back and forth regularly over the same ground. Scarcely anyone ever left the village, and practically no one ever came. An itinerant merchant visited once a year with donkeys laden with goods, bartering salt, sugar, cloth and other things for grain. He was the only visitor except a few from one or two nearby villages. The direction in which Jattu gazed was thus simply the way by which one would leave the village. Far beyond the hill lay the big world: how many miles away, and at the end of how many days' travelling, Jattu had no idea.

On the opposite side of the village there stretched a high range of hills covered with thick jungle. No one ever went in that direction. This entire inaccessible region was known to the outside world as *Adipradesh*—the Land of the Beginning.

Jattu often wondered if Kalluri would ever return. Before he left Jattu used to be constantly at his side. Kalluri knew things no one else in the village did. He knew the eggs of various wild birds, and the properties and uses of many roots and tubers. When Kalluri told him tales of ghosts and spirits, Jattu listened enthralled.

People said Kalluri would never return. Once you left the village it was difficult to reach the outside world, and if you made it there was little chance that you would return. But one day, as Jattu was on his way to the stream for water, he heard the news: Kalluri was back. Abandoning his earthen pot by the side of the path Jattu ran towards Kalluri's hut.

Kalluri saw Jattu and smiled. He was fond of Jattu. Kalluri had always been lean, but now he was even thinner. He looked darker and somewhat wizened. But his eyes were bright, and his movements as quick as ever. Jattu showered him with questions, wanting to know if he had seen the carts that moved without being pulled, and the black, unbelievably strong demon that blew smoke and could pull a whole chain of carts. After a while Jattu discovered that Kalluri wasn't answering him freely. He seemed evasive about his journey. Kalluri had always been somewhat mysterious, and now he was even more so.

Villagers gathered one by one and sat down to talk. Many of them were disappointed to discover that Kalluri had brought few novelties with him from the outside world. They knew, however, that Kalluri wasn't a practical, sensible man. A little later Elha appeared calling for Jattu, carrying the waterpot that he had abandoned on the way. Jattu made a face as he got up. As he was leaving, Kalluri whispered to him: 'Come back in the morning. I've got something to show you.'

Jattu scarcely slept that night. He kept thinking of what Kalluri would show him the next morning. Early at dawn he hurried towards Kalluri's hut.

Kalluri untied his ragged sack; his teeth glistened as he held a box-like object before Jattu. Jattu took the black box gingerly in his hands and scrutinized it. It was small, about the span of Jattu's fingers in length and half a span in width, and appeared to be covered in leather. Jattu felt it and decided that it wasn't in fact leather. Part of the box was bare, and sounded hollow when he tapped it. Though it looked like metal, it really wasn't, Jattu thought, or perhaps it was some kind of metal he didn't know. When Jattu tapped on the strip of transparent glass on one side of the box it didn't sound like glass either. Everything about the box seemed strange. The leather, the metal, and the glass were of a kind that Jattu had never seen before. Something was scrawled behind the strip of glass. Jattu saw two knobs on one side of the box and thought they were for opening it. He tried but couldn't open it, and asked Kalluri.

Taking the box from Jattu, Kalluri said, 'It doesn't open.' He turned a knob, and Jattu's sharp eye noted that a vertical white band behind the strip of glass moved to the left. Then the box made a sound as though it were clearing its throat, and suddenly spoke in a human voice. Even when Kalluri took his hand off the knob and the white band stopped moving, the voice continued to speak. Jattu listened in wonder.

At first it seemed to Jattu that the box was speaking in a foreign language. But after a few moments he recognized one or two words, and in a short while he found that he could make out quite a few. The box spoke Jattu's language, though in an unfamiliar fashion; it used many words that Jattu didn't appear to have grasped much. The two became absorbed in listening to what they couldn't understand.

After some time Jattu was amazed once more when the box suddenly began to speak in a female voice. He didn't know how the box could totally alter its voice in an instant. It was a sweet voice, though; none of the women in the village had a voice like that, Jattu thought. The box spoke for a while in the female voice and then started singing. Leaning forward Jattu listened closely. The box not only sang, but also made instrumental sounds. The singing was beautiful—so different from the songs sung at village festivals. The music was marvellous too: Jattu made out the sound of the drum, but didn't know the other instruments.

From that day onwards Jattu spent most of his time in Kalluri's hut. The news of the talking box spread, and everyone in the village paid a visit to Kalluri. A few men always turned up to listen each evening. Like Jattu others found the words hard to follow at first, but soon began to understand a good deal.

Jattu learned that the box had two mouths. One of them spoke when the white band behind the glass was at a point on the left, and the other when the band was at a point on the right-hand side. Kalluri discussed this phenomenon with some of the villagers. From their discussion Jattu learned that the box didn't speak by itself, but that words which were uttered far away issued magically from the box. The men didn't know if the voices came from two different places or only one. Both voices spoke their language, but the villagers felt that the speech with the band on the left-hand side was more like their own. Moreover, the voices from that side came in loud and clear, while the voices they heard when the band was on the right-hand side often sounded blurred. The men therefore preferred to listen to the voices from the left.

One day old Ettanna, who had lived in the outside world many years ago, came to listen. He explained that the voices came from different cities. The right-hand voice came from Hastipur—the capital of their country, as he reminded them— while the left-hand voice came from Hakimabad, the capital of Shufaristan. Someone immediately expressed a doubt: the left-hand voice sounded clearer and louder, and its language too was close to their own; how could it come from the capital of another country? The voice from the capital of their own country should be clearer, and nearer to their own speech. Ettanna replied that their village was situated on the border of Khauradesh, their fatherland; the territory of Shufaristan began just beyond the hills behind their village. Since Shufaristan was a smaller country, its capital was closer to their village than that of Khauradesh. That was why Shufaristani speech was more like their own, and why the voice from Hakimabad sounded clearer.

None of the villagers knew enough to question this explanation. Most had never heard of Shufaristan and its capital, and many didn't even know the capital of their own country. A youth named Komwa asked: 'I used to think that different countries spoke different languages; that would make sense. If Shufaristan speaks the same tongue we do, why do we have two countries? Wouldn't it be more natural for us all to belong to one country?' Ettanna laughed and said: 'There's sense in what you say; however, things aren't that simple in the outside world. Ignorant hill-folk like us can't understand civilized minds.' He added after a pause: 'I'll tell you something even more astonishing. Khauradesh and Shufaristan speak the same language, as you know. That langauge is called Khaurabhasha in our country; in Shufaristan, however, it goes by the name of Rufidi. Can you believe it?' The men sitting around laughed, and marvelled at the ways of civilization.

## 2

Days went by and people got used to the talking box. Jattu learned the hours when songs came from the box, and arrived at the right time. Others too had no interest in listening to mere talk, and waited for the songs. Only a few old men sometimes sat listening to the talk with grave and studious faces.

One day Kalluri revealed to Jattu one of the secrets of the talking box. When he removed part of the frame from the back of the box, two red cylindrical objects fell out. Jattu picked one up; it was small but heavy. Then Kalluri showed him that, when the cylinders were out, the box couldn't speak. No matter how much you turned the white band behind the glass no sound came. As soon as the cylinders were put back in, the box came to life again. Jattu was intrigued. 'The magical power of the box rests in these cylinders,' Kalluri said. Pointing towards his own testicles, he added: 'It's like one's manhood, which is contained in these. Removing the cylinders is like castrating the box. We pick up round stones on the bank of the stream, paint them and turn them into gods; some magician has charged these cylinders with power in the same way. Nobody in our village is powerful enough to make a talking box like this. It must be a great magician who made this one.' Kalluri gazed at the box. He himself had some knowledge of magic and charms, and had cured a few sick people. Looking at him Jattu thought Kalluri was pondering how he could acquire extraordinary magical powers like those of the magic box.

Although the sound was better when the white band was on

the left-hand side, Jattu preferred to listen to the right-hand side. On the left there was lot of talk and little singing, while songs and music came more regularly from the right-hand side. Then Jattu learned that Kalluri had become interested in something else. On the left hand side strange sounds came from a point close to where comprehensible voices were heard. The unusual sounds were like someone whistling or babbling incoherently. Jattu was amused by them at first, but soon lost interest. Kalluri, on the other hand, appeared to be more and more fascinated by them. Ignoring the songs and the talk, he often sat by himself listening spellbound to the weird sounds.

Kalluri puzzled over the source of the sounds. He decided they weren't human voices. Then he recalled the sounds that Turakkal the shaman made when possessed by spirits. He also thought of the burial ground between two hills behind the village, where he had walked on many dark nights amidst mounds topped by large or small stones, in connection with magical rites. There too Kalluri had heard the weird babbling and whistling of the spirits haunting the place. Listening to the sounds coming from the talking box, Kalluri became convinced that these came from the same source: the magically powered box had a link with the spirit world. The voices were alien, orphic messages, Kalluri was like a determined astronomer hoping to make a chance connection in the vast intergalactic spaces.

Kalluri spent hours every day listening to those sounds. He found that they didn't come with the regularity of the human voices. Sometimes they were loud and insistent, and at other times broken and barely audible; there were times when they disappeared entirely. Kalluri wasn't surprised: after all they were voices of spirits, who spoke when they pleased and had no obligation to speak at appointed hours like human beings. Kalluri also noted that the human voices from both sides ceased at a particular hour every evening, while the supernatural sounds continued in the night and in fact were more powerful then. This was natural, night being the time of the spirits: they took over the box when men retired to bed. Listening to their voices and observing the repetition of many sounds, Kalluri came to believe that they had a language of their own. He felt that if he could make out the sequence of various sounds and their configurations, he would be able to grasp the language of the spirits. If he did in fact manage to do so, what a treasure-house would be open to him! The idea thrilled him. Now he listened to the voices in total absorption. He was miserable when they didn't come.

At the beginning of the rainy season clouds gathered in the sky. As lightning flashed, the spirit voices in the box became louder and more urgent. Kalluri imagined that the ancestral spirits living high above had descended on the clouds and were clamouring in their excitement. He listened intently. He had listened to the voices for so long now that he felt he was on the threshold of deciphering the language. He had grown familiar with its turns, its ups and downs, and was becoming confident that one day everything would suddenly fall into place and make sense. Now the spirits were shouting in the cloud-covered sky, as though they were desperately trying to tell him something that in his ignorance he was unable to understand. He felt helpless as he listened; tears welled up in his eyes. Box in hand he stared through the door of his hut at the rain-filled clouds. There was a loud thunderclap and the first showers fell. It wasn't possible to hear the voices clearly in the heavy rain. Turning the knob Kalluri shut off the voices and, putting the box away, went outside. He stood in front of his hut, his empty palms stretched out in the pouring rain.

The spirit voices were strong throughout the rainy season. On the other hand, the human voices on the left and right sounded feeble. The spirit voices appeared to have prevailed over them. Jattu's interest in the box diminished when songs were not properly audible. What's more, Kalluri was now engrossed in listening to the weird sounds for hours on end. He seemed to care for nothing else, and was lost in a dream world. He began to look drawn and weary because he had almost ceased eating. He rarely spoke to anyone, even to Jattu. Jattu's visits to his hut became less and less frequent.

It grew cold when the rains were over. As was customary at this time of the year, the old bearded merchant arrived one evening in the village with his donkeys. Along with his salt, sugar and so on, he normally brought coloured beads each year, which the women of the village coveted. He didn't have them this time. He said: 'I used to bring them from Tasaria in Shufaristan. Until this summer you could cross the border without any problems. People went back and forth as they pleased. But now soldiers have been posted all along the border. They seldom let anyone cross into Shufaristan. I've seen them patrolling the hills too.'

The merchant heard about Kalluri's talking box and came to have a look. The spirit voices had grown weaker since the rains ended. When the merchant came in, Kalluri was turning the knobs to see if he could pick up the voices. Instead, he heard only the voices that came when the white band was on the left-hand side.

'They call it a radio,' the merchant said, casting a glance at the box. 'Looks like you've been listening to Hakimabad. People in our country nowadays avoid listening to it, you know. The government frowns upon it; I've heard there's even an order forbidding it. But of course in your isolated village you needn't worry.'

When Jattu came round a few days after the merchant had left, he found Kalluri worried. Kalluri showed him that, no matter how you turned the knobs, the voices didn't come out clearly. He said he feared that the magical force in the box was running out. The box was dying.

Day by day the box lost strength, the voices grew weaker. Forlorn, Kalluri watched the box dying before his very eyes. He saw plainly that the spirit voices would soon abandon the box, as the soul casts off the body it has used. Overcome by a feeling of helplessness, he sat gloomily in his hut.

3

Lately Jattu had taken to roaming about instead of going to Kalluri's hut. He often went and sat upon the boulder at the edge of the village. One day, as he stared into the distance from his high perch, Jattu saw some men approaching. He was startled. Visitors were an unusual event. Narrowing his eyes he watched the strangers riding towards him on horseback. They all wore khaki clothes, and each of them carried something with a long, shining barrel on his shoulder. As they descended the hill and came up the slope in front of him, Jattu jumped from the boulder and ran towards the village.

The villagers were surprised to see soldiers visiting them, for it happened only once every five or six years. The soldiers' commander asked a question, which no one seemed to understand. One of the soldiers then came forward and asked the same question in a different way, whereupon the villagers gathered that the soldiers wanted to see the man with the talking box. The visitors were taken to Kalluri's hut.

The soldiers dismounted, and Kalluri was called out. The commander, who had a boyish, well-to-do look, examined Kalluri's talking box. 'It's made in China,' he turned and said to one of his companions. 'We don't import Chinese radios, of course. He must've got this in Shufaristan.' Then the commander began to question Kalluri: where had he been the year before? What was he doing there? Kalluri thought they suspected that he had been listening to the spirit voices in the box and had acquired great magical powers. He felt he must conceal the fact that he had listened to the voices. 'No, no, I didn't listen to the spirit voices,' he said. 'I used to listen to the voices of men here.' He pointed toward the white band standing on the left side behind the glass. The commander asked him what he had heard on that radio station. While Kalluri deliberated, the commander turned to some of his men and said, 'Ask the others in the village. Try and find out what they've been listening to on the radio.' The soldiers spread out and began to interrogate the villagers. Returning in about half an hour one of them reported: 'They don't seem to have listened to any Shufaristani propaganda. The people are absolutely ignorant here; I doubt if they understand anything they hear on the radio.' 'They might be ignorant,' the commander said. 'But we must be on guard. Shufaristani agents have infiltrated this region.'

The commander ordered his men to round up all the adult males in the village. The villagers were herded together in an open space. Mounting his horse, the commander addressed the crowd squatting before him:

'People of the Urukhiphal valley, always remember that you

are citizens of Khauradesh. If you have listened to anything said agains our great country on this radio'—he held up Kalluri's radio —'or listen in the future on another radio someone might bring to you, you can be sure that they are lies. Shufaristan is carrying on a vicious propaganda campaign against us at present. Within these hills'—he waved towards the hills behind the village—'oil has been discovered. It's a great boon to our country. This district, which unfortunately has been neglected until now, will soon be developed; you will all profit from the new plans. Shufaristan was never particularly troublesome in the past; since the discovery of oil, however, they have been making bold claims to your tribal land. Hakimabad has constantly been making broadcasts, trying to brainwash you. They say they want to free you, which is nonsense. They call themselves socialists and defenders of the poor; their government is in fact nothing but a ruthless dictatorship. People of this valley, never forget that your future lies with Khauradesh. Long live Khauradesh!'

'Long live Khauradesh!' shouted the soldiers, and some of the villagers also made an effort to join in. Scarcely anyone had understood the commander's speech, but no one betrayed their ignorance. The women and children had formed a circle around the congregated men and Jattu was among them, alternately casting glances at the stranger speaking from horseback and at Kalluri standing by his side.

Then the soldiers prepared to leave. Kalluri was put onto a horse behind one of the soldiers. The village children ran shouting after the soldiers for part of the way. Jattu was among them. One by one the boys dropped back; Jattu alone continued to follow the departing visitors silently. He looked at Kalluri all the time, but Kalluri never turned towards him once. Kalluri sat staring vacantly straight ahead.

The soldiers came to the edge of the village. The commander took Kalluri's radio from his coat pocket and, handing it to one of his men, said, 'Keep it with you, sergeant.' Taking possession of the radio the sergeant looked it over idly. He turned a knob, held the radio close to his ear and listened. 'The battery is almost completely worn out,' he said. Then he opened the radio and took out the battery cells; after a casual glance at them he threw them both away. Then he closed up the radio and put it away in his canvas bag.

Jattu halted, and watched the horsemen pass. They went past the boulder and dropped from sight as they rode down the slope. A little later their figures, grown smaller, could be seen climbing the hill. They crested it and began to descend on the other side. When their heads disappeared under the hill, Jattu rushed forward. He picked up the two bright red cells and, clutching them in his hand, ran for home.

# the terrorist

## 1

I arrived here in late summer. After searching for a couple of days, I found a room. It wasn't large, but it had a private bathroom, which seemed important to me.

For the first time in my life I was hit by truly searing heat, never having been north before. Accustomed to the humid coastal weather of the south, my nose felt constantly dry. The walls of my room were hot to the touch, and so was my bed at night. Sleep seemed impossible. I got up early each morning, took a bath, and left for work. I got into the habit of looking in the window of a shabby restaurant on the way. On a board in the window I saw a large aluminium pan heaped with boiled sheep's heads. The skin had been loosened by cooking, further exposing their teeth, so that they appeared to be grimacing with dilated eyes. The restaurant boy used to skin the heads one by one, leaving the skulls bare. He gathered everything—skin, brain, tongue, eyes, and the rest—on a plate, and carried it to the unkempt customer awaiting breakfast with sleepladen eyes. (The thought of the mucous inside the sheep's throat and nostrils invaded my mind.) Then someone told me that the heads were boiled all night to cook them through and through. Tossing about on my hot mattress at night, I thought about the boiling sheep heads, and on the way to work in the morning I met the gaze of the eyes in the window.

I went to the Central Post Office my first week in town. I had to go to a first-floor office to rent a post-office box. I had no intention of renting it for more than six months, but it turned out they could only be rented for a year at a time. I paid the rental fee and received my key. I looked at the number: 526. Five plus two is seven: seven plus six, thirteen: three plus one, four. An even number. I was pleased. I have a fear of odd numbers. Then I smiled to think that I was still caught up in such superstitions.

I came downstairs and went over to the post-office box area to take a look at my own. The boxes were in a hall to the right of the main lobby. There were about ten rows of them, and the top row was well above my head. Anyone who had a box in that row would have to grope blindly about inside it. Not very pleasant, I thought, to feel about in an empty box above your head, your fingers shrinking from the cold touch of the metal, with perhaps a shiver travelling down your spine if you scraped the surface with your fingernail. On the other hand, the bottom row was only knee-high, which seemed equally awkward. You'd have to bend down with your hands on your knees, and peer into a mouse-hole. Luckily my box was about shoulder-high. You opened it and looked straight in. I felt about inside the box, for no particular reason. A little dust remained on my fingers. Wiping them off I blew the dust off the bottom of the box. Then it struck me that I was being foolish. What was the point in examining my box? I certainly didn't expect to find anything inside. I was acting like someone looking over an apartment he was going to move into.

## 2

It was the first time I had been away from my home town, and at first I felt a little lost. But I soon got to know my way around. The town had been laid out according to a very simple plan. There was a long main street from east to west, intersected by another long, wide street with a network of smaller, parallel streets. The people looked different from people in the south. They were stocky and rugged, and not particularly polite, as I soon discovered. Walking through the streets was an annoying experience at first. People didn't pay any attention to where they were going and seldom made way for others. I was constantly being bumped into, and my slight build made matters worse.

Then I hit upon the idea of walking with my fists clenched, which is normally taken for a sign of anger, but in my case it was simply a practical measure. Your arms stay tense when your fists are clenched; they don't just hang down and get knocked about when someone bumps into you. On the contrary, it's the other person who is more likely to feel the effects of a collision. I've got used to walking with clenched fists now. When I see someone approaching and think that he might bump into me, my fists tighten instinctively, and I only relax when he has passed me by. Sometimes I keep my fists clenched even when there is no one around.

The town is neither large nor of any particular administrative or commercial importance. But since the Russians built a giant ammunition factory nearby, it has gained some prominence. A few subsidiary factories have been developed, and the population of the town has risen sharply. They say there are some five hundred Russians here. You don't see them much around town, since they live in a camp close to their factory. Their wives are often in the market though. I was in a grocery store once, with two Russian women beside me. A bag in one of the women's hands hit something, I heard a bottle break and then my nose was assailed by strong fumes of alcohol. The woman opened her bag in embarrassment, and liquor trickled out. 'Oh madam, madam,' the shopkeeper cried out in feigned shock, and began to make fun of the woman. The local liquor, powerful and clear, resembles vodka; the Russians seem to prefer it to beer or whisky.

As in the south, military police are posted at most street-corners here. I've been asked to show my identity card a few times. When they see that I work in a box factory, they let me pass on without questions. I've noticed that regularly employed local residents aren't normally asked to show their cards, nor are white foreigners. It's those who look like strangers in dress or appearance who get stopped for the most part. Also, men between twenty and thirty-five years of age are often questioned. I'm in that age bracket, and, worse still, as a southerner I stand out in a crowd. I realized that I'd be asked for my identification card frequently. Not that it matters, for my papers are in order.

At the post-office entrance there is an ordinary policeman,

who checks briefcases, bags, etc. I don't carry a briefcase; on one or two occasions I've had a paper bag with something I'd bought on the way, which the policeman checked.

## 3

For the first few days after I got a post-office box I went to check it anyway, though I didn't, of course, expect any mail. Once or twice I peered into the area behind the boxes through my box. There were long tables piled with mail back there. Of course I saw only a small part of that area. The woman who sorted the mail sat right in the middle of that part of the hall that I could see. Facing the rows of boxes she sat back against a wall, working briskly away. Once, as I watched her, my gaze must have distracted her. She looked up at me and smiled. I smiled too, and closed the box. Her smile lingered in my mind as I walked out of the post office. Then it occurred to me that, although I'd seen her face and part of her body, she had only seen my eyes and nose through the box; she hadn't seen me smile. I was a little upset at this and wondered if I should've raised my head and smiled so that my lips would have been visible in the box. But to smile while stupidly staring at the closed box above mine would have been absurd, and she too might have found it comical to look at a pair of lips smiling in a box. When I thought of this I laughed aloud, though I'm not the type who often laughs to himself in the street.

The first letter I received from the organization came from 'Joseph George', a choice of names which I admired. It was a safe one, since the Christians formed a minority community which was normally above suspicion. The letter was in response to the one I had sent upon my arrival, and which I had filled with superficial personal news. Now I wrote back to 'Joseph George' in the same manner, except that I worked in a few significant details here and there.

When I came here I had thought that shortages would be less in evidence. In the south they are the order of the day of course, but I was in the north now, in a city close to the capital. Yet as winter approached, powdered milk disappeared from the market, eggs became scarce, and so on. Once I went to the grocer's to buy some detergent; in place of the familiar Camel brand I saw boxes of a new Lion brand labelled 'New More Powerful Detergent', with the word NEW printed in bright, bold letters. I thought to myself that the government called itself socialist, yet flaunted this sort of capitalistic advertising on products from its factories. I discovered that the new brand was more expensive. Then it dawned on me: since they claimed that there was no inflation in their regime they couldn't raise the prices of the old products, so they had simply taken the old brand off the market and replaced it with a new, costlier one; people would think that the brand was more expensive because it was 'new' and 'more powerful'. What can really be new about detergent?

During my first few weeks here I used to go for a walk along the main street in the evening, a street which is lined with bars. They drank a lot of beer here. It's normal to order two or three bottles of beer immediately upon entering. Like other things beer is often in short supply and a bar may run out of it early in the evening. So people order all the beer they want all at once. Of course it is frustrating, when you've had a bottle or two and want more, to learn that they're out of beer.

Though bars are crowded in the evening, the town shuts down early. Shops and restaurants close by ten o'clock. People drink their beer quickly, then eat and go to bed.

I sometimes wandered about late into the evening. Since most places were closed, the streets were dark for the most part; the tailors' shops, however, stayed open past midnight. Beneath glaring fluorescent lights they patiently carried on with their cutting and sewing. People are fond of clothes in the north; they're forever having loud, flashy suits made. I fancied that the tailors, diligently studying measurements and marking lengths of cloth, were in fact devising plans for an uprising: some day they'd switch off their brilliant lights all at once and step out into the shadowy streets clutching their long, shiny scissors.

# 4

One day I was about to open a letter I'd received when I glanced at the name on the envelope. It wasn't mine. I was puzzled for a moment, but then noticed that the post-office box number was 536. The letter had obviously been put in my box by accident. I thought at first of going into the office to return it, but then I saw that the woman who did the sorting was nearby distributing the mail. To save trouble I knocked on the side of the box and drew her attention. 'This isn't for me,' I said. 'Thanks,' she replied and smiled. That smile again.

Two days later when I went to check my box I saw her sorting the mail. There was nothing in my box. I knocked on the box and said hello loudly. She looked up and waved with a smile. I'd been a little forward, but she seemed to be warm and responsive. Soon I got into the habit of looking for her when I went to the post office. Occasionally I said hello; I felt let down when she wasn't around. A few times I saw men talking to her. There was a door to her right that opened into another part of the office, where these men apparently worked. One time I watched a man standing beside her whom I'd seen with her before. He was partially bald and had bushy eyebrows. I shut the box after a minute or two, not wanting to attract his attention inadvertently.

Once when I opened my box, I noticed that she was just distributing the mail. Since my own box was empty I knocked and asked, 'Do you have anything for me?' I heard her footsteps, then her face appeared on the other side of my box. 'Let me see,' she said and checked the bunch in her hand, 'Sorry, I don't have anything for you today.' I stayed talking for a minute or two. A few days later this happened again. One day I brought her a bar of Kit Kat, an English candy that boys sell in the street; it's smuggled, and therefore expensive. I reached my hand into the box and gave it to her. Saying 'Thanks,' she unwrapped it, reached back into the box, and offered me a piece. 'I don't know your name yet,' I said. 'Dolores,' she said. She was a Christian then. There's a large Christian population in the town, which has apparently been there for many generations. Most of them live in an older part of the town. I had wandered in that direction once and had seen their peculiar old-fashioned houses with roofed balconies.

'Dolores,' I said, sucking on the candy. 'Nice name.' She smiled. Then I said, 'Don't you want to know my name?' 'But I've seen it on your letters!' she replied. I laughed, seeing how stupid I'd been. 'Dolores,' I said again turning the candy in my mouth. 'Beautiful—but Christian names don't mean anything, do they? Names like John and Mary.' 'My name has a meaning though,' she said, and seeing the question on my face added, 'Dolores means sad.'

'Sad!' I almost shouted, 'Good God, how could your parents give you such a name? And you're always so cheerful and happy.' 'Oh well, we have names like that,' she said. 'But tell me about *your* name. In your case every name has a meaning, I know. And you have so many names with different meanings.'

'My name means one who lives in happiness and luxury,' I told her. 'Oh, that's wonderful', she said. 'Mr Happiness-and-Luxury!' I exlaimed with a tinge of bitterness in my voice. 'To tell the truth, my name is a more accurate reflection of my parents' naive optimism than of reality. My life—but enought of that.' She didn't say anything, but I thought I saw a certain understanding in her eyes. Then I laughed loudly and said, 'You see, both our names mean precisely the opposite of what they ought to!'

I spoke to her a number of times after that. When she was busy at her table, at least she'd smile and wave. I didn't want to disturb her every day, so I only went to the post office on alternate days. I was restless on the days I didn't go. I didn't have much work at the office. Once in a while I entered deliveries in a huge register; the rest of the time I just sat around. I didn't talk much with anyone at the office.

One day when I knocked on the box Dolores got up from her table and came to me. 'Here,' she said, 'I had a letter for you just now.' She stretched her hand into the box; instead of taking the letter, I clasped her hand. I held it, warm and soft. 'Don't be silly . . .' she said, but made no effort to withdraw her hand. To be sure, it was rather ridiculous holding hands with our arms upraised, standing on either side of the rows of boxes. Then I heard someone entering the hall behind me and let her hand go. I left without saying a word.

## 5

Dolores handed me a letter through the box personally on another occasion. 'Joseph George must be a close friend of yours,' she said. I was startled for a moment, then said, 'Yes, we were classmates.' She looked pleased that my friend was a Christian, but I went away with an uneasy feeling. On the one hand, I was pleased that she took enough interest in me to notice who wrote to me: on the other, I was worried by the thought that this might possibly jeopardize my mission.

I corresponded regularly with Joseph George, responding with long-winded letters to the equally lengthy ones that I received. Matters of substance can be adroitly inserted in a long drawn-out letter; they might be conspicuous in a short one. It was fair to assume that the censors didn't spend much time over a meandering letter, especially when it appeared to be casual and personal. Hence J.G. and I always incorporated a great deal of fictitious matter into our correspondence. J.G. sometimes invented quite absorbing stories, and I in turn tried to match him in imaginative flights. Returning from work, I spent long hours at my desk composing letters.

I had hinted that my mission in this town was not likely to prove difficult. The policeman at the entrance to the post office didn't check people very conscientiously, and even allowed them to pass completely unchecked on many occasions. It would be no problem to smuggle in something in a carton of tea or biscuits. I had placed the brown paper package that I brought along when I came here at the bottom of my trunk. It was just the right size for my post-office box. Once I had it past the guard, the rest would be easy. I would leave it in the box in the evening; Dolores left at five, and no one was there after that. There'd be no chance of anyone observing the package from inside the hall.

I had indicated my readiness to carry out my task at any time, but Joseph George counselled patience. He pointed out that a number of things had to be considered before choosing a date. It was essential to coordinate the activities in different cities with care, for the entire plan would be in jeopardy if the mission in one town were executed prematurely. I confess I was eager to finish the job: the package at the bottom of the trunk weighed on my mind. On the other hand, I was also grateful for each passing day, for I knew that once I had left the package in my box I'd never see Dolores again.

Watching or talking to Dolores, I was always aware that her face would one day disappear for ever from my sight. Once I asked her, 'Could I see you after work this evening?' She smiled as usual and said, 'No, I'm sorry, but our friendship should stay right here.' I never asked her again. I knew I'd see her only behind an iron wall of boxes. It occurred to me that I had never really had a good look at her. When she was at her table I could see her entire figure, but only from a distance; when she talked to me at the box, I saw just her face, and that too imperfectly, her chin out of sight when her forehead was visible, and vice versa. The inescapable rectangle of the box gave me the choice between seeing her fully from a distance, or seeing a close-up of her face alone.

## 6

Dolores had told me that the censors' office was located behind her. Incoming mail was censored there, while outgoing mail was handled in another part of the building. I had noted that aerogrammes often appeared to make it through unopened, while envelopes were almost always investigated, and large packets invariably.

I had seen the balding man with bushy eyebrows a number of times with Dolores. Lately he seemed to have got into the habit of gossiping with her. He'd be standing near her—quite close at times—or leaning against her table, with his back to me. Once I saw them drinking coffee (Dolores didn't drink tea).

I worked from eight to two; sometimes I went home for lunch first and then to the post office, at other times I went there straight from the office. Not many people came in to check their boxes in the afternoon. This gave me a better chance to watch or talk to Dolores. As winter approached the afternoons became pleasant. Enjoying the warm sunshine one day, I walked from the factory to the post office. I opened my box and peered in. Her chair turned away, Dolores sat almost with her back to me, and the balding man leaned against her table; they were laughing. As I watched, the man threw back his head in laughter and pressed Dolores's shoulder. His hand lingered on her neck for a moment and then slipped over her breast. Dolores got up immediately, saying something. The man moved from the table too and, patting her gently on the cheek, went inside. Arranging her hair, Dolores was about to turn round when I shut my box. I went out and walked briskly home. On the way I bumped into someone so hard that I nearly knocked him over.

I came home and threw myself on the bed. I lay for over two hours with my eyes open. I didn't eat. Then it was evening. I got out of bed and made myself a strong cup of tea. I didn't feel like staying in my room. A half-finished letter was lying on my desk, but I was in no mood to continue it. I went out.

I thought I'd go to the movies. I'd been to a six-thirty show twice before; it was usually crowded, and everyone ignored the 'No Smoking' sign. The smoke and the noise annoyed me, and now I thought the nine-thirty show might be more pleasant, since it wouldn't be as crowded. I decided to wander about in the meantime. Passing through the goldsmiths' lane, I stopped and stared blankly at the glittering showcases. A few Russians were also scrutinizing the jewellery in the company of their pale, plump wives. The Russians are always hanging around the goldsmiths' shops.

I washed down a felafel sandwich with a Pepsi and went to a picture. It didn't appear to be a popular film: the theatre was practically empty. When the title flashed on the screen, I saw that it was a gangster film. Soon after the picture started, I heard a noise at my feet. The audience at the earlier show had scattered empty packages of chips and husks of dried watermelon seeds on the floor and now, since most rows were more or less vacant, rats had come out to nibble at the crumbs. They scampered away when I tapped my foot, but were back in a few moments. Once I felt a soft, furry touch on my left foot; after that I put my feet up on the seat in front of me. The picture was dull, and I hardly watched it. I would've left, but since the incident at the House of

Culture no one was allowed to leave an auditorium in the middle of a show, for fear that they might slip away in the darkness and leave a bomb behind. I was forced to sit through the entire show.

That night I dreamed I sat alone in a theatre, while someone resembling the balding man in the post office raped Dolores on the screen. Rats came and began biting my feet in the dark. I ran through the empty rows, with rats scurrying after me. Stumbling past vacant seats, I raced back and forth on bleeding feet, but couldn't get out of the theatre. None of the doors would open, though I pounded on each in turn. The theatre resounded with strident music.

7

One day I noticed that the familiar picture of the President, which hung in every shop and office in the city, was being replaced. The stern-faced figure in military dress, bedecked with ribbons and medals, had reappeared in a white silk suit and a broad smile. Entering the post office a few days later, I saw a notice posted on the door: 'For your security this section will henceforth close at eight p.m.' The main hall in the post office is open until late at night for the telegraph service; the section with the post office boxes used to close at midnight. The change in closing time didn't seriously affect me; I could easily carry out my task between six and eight in the evening. Nevertheless, the next day I wrote to Joseph George: 'Auntie had twelve eggs to hatch, the hen has broken four; now there are only eight. If they do not hatch soon, they will all be gone.'

My correspondence with Joseph George was becoming increasingly labyrinthine. To give his letters an innocent look J.G. filled them with more and more irrelevant detail, and with fictitious characters and situations that had begun to assume a reality of their own. I often felt that J.G. was getting carried away by his imaginative impulse, and elaborating stories needlessly. I admit that I found his letters more absorbing now, but I was often at a loss to separate the true substance from mere fabrication. I spent a great deal of time pursuing different interpretations of each letter. My own letters may well have acquired a similar character, for I had the impression that J.G. often missed my point. Our correspondence seemed to have lost its essential linkage, and I felt as though I were groping in the mist. Fearing that a misunderstanding might wreck everything, I hoped my mission would soon be concluded.

I continued to see Dolores as before. I gave her a silver paper knife for Christmas. 'You can use it for censoring my mail,' I said in jest. One day she said, 'You have circles under your eyes. What's bothering you?' 'I have a lot of work at the office these days,' I said. It suddenly occurred to me as I was leaving that she'd only seen my eyes, nose, and mouth, and touched my right hand. She doesn't know whether I'm fat or skinny: for all she knows I could be missing a leg.

I didn't speak much to Dolores last month. I merely looked at her, and stood watching her when she didn't see me. At home, composing letters at my desk, I often sat without putting anything on paper, her image hovering before my eyes. One day, after I had conjured her up as I sat at my desk, I asked her to come closer. Then I stretched my arm as far inside the box as I could and touched her, caressing her hair, her cheeks, her neck. Thrusting my fingers inside her dress I made an effort to squeeze one of her breasts. But I couldn't get my arm far enough inside the box, my elbow kept bumping against the side of it, and I couldn't move my hand the way I wanted. I struggled uselessly with straining fingers. And it was quite impossible for me to reach below her waist, though there were things I wanted to do to her. I wanted to thrust my hand between her legs and clutch her pubic hair. I conjured up countless visions, but the wall of boxes always appeared before me. All my dreams were futile in the face of that wall. At times I was filled with rage and wanted to smash the rows of boxes to pieces.

So many images of Dolores were crowding before my eyes that they began to seem real to me. I often woke from a reverie only to discover that it had all been in my mind. My visions were becoming so confused with reality that I sometimes wondered if I'd really ever seen the balding man caressing Dolores, or if I had in fact held her hand. But I didn't allow such doubts to run away with me.

Talking to Dolores two weeks ago I had thought she looked at me strangely, as though there were something on her mind. I was troubled by the thought that the censors might have become interested in my correspondence and that she had learned about it. I received two letters from Joseph George after that, neither of which made much sense to me. I began to wonder if, instead of working out a brilliantly conceived plan, we had simply been engaged in a trivial exchange all this time.

## 8

Curfew was suddenly declared all over town two days ago. I was perplexed, not having the least idea why this had happened. As far as I could see there had been no signs of unrest or rioting. That the town should be put under curfew when things appeared to be normal was extremely suspicious. Haunted by apprehensions, I was almost convinced that the government had got wind of a far-ranging plot and had taken measures to thwart it, including seizing the suspects.

The curfew is lifted for two hours each evening, so that people can hastily buy their necessities. I made a quick trip to the post office yesterday as well as the day before. Since the curfew is not lifted until five, I had no hope of seeing Dolores. I wasn't even sure if she had come to work in the first place. Staffing continues for essential services, but I don't know if her work falls into that category. The pile of mail that I saw on her table the day before yesterday was there yesterday too, and in fact seemed to have grown larger: she probably hadn't come in.

I've been confined to my room for two days, and am becoming increasingly troubled. The streets are quiet, except for the occasional sound of a passing jeep or truck. I find myself missing Dolores. Her face looms before my eyes, outlined by the rectangular box as by a picture-frame. She merely looks at me. Once or twice I thought I saw tears streaming down her cheeks. I wanted to tell her not to cry. Sad Dolores. I must see her, talk to her.

I've debated with myself if I should take the brown paper bag to the post office before it's too late. But what about Joseph George? Perhaps some critical message from him waits in the pile of mail on Dolores's table. I don't know what to do.

Today is the third day of the curfew: images have been rising and fading into one another in my mind. I see the ruined post office with Dolores's face emerging from the wreckage, or her face forms first and then disappears in an explosion. In addition, since yesterday I've been hearing footsteps. Heavy boots climb the stairs, the footsteps grow louder and cease before my door. I listen tensely for a knock which doesn't come. It has happened several times in the last twenty-four hours. This morning I saw that my hands were shaking. At breakfast the cup of tea rattled in my hand: just then I heard the sound of steps climbing the stairs. The tea continued to slosh about as my grip on the cup tightened. The steps halted before my door. A few seconds passed, and then the cup in my hand clattered to the floor. Now it's noon. From time to time I'm seized by a wild desire to open my door, rush down the stairs, and dash through the deserted streets as far as I can. But then, as one might either concede the truth or delude oneself utterly in a moment of helplessness, I persuade myself that the thought of being tracked down is absurd, for I've never joined a plot, have seldom received any mail, and have nothing of consequence in the brown paper bag at the bottom of my trunk. As I spent my life in the south making few friends and shunning relatives, I'm living now in the north, stuck with a dull job and caught up in confused dreams of love or freedom, like hundreds of other people.

# a tale of two generals

## 1

Turning on his right side, General Kurma glanced at the bedside alarm clock. In the dark, the minute hand glowed a phosphorescent yellow. It stood straight vertically, like an upright sword in the hand of a soldier at a guard-of-honour ceremony. The hour hand was nowhere in sight. Which meant that the hour hand stood exactly behind the minute hand. Which meant that it was midnight.

Or was it really? What if the hour hand had simply disappeared?

People disappear in the middle of the night, never to be seen again. Had the hour hand suffered a similar fate?

For a moment, General Kurma was filled with anxiety. What if the hour hand had indeed vanished? What could one do with the minute hand alone? How could he, General Kurma, carry out the time-table for the coup without the hour hand?

The hour hand advanced imperceptibly, and was visible on the left side of the minute hand. General Kurma clapped silently.

Long live the hour hand! Long live the revolution!

It seemed to General Kurma that in front of him, too, stood a minute hand, in the shape of General Pulav, covering and obscuring him. The minute hand inside the clock had moved away in a few seconds, but the minute hand that stood in front of General Kurma refused to budge. It was time to shove it aside. It would be pushed aside, and everyone knew that the hour hand rules the clock.

Long live the hour hand!

The minute hand slowly sank inside the clock. General Kurma impatiently waited for the moment it would reach its nadir, with its nose touching the ground, so to speak. It should stop right there, for ever, General Kurma thought.

Long live the hour hand!

General Kurma turned to the other side of the bed, and looked at his wife. Enormously large, she was fast asleep. The breasts atop her huge body seemed to be spilling out in opposite directions. With each inhalation, the breasts heaved up, as though they were eager to jump off and run away. Her belly, too, heaved up and down with each breath, and the belly button expanded and contracted like a crater. The moonlight coming in through the window illuminated her body from the neck to the buttocks, leaving the head and the legs in darkness. It seemed to General Kurma that the attraction of the moonlight was creating unusually high waves upon his wife's body.

General Kurma knew that sleep would not come for at least two more hours. He rose from the bed silently, and went into the kitchen. Without switching on the light, he located the refrigerator, and fumbling a bit, opened its door. He took out a packet of peanuts, and began to eat the peanuts one by one. He liked chilled peanuts. His wife didn't allow him to eat too many peanuts. General Kurma decided that, once he had successfully executed the coup d'etat, he would eat peanuts to his heart's content. When your husband is the president of the country, what wife would dare to dictate to him?

To get a little light, General Kurma had kept the refrigerator door slightly ajar. The low hum of the refrigerator mingled with the sound of the crunching of peanuts. As he ate, General Kurma looked into the refrigerator. Inside the refrigerator there was a different world. A secret world. Cold, indifferent, like an alien planet. Suddenly, General Kurma felt very lonely. Would the other officers of the army, and the soldiers, fully back him?

Drinking some water out of the refrigerator, General Kurma returned to the bedroom. For a while he stood beside the bed, then went towards the balcony door. He walked onto the balcony.

Bright moonlight spread everywhere. There was no trace of clouds in the sky. But it was the end of May; the monsoon was at hand, and it could rain any day.

He must carry out the coup d'etat before the arrival of the monsoon. A revolution must be carried out in summer, when people's heads are still hot. All the revolutions in the world took place in the summer. Once the rains come and people's heads cool down, there was not much scope for a revolution. General Pulav, too, had come to power after a revolution four summers ago.

He who comes to power in the summer goes in the summer.

Once he came to power, General Kurma intended to abolish the summer. There would be no more summer; no one would ever talk about summer. That would be his first decree.

General Kurma surveyed the courtyard of his bungalow. His eyes lingered over the statue newly erected in the centre of the garden—the statue of President Pulav.

General Pulav and General Kurma had passed out of the military academy together, and had been close friends over the years. Four years ago, General Pulav had staged a coup, and had become President. Even then, General Kurma continued to call him 'General Pulav'. President Pulav used to tell him, 'General Kurma, I am President now. You must call me President Pulav.'

'What to do, General—sorry, President Pulav, I cannot break the habit of so many years.'

'Tut, tut,' President Pulav said with a chuckle. 'If you weren't such a useful person, General Kurma, I would have hanged you for treason.'

On his part, General Kurma had firmly decided that he would compel everyone to call him President Kurma once he became president. There would be no excuses, absolutely.

Watching President Pulav's statue in the garden, General Kurma's brow became puckered. He was tired of seeing President Pulav's statues in all kinds of places. And now, one had sprouted right in the middle of his courtyard.

For the past two years, President Pulav had started a virtual campaign of erecting his own statues. Every square in the capital displayed his statue. Every government building, every school and college, every hospital and stadium bore his statues. Not content with that, President Pulav had recently issued a decree that even private residences of important persons must display his statue. A factory of statues had been set up at one end of the town, and hundreds of statues emanating from it had invaded the city.

All the statues were absolutely the same. They were made of cement out of the same mould. The face, the hands, the clothes, the ribbons were all painted to look like the real President Pulav. Realism is the forte of dictators. President Pulav believed that every citizen should feel that he, President Pulav, was actually watching over their every action.

There was a whirring sound in the sky, and General Kurma looked to his left. A helicopter was passing from west to east.

President Pulav's nightly runaround. It had increased in recent days.

President Pulav had nine palaces in different parts of the capital. He spent each night in any of the nine residences. Nobody knew in which palace he would spend a particular night. In this way, President Pulav hoped to elude assassination.

But the fear of assassination kept growing, and he found it unsafe to spend an entire night in one palace. So he began to change residence in the middle of the night. This grew to the extent that he changed palaces three or four times in one night. It came to the point where he spent hardly an hour in one residence. He did the round of all his nine palaces in a single night. As a result, he got very little sleep.

How small and insect-like appeared President Pulav's helicopter in the sky! General Kurma wanted to grab it in his fist like King Kong, and crush and throw it away.

President Pulav's king-size insomnia disappeared over the horizon. General Kurma's would-be king-size insomnia paced about the balcony. Between the two insomnias, the moon sang her historical song.

## 2

At the southern end of the capital there was the Great Slum. Some people claimed that it was larger than the city proper.

Most citizens didn't want to believe that. But everyone agreed that it was the largest slum in Asia.

The Great Slum had grown over marshy land, and was always muddy. The mud went very deep. If an ordinary citizen entered the slum area, he slowly sank into the mud and disappeared. The denizens of the slum were the destitute hordes that had migrated from the villages to the capital. They were so emaciated, and weighed so little, that they didn't sink into the mud as they walked about. Over the narrow, twisted paths of the slum, these sawdust creatures floated effortlessly. The huts they had built were also lightweight. Their possessions were scanty, such as a few aluminium pots. Even so, during the monsoon, when mud became softer, several huts went under the mud. Sometimes, sleepers in a hut slowly sank into the mud overnight and disappeared. Some residents of the slum, who worked in the town, made good money, ate well, put on weight, and, as a consequence, sank into the mud as they slept in their huts at night. Such population loss was made up by fresh hordes of the destitute moving in from the countryside.

The respectable bourgeoisie of the capital never went near the slum. Even the police and soldiers didn't enter the slum, for fear of sinking. In case of extreme necessity, the police would go in holding huge gas balloons in their hands. The balloons enabled them to walk lightly over the mud. But, with balloons in hand, they were unable to make free movement, and were consequently largely ineffectual. Once, urchins hurled small stones at the balloons; with his balloons bursting, the policeman sank screaming into the mud and disappeared. In a way, there was about the slum a far greater air of freedom than about the city.

Having peppered the city with his own statues, President Pulav was unhappy about one thing—there wasn't a single statue of his in the Great Slum. The Department of Statues had made many attempts to put up a statue there, but had no success. They tried to erect a statue over a solid foundation of stones and cement bags; but the mud was so deep and invincible that the statue, along with its base, inevitably went under. The illiterate residents of the slum claimed that the mud stretched right up to the centre of the earth.

Then the Department of Statues dropped a statue from an aeroplane, with hundreds of gas balloons attached to it. Owing to the balloons, the statue hung above the mud, just touching it. As the balloons moved with the wind, the statue swayed about. With hundreds of balloons tied to its hands, the statue looked so funny that the slum-dwellers began to call it the Balloon Man. Then the urchins began to steal the balloons by breaking the strings; with the number of balloons diminishing, the statue began to go under. Very soon, the Balloon Man had disappeared entirely.

President Pulav continued to insist that his statue be erected in the Great Slum. As it is, his rule over the slum area was less than absolute. Erecting statues would at least give him a psychological edge. He sent word to the top officials of the Department of Statues that they had to find a way of accomplishing their job, or else they would lose their hands.

The officials of the Department of Statues were frightened to death; they didn't know what to do. To buy time, they replied: 'The monsoon is at hand. There is no use making attempts during the monsoon. We will submit a plan as soon as the monsoon is over.'

President Pulav agreed.

### 3

On the day of the first rains, General Kurma effected a coup with the help of some senior military officials and dethroned President Pulav. General Kurma now became President Kurma.

The ousted president made an attempt to flee to a neighbouring country in a helicopter. But the helicopter was shot down at the foot of the mountains west of the capital. The helicopter burst into flames a few moments after it crashed. President Pulav's body was never found. It was concluded that the body had been incinerated.

One of the things President Kurma did as soon as he had established himself was to remove President Pulav's statues in the capital. It took a few weeks to bring down and cart away hundreds of statues. The statues were dumped on the barren land west of the capital, near where President Pulav's helicopter had crashed.

The statues were gone, but the pedestals remained. President Kurma's colleagues said, 'Presidentji, we can now erect your statue on the pedestals.'

Affecting indignation, President Kurma said, 'Oh no, I have no wish to see my statues erected all over the place.'

So the city was left with empty pedestals everywhere, which looked very unsightly. President Kurma's colleagues said, 'If you don't want statues, Presidentji, let us demolish the pedestals.'

After a moment's thought, President Kurma said, 'Let the pedestals be. The statues have gone, haven't they? What harm are the pedestals doing to anyone?'

President Kurma's colleagues figured that, despite his denials, the President probably intended to have statues erected in course of time 'by public demand.' So the pedestals remained. The people were fed up of seeing the vacant pedestals, but there was nothing they could do about it. In private, people used to refer to President Pulav's rule as the Reign of Statues; they began to call President Kurma's reign the Reign of Pedestals.

The monsoon was over, winter too passed; but the summer never came. For, before the winter was over, President Kurma had, by a decree, abolished summer. As summer no longer existed, there was no summer vacation for anyone. But the temperature of the capital kept climbing. Everyone, students and government officials particularly, were annoyed that they couldn't go to the hills for a holiday. Public unrest grew. President Kurma's Intelligence Department advised him that the public, enraged at the abolition of the summer, might rise up and precipitate another coup.

President Kurma was himself keen on going on holiday to his palace in the hills. He issued a decree reinstituting the summer. Everyone was happy, including President Kurma. He packed his bags, and, in a convoy of Mercedes cars, headed for the hills.

## 4

President Kurma now spent a lot of time in the kitchen. His astrologer, Swami Agnimandya, had warned him about the danger of poisoning. As a result, President Kurma had started doing his own cooking. Since his assumption of office, his wife's physical dimensions had grown further, and she was incapable of any work. President Kurma didn't trust any of his other relatives or retainers, and hence resorted to self-help. His advisers complained that he did not spare enough time for the business of the state, but President Kurma didn't change his ways.

During his stay in the hills, the ambassador of a small Himalayan kingdom came to visit President Kurma. President Kurma was rolling chapattis at the moment. (He ate a lot of chapattis, ten per meal.) President Kurma entered the drawing room with a rolling pin in hand. The ambassador, whose own wife used to frequently emerge from the kitchen with a rolling pin in her hand with consequences that the ambassador did not remember with pleasure, took fright and ran out of the palace, never to return.

President Kurma chuckled, and went back to the kitchen. He was cutting vegetables. President Kurma looked out of the kitchen window; what he saw startled him. There, in the stony land beyond the barbed wire fence stood a person watching President Kurma. For all he knew, the person was none other than ex-President Pulav.

At first President Kurma thought it was the ghost of President Pulav. But then he recalled that President Pulav's body had never been found. Perhaps, surviving the crash, ex-President Pulav still lived in hiding. Pulav was alive!

Rushing out of the kitchen with the vegetable knife held high in his hand, President Kurma ran in the direction of General Pulav. General Pulav turned and bolted. By the time President Kurma had circumvented the barbed wire, the fugitive had gained considerable distance.

General Pulav dashed down the hill taking big strides. President Kurma ran after him, disregarding the stones and the thorny bushes in the way. In a few minutes, General Pulav reached the edge of the plain on which were scattered hundreds of his own discarded statues. By the time President Kurma had reached the bottom of the hill, General Pulav had entered the Forest of Statues.

Panting heavily, President Kurma stopped at the edge of the Forest of Statues. As all the statues had been shaped and painted to look exactly like General Pulav, it was practically impossible to find the real General Pulav from amongst them. If General Pulav had made some movement, his presence would have been revealed. But, obviously, the General was keeping perfectly still.

'General Pulav!' President Kurma shouted, raising the kitchen knife high above his head. 'Come out like a man! We will fight a duel.'

Under the midday sun, waves of heat billowed over the Forest of Statues. Then a loud sound came out of the Forest: 'Ha! Ha! Ha!'

Grinding his teeth in anger, President Kurma looked around. He couldn't locate the precise source of the sound. The sound reverberated again; 'Ha! Ha! Ha!'

Boiling with rage, President Kurma entered the Forest of Statues, and began stabbing at the statues at random. Striking the cement, the knife got blunted and twisted; but he went on jabbing at the statues furiously. By this time, soldiers had reached the place; they pacified the President and took him away. The doctor gave him a heavy dose of tranquilizers.

The next morning, President Kurma returned to the capital. The problem of General Pulav cried out for an immediate and satisfactory solution. One was to drop a bomb on the Forest of Statues. But what if the fugitive still escaped? Besides, President Kurma wanted to capture General Pulav alive, and torture him personally.

Then the Intelligence Department brought news that all the statues on the plain had risen and were marching towards the capital. The statues moved slumberously, as if they had trouble in shaking off their long sleep. Crows and statues enjoy a congenital association; crows love to perch upon the heads of statues. The statues had suddenly abandoned their statue-dharma, thus alarming all the crows that nestled in the Forest of Statues. Hundreds of crows flew in the direction of the capital. The citizens of the capital were alarmed at this invasion of cawing crows aimlessly flying about. The appearance of a crow traditionally signifies the imminent arrival of a visitor. The citizens wondered what army of visitors was planning to visit them.

The President figured that General Pulav himself was obviously among the ambulant statues, leading them. With hundreds of statues scattered over a vast area, it would not be possible to bomb them effectively. Nor would bullets have much effect on the cement statues. President Kurma became extremely worried. The statues were advancing moment by moment.

Then President Kurma smiled. He gave an order to remove all the empty pedestals in town, and to cart them to the edge of the city.

All army and civilian vehicles were mobilized on a war footing, and the pedestals were placed near the edge of the city. Standing atop a watch-tower, General Kurma surveyed the plain. He had given orders not to shoot at the army of statues, leaving the soldiers wondering.

The army of statues arrived at the place where the pedestals stood. Seeing the empty pedestals, each statue climbed up on one. As President Kurma had anticipated, the sight of empty pedestals had awoken in the statues their statue-dharma, and, following their dharma, they were now reassuming their position upon the pedestals.

President Kurma watched all this happening with a triumphant air. He knew that he would achieve his objective when all the statues had regained their place upon the pedestals. Only General Pulav—the real General Pulav—would be left standing on the ground. Then he would be an easy target.

All the statues took their place upon the pedestals. Only one figure was left standing in the empty arena. The officer who led the soldiers looked back and shouted, 'President sir, it's only a cement statue!'

'Eh?' President Kurma said. He realized that the real General Pulav had occupied one of the pedestals, and therefore this last statue had been left standing on the ground helplessly.

'Shaitan!' President Kurma muttered. Then he shouted at the soldiers: 'Shoot at every statue!'

The soldiers began to shoot. Splinters flew off the cement statues. Seeing that they are being shot at, the statues jumped off the pedestals, and drew their pistols and began to shoot. But there were no bullets in their pistols. The statues began to run helter-skelter. Standing amidst the statues scurrying about, General Pulav reflected upon the situation. It would not have been difficult for him to save his life by joining the fleeing statues. But a different question pre-occupied him; was he the real General Pulav, or just a statue? He wasn't sure any more, and this troubled and vexed him greatly. He touched and pressed his own flesh; but, since the helicopter crash, his body had become hard like cement. The suspicion grew in his mind that he was just one of the statues. Running away from the field would not be the solution to this problem. If he had marched ahead and faced the bullets, the question would have been resolved. If he were a statue, only splinters would fly off; if he were the real General Pulav, he did not want to die alone. He would kill President Kurma too.

General Pulav stepped out of the crowd of statues with measured steps. Observing him from the watch-tower, President Kurma ordered his soldiers to stop shooting. The guns fell silent, and the statues too stopped in their tracks. It suddenly became unusually quiet and still. In the midst of the stillness, General Pulav continued to advance step by step. Arriving at the foot of the watch-tower, he looked up at President Kurma. Behind the still figure of General Pulav stood the statues, equally still; with finger on the trigger, and guns pointed at General Pulav, the soldiers too were perfectly still. Amidst the host of men and statues, General Pulav felt completely alone. It was the terrible loneliness of one who didn't know if he was himself or not.

'President Kurma, I—I am General Pulav!' General Pulav shouted. He found it funny to make the claim with such confidence.

'Ha! Ha!' President Kurma laughed from the tower. 'Will you surrender, Pulav?'

'No, I will not surrender,' General Pulav replied.

'No? In that case, General Pulav, I myself shall send you to Jehannum.' President Kurma drew his pistol, and fired.

The awareness that the bullet had pierced his heart, and that he was dying, was accompanied by the knowledge that he was indeed the real General Pulav, and it filled his mind with a singular satisfaction. As he fell, General Pulav summoned all his strength, and lifted and fired his pistol. The bullet hit President Kurma in the chest, and he fell from the watch-tower in slow-motion.

## 5

With the death of the two generals, the country underwent a period of anarchy. There was no general powerful enough to become President. Things worsened to such an extent that some people began to openly talk of bringing democracy to the country.

About this time, the natural evolution of the people in the Great Slum reached its acme. For years, the people of the slum had continued to become more and more insubstantial. Now, their internal organs and flesh and skin withered away completely, leaving only skeletons behind. They had become skeletons without undergoing death, and went about their business as usual. Of course, they could not procreate; but, as they were already skeletons, they didn't die either. These beings came to be regarded as a new caste; the caste was rated higher even than the Brahmins, as the skeletons not only looked fair, but boasted of a rare purity, and purity was the goal of all the castes.

Seeing the anarchy in the country, the skeletons decided to take over the reins of government. In this, they encountered little opposition. Who would fight with skeletons, which would be like fighting with waves?

Since the skeletons needed no luxuries for themselves, not even food, they brought the rule of equality and justice to the country. There was no possibility of anybody attempting a coup against the skeletons. Swami Agnimandya, who had been re-appointed as state astrologer, has predicted that the Reign of Skeletons shall last forever.

# tree of death

*In every boundary tree*
*The crowds of birds delight;*
*And heaven is wrapped in darkness*
*That soon will show its strength.*

Martand came out of the university library and walked towards the Genghis Kubla Art Gallery. He didn't expect to find a new exhibition there, but he thought he might use the men's room. It cost ten paise and you even got an admission ticket. Pay toilets were not common in Bombay. In a poor country like India few could afford to pay for small pleasures.

Martand could have used one of the men's rooms in the university; not that he had money to squander in men's rooms. He just couldn't stand the smell of the university toilets.

Bhadra sat in the gallery restaurant stroking his beard. He appeared pleased to see Martand. There was nothing but a glass of water before him on the table. Martand ordered two cups of tea. 'Now in exchange for the cup of tea—and a Char Minar cigarette, if you don't mind—I'll tell you a story about flies, a subject that fascinates you,' Bhadra said. 'I was in my studio at night, brooding in front of a blank canvas. A fly kept landing on the canvas, crawling about like it was looking for something. I was annoyed, and couldn't figure out what it was up to. Then I caught on—the fly thought that the canvas was an open window! It just wanted to get out of the room. Flies can't see well in artificial light, and it had mistaken the white canvas for light shining in through a window. Then I swatted it with my brush. Killed it with one blow.'

'Why didn't you enter the stained canvas in an exhibition?' Martand asked. 'The critics would have loved it.'

'You can forget about exhibitions, man. I'll have to start painting billboards soon,' Bhadra said.

'So what have you been doing lately?' Martand asked.

'Killing flies mostly,' Bhadra replied. 'Still, a job came up last week. Mr Jain, who owns the Shankar Cotton Mill, wants me to do a large portrait of Vishwaroop Baba. Of course, it means good money.'

Leaving the Art Gallery, Martand wondered if he should go back to the library. It was a quarter past four. He was supposed to be at the railway station at five-thirty to see his girlfriend Maitreyi off, so he didn't have much time. What could he accomplish in an hour?

He was looking for an excuse to get away from his desk anyway. He had been working on his Ph.D for the past six months, a Ph.D he didn't really want. He already had an MA in Sanskrit, and good grades, but he couldn't get a college teaching job. He had been willing to go to a small town, even to some godforsaken little place, but there just weren't enough openings for a lecturer in Sanskrit. He didn't want a business position. Once he began working in an office, his chances of getting a teaching job would be even slimmer. He didn't know what to do. Then he was offered a government scholarship for the Ph.D. There wasn't much competition for this particular scholarship, because it didn't pay much. But Martand took it, thinking that it would at least keep him in academics. He could do research until something better came along.

Martand strolled towards the Gateway of India. Standing by the parapet, he watched the waves breaking upon the wall. Idly he sought some pattern in the breaking waves. He remembered an American film in which every seventh wave was higher than normal; a prisoner on an island had jumped from a cliff into just such a wave and escaped. Martand still remembered the final shot in the movie, with the man shouting, 'I'm free!' against the vast background of the blue sea.

A flight of steps along the wall of the Gateway of India descended to the sea. Someone had defecated on one of the steps. A big wave rose, broke high on the stairs, and washed the turd away.

Maitreyi was waiting right under the huge station clock at Victoria Terminus. 'Maitreyi, did you fix up a meeting here so that you can promptly note how late I am for the appointment?'

'Enough of your sardonic talk, Martand.'

They went to a nearby restaurant.

'Packed your things?' Martand said.

'Yeah.'

Both sipped the coffee in silence.

'I am going away for a long period, Martand,' Maitreyi said, looking into Martand's eyes.

'I know.'

After a few seconds, she said, 'Maybe for good. If I like it at Jawhar, I plan to spend two or three years in the tribal area doing healthcare work. Guruji has built up an excellent organization there, with some dedicated people. There are women too.'

'Sounds fine.'

'That's all? You have nothing more to say?'

'Not really.'

'You want me to go away just like that? Don't you want me to stay here?'

'Oh, I will be happy if you remained here.'

'Oh Martand,' Maitreyi said, putting the coffee cup down. The spoon in the saucer toppled over, and clattered upon the bare floor.

'I can't live in this city. It's like Blake's London.' Maitreyi had just finished her BA exams. 'What does that guy say? ... "Mind-forg'd manacles." Yes, that's still true. After two hundred years, even more so, with all those MNCs, and the media opium.'

Martand didn't say anything. Maitreyi spoke again: 'You know Martand, I have a feeling that you'd react like that fellow in your favourite novel if I asked you *the* question. I mean *the* question.'

Martand looked up quizzically.

'The guy said "No" simply, didn't he?' Maitreyi said.

'Oh, that would be an overstatement.'

'What do you mean, Martand?'

'I mean one doesn't have to look at things in the Either/Or spirit.'

'Then what?'

'I mean, in the world there are only possibilities, ill at ease.'

'Come on, Martand, thousands of people fall in love; or they fall out of love. They know their minds.'

'Look, Maitreyi. I don't know which is the most abused word in the world—love, or freedom.'

Maitreyi's train moved ponderously. Martand was left alone in the departure din. He walked out under the domes of Victoria Terminus. He savoured the words in his mind: *Victoria Terminus*. They had a nice air of sombre finality.

Emerging from the stone edifice of the station, Martand stood briefly in the glare of the sun, blinking.

*Victoria Terminus.*

Now that Maitreyi was gone, Martand had lots of spare time. He hadn't seen Bhadra in the restaurant of the Art Gallery for a long time. He guessed that he was busy working on Baba's portrait. Then one day Nisshank told him that holy ashes had begun to emanate from Bhadra's portrait, and that people were flocking to Mr Jain's home to watch the miracle. This was not, in fact, so surprising, since Baba was well-known for miracles, including the mysterious production of wristwatches, gold rings, holy ashes, and the like.

One day Martand at last saw Bhadra at the Art Gallery. He was a new man. He carried a pack of Marlboro cigarettes.

'You know, when the portrait started emanating holy ash, Mr Jain gave me an additional two thousand rupees. Then I painted another portrait for one of Baba's devotees, Yeshwant Rao Jejurikar, the state minister for the Abolition of Blind and Bad Faith. And it produced ashes too! Now I have so many orders for Baba's portrait that I have to work day and night to keep up with them. But I'm making a fortune.'

'It's great that you have made it at last, Bhadra.'

'And what about you, Martand? Has kismet begun to shine on you?'

'Oh, I am doing little jobs. I am writing notes for the encyclopaedia of Indian literature for the Academy.'

'Oh, I am sure they pay a pittance.'

'They do.'

'Martand', Bhadra placed both his elbows upon the table. 'Why do you want to cling to Lit. Crit.? There is no money in literature, Martand. Nobody makes money by writing. Or by writing about writing. The papers don't even publish book reviews any more.'

'True.'

'If you want my advice, Martand, instead of trying to be a literary critic, be an art critic; write reviews of art exhibitions.'

'I don't know much about art.'

'Who does? You have the facility with language. That's sufficient.'

'You think so?'

'Yeah. Look, you write a book review; the writer gives you nothing, because he makes next to nothing on his book. You write an art review, and things are different. The artist hopes to sell. For a good review, you can leastways expect a lavish dinner from the artist. With drinks.'

'You know I don't drink.'

'Never mind. Once you make a name as an art expert, you can cultivate the famous artists. As you know, they make lakhs of rupees. Even crores, nowadays. Approach them for writing an appreciation for their catalogues. A few thousand rupees is nothing for them. Of course, you have to be all praise. Eruditely.'

'You mean, I can't milk literature, so I should try to milk art.'

'Precisely.'

Bhadra's hard-headed analysis of culture left Martand speechless. He looked away vacantly, where beyond the wire mesh, tender green plants made timid movements. Some snatches of lines floated vaguely through his mind: 'A frond of seaweed . . . a dragonfly already . . . these signify excessive suffering.'

'Think about it, Martand,' Bhadra said, collecting his packet of Marlboros and gold lighter. Martand stared at his receding figure, growing smaller. Already.

That same week Martand got a job tutoring a boy in Sanskrit. The boy's school exams were coming up in a month, and Martand's job was to prepare him for them. The boy happened to be particularly dull, or uninterested, and Martand had to take great pains with him. He couldn't afford to let the boy fail, for he was a distant cousin of his Ph.D adviser. For two or three hours every day Martand struggled to hammer some Sanskrit into the boy's head.

One day the boy said, 'I hate this. What's the point of breaking one's head over a language that's of no use?'

'Well, it is the language of the gods.'

The boy sniggered.

Once the boy's exams were taken, Martand returned to his research into the grammar of Panini. (Martand had majored in Sanskrit, because he had a fascination for Sanskrit poetry. But his Ph.D adviser, before recommending Martand for a scholarship, insisted that he do research into Panini.) Martand now had more leisure, too. He noticed that the air in the city seemed clouded, and at first he thought it was simply dust. But on closer inspection he discovered that the air was full of particles of ash. He remembered when he had lived behind the crematorium by the sea at Shivaji Park. A thin film of ash used to settle over everything in his room, and sometimes he could smell burned flesh. In Martand's mind that smell was inseparably associated with the ash that invaded his room, and now he automatically sniffed the air. There was a distinct odour all right, but it was not the familiar smell of burned flesh. It was a sweet smell, sickly sweet. And how could ashes rising from the crematorium travel so far? He lived miles away from it now. However, where there's smoke there's fire. He just didn't know from which fire-pit these ashes arose. They came from somewhere, and drifted quietly in the air.

Days passed, and the ash in the air increased. Gradually, everyone, including Martand, discovered the source. Bhadra had made and sold innumerable portraits of Baba, and holy ash was trickling from every one of them. The ashes emanating day and night from so many portraits had slowly begun to permeate the atmosphere of the city.

It seemed unlikely that Martand would see Bhadra again, for

Bhadra's life had changed. However, Martand still received news of him from friends like Nisshank. He learned that he now had a large new studio, and was practically turning out portraits of Baba on an assembly line. Others had tried to follow in his footsteps, but no one else's painting produced the holy ashes. Bhadra seemed to have acquired a divine monopoly, and he was making money like a Bollywood superstar.

The ash spread.

\*

*The beams of heaven have been eaten*
*By the termites of darkness;*
*Through their holes now falls the sawdust . . . .*

Martand put the book down. He had been reading Vidyakara's *Treasury of Verse*. The lines he read were by one Murari, from the ninth century. Who was this Murari? How come this poet wrote such striking lines about darkness, rather than about love and young women and enjoyment, as most of his fellow-poets had done? So many of his verses spoke of darkness, or shadows. 'You speak to me, Poet of Darkness,' Martand said to himself, and rose to go for a stroll.

Martand went out of the library, and walked aimlessy. The Chengis Kubla Gallery was closed. Art had bowed before almighty ash, and had withdrawn.

Day by day the city's appearance changed. Ash settled over the buildings, the cars, and the roads. It fell upon trees and statues and playgrounds. The ties beneath the railway tracks disappeared in ashes, though the tracks themselves still shone above it. Everywhere layers of ash grew imperceptibly. The whole city was turning grey.

Pedlars who displayed their wares by the streetside found their business threatened, for their wares quickly disappeared under ash, and they had a hard time dusting off the goods. On the other hand, shoeshine boys did a roaring business. Some people had their shoes shined every two or three hours. Later, when the streets were covered with two or three inches of ash, people no longer bothered. Office-workers who parked their cars at work in the morning had difficulty locating them in the evening; they were almost indistinguishable under their blankets of ash. Lovers parked and waited until they were hidden behind ash-covered windshields. But policemen made peepholes in the ash with stealthy fingers and still peered in. At a local soccer match between teams in red and green, ash quickly turned the sweat-soaked shirts grey, the ball was constantly passed to the wrong man, and the game was a shambles. Things were even worse at cricket matches. Sometimes clouds of ashes floated over the field, and the batsman and the bowler disappeared from view. The fielders watched for the ball to emerge suddenly from the grey clouds. One match had already ended and both teams had gone before one of the fielders finally realized the game was over.

The ashes rose higher on the railway line, and now you couldn't see the tracks at all. It was useless clearing them, for in a few hours the ash settled in again. Anyway it was impossible to clear miles and miles of tracks daily. So traffic on the railroad had virtually come to a standstill. Streets simply had to be kept free, and the municipality cleared the roads of layers of ash each morning. Snowploughs were brought in especially from America— by air, on a MOST-URGENT basis.

Almost every person in the city was intoxicated by the fragrance of the holy ash. No one complained about air pollution. Bhadra was still turning out portraits, and they were hanging in more and more houses. The ash increased at a faster and faster rate. Of course there were people who would have been happy to put an end to the whole affair. But how to do it? The production of ash could be stopped by smashing the framed pictures of Vishwaroop Baba, but no one dared to do so. One man who smashed a picture was said to have died the next day of heart failure.

Martand received a letter from Maitreyi. It read:

Life with the tribals in Jawhar is so wonderful! They are such innocent, honest and happy people. Martand, why don't you taste this life once? Why do you want to live in that ash-covered city, as if it were already a city of the dead? And why do you choose a loveless, unfree life? I

don't understand, Martand. With love, all the same,
Maitreyi.

Martand pored over the letter a couple of times, then put it
away. Then Bhadra came to see him in the university library one
day. Martand was surprised.

'How did a famous man like you find time to visit me?'
Martand asked.

Bhadra took Martand to the Khyber restaurant. Martand found
out that Bhadra had bought a large house on Malabar Hill near
Baba's palatial villa. Bhadra was closely associated with Baba
now, and gave twenty per cent of the money he made on paintings
to him.

'Martand, I have it made for life thanks to Baba, and now
you've got the same chance. Baba wants his biography written.
He asked me if I knew somebody who could do it. I thought of
you. You're a Sanskrit scholar, I thought, so you should be able
to write in a chaste, dignified style. I'll do the illustrations for the
book myself. Will you take the job?'

Martand didn't speak for a minute. Then he said yes.

'Good,' Bhadra said. 'I knew you wouldn't pass up an offer
like this. It's a lot better than wasting your life in a miserable
library. Can you come to my house at four on Friday? I'll take
you to Baba's place.'

On Friday afternoon Martand walked up the hill. There was
much less ash in the air up there. The breeze from the sea blew
the ash down towards the city. Here the air was fresh. From the
hill one had a blurred view of the enveloped city.

Sunderlal, Baba's personal secretary, asked Bhadra and
Martand to wait in the hall. Baba was talking to some important
visitor. There were many expensive and beautiful things to look
at in the hall, so Martand was not bored.

Then Baba entered. Martand looked for a halo around his
head, but didn't see one. Still Baba had a radiant face. Bhadra
introduced Martand to Baba.

In his younger years Baba had been an assistant in a butcher's
shop. One day, while chopping up a leg of mutton, a splinter of
bone flew up and struck him in the middle of the forehead, cutting

him deeply. At that moment Baba had a revelation, and his life was changed. He travelled about, sharing his enlightenment with the people, and his fame spread. He was at first known as Kasai Baba, but later changed his name to the present one.

Baba had received divine wisdom, but for the rest of his life an excruciating pain often recurred at the very spot where the bone had struck him. The only thing that relieved this pain was the yogic headstand. So Baba spent a good deal of his time upside down.

'You know, Martand,' Baba said, 'You'll have to use your imagination to write this thing. You won't find out many facts. You had better not look for them, in fact. Ask Sunderlal for the available information. He'll give you a list of my important devotees. You can talk to them, and use their comments in the book.' Baba paused, and looked at Martand with his piercing eyes. 'The biography must be well-written. Make good use of your Sanskrit. Look up the lives of the great seers of the past, and produce a nice mix of their life-stories. Write in Marathi or English, as you wish. Of course the book will be translated into about fifteen languages.'

Then Baba asked a servant to bring the drinks. 'Let's go and sit on the veranda at the back,' he said.

They sat on cane chairs on the veranda. The servant brought glasses of whiskey.

'What you see in front of you is the Tree of Death,' Bhadra informed Martand.

There in the courtyard, the Tree of Death was flourishing. Its trunk and branches consisted of gigantic spinal columns. The discs were huge at the trunk, and became smaller as they mounted. Large and small skulls hung upon the branches. When the tree swayed in the wind, the discs made a grating noise. The wind blew through the hollows of the skulls and made a sound like laughter.

Martand hadn't had a drink for a long time. All he could afford in his present condition was cheap 'country' liquor, which was absolutely revolting. So Martand had practically given up drinking. Now he greedily gulped down the expensive Scotch he had been offered.

Martand watched the Tree of Death, while Bhadra talked business with Baba. Then, from the right wing of the villa, a little girl came into the courtyard. She wore a dark red silk skirt. Frolicking, she approached the tree. She looked up at it. Then with her tiny hands she shook the trunk. The discs ground together. Skulls swayed to and fro, and a few teeth fell from them.

The girl walked round the tree, and picked up the teeth which had fallen to the ground. Then she shook the trunk again. A few more teeth fell. She gathered them as well. After a while the girl left, a handful of teeth cupped in her hands like an offering of flowers.

Putting teeth back into the skulls must be a major job for the gardener, Martand thought.

It was getting dark and, one by one, crows came and sat on the branches of the tree. They cawed. The pigeons, fat and white, which Baba had kept nestled in the ornate cornices of the villa, sat still and silent, brooding.

As he talked to Bhadra, Baba's face suddenly turned red and the veins on his forehead stood out. The pain had struck. Vishwaroop Baba rose and stood on his head upon the carpet. Bhadra and Martand sipped their whiskey silently.

Standing on his head, Baba saw the inverted Tree of Death. Its branches had become giant roots embedded in the grey thickness of the sky. The tree grew up into the earth. There must be an altogether different expanse of branches and foliage and fruit spreading beneath the ground. Observing the tree, Vishwaroop Baba rejoiced in the knowledge that he alone had perceived the true nature of the Tree of Death.

When the pain subsided, Baba was on his feet again. 'Carry on,' he said to Bhadra and Martand, and went inside.

With Baba out of sight, both Bhadra and Martand relaxed.

'Now I'm planning on slowing down with Baba's portraits,' Bhadra said. 'I haven't painted anything else for months. I want to take time off to work on other things. Like landscapes. The sea, or mountains.'

The sandwiches beside the whiskey glasses had attracted a few crows. They came down and hopped around on the railing, but didn't dare come any closer. Bhadra tried to shoo them away.

They flew off each time, but came again.

In Martand's catatonic soul, giant slumbering Komodo dragons were stirring, resurrected by the hallelujahs of alcoholic blood. Martand dipped a piece of bread in the whiskey, and threw it to the crows. One of them quickly swallowed it. Martand went on making little balls of bread, soaking them in whiskey, and throwing them to the crows. The number of crows grew rapidly. They raised a din on the veranda. Martand was playing—a gratuitous act—with the crow, the doer.

After a while the whiskey began to have an effect. The crows flew and hopped about groggily. Alighting on the tree they lost hold and fell, then flew about helter-skelter, perplexed and alarmed.

One of the sozzled crows, as it flew about, lost its balance and alighted upon Bhadra's head. It flew off again, but this time carrying in its claws the wig that Bhadra wore over his bald head.

'O my toupee!' Bhadra wailed, gesticulating after the fugitive crow with the wig entangled in his claws.

Bhadra suddenly turned to Martand, his eye blood-shot.

'Martand, you son of a dead egg!' Bhadra screamed. 'Because of your prank, I have lost my precious Parisian wig!'

Before Martand could respond, the wig-encumbered crow flew in the direction of the tree, wobbling even more than before. In a desperate attempt to gain altitude, he fell into a heap of ash, which the gardener had swept together in a corner of the courtyard. In greater panic, the crow tried frantically to get out. When it finally managed to rise, it had been transformed into a grey-white ghost. But it had got rid of Bhadra's wig. The immersion in the holy ash had terrified the crow so much that, beating its wings widly, it flew away from the tree and, alone, disappeared into the white darkness.

The spectacle of the crow had dispelled Bhadra's ire. He gave in to splits of laughter. Martand, too, laughed. He laughed so soul-wrenchingly that tears came into his eyes.

# V

# Visions of Nirvana

The fair tree of the Void abounds with flowers,
Acts of compassion of many kinds,
And fruit for others appearing spontaneously,
For this joy has no actual thought of another.

So the fair tree of the Void also lacks compassion,
Without shoots or flowers or foliage,
And whoever imagines them there, falls down,
For branches there are none.

—From Saraha, *Dohakosha* (Treasure of Songs,
9th Century AD)

# the phonemate

## Friday, 8 January

It's a nice room. (After all, this is an American hostel.) Well furnished. Closet with a sliding door. Large mirror, carpet. A large window, which is one thing I particularly like. There is a phone in a wooden box set in the wall, which I am to share with the chap in the next room. The box has shutters on both sides, and you can turn the phone both ways. This is an ingenious idea. They say there used to be a phone in every room. But, when the phone rates went up, they installed a phone between every two rooms to save money. . . . I don't yet know who lives in the next room. Doesn't have his name on the door. Haven't seen him in the corridor either. Hope he's a nice chap . . .

## Tuesday, 12 April

The phone rang around eleven in the morning. It was for Alfredo. Rather surprising. Alfredo seldom gets a call. Even this time it probably wasn't a friend. 'May I speak to Mr Navarro?' the guy asked. 'Just a second,' I said, and knocked on the other shutter. I knocked rather hard and the shutter opened. I peered through. Alfredo lay on the bed, eyes shut. 'Alfredo,' I said. 'Alfredo.' He didn't open his eyes. I knocked again, he didn't stir. I was perplexed. I didn't know what to do. Finally I said to the man on the phone. 'He's not in his room,' and hung up. I reached into the box and opened wide the other shutter. Stooping a bit, I looked into Alfredo's room. He lay still. A bedsheet up to his chin. Eyes shut, I knocked sharply on the side of the box again. Then I thought: maybe he's dead. What a thought, I shuddered. But the idea stuck in my mind. Couldn't think of any other explanation. I paced about the room. Looked through the box again. Paced again. Looked at the clock. Time for class. Picked up my overcoat and left.

Couldn't pay much attention in class. In the afternoon after classes I virtually ran back. I opened the door, flung my books on the bed and looked through the box, heart pounding. There he lay on the bed. Just like in the morning. Not a wrinkle of the sheet on his body seemed altered. I stared.

He's dead as a dead pigeon.

This awareness slowly filtered into my mind. My God! I thought. He's really dead. No shit.

I had broken out in a sweat. I sat down on the bed. It took me a long while to assimilate the fact that Alfredo was dead. Then I began to wonder what I should do. From the viewpoint of responsibility, I should have gone and told the dorm Resident Assistant, or notified the Manager's Office. But, for some reason, I couldn't do that. I just sat.

I was sure it was suicide. Alfredo hadn't seemed ill. Must have taken sleeping pills.

I never knew much about him. He was from Venezuela, but not at all like other Latin Americans. Latin Americans are so talkative. They always stick together. What a racket they make in the dining hall, sitting in a group. But I rarely saw Alfredo among them. He sat mostly by himself. In the last three months I spoke with him barely three or four times. He never seemed to have a friend—man or woman—in his room. He had a record-player. And he had a Spanish record which he often played. The same record again and again.

Now he was dead. Alfredo.

I remembered reading in the *Daily Student* over a month ago that in another dorm a student was found dead in his room. And once someone said that, last semester, a guy jumped from the fourteenth floor of this very building.

And now it was Alfredo, my own phonemate.

Couldn't eat much at dinner. Also forgot to watch the news on TV.

Sat down to study, but couldn't concentrate. I felt funny. Thought I might have a drink, but there was nothing in the room. The vodka had finished the day before yesterday.

It's cold tonight. So I don't feel like going outside to buy something. I think I'll go to bed early.

But what about tomorrow? Tomorrow at least I must go and inform the office.

*Wednesday, 13 April*

Couldn't fall asleep for a long time last night. Thinking about Alfredo. Myself lying on my bed in the dark, and Alfredo in his bed in the dark on the other side of the wall.

My first thought in the morning was of Alfredo. For a moment I thought he may have woken up, gotten out of bed. I jumped up and opened the phone-box. He was still there in the bed.

I know I can't go to the office and inform them. Now what? When will people realize that Alfredo is dead? He doesn't seem to have any close friends. So no one will notice that he is not around. Nobody will miss him in class either. So he's just going to be lying there! But the maid comes next week, on Monday, to clean the rooms. When she opens the door with her master key, she is going to find him dead. God, how shocked she will be! Must stay in the room to watch the fun. Once I have pulled the shutter closed from the inside, nobody can say that I knew Alfredo was dead.

At lunch Rakesh asked if I wanted to go to California with him this summer. I said I'd see. I'd rather go to the East Coast, I think. But there's plenty of time yet.

In the afternoon I went to see Martha Franzman, who sits in the lounge of the Main Library selling buttons with messages. She gave me a button with a message in Marathi. She copies the message, 'War is not healthy for children and other living things,' in various languages. She once showed me a long list of languages she had done. She didn't have Marathi, so I gave her a translation in Marathi. For doing the translation, she gave me a free button with the message. She has copied my handwriting so precisely. I wish I had written it out for her in a better hand. But it didn't occur to me that she would make an absolutely exact copy.

Now if I wear this button, who will be able to read it? That's great, wear a message in a language nobody around you can understand. BIG MESSAGE. Must get a button in Swahili or Korean from Martha to wear in Bombay.

Wasted a good deal of the afternoon reading the *New York Times* in the magazine section.

Saw Judy in the Library. I didn't say much. Just 'Hi, how are you,' and the like.

Dinner was worse than usual. Must think seriously about moving into an apartment this summer.

Just returned from eating at the 'Steak House'. Saw Shankaran sitting there with Cathy. He is married, but always running after girls. He'll have to stop fooling around when his wife comes here next semester. The other day I was talking to Cathy and I deliberately said to her that Shankaran is married. He might have found out about that. While leaving, he pretended not to see me.

Peered through the phone-box three or four times during the day. Now one last time.

*Thursday, 14 April*

At eleven the same man called again asking for Mr Navarro. I said I'd see, and knocked on the box. Told him N. wasn't in his room. He wanted to leave a message: 'Please come and see Mr Thompson in Bryan Hall 121.' I dutifully slipped the message under Alfredo's door.

Nice weather today. Over 70 degrees. It was strange to go out without a coat after three months. Even saw some flowers in one place. Yellowish white. Dogwood, Mark said.

Had a letter from Prakash. Wants to come here: asks what things are like. Am going to tell him that things aren't good, there might be a cession, so it's risky to come looking for a job.

Saw Bhatnagar on 10th Street. 'Feel free to come any time,' he said. This 'feel free' is a big joke. Married people seldom invite us dorm-dwellers to eat; if you see them they say 'feel free', but never invite you on a specific date. We cannot entertain them, but shouldn't they care about us?

I was reading this afternoon, and it occurred to me that there are around eleven hundred people in this building in their rooms, and in only one room is there a dead man. And I alone know which room he's in.

Went to Jeff's party in the evening. Around midnight the girls left, and we went on drinking. I had seven cans of beer—crossed the six-can limit. Came back and, instead of going to bed, sat in the chair listening to the *Pakeezah* songs on tape. It was around two-thirty. I played the tape pretty loudly. Didn't give a damn if Gary in the next room got annoyed. I was really high. The music was melting in my head. Then I got up and opened the phone-box. I looked through. In the dark I could vaguely make out Alfredo's face. He was beginning to smell. It was a heady smell. I watched him for a long time, sniffing at him from this distance. I felt so light in the head. I was beginning to see double because of all the drink. I saw two images of Alfredo, mingled with each other. Two faces. When the tape ran out, I shut the phone-box. Everything in the room was struggling to double itself. Two tape recorders, two lamps, two ashtrays. As if all things were unable to bear being alone any longer, and were looking for another like themselves. I looked in the mirror. I could see two images of myself. I raised my arms. Four of them. Like some god. I laughed.

I lay in bed and in a few minutes I felt I was going to vomit. Got out of the bed in a hurry and looked around for a glass or something, when I threw up right on the carpet. There was something red in it, which frightened me for a moment. Then I realized it was the tomato paste in the pizza I had eaten. Went down the hall to the toilet and washed my mouth and went to bed.

*(Wrote this last part on the 15th.)*

*Friday, 15 April*

Got up at eleven. A mess on the carpet. It had begun to stink. Is

Alfredo's corpse going to stink like this, I wondered as I took in the rich, rank odour. The odour of contrition.

This was a pain in the ass. Once in January I had vomited on the carpet. I had a hard time cleaning it up then. So I had decided to be careful and vomit in a glass if it came to that. Still, this happened last night.

My head was in a bad shape. Took some Alka Seltzer. Missed breakfast, of course. Then I started cleaning up. Once the carpet absorbs dirt, you can't get it out easily. Got some water in a bowl and started scrubbing with balls of newspaper. Cleaned it up as well as I could.

Missed Flanigan's class.

Saw Mike in the elevator; his hand was in a cast. Said he broke it playing volleyball.

Like a devout man saying his prayers at regular intervals through the day. Or did I expect Alfredo to ascend bodily to heaven?

Had a date with Karen in the evening. Went to 'The Magic Flute'. This was my fourth date with her. Thought she would sleep with me this time. Last time she allowed some petting, but wouldn't go all the way. This time she came to my room.

At one o'clock I said goodbye to Karen at the elevator. Came back, opened the phone-box and smiled at Alfredo. That was crazy.

*Saturday, 16 April*

Had a long-distance call from Dilip in Iowa. Said he was going to Chicago in May and would like to come down here. I said fine.

Read a sign on the notice board: Portable Olympia for sale. Must go and have a look.

Saw Rakesh. He said three guys' rooms were burglarized on his floor last night, while they were asleep. It's stupid to go to bed without locking your room.

Got out of the elevator on the seventh floor by mistake and went to the room exactly below mine. Almost put the key in the door before I realized that I was at the wrong room on the wrong floor.

Went to the College Mall in the afternoon. There was a sale going on. Bought a pair of blue jeans. In this country if you want to buy something, you have to wait for a sale. You have to always remember that you are a consumer nothing more.

Called Ashok on the phone. He's leaving for home next month. Must throw a party for him. Helped me a great deal when I first came here.

There was news of drought in India on TV.

For almost a week now, I have been thinking about that corpse in the room. Walking down the street, or talking to someone, the image of that body floats to the mind's surface. As one might do a wash for a water colour, these days have acquired the colour of the corpse. I am beginning to feel as if that body has been in that room for years and that it is going to remain there years longer. That's going too far. Yet there is a corpse in the other room, like a secret flower.

*Sunday, 17 April*

Stayed in my room all day. Went down to eat and so on. That's all. Have been trying for the whole day to write a poem. Wrote about a dozen lines. No good.

Tomorrow the maid comes.

# letters from nikhil

At a quarter-past ten I stand at the window, waiting for the mailman. The mailman comes around half-past ten. He doesn't always have a letter for me. And sometimes, even if I have a letter, I am disappointed. A doctor lived in this room before I moved here. It's three years since he left. Yet a number of pharmaceutical companies still send medical literature in his name. At least twice a week this kind of mail comes. I run to the door and grab the envelope, and all that it contains is recommendations for some unheard-of or unpronounceable medical products: 'TANDERIL, Rapidly Reduces Inflammation Conditions', 'BUTAZOLIDIN, Dramatic Response in Acute Rheumatic Conditions', 'EURAX-HYDROCORTISONE, the Simple Solution to a Complex Dermatological Problem', 'KENAMINA for Better Control of Allergies', etc. This kind of thing frustrates me. But I cannot work up enough enthusiasm to write to all these companies and tell them that the doctor does not live here any more. So I still receive his mail.

Of course there are times when I get letters I really look forward to. On rare occasions, there is a quite unexpected one. A few months ago I had such a letter. It read:

16 October

Dear Brahmadatta,

I know you will be surprised to see this letter. Probably you don't remember me at all. Whether you do or not, I had to write to you. This is about the report I am putting together.

The General Manager wants the report no later than 15 December. Which leaves me just two months to work at it. Also, I must set aside ten days or so for typing the report. I cannot ask anyone else to type it, obviously, and I can only type with two fingers. So it's going to take a good deal of my time.

Come to think of it, this isn't my first report. I have prepared reports in the past. But I have never done a report like this. Everything hinges upon this report. I'm not sure, of course, that the General Manager will give me a higher position if he is happy with the report. Also, who can be certain that the GM will like the report? Sometimes one finds him very pleased with a poor, quickly written thing that may be full of contradictions. One can't blame him, though. For he alone knows the specific purpose that a report is meant to serve. We might find him inconsistent, because we don't know enough.

Yet I must prepare this report with care. Two or three other persons have earlier submitted reports on this very problem. (Naturally, I have not been able to see those.) If there is some discrepancy between our reports, the GM is bound to make further investigations. Also, there is a rumour that one or two others are going to write reports on the same problems as mine. Inevitably mine will be compared with theirs.

What I'm particularly unhappy about is that, once the report is finished, no trace of it will be left in my possession. We do not have permission to keep a copy of a report. We have to send away even the preliminary notes, the early drafts. One produces a report with so much labour, so much care, and one can't even keep a memento.

That is why I write to you. This is a foolhardy notion, maybe. Some people might think it sheer lunacy. I cannot say what I shall have to face if my plans go wrong. I'm prepared for anything. The idea is, I shall secretly send a copy of the report to you. The company has data on all my relatives and friends. So it would be unwise to send it to any of them. If I leave it with you, there is much less risk. So will you do this much for an old schoolmate?

I do not write my address. I don't want the company to get wind of this. Also, I don't want the Punjwani Syndicate to get hold of my address. (They probably have it already, though.) The Punjwani Syndicate is after some of our company's industrial secrets. They try to keep track of all our correspondence. So I shall write to you in a few days and let you know at what address you could write to me. That's all for the moment.

Yours,
Nikhil Dev.

Dev. At first the name mystified me. But the words 'an old schoolmate' rang a bell. Nikhil Dev was my classmate for two years in elementary school at Jamshedpur. I wasn't very close to him really. I have now forgotten even my close friends of those days so how could I instantly remember Nikhil? Straining my memory, I faintly recalled a thin boy wearing glasses. He was the only boy in the class with glasses. That's what fixed him in my memory.

It was a typewritten letter. Even the signature was typed. I tried to read the postmark, but it was very faint. So I couldn't figure out where the letter was mailed.

What do you do if you receive such a letter? I read it three or four times and then put it away in the desk drawer.

About two weeks later, I had another letter. It read:

28 October

Dear Brahma,

These four days, I've been looking for a chance to write to you. This is the moment. I must finish in thirty-five minutes.

Probably I wrote to you about a report some days ago.

Actually, I'm not writing a report of any kind.

This doesn't mean, though, that what I wrote to you was untrue.

Perhaps I also mentioned that I've been travelling from place to place. Don't be surprised if I tell you that I've spent the past three months in this room. Sometimes, when you are on the move night and day, you begin to think you are at one spot. Not that it makes much of a difference.

So much for misinformation (which is what usually passes for information in this age of ignorance).

What I'm busy writing is a letter demanding clarification. It's time I asked for clarification on some vital matters. I have been in service these many years, and as yet I have no idea of service conditions.

I intend to raise the following points:

1. Please clarify which officials rank above me and which below me. I suspect that some officials who give me orders rank below me. I ignore their orders. Sometimes officials to whom I give orders ignore them. Probably they rank above me. Yet it is not impossible that some whose orders I disregard actually rank above me. And that some who disregard my orders actually rank below me. So who should obey whose orders?
2. Another point in the context of the above: are there any officials with the same rank as mine? If so, how many? How should one treat them? What behaviour should be expected of them?
3. One of the circulars we have received states that one's entire salary will be paid at the time of one's retirement. What if someone resigns prematurely? Does he get anything? How much?
4. Is there any objection to having my desk face south?
5. May one use red ink?
6. Must one scrutinize the watermark on every piece of paper?
7. How long must one make applicants wait in the line?

I'm sure there are a few more questions stirring in my mind. They haven't yet taken shape, so I cannot put them down here. But I should be glad to know your opinion on the points listed above.

Yet another matter of importance. I've been planning to

demand a clarification, and yet I have not the slightest idea as to the best season for this enterprise. To my mind, the monsoon is the best. Buildings are gray and wet, umbrellas float in the street. And a crow at your window.

But some say winter is the best, really.

What is worse, I'm not sure what season it is at present. I wrote 28 October above, but that doesn't mean much. When I look out of my little window, the sky is mostly cloudless. One cannot say it's very warm these days. At the same time, it's not particularly cold either. Is this summer then? The beginning of summer? Or the end? Three days ago a cold wind blew in the evening. Yes, I even asked for a sweater. I felt better when I put it on. But I woke up in the night, perspiring heavily. It was very warm. I took off the sweater and threw it away. I didn't need it again. Yet, who could swear that this isn't winter? Often, the winter isn't cold at all.

If this is winter without cold, could it not be the monsoon? A monsoon without rains?

Not quite without rains, maybe. Yesterday, I looked out of the window early in the morning, and noted that the square was thoroughly wet. I looked at the walls; but walls absorb water quickly, so I couldn't tell. Perhaps they washed the square early in the day. But I remember they have virtually given up washing it these days. True, they may have begun washing it again. In the past they washed it every other day. So if tomorrow I find the square wet, it must mean they have begun washing it again. It's possible, though, that they are going to wash it just once in a while. So I really can't be sure if it rained yesterday or if they washed the square.

No more shall grief of mine the season wrong.

So it'll be nice if you can help me out of these puzzlements. You live in Bombay, so you must know a great deal about such things. By the time I hear from you, the letter I'm planning to write will have taken a more definite shape in my mind.

Needless to say, I cannot write my address this time

either. In my last letter, I explained why. One shouldn't need to offer fresh excuses every time.

So I shall let you know in a few days how you may get in touch with me. The outlook is good.

The season wrong.

The letter ended at this point, as if it were left unfinished. There was no signature. It was written on blue notepaper, in a thick, slanting hand. I can't be sure, but I had the feeling that the writer was attempting to write in an uncharacteristic hand deliberately.

I could read the postmark on this letter. The town's name appeared to be the same as on the last one.

This letter, too, I read three or four times, then put it away.

In a few days I received another letter:

Dear Brahma,

I'm preparing to resign. I'm through.

The thing that I have been trying to put together in my mind since the day I got this job was nothing else—I now know—but this letter of resignation.

Could I come over to live with you after I resign? I think we'll get along very well.

Think it over.

Will write again.

The letter was not dated. It was in a different hand this time: rounded letters, great gaps between words, so that each word seemed an island.

I pondered over the letter. I was even annoyed. What gave him the right to come and live with me? This was unfair, to say the least. Do you go and live with someone just because you've got hold of his address? What does he know of me? Does he know if I have a job? If I'm married or not? How many kids I have? How many daughters? Their age? What my house is like? How many rooms it has? If my father is alive? My mother? What my financial situation is?

Letters are all right. But a man in the flesh!

I checked myself. What if he really comes and lives with me,

I asked myself. I have lived by myself in this room for the past three years. Nobody ever slept in this room, besides me. I go to bed stark naked. How could that be possible if he came to live here? I couldn't get to sleep with anything on my body. Which means staying awake night after night.

I kept worrying. Another letter arrived within two days.

Dear Brahma,

When I got this job, I had some idea that it was silly to even think of resignation. Then why did I keep thinking of resignation? To keep up my spirits, perhaps. But was I really thinking ahead to a letter of resignation? What did I want? What were those words doing in my head?

By now I'm more or less convinced that what I meant to write was quite different. In truth, I was striving to give shape to a letter of accusation that would put everything in the right perspective.

One has to be careful in such matters. You have to weigh every word. You have to check your facts over and over. I believe I now have the maturity to carry out such a task. That is why I'm determined to see it through.

The past few months, I've been closely studying the affairs of the Company, and especially the GM's conduct. Recently, the Punjwani Syndicate got hold of some of our industrial secrets. They have even begun production. Every day I'm more and more convinced that the man behind this is no one else but the GM himself. There are other things, too, that I've noted.

So I'm planning to send a long letter, fully documented, straight to the board of directors.

Here, I need your cooperation. It's not safe for me to send this letter. So I'll mail it to you. You have to type it out, mail it, and burn the original.

There were other things I wanted to write about. But there is little time left.

Yours,
Satchidanand.

The letter was typed, except the signature.

It's strange, but now I felt sad that he wouldn't come and live with me! I would have gone to the railroad station to receive him. I would have carried his suitcase. I would have hung his jacket on the only clothes-hanger in my room. If he hadn't remembered to bring a toothbrush, I would have rushed downstairs and bought him one. I would have taken him to the movies. I was so eager to ask him questions, to exchange views with him!

For two-and-a-half months; I had no letter from him. I decided I had better forget him. Then, one day, there was a letter:

2 February 1967

Dear Brahmadatta,

Everything is beginning to fall into place. I wonder how I ever thought of writing a letter of accusation. An accusation!

I sat down to write what I thought were accusations, and soon realized that I was writing to beg forgiveness.

Yes, I begged for forgiveness.

For looking up while I sharpened a pencil, for looking back at the third bend, for reading *The Lotus of the True Law* before washing my mouth in the morning, for keeping an apple on the window-sill to rot, for smelling the fresh newspaper, for failing to touch the lamp post, for drinking out of a green glass, for speaking the name of Devidas Bakshi, for hiding the nail, for wishing to write nursery rhymes, for erasing the written word, for blowing upon the mirror.

For writing letters to you.

This is the last.

On my part, I can say that I never wrote to you without cause. I'm writing this one to say: burn all my letters, counting this one. I have gone through so much.

[signed]

The letter was signed in English, but I couldn't read the signature. The first letter of the first name was either C or G.

I must really forget about him now, I said to myself. I could not bring myself to tear up the letters. I put them away at the bottom of the desk drawer.

Then I began to work at making paper bags and forgot all about the letters. After a month, I received a letter:

Brahma,
    I began to write. I didn't seem to get anywhere, so I tore up the sheets. I sat down again. Tore up the sheets again. Now I'm getting down to it once more, after racking my head for days. This time I'm more sure of myself. I want to write about myself. All about myself. Perhaps for myself alone.

It's plain what lies ahead for me. I'm not in the least concerned though. Only the other day, I learned that our board of directors is largely made up of men from the Punjwani Syndicate. It does not matter to me anymore. I want to ask a last request of you. This piece I'm writing about myself, I do not want it to fall in the hands of our company / the Punjwani Syndicate. Can you come to this place and take it away? I cannot send it by mail. Come to the address below after three days. I will have finished by then.

The address is: 'Saphalya'
Dr Ambedkar Road
Old Andhavana
Sahibganj, BIHAR

In my room you will find a notebook in the desk drawer, Nehru's picture on the cover. The sheets are not ruled. This is what you are to take away.

I write this, because I probably won't be here when you arrive.

The letter was undated, unsigned. It was written on a sheet torn from a notebook. Very cluttered writing. You felt that each letter of each word was written slowly, with great difficulty.

I was in a fix. I didn't know what I should do. Should I go to Sahibganj? On the one hand, I was eager to go. On the other, I wondered if it wouldn't be just foolish. Could I really trust his letter? It might mean only a long, fruitless journey. I wasn't in a position to squander money on a wild goose chase. True, I had made some money making paper bags.

For two days I vacillated. I lost sleep. On the morning of the third day I got up, washed, stuffed a few things in a suitcase, and went to the railroad station.

I got off at Sahibganj station and entered the town. It seemed a sordid town. The roads were tarred, but very narrow, and full of dust. I felt cramped from the day's travelling. My eyes were heavy. It was almost evening, but the air was still warm and dry.

It took some time to get to Ambedkar Road. Nobody would give me proper directions. The people were slow and careless. They squatted idly on the steps of houses, or on string beds in courtyards.

Old Andhavana, I was told, was the oldest part of the town. A wooded, desolate outlying area which, apparently, inherited its name from the time of the Buddha. 'Andhavana', I believe, means 'The Forest of the Blind'. Now the town had enveloped it, under the pressure of 'development'.

I reached Ambedkar Road just as daylight was disappearing over the house-tops. There was a restaurant at the corner of the street. A little further up, a grocery store. On the left, a strip of smoke swayed slowly in the sky. I made my way through boys gathered around a dead crow in the street. On the right, I saw a sign at a gate: SAPHALYA. It was a one-storey house that must be quite old, but was recently painted. I entered the gate.

I waited on the porch for a few seconds. It seemed quiet inside. Then an old man came out.

'Is there someone called Dev here?'

'Who are you?'

'A friend. Brahmadatta.'

The old man shook his head. He motioned me to wait, and went inside. He came out with a bunch of keys, and then motioned me to follow him upstairs on the back stairway.

The old man's voice filtered through the creaking of the wooden stairs: 'The hospital people took away the body in the morning. He had asked that the body be given away to the hospital.'

The old man opened the door of the room. I stepped inside. I looked around. A bed. A desk. Books. A lamp on the desk. An ashtray. Two packets of cigarettes. Shirts and trousers hanging on two pegs on the wall. A large trunk in a corner.

I was amused to find myself a little disappointed at this. As if I had expected to see something weird—some tantrik thing, or something Poesque—in this place.

The old man stood beside me in silence. I stepped forward. I pulled out the desk drawer. Papers, notebooks, pens and pencils, some small change. I looked over the notebooks and took out the one with Nehru's picture on it. I put it in my suitcase. I locked the suitcase. I looked at the old man. He stepped aside to make way for me. I stepped out of the room. I walked down the stairs as the old man locked the room.

I didn't take out the notebook on the journey. I opened it only when I got home.

The notebook was all blank. On the last page was written, in a clumsy hand: 'NIKHIL'.

I went through the notebook again, turning each page. Was this the notebook he had mentioned? There was Nehru's picture on the cover. But had someone been inside the room before me, and had he—or they—taken the right notebook away? Could I trust the old man? I had a feeling that someone had rummaged in the drawer before me. Or at least I felt now that I had felt so then. I could have been mistaken. Or perhaps somebody did search through the drawer, perhaps the old man did, for money.

I turned again to the last page of the notebook. Was this his own hand? I couldn't be sure of even that! His first letter had a typed signature. Afterwards I had letters under different names in different hands. Could I swear that all these letters were written by him, were written by one man? If I had shown all the letters to someone and if he had said, 'You've written all these yourself,' how could I prove it wasn't true? It was perfectly possible for someone to say that those letters had materialized *ex nikhilo*, so to speak.

The notebook is still with me. Constant thumbing has made its pages dog-eared.

# the life and death of
# manu

*Who speaks, who listens, and what is confided?*
*Like the dust in a dusty tunnel,*
*That which arises in the heart goes to rest in the heart.*
—Saraha, *Dohakosha*
('Treasury of Songs', 9th Century)

## 1

It was a big room with a high ceiling, in the centre of which an electric bulb burned day and night. An electric clock hung upon one wall, opposite a huge portrait of Queen Victoria. A telephone stood on a large desk beneath the picture. There was a chair beside the desk, and Manu had arranged several stacks of books next to the chair, each stack a little shorter than the next, making a sort of a staircase. Walking up these stairs of stacked books, Manu used to reach the seat of the chair. Then he climbed up one of the rails on the back of the chair like a monkey and alighted upon the wide plateau of the desktop. The receiver lay beside the stand, with a fat telephone directory on the other side. Sandwiched between the two, the receiver rested on its back. Manu had moved a small diary near the directory, by means of which he climbed to the top of the directory. Then, walking across the directory, he hopped onto the grip of the receiver.

Manu ought to have walked to the mouthpiece first and said hello. But he walked to the other end instead and listened. He had learned that the Confabulator at the other end was often already on the line. If Manu's hello interrupted his monologue, the man used to be annoyed. That's why Manu always went to the earpiece first and made sure that the man was not already there. Then he walked along the handle of the telephone towards the mouthpiece, and shouted, 'Hello, hello.' Then he went back to the earpiece and listened. He heard the man say, 'Hello, good morning.' Then Manu walked back to the mouthpiece and said, 'Good morning, Father.' Sometimes Manu's first hello elicited no reply from the other end of the line. Then he waited for a few minutes, and said hello again. He went back and listened, his ear close to the rim of the earpiece. When he had gone through this a few times, he usually heard a voice from the other end. But there were times when he had to keep trying doggedly.

Did it ever occur to Manu that however much he shouted there might be no answer from the other end? No, such a thought never occurred to him. In some vague way, Manu thought of his hellos as exerting a kind of pressure; when enough pressure had built up at the other end, there would be a voice in response. At times you needed a greater pressure, that's all. But there always had to be an answer, so long as you could say hello; Manu remembered one day when he had gone on saying hello for hours; at four in the afternoon he had at last heard a reply from the other end. That night he was dog-tired from walking back and forth on the telephone all day. To make matters worse, walking on the slippery, narrow handle of the telephone wasn't easy. Once, carried away by the conversation, and practically running along the handle, Manu slipped and fell on to the desktop. He was lucky to get away with minor bruises. Since then Manu was careful to walk cautiously upon the telephone handle.

Such hazards arose from the fact that the receiver lay on its back. It would have been a different story if it were lying on its side, for Manu could then have walked on the desktop between the mouthpiece and the earpiece, and would have been spared the strain of walking on the telephone handle. Manu wondered if he could turn the telephone on its side, but, in spite of all his efforts, he wasn't able to move either the stand or the telephone book. He had to accept things as they were. It wasn't so bad, after all: what if the receiver had been lying face down?

It usually took Manu a few seconds to walk from the mouthpiece to the earpiece. Manu had pointed this out to the Confabulator, who therefore normally waited for a few seconds after Manu had finished talking before replying. But the Confabulator was often carried away by the subject of conversation, and began to speak the moment Manu fell silent. Naturally, Manu missed a few of his words, and sometimes he was plagued by the feeling that he had missed something important. Yet Manu never dared to ask the Confabulator to repeat himself. Only once did he make such a suggestion in an oblique manner; his heart was beating loudly as he went over to the earpiece to listen to the reply. There was complete silence for four minutes, then the Confabulator began to speak about something entirely different.

Sometimes, as the Confabulator spoke, Manu could hear songs from Hindi films in the background. The sound was rough and screechy, like records played on a juke box. Manu wondered if the Confabulator was talking from an Irani restaurant. It was difficult to hear him against the background of noisy music, but that was nothing compared to what Manu had endured some months ago. For almost an entire year, the roar of huge machines came over the phone, and Manu could scarcely hear anything said to him. That was a time of great mental anguish for Manu. Then, about two months after the roar of the machines had ceased, a curious thing happened. The Confabulator complained that he heard the clatter of a typewriter from Manu's side, and demanded that the typist be asked to move further away. Manu was naturally surprised, and hastened to assure him that there was no typist anywhere around. The Confabulator didn't bring up the matter again, but Manu kept puzzling over it. Had the man made a deliberately false accusation with some unknown ulterior motive? Or did he actually think he heard the sound of a typewriter? Manu was fascinated by the idea that one could have acoustical hallucinations. If he thinks he hears a typewriter, Manu thought, perhaps he is also only thinking he's listening to me? Perhaps he thinks he is manning a helpline? They were wild ideas. What was certain is that there he was, Manu, talking over the phone.

By and large Manu's conversation with the Confabulator was entertaining. No doubt there were periods of boredom, especially when the man took to philosophizing. At such times he talked for hours. On one occasion the Confabulator expatiated upon the prospect of being without ears, without voice, without breath, without measure. At another time he assailed the belief that the Self is everything. The sage Yajnavalkya maintained this belief, just as 'of all pleasures the uniting point is the phallus, and of all evacuations the uniting point is the anus'. The Confabulator conceded the point regarding the phallus, but claimed that the argument for the anus was nonsense. What of urine, and spittle, and snot, he asked, and of the orifices from which they emerged? They had their character and mystery, and it was unjust to say that they were no different from faeces. How could you reduce everything to an undifferentiated mass of shit? At this point the Confabulator paused dramatically, as if challenging Manu to contradict him. Manu modestly commented that he was not, unfortunately, qualified to say anything on the point regarding the phallus, not having the relevant experience, but that he was inclined to agree with the man's views on the second point. It was a fine and compelling argument, he added.

The man wasn't without humour though. He knew plenty of jokes. Whenever he told one of his jokes, Manu walked to the mouthpiece and laughed into it loudly, but always with a rather uncomfortable feeling. It's all right to laugh the moment a joke explodes in your mind, but to walk, cautiously, along the handle of the phone and then burst into laughter didn't seem quite sincere. Yet Manu tried to make his laughter sound as hearty as possible. In the flow of conversation Manu sometimes attempted to ask searching questions, but always received cleverly evasive answers. Yet the man was not averse to speaking about himself. On many occasions he talked about his life, his childhood, and his plans for the future. Manu listened, deeply engrossed, but with a vague feeling of unreality. On the other hand, Manu seldom got away without giving complete replies to the questions put to him. The Confabulator had a way of forcing out of him, gently but firmly, what he wanted. The Inquisitor, the Confessor, the Hierophant, the man was like a many-headed god or demon. In the infinite well of nothingness, you could still hear him as the primal voice, the sacred Speech-Bearer.

Each morning at half-past ten, Manu would climb up the staircase of books to the seat of the chair, and then to the desk-top. He carried a small lunch box and a container of water. He did this to avoid climbing up and down more than once in a day. There used to be a break in the conversation from one to two in the afternoon, and then Manu ate his lunch. The conversation ended for the day around five-thirty in the evening, and Manu descended from the desk. One day a question occurred to Manu: Does the conversation really end at five-thirty? Does it really begin at a half-past ten in the morning? What basis was there for assuming the line was silent when Manu was not on the phone? Perhaps the line was operational, when Manu was not on the phone. This idea destroyed Manu's peace of mind. One night he rose from the bed and, with sleepy eyes, climbed up on the desktop. He applied his ear to the earpieces, and listened for some minutes. There was no sound on the phone. Then he went to the mouthpiece to say hello, returned to the earpiece and listened. After another five minutes he repeated his actions. Then he said to himself, 'This is silly, I've got to forget the whole thing.' He went back to bed.

He thought that was the end of it, but it wasn't. The idea stuck in his mind. Later, he went through the same experiment a number of times. And then one day it happened: he heard a voice on the phone; it was at half-past seven in the evening and there was a voice on the phone. He listened. The man was speaking about Alexander's campaign in India. After a while the man asked a question, as though he were sure Manu would be listening at his end. Manu was so confused that he didn't even feel surprised. He hastened towards the mouthpiece and did his best to answer the question. When he went back to the earpiece, the man had nonchalantly continued his discourse, as though it was perfectly normal for Manu to be on the phone at this hour. That night they conversed for a long while. At a quarter-past ten the man uttered some incoherent sentences and fell silent. Manu remained at the earpiece for a few minutes, and then climbed down.

This happened three or four times during the next few days. One day the caller asked Manu to be on the phone at seven in the morning; he continued to make such requests frequently. Sometimes he demanded Manu's presence in the middle of the night, or in the small hours of the morning. Manu became aware that these frequent appointments at odd hours put him under a great deal of mental and physical strain. Yet he didn't think of complaining. For one thing, it was the caller who did most of the talking now. Manu didn't have to say much. He used to rest his chin on the rim of the earpiece and listen languidly. A time came when Manu was on the phone practically day and night. With weary limbs and swollen eyes, he made the rounds between the mouthpiece and the earpiece. Only with reluctance did the caller allow him a few hours for food and rest. Manu did not know that this is what happened at all the call-centres all over the world.

### 3

And one day, while leaning over the rim of the mouthpiece to answer a question, Manu lost his balance and fell inside. The plastic covering of the mouthpiece was broken, and Manu went straight down, like Alice in the rabbit-hole. He found himself in darkness, and at first didn't even understand what had happened. He lay stunned, staring at the circle of light above his head. After a moment of struggle he realized that he couldn't get out of the hole on his own. For an instant he was paralysed with fear, but then he remembered that, by great good fortune, he had fallen into the mouthpiece and not the earpiece. He spoke up and gave an account of the incident, demanding to be rescued immediately. Then he lay back quietly, sure that someone would turn up in an hour or two. Two or three hours passed. Manu repeated his plea again, and waited. No one arrived. Manu was annoyed at first, then he became angry, and finally terrified. He literally howled into the phone, with a voice as screechy as a crow's. He lay inside the hole in a stupor.

After a long interval Manu regained consciousness, and spoke into the phone with difficulty. He did so twice more at intervals. Then he was unable to speak any longer. It took him six more days to die, though.

Two men arrived the day after Manu died. They wore heavy woollen overcoats, with belts tightly strapped. It was rather odd, to say the least, to go about in such dress in a tropical country. It was as though the men wanted to preserve in their heart the great and bitter cold of the country from which they had come.

They climbed the stairs. One of the men opened the door and stood by, while the other entered the room and went towards the phone. He peered into the mouthpiece. Then, very gently, he lifted Manu's body out and held it in his palm, he stared at it for a few seconds, then dropped it inside the left pocket of his overcoat and buttoned the pocket. He took out a small notebook from his right-hand pocket, looked at the dial of the phone, and jotted down the phone number. Then he lifted the receiver and replaced it on the phone. He turned to the door.

The phone rang. The man stopped and turned back. He picked up the receiver, listened, and nodded. Then, instead of hanging up, he placed the receiver on its back between the stand and the phone book, as it had been. He went out, and the other man shut the door behind them. Their boots clattered on the staircase, and then the sound of the departing van dissolved into silence.

# the departure

## 1

A fuse was burning before my eyes. Emitting small sparks, it burned from right to left. It wasn't really a dream; it was one of those images that float in your mind's eye just before you wake up. I immediately realized that it was a scene from a movie I had seen the day before. In the movie it had been a burning dynamite fuse that a few moments later blew up a huge dam.

The fuse continued to burn before my closed eyes. I wondered when it would reach the sticks of dynamite. Although the fuse burned on and on, the burning point itself always remained in the centre of my field of vision. Which meant that the image was being tracked as in a movie, from right to left. In the cinema, when you watch a close-up of a burning fuse, you automatically tense up a bit, knowing that in a few moments there's going to be a big explosion on the screen. But the fuse that now burned before my eyes seemed to be endless. Was it going to burn on for miles and miles like that? It held me spellbound. Leaving a black thread behind, the point of fire was speeding ahead. Was it all one fire—that which had burned out, and that which was burning on? Or was it a series of separate, temporary fires? The whole of the fuse wasn't burning all at once; at a given moment, it burned only at a particular point. On the other hand, the burning of the fuse at a particular point was part of a general burning, and it didn't seem right to regard it as a separate fire. I puzzled over the matter. Then I thought to myself, all one can say at any particular time is that the fire has, at this moment, burned up to this point. While

I was saying this to myself, the fire had of course burned onwards.

After a while, the strain of concentrating upon the burning point became intolerable, and I opened my eyes. Even then, the fuse continued to burn before me for a few seconds. Without moving, I remained in bed staring at the ceiling. Then I got up, tossed the shirt and trousers that I had thrown over the back of the chair onto the bed, and sat on the chair. After resting in the chair for a few moments, I went to the toilet. Coming back, I threw the shirt and trousers lying on the bed over the back of the chair, and leaned back in the bed. That's the way it is with my shirt and trousers—from the bed to the chair, and from the chair to the bed. Sure, there's a closet in my room, and there are clothes-hangers in there. But I don't have the necessary enthusiasm to put my clothes on the hangers, and to hang them in the closet. Anyway, you always put the clothes that you take off on again, the next day if not on the same day. So what's the point in bothering to hang them up in the interval? Maybe clothes hate to be cooped up in a dark closet; perhaps they like it better out in the open. It's nice for the wearer, too. Lying in bed you can watch your shirt and trousers suspended over the back of the chair, or, sitting in the chair, you can watch the clothes lying on the bed. Why condemn them to hang in a dark closet like lonely ghosts?

As I lay back in the bed, I looked around my room. I had practically completed packing my things. I was going to leave most of them with my landlord Maganmal. It was from him that I had borrowed the cardboard boxes for packing. I still hadn't put anything much in the suitcase that I was going to carry. For one thing, I didn't intend to take a lot of things along. And then, one can pack a suitcase in a matter of minutes. Besides, you can't pack things like your toothbrush on the day of your departure. If you're starting very early in the morning, you have to brush your teeth quickly and stuff the toothbrush into the suitcase in a hurry. Even if you dried the toothbrush carefully on a towel—in the rush of departing you don't usually have time for that, anyway— the bristles still remain damp at the roots.

This business of packing had made my room look bare, but it had also resulted in a large pile of things rising upon my desk. I had come across so many things that didn't seem worth taking along with me, but which, on the other hand, I didn't feel like tossing into the boxes I was going to leave with Maganmal. I had been throwing such things onto the desk, as a result of which the desk now looked awfully cluttered. If I didn't want to leave these things with Maganmal, what was I going to do with them? That was a problem. I rose from the bed, walked over to the desk, and surveyed the heap. My bank book, a few certificates, the passport that I had taken out years ago when I was planning to go to America. As a matter of fact, the passport had expired long ago. I opened it now, and scrutinized my photo inside, noting how different I looked then. I read the information about myself, then read the long list of countries one was permitted to visit that had been stamped inside. It was gratifying to read the long list of countries I was free to visit. But what was more interesting were the names that were missing from the list. I noted the absence of both Israel and the Republic of China. I shut the passport and tossed it back onto the heap on the desk. There were some old letters, and an album of photographs. I opened the album. Turning its black pages, it seemed to me that I was, for no good reason, disturbing the sleep of these images settled in the depths of an ever-lasting night. I laid the album down gently, then fussed about with a few more things. Then I just stood there, unable to make up my mind what to do about the heap upon the desk. Annoyed, I turned back towards the bed. Picking up the ashtray on the desk, I set it down beside me upon the bed. I noticed that the parings of nails that I had dropped into it the day before had already disappeared beneath a fresh layer of ashes.

And suddenly it struck me with unexpected force that, at last, I was going to leave my room, that I was going to leave the city. Tomorrow I would be travelling. After such a long time I was going to travel again! My last trip was when I had come down to Bombay. Since then, I hadn't gone anywhere at all. I looked around my room again, examining each nook and corner. I had lived in this room for three years. Several others had lived in it before me, had slept in the bed that I slept in. On the mattress, beneath the bed cover, there was a hive of yellowish black stains at the level of the loins. The thought came into my mind that someone somewhere must be making a list of the persons that had lived in this room one after the other. But why would anyone make such a list?

Before I rented this room, a man called Jadeja had it. When he started bringing women to his room at night, Maganmal asked him to leave. I had visited the room once before Jadeja left. The walls were covered with pinups from hard-to-obtain foreign magazines like *Playboy*. Those pictures of nude bodies now floated up in my mind. Then I turned and looked at the clock, and noticed that it was past a quarter to eleven. Junnarkar was due to arrive at eleven. Hurriedly I went in for a bath. There was knock at the door while I was still in the bathroom. 'Jagtap, Mr Jagtap . . .' Junnarkar shouted. I hate anyone to call my name out loudly. Drying myself quickly, I came out of the bathroom and opened the door. Asking Junnarkar to sit down, I put on my shirt and trousers. Junnarkar surveyed the room. He was looking it over in the peculiar manner in which people survey a place they are planning to move into. People get quite engrossed in planning things—let's move the desk over there, put the bed on this side, let's shift the cupboard into that corner, and so on. It's strange.

Junnarkar worked in a solicitor's office on the floor beneath the office where I had worked until a few days ago. I used to run into him on the stairs, or in the corridor. When I told him that I was leaving my room as well as my job, he asked me if he might rent my room. He had visited it once to look it over, but Maganmal hadn't been in his shop. I had spoken to Maganmal about him in the meantime. Now, on Sunday, I had asked him to come over again. I had told him that I was leaving on Monday.

I dressed, and sat on the bed. A spasm of dry coughing seized Junnarkar, and he kept on coughing for a minute or two. Then he stopped and said, 'Looks like you haven't finished packing yet.'

'I don't have much to pack, really,' I said. 'And I'm not taking all my things along. I'm leaving them downstairs with Maganmal for the time being. He has a large storeroom at the back of his shop, and has agreed to let me store my belongings there for a while. I'm just taking a suitcase.'

'You're doing the right thing. There's no point in taking all your belongings right away. I assume you'll spend the first few days in a hotel, and the packages would only be a bother.'

Then Junnarkar asked me what the new company I had told him I was joining was like, what my prospects were, and so on. I told him I had excellent prospects.

Another fit of coughing seized Junnarkar. When he had stopped I said, 'That's a nasty cough.'

'Yeah,' Junnarkar puffed. 'It's been like this for over a week now. It just won't go away.'

'Why don't you take some tetracycline tablets then?' I said. 'That'll make you well in a couple of days. Tetracycline is the best thing for infections like that. It's really effective. If you like, you can buy some from the druggist round the corner here. He'll give it to you even without a prescription.'

'Oh, no,' Junnarkar shook his head. 'I avoid taking medicines as a rule. Especially these new-fangled antibiotics and what not. One should give one's body a chance to get well naturally, on its own strength. I'm sure the cough will go away in a week or two. The more you allow your body to fight germs, the stronger it becomes. Don't you agree, Mr Jagtap?'

He looked at me. I remained silent. I thought to myself, he's the sort of guy who drinks a lot of milk and exercises daily, and that sort of thing. He'll keep on coughing determinedly and will get well through sheer tenacity. That'll give him the satisfaction of having proved something.

'I don't think I'll stay in this room for long,' Junnarkar said. 'I've invested some money in an apartment in a co-operative housing society at Andheri. The building will be complete within a year or so. Once I move into my apartment, I plan on getting married too.'

'Ah, that would be nice,' I said.

'I think you ought to do the same thing, Mr Jagtap—I mean, get married once you're settled in your new job. There's no point in living like this.'

'I'll think about that,' I said, looking out of the window. When I asked Junnarkar if he'd care for a cup of tea, he said he'd prefer to go see Maganmal right away. Straightening his back as if to rise, he looked at me. Suddenly I said, 'I meant to leave tomorrow, but it looks as though I'll have to be around another two or three days.' 'No problem,' Junnarkar said, 'I've lived in a hotel for so long anyway, I can easily wait another three days.'

As we walked downstairs, I thought over what I had just said. I hadn't really been planning to postpone my departure by two or three days. I'd only said so on the spur of the moment. I'd said I'd keep the room for another three days, and Junnarkar paid Maganmal in advance for a period beginning after that. So what had been said quite unexpectedly became a definite thing.

## 2

I went out for a stroll that afternoon. In the last few days—the few days that I was to spend in the city before leaving it for good—I had taken to wandering around in different parts of the city, as though I wanted to have a last look at every part of it before I bade it goodbye. On this day I went to Malabar Hill by bus. Standing near the edge of the Hanging Gardens on the hill under the midday sun, I watched the sea and the city spread below. In the distance beyond the bay, on the far side of Nariman Point, stood the jungle of new skyscrapers that had led some people to call that area the Manhattan of India. How cities change, I thought. And the city would continue changing after I was gone.

I descended from the hill, walked along the Chowpatty beach, then along Marine Drive, turned left at Churchgate Station and came to Flora Fountain. It was a long stroll, and I walked the streets peering at the surrounding buildings as though I were seeing them for the first time in my life. As it was a Sunday, the downtown area was more or less deserted. At this hour of the day, the heat was burning me, and it seemed as though the city too were burning. And it would go on burning, burning.

Passing by the Yellow Gate near the docks, a man accosted me, and, furtively opening a paper bag that he carried, said, 'Have a look at this trouser-piece, saab. Genuine English cloth, saab. Smuggled out of the docks.' I told him I didn't need new clothes any more.

I ate something on the way, then returned to my room. For an hour or two I sat in bed smoking cigarettes. As usual my mind turned to my impending departure. I was going to buy a ticket straight through to Delhi. Of course I had no intention of going to Delhi. I'd get off anywhere on the way at some small, unimportant station, go into town with my suitcase—a suitcase that carried no name or address—and rent a room at some out-of-the-way hotel. What would that room be like, I wondered vaguely.

Suddenly the light in my room went out. The darkness was total, for all the lights in the area had gone off. If my light alone had blown a fuse, the room wouldn't have been so dark, what with the lights from the other apartments and from the street. Now I'd just have to sit still, and wait for the lights to come back on. In this total darkness, only the burning point of the cigarette in my hand was visible. Then I realized that I had left the ashtray on the bed, but didn't remember exactly where it was. I could have groped around for it, but I was afraid that I might overturn it, or get my fingers covered with ashes. I didn't have any matches handy either. I sat still, flicking ash onto the floor. After a while I wondered if the cigarette had burned down close to the end. I didn't know for sure, because, in the darkness, I didn't know how far the burning point was from my fingers. Maybe I was going to get burnt. Straining my eyes, I watched the burning point of the cigarette, and said to myself, the cigarette has burned up to here. But where was here? Since I didn't know, there was little point in saying 'here'.

After some time my fingers felt the warmth of the cigarette, and I knew that now I had to put it out. Should I extinguish it on the floor? I thought for a few seconds. Then, holding the cigarette between my thumb and forefinger, I brought it close to the bed, and moved it around in the air. In the faint light of the cigarette, the round ashtray gleamed on the bed. It had shown up so quickly because it was made of thick, patterned cut glass. Some time ago, when Kamalakar had come over from America for a visit, he had presented me with this beautiful, expensive ashtray.

It had never occurred to me that a cigarette could be a source of light. It was as though the cigarette, on its own, had discovered its ashtray. I held the cigarette close to the ashtray, and, bringing my head nearer, observed the round ashtray in the dim light of the cigarette. The ashtray glowed in the faint light, appearing even more beautiful in the surrounding darkness. Twisted cigarette butts and burnt-out matches nested upon the ash in the hollow at the centre. I moved the cigarette in a circle above the round ashtray as though I were making a gesture of benediction. It was a strange sight in the darkness, like watching a burnt-out city from the sky. After a moment, with small sparks flying up, the ashtray shone brighter in the darkness, and then was drowned in darkness like a cluster of stars dying out in the vastness of space. As I remained with my head lowered over the ashtray, a smell arose as though of burning flesh. The cigarette had burnt the nail parings resting beneath the ashes.

I picked up the ashtray, placed it on the bedside table, and sat in darkness. Then I stretched out and fell asleep. At some point late in the night the lights came back on and, since I had forgotten to switch it off, the light in my room woke me up. I got out of bed and turned it off. I don't know if it was because my sleep had been interrupted, but I was unable to fall asleep again; I remained awake in bed for the rest of the night.

# notes of a working writer

## i. *The Making of the Text*

Most of the stories in this volume were written in Marathi. Subsequently, they were re-done in English. I say 're-done' because what I did cannot exactly be called translation. The final draft of each story was done without consulting the original, for, at that stage, my main concern was to see that the story worked in English. This was rendered easier, because when I write in Marathi, I often mentally translate sentences that were formed in my mind originally in English. As an extreme example, I may cite the long sentence at the end of 'The Terrorist'. This elaborate, syntactically convoluted and, to my mind, crucial sentence was composed in English, then laboriously re-done in Marathi. I had to compose it in English first, because such involved syntax is much easier to manage in that language. In the Marathi language, the concluding verb needs to come at the end of a sentence, hence the tendency in Marathi is to write short sentences. I remember that I struggled for an entire morning in my tiny apartment in Basra to rework that long, final sentence into Marathi. It is then that I began at the beginning to write the story (in Marathi). For the same syntactic reason I have cited above, reworking the stories in English meant a great deal of stylistic recasting. I like to think—presumptuously I guess—that I am more attuned to the rhythms of English sentences, and have greater facility with diction in English than with Marathi. For example, a sentence from 'The End of History': 'It is in this manner that they make the roads we saunter over.' In the context, *saunter* is, I am certain, the *mot juste*, a gift from the goddess Saraswati; the original Marathi is the pale equivalent of *walk*. In the case of quite a few stories, I could not resist the writerly impulse to modify, or to insert new material. Some stories have large chunks that were written in English (e.g. 'An Excursion'). The stories in *Fair Tree of the Void* thus stand halfway to composition in English. But I thought it prudent (especially since I was sending the stories to American journals) to take the help of my friend Breon Michell, professor at Indiana University. In those early days I was apprehensive and unsure, and Breon was a great confidence-booster. He polished the verbal surface of the stories, without taking excessive liberty. I am deeply grateful to Breon, although I have, over the years, drifted closer to English, which thankfully, has now a more distinct Indian identity, which it did not in the 1970s.

## ii. *The Long and the Short*

It's curious, in English, the short story as a form is scarcely taken note of, is seen as marginal. In the Indian languages, on the other hand, short fiction is taken seriously, on par with the novel. Many prominent Indian writers have produced the main body of their work in the *katha* form.

This has to do mainly with the economics of writing. In England or America, a writer can hope to survive (and even become wealthy) by writing. But only novels bring in profits; short story collections, like those of poetry, seldom do. In the Indian languages, writers can rarely survive by writing alone. Whether it is novels or short stories, the economics are largely the same, which is to say, negligible.

The mode of literary production and the career graph of a writer are different in the West. Observing the credit page in my 1990 collection, *Fair Tree of the Void*, a British friend noted with some surprise that the stories were written over a period of fifteen years. For the professional writer in the West this would be woefully low output. Yet, if you compare it with the work of a poet, it wouldn't seem so aberrant. Three hundred pages of poetry is substantial work for a lifetime. So it may be with the fiction artist.

The trouble is, we don't quite think of fiction as art. Literature used to be counted among the arts: but the novel, from the beginning, has retained an ambivalent character. The novel is part literature and part sociology (which is why it is the favoured form for Marxist critics). The novel is commonly a combination of social chronicle and biography. Usually, large chunks of the life-history of the central character(s) are narrated over several hundred pages. As a literary form, the USP of the novel is information; information about social mores, chiefly, but also about different regions and countries, about various professions, and various fields of knowledge, such as history. There used to be a theory of literature as the sugar-coated pill. Today what the sugar-coated pill makes swallowable is not morality, but information. Lucien Goldmann, a Marxist critic, puts it bluntly; in capitalist society 'art is merely an inferior form of knowledge'.

No doubt, the novel is multi-purpose, which is the reason for its survival in an age where information has gone high-tech and the modes of dissemination are numerous and extraordinarily competitive. One purpose that the novel serves is what Freud told us about a long time ago: daydream. (Only the cinema can beat the novel here.)

But the mainstay of the novel is still information. This is pretty accurately reflected in the gauging of public taste: there is a best-seller list of fiction (meaning the novel) and that of non-fiction. The two are on par; in fact, interchangeable. The two categories fulfill the same need: information. An obvious connecting link is biography, which is acknowledged to be a major component of fiction. Biography—especially autobiography—is also a prime subdivision of non-fiction. Non-fiction provides information without the addition of fictional embroidery. But in popular perception, there is little difference between the two. A reviewer in *Time* magazine (13 September 2004) speaks of the novel becoming a 'Trojan horse of non-fiction'. This reviewer remarks that Amitav Ghosh, the Indian English novelist, is a purveyor of facts about some academic discipline, with the facts being suitably 'sugar-coated in fiction'. The *Time* reviewer was perhaps unaware that he was using a concept that has its origin in Horace and Lucretius, with only a little change in the terms of reference.

So if you see a lot of tourists inspecting churches for hidden clues to the life of Christ, don't be too sure it is under the influence of some non-fiction work; it might be a novel.

The strength of the novel is length. (The law of diminishing returns begins to apply the more the length stretches; but novelists believe there are other factors which counterbalance it.) To achieve length, the novel has to carry a lot of excess baggage, which, anyway, is built into the form as biography and social chronicle. But this precludes the kind of intensity and concentration—the 'critical pressure'—that most art forms strive for. (Edvard Munch's 'The Scream' is a classic example of critical pressure. So are many lyrics.) The short story is more proactive and fastidious on this front: information, yes, but the most cunningly chosen. The short story writer can legitimately aspire to write the 'perfect story'. No novelist hopes to write the 'perfect novel'.

But aesthetic appeal is not—or should not—be the supreme goal of the short story. The short stories of Kafka do not seem to care much for aesthetic perfection. Nor do those of the early Hemingway, or of Borges. What these writers focus upon is not beauty of form, but a kind of knowledge. (Not the 'inferior form of knowledge' which Goldmann speaks of.) Great short story writers offer us a singular vision. The short story gives us knowledge, but not knowledge as information. The short story at its best goes beyond sociology, or biography, or information of any kind. Twisting the words of Aristotle around, we might say that most novels are closer to history than to philosophy. The short story, on the other hand, is apt to become obsessed with pursuing a vision, frequently treating the business of (hi)story-telling with scant regard, at times almost playfully. However, if fiction is to be taken as an art form, it cannot be straightforward philosophy, or history; it must transcend these spheres of human understanding.

## iii. *The Short Story Writer as a Guerilla*

The French writer Alain Nadaud declares: *La Nouvelle, c'est la guerilla.* ('The Short Story is a guerilla force.') That is a fetching description, and it does zero in on the perpetual mission of the short story. In the literary ethos we are familiar with the short story has been seen as nothing more than 'a slice of life', to be enjoyed briefly over one's afternoon cup of tea. But it has not always been regarded in this way; not in France or Germany (think of Maupassant or Kafka), or Latin America (Borges, Cortazar). Not so in the Indian languages, where the explosive potential of short fiction is recognized and respected. In these regions of the world, the short story writer lives up to the title of a guerilla fighter who strives to go beyond the limits, to find chinks in the walls, to discover virgin modes of synapsis. Sometimes, the writer succeeds. After Kafka's parables and snippets, all fiction, novel and short story alike, had to adjust the alignments. Ditto with Borges.

This conception of the role of the short story is at variance with the idea of short fiction as fodder for magazines. It is important to appreciate the vital role that the short story can play in the ecology of literature. Nadaud's words quoted above echo Eliot's words in the *Four Quartets*: 'Each venture / Is . . . a raid on the inarticulate.' Eliot's reference was to poetry; that is not irrelevant. There is much in the make-up of the short story that is close to poetry. At its best, the short story functions like poetry. I'm not talking about 'poetic', or lyrical, stories. The short story writer's approach to his material—clinically speaking—is similar to that of the poet. It is significant that Edgar Allan Poe, who believed in the *intensity* of poetry above all, and maintained that a long poem (like a novel, you might say) is impossible, is one of the first guerillas of fiction, breaking new ground. Poe believed in 'pure poetry' (an idea that was taken up by the French Symbolist poets); he might have spoken of the short story as 'pure fiction'. And, indeed, the novel, however great, cannot but be 'impure fiction' since nobody can keep up intensity and concentration at such length. Only a few novellas, such as *The Old Man and the Sea*, can approximate the 'purity' of short fiction.

The French Symbolist poets (especially Rimbaud) had faith in writing—with the special French notion of *ecriture*—as a ceaseless exploration (from whom Eliot inherited the idea), and the guerillas of prose fiction were driven by a similar impulse. The transcendentalist impulse is very pronounced in the guerillas of fiction: Joyce with his Gabriel aspiring to 'his journey westward', and Stephen to become 'refined out of existence'; Kafka with his endless winding stairs and the inaccessible castle; Hemingway, with his vision of the luminous peak of Kilimanjaro (like Mount Kailash); Borges with his magical Aleph.

But it is not philosophical transcendence that is of consequence; what matters to us is the down-to-earth project of devising ways to trap what may facetiously be called the unusual suspect, or what Eliot gravely calls the inarticulate. (It is not insignificant that Poe was the inventor of the detective story.)

Time and again, the guerillas of prose fiction have initially been treated as pariahs, or at best as contemptible irritants. Poe is the quintessential guerilla; generally dismissed as a phony, he was honoured as a prophet in a far country; when Baudelaire and Mallarme lauded him, the English-speaking world grudgingly admitted that Poe might, indeed, be a 'genius'. Hemingway, in his pristine Parisian poverty, had his stories rejected by editors, who dismissed then as mere 'sketches'; this particular guerilla went on to change the fictional prose style of English for good.

Countries like France have specialized in exporting revolutions of all kinds; the English temperament has been skeptical of the Che Guevara type (except in the brief Romantic era). We do not find guerillas of short fiction in England with the originality of Poe, Hemingway, Kafka or Borges. The names of short fiction writers in England—E.M. Forster, H.G. Wells, Kipling, Katherine Mansfield, V.S. Pritchett—are of a different order.

But even in the staid climate of English letters it is the rare guerilla who has tried to explore new territory. There was Joyce with *Dubliners* (he was, of course, Irish), and Virginia Woolf; more recently, a writer like Ian McEwan. Generally, the English have been unfavorable to the new. (Auden, who briefly saw a vision of 'new styles of architecture', went on to retract, and to insist, 'I love *old* styles of architecture.') The English tradition was never very comfortable with Modernism. Looking back on the twentieth century, Frank Kermode says, 'It once seemed that there was going to be a major technological revolution in the novel, but it didn't happen. Even Joyce didn't cause one.' (*The London Review of Books*, 25 April 2002.)

Joyce didn't succeed, because the novel is the prisoner of the marketplace. Not many novelists would be willing to work laboriously, in impoverished conditions, on one or two novels over a lifetime. But Joyce, with *Dubliners*, was a true guerrilla, though he has had more influence outside of England.

The symbiotic relationship between the short story and the novel needs to be taken seriously. Very often fiction writers have played the guerilla role before going on to longer projects. Great short stories—you can take your pick—serve as a kind of Arnoldian touchstone for fiction writers of all varieties.

Indian English writers have chosen to tread in the footsteps of British models. To quote Kermode again: 'Their allegiance is to the English novel of the nineteenth-century tradition, and their work has little in common with deviant strains, whether of Modernism or Postmodern magic realism.' Little wonder, then, that the Indian English short story has been unadventurous. We don't have classics such as 'The Killers', or 'The Great Wall of China', or 'The Dead', or 'The Overcoat'; nor do we have unitive collections which may serve as primers for budding writers, or reward readers who desire to venture beyond bestseller opium, e.g. Sherwood Anderson's *Winesburg, Ohio*, Borges' *Labyrinths*, *Nabokov's Dozen*, Robbe-Grillet's *Instantanes*. Does Indian English literature hope to produce a *War and Peace* before it has attempted something like 'How Much Land Does a Man Need?' or 'The Death of Ivan Ilyich'?